For Polly and Joe, with love and gratitude

Something BLUE

rosie orr

ISBN 9781910939239

ACKNOWLEDGEMENTS

Huge thanks to everyone at Accent Press, especially my brilliant editor, Rebecca Lloyd. Also to Oxford Writers' Group, for all their support and encouragement, and to Matt Fitton for his endless patience when explaining technical matters.

Last – but never, ever, least – to Michael, for always laughing at the funny bits, and for the unfailing supply of Maltesers.

CHAPTER ONE

Anna Hardy pushed her way through the crowd of lunchtime shoppers thronging the aisles of the menswear department in Marks & Spencer's gleaming Brighton store, wishing she had a double buggy, or at least a wheeled shopper to assist her progress. As she glanced at her watch – twenty-five past twelve already! – an enormously fat woman trod on her foot. Anna smiled at her to show no harm had been done; the woman swore loudly and steamed on her way. Mentally adding a pair of whirling scythes with extremely sharp blades to the axles of her imaginary buggy, Anna pressed on.

Footwear … hosiery … at last – lingerie. Rack upon rack of stockings, slips, night-dresses and housecoats faced her – no sign of bras, let alone suspender belts. Ah, there they were, beside the thermal vests, which were actually rather pretty, especially the coffee-coloured ones with the … *Not now*, vests weren't what she was looking for. She smiled; they *definitely* weren't what she was looking for …

She flicked quickly through the rails of lacy underwear. The black? Or maybe she should go for the champagne. Would that suit her complexion? Better check. Seizing a set of each colour in 36B and the thongs decorated with elaborate lace flowers, she headed for the nearest mirror.

As she tried to separate the hangers, which seemed to have mysteriously welded themselves together as she took them from the rail, she realised she'd unwittingly taken an extra set. This one was a deep carnation red, with delicately scalloped straps and richly embroidered flowers highlighting strategic areas. She held one of the flimsy scraps up to her face. She'd run all the way from Avant Art's coffee bar; her cheeks were pink, her brown eyes glowed, her black curls had escaped from their

1

combs and tumbled over her shoulders. The deep crimson suited her perfectly. Hell, she'd buy it.

She was about to put the unwanted sets back on the rail when she hesitated. She'd never worn red underwear in her life. Maybe champagne – or the black, it really was very nice – would be more suitable? She caught sight of herself once more in the mirror. Was she *mad*? Today was no time to be playing it safe; today was a day for throwing caution to the wind – for *celebrating*. Today was a carnation-red day if ever there was one.

She hurried to the pay desk where the elderly assistant was crouched motionless over the till like a giant spider, watching her suspiciously. She placed her purchase on the counter and found her purse. With agonizing slowness the assistant lifted the bra to within an inch of her rakishly diamantéed spectacles and scrutinized the washing instructions on the tag. She frowned. 'Course, you seen this is non-iron, haven't you?'

'Oh yes, that's fine –'

'Only you wouldn't credit the number of customers who run amok with a hot iron then come running back complaining the underwire's melted.'

'No, really, it's –'

'I always make a point of saying to them –'

Anna glanced at her watch. Twenty-five to one. God, that only gave her forty minutes before Jack …

'Please don't think me rude, but I really am in a terrible hurry –'

The elderly assistant reared back as if Anna had spat at her, pursed her lips and began a lengthy examination of the price tag. Tough measures were clearly called for. Anna drew a small black notebook from her bag. It was last year's diary, but only she knew that. Placing two twenty-pound notes on the counter, she leaned forward. 'Look, I shouldn't be telling you this, but –'

'Euro this and euro that! If you want my opinion –'

Anna flipped the diary open officiously. 'I'm part of a team of time-and-motion inspectors vetting the southern branch – er – sector.' She ran a finger down the list of last year's bank holidays, and suddenly drew in her breath sharply. 'Oh dear. I'm very much afraid Lingerie's got three black stars beside it.'

The assistant's watery eyes bulged. 'Black stars?'

'Urgent action required.' She shook her head regretfully. 'I can see what a keen interest you take in your work, and I'd hate to be forced to mark you down. However, the pace of modern life being what it is, speedy service is of the essence.' Frowning, she scribbled *happy birthday, Jesus* in the space for Christmas Day and looked up. 'The absolute essence.'

The result was gratifying; the underwear was shoved into a bag and the change thrust into her hand before she had time to blink. 'Excellent. That's exactly the kind of response we want to see.' Anna grabbed the green plastic bag and dropped the change into her pocket. She made a show of scanning the name badge pinned to the woman's meagre bosom. 'I shall make a point of mentioning you in my report, Evadne.'

Leaving Lingerie at a run, she sprinted downstairs to the Food Hall, seized a wire basket and sped to the sandwiches and snacks, praying it wouldn't turn out to be one of those days when the Powers That Be had amused themselves by decreeing that all the produce be moved to entirely new locations on the shelves. Anna always wondered if the staff took turns to watch on the security monitors, laughing uproariously as the bemused customers trailed about desperately searching for their prawn cocottes and ocean pies. Thank God; she was in luck. A pack of roast beef and horseradish sandwiches and another of ham and Swiss cheese, and she was off to desserts. Pushing in front of a couple of nuns deliberating between cherry cheesecake and tiramisu, Anna grabbed a pecan pie and headed for the self-service checkout.

Three minutes later she was outside; by twelve forty-five she was at the bus stop. Six minutes later, her bus still hadn't come. Anna glanced at her watch again, sick with impatience. Three buses lumbered past in convoy and stopped at the next bus stop, closely followed by two more which, though they idled provocatively to a halt beside her, proved to be Out of Service.

She began to run.

Ten minutes later, she turned into Hanover Terrace, a narrow row of wafer-thin late-Edwardian houses. Her throat burning, the carrier bag containing the pecan pie banging painfully against her hip, she put on a final spurt to reach number twenty-eight. With a cursory wave to Mr Simwak, her Thai lodger, as he did something scientific to the herbs in his basement window box, she sprinted past the area railings and up the steps to her own front door. Flinging the food bags down on the hall table, she took the stairs two at a time, peeling off her velvet waistcoat and unbuttoning her blouse as she went. One o'clock. With a bit of luck she might just make it. They always made love in the kitchen at lunchtimes, so there was no need to tidy the bedroom. Thanking God for small mercies – the patchwork quilt lay crumpled on the wooden floorboards, underwear spilled from the open drawers of the old pine chest of drawers, a mug containing the bluish remains of last night's cocoa sat on top of the pile of paperbacks on the cluttered bedside table – she yanked off the rest of her clothes, dropped them on the floor and headed for the bathroom.

Twelve minutes later she was in the kitchen, teeth cleaned, legs shaved, hair brushed, make-up freshened and body spritzed liberally with the Diorissimo Jack had given her for Christmas. As yet, only she knew that beneath her outer layers of clothing she wore the sexiest underwear she'd ever seen. She glanced round, checking that the place was reasonably tidy. With its blue-green Shaker units and picture window overlooking the walled back garden, the kitchen was Anna's favourite room. She'd washed up her breakfast dishes in the morning, and given the table a quick polish. Yup; everything looked fine. Flinging a Nina Simone CD onto the player, she ripped the wrappings off the sandwiches, put them onto a plate, turned on the oven at mark nine (making a mental note to remember to lower the regulo as soon as it had heated up) and thrust the pecan pie into its cavernous depths. She was setting out wine glasses and cutlery when she heard the sound of a key in the front door.

Her heart leapt.

Jack.

She took the jug of daffodils that stood on the windowsill and placed them in the middle of the table, smoothed her jeans over her hips with one hand and fluffed up her curls with the other.

'Hello, angel.' Jack stood in the doorway, carrying a bottle of wine.

Anna turned – and the question she'd been waiting all morning to ask died on her lips. He looked as handsome as ever: his dark hair with its stripes of grey falling into his eyes, and the lopsided smile deepening the worry lines etched on either side of his mouth. But today he was grey with exhaustion; his tie drooped at half-mast over his crumpled shirt and one of the buttons on his grey tweed jacket was hanging by a thread. It was obvious that things hadn't gone well. Better not to ask him anything until he had some food inside him.

'Jack? You OK?' She went to him and put her arms round him.

'Wasn't.' He nuzzled her neck. 'Mmm. Am now, though …'

They kissed, and when he held her away from him to look at her he looked a lot happier. 'Angel …' He kissed her again.

Heartened, Anna took a deep breath. As she opened her mouth to speak, he let go of her.

'Hell of a morning.' He dropped his briefcase and threw himself down into a chair.

Anna closed her mouth again. This clearly wasn't the moment. She took the bottle opener from the drawer and handed it to him. 'Fourth years playing you up again, hon?'

'Little bastards.' He yanked the cork from the bottle. 'Made a start on *Romeo and Juliet*. Christ, Anna, the only one of 'em who'd admit to having even *heard* of Shakespeare was Hayley.'

Anna tried to think of something encouraging to say. 'Well, I suppose one's better than nothing.'

'Not when that one thinks Will Shakespeare is a character in a film played by Joseph Fiennes.' He splashed wine into the glasses. 'Or "that wicked dark bloke with the sexy bum", to be

5

more precise. I dunno. Sometimes you wonder why you bother.' He pushed one of the glasses towards her. 'Anyway, enough about me. How was your morning, love?' He pulled off his tie and threw it over the back of the chair opposite.

Anna sat down at the table and passed him the sandwiches, considering her morning. Actually it hadn't been bad as mornings went at Avant Art, 'Brighton's challenge to Tate Modern', as Alastair, the gallery's whizz-kid young director, liked to put it. Anna had worked in the coffee bar for the last fifteen years, and been supervisor for the last nine. The work was often tiring, but never dull. She and her assistants, Roxy, Trish and Susie, were always too busy to be bored. Their customers ranged from matrons making a daring foray into the world of espressos and croissants because the café at BHS was full, to students from the local art college who came with the express purpose of talking loudly about their own work's superiority to that currently on show in the coffee bar, where smaller installations were displayed. Most of the customers were polite, and as far as Anna was concerned, all of them were interesting. 'Not bad. Had that bloke in again, you know, the art-history tutor from the uni –'

Jack raised his glass, and drank deeply. Anna stared at him, dismayed. He hadn't made their usual toast. They always clinked glasses and drank to their future – it had become a ritual. Did that mean …? No, of course it didn't; he was just distracted because he was upset. She wouldn't push: let him tell her about it in his own time. She took a sip of her own wine, and carried on. '–versity, the one with the lisp who always changes his mind at least three times about the kind of tea he wants no matter how long the queue is. You remember – the one who wouldn't let Trish serve him because he said her eyebrow studs made him feel faint?'

She handed him the plate of sandwiches. He took one. Anna smiled, relieved. Everything must be all right if he was eating.

'Well, this morning Roxy'd had enough, so she got some of the fancy teas down and asked him if he'd mind reading out what it said on the boxes, because she hadn't got her contacts in and she wanted to be sure to get his order right.'

He bit into his sandwich. 'I didn't know Roxy wore contacts.'

'She doesn't, that's the point. Anyway, I know it's cruel, but honestly, if you could have heard the way he said the names – "Lapthang Thouchong", "Aththam", "Jathmine". I mean the whole queue just –'

'Mmm, beef's good.'

Anna drank some more wine. The fourth years had clearly got to him more than ever this morning. He'd been pretty low last Thursday, now she came to think of it. He'd been teaching Lawrence's poetry and some bright spark had asked if 'this was the same bloke what wrote Cunts 'n' Lovers what had been on telly'. No wonder the poor man was down; she mustn't start reading things into his behaviour. He took another sandwich, cheese and ham this time, and topped up their glasses. 'Young Alastair still having tantrums because Damien Hurst refused his invitation to show?'

She grinned. 'He's moved into "Huh, See if I Care" mode as of this morning. Susie overheard him saying that he reckons Hirst simply doesn't feel ready for Brighton yet. Actually "Bugger can't get it up sarf of Watford, right?" is how Susie said he put it.'

She was fond of Alastair, despite the Cockney accent he affected in a vain attempt to disguise his upper-class origins and Cambridge education, and the savagely ripped rainbow-striped dungarees and purple tattoos he wore in the fond belief that they were the garb of the working-class artisan. He was constantly engaged in art-world feuds, and loved nothing more than a good fight with the press, as a result of which the little gallery was frequently the subject of headlines in Brighton's *Evening Argus*. But he had an excellent eye for new talent, and since his appointment last year the gallery had enjoyed a steadily increasing reputation.

Jack grinned back, and Anna relaxed. Maybe she'd have a sandwich herself.

7

'So.' Jack raised an eyebrow. 'Here's to getting it up.' He set down his glass. Got slowly to his feet, and moved to stand beside her chair.

Anna put down her sandwich.

He stood looking down at her, then reached out and touched her hair. '"Come, madam, come ..."'

Thank god. It really was all right. The John Donne poem had been a prelude to their lunchtime lovemaking ever since that first time Jack had arrived full of despair over the kids' response to his efforts to interest them in poetry of any kind. When, in an attempt to cheer him up, Anna had asked him about his own favourite writers, he'd launched into the Donne, which had speedily led to other things.

He took her hand and drew her to her feet. '"... until I labour, I in labour lie."'

She smiled, and for the first time since he'd arrived, allowed herself to relax.

He trailed his finger slowly down her breast. '"Off with that girdle, like heavens Zone glistering ..."' He began to unbutton her waistcoat.

Anna closed her eyes. At last she could allow herself to think of the future. Maybe he'd be able to move in straight away. Well, not tonight, obviously, there'd be things he'd have to do, stuff to sort out ...

'"Unpin that spangled breastplate which you wear ..."' He fumbled clumsily with the fastening at the high collar of her blouse.

She imagined them going to bed together every night, instead of Jack having to rush off at midnight like Cinderella. Waking up together. Breakfast in bed on Sundays with the papers. No, forget the papers, they'd be too busy making –

He'd finally got the hang of the hooks and eyes and was unfastening the tiny pearl buttons at record speed. '"Off with that happy busk ..."'

She opened her eyes as he slipped the blouse down over her shoulders. She wanted to see his expression when he saw the –

He drew in his breath sharply. 'Jesus Christ, Anna.' He was gazing at her breasts as they spilled over the artfully sculptured cups of her red bra. Her *carnation-red* bra. He swallowed hard, and ran his hands over the gauzy fabric, lingering over the delicately embroidered flowers. 'You look ... you look ...' As they kissed, he undid her jeans. '"Your gown going off, such beauteous state reveals ..."'

The first thing they'd do was repaint the bedroom, make it theirs, not hers. Maybe Indian Red – it needed a shade with real warmth. As Jack slid her zip down slowly, she shivered. Forget warm, hot was more like it. Indian Red, that was the colour; she'd seen it in a book of Indian miniatures once, used as a background against a couple making love on a heap of striped silk cushions. Maybe she'd make some cushions, and a new cover for the bed. It would look fabulous. And they could make a start on the herb garden it turned out they'd both always wanted but never had; she'd seen some huge terracotta pots for sale in the flower shop at the bottom of the hill, they could...

Jack began to ease her jeans down over her hips. Catching sight of the practically non-existent panties, he pulled her to him with a groan and buried his face in the filmy lace. After a moment, he looked up at her, breathing hard. '"Off with that Coronet and shew ..."' he pulled off her jeans and tossed them in the corner '"... the hairy Diademe ..."' he began to slide the panties down '"... which on you doth grow."' He gazed at her adoringly, then pulled her to him.

At last she'd be able to do all the things she'd longed to do for so long. Wash his socks. Iron his shirts. All the little things, the domestic things that formed the glue of any –

'"Licence my roving hands, and let them go ..."' His voice was hoarse. '"... before, behind, between, above, below."' He began to suit the actions to the words.

Anna closed her eyes again and gave herself up to the pleasures of sensation, all thought of cushions and terracotta pots forgotten.

'"Full nakedness"!' He was removing his own clothes, now, and fast '"all joys are due to thee" – give me a hand with this buckle, would you darling, the damn thing always sticks.'

They subsided onto the floor.

'"... As souls unbodied ..."'

Breathing as hard as he was, now, Anna struggled with his belt buckle while he shucked off his shirt with frantic haste.

'"... bodies uncloth'd must be."'

She was easing his zip down when she caught sight of him casting a covert glance at his watch as he unbuttoned his cuffs. God, how she hated that watch. Still, they wouldn't have to live like this for much longer. She kissed him, took hold of his corduroys and began to tug them downwards. '"To taste whole ..."'

She licked his chest.

He groaned. '"... joys". Christ, Anna, that underwear – it's bloody fantastic.'

Smiling, she slowly travelled lower. 'Won't it be great when we don't have to keep meeting like this, Jack? When we can take as long as we want? As often as we want?' Lower still.

He groaned again, and thrust his hands deep into her curls. 'God, yes. Can't wait...'

Everything must be all right, then. Oh God, she couldn't wait any longer either. She had to know – had to hear him say it. She'd ask him now; get it out of the way – they'd enjoy making love even more then. She raised her head. 'Jack? What happened? ... How did Ruth take it?'

Jack recoiled as if she'd hit him, and snatched his hands from her hair as if it had stung him. Anna looked down at his slowly wilting penis, and sat up. 'Jack?'

He looked away. 'Anna, it's not as easy as you –'

'Easy? Nobody ever said it was going to be *easy*. You promised you'd tell her last night – you promised! Jesus, Jack, it was your idea to tell her you wanted out!'

'And I do want out, you know I do!' He looked at her pleadingly. 'You know I love you – it's just harder than you realise to actually tell her. I did try last night, honestly, when she came back from her aerobics class. I offered to get her a glass of wine, you know, to get her in a good mood. It always worked a treat when we were first –' He saw the look on Anna's face, and stopped. 'Yes, well, anyway. By the time I'd brought it into the living room and gone back to the kitchen to get the peanuts she wanted and been sent back *again* because I'd brought the wrong ones, she'd started to watch some documentary on euthanasia. She shut me up as soon as I started to speak.' He frowned. 'Between you and me, I reckon she's just waiting for the law to be changed so she can bump off her mother. Old bat annoys her even more than I do, apparently, though I can't see the problem myself.' He put a hand on her thigh. 'The kids are always around, for another thing. In fact the only time I see Ruth alone is in –'

She pulled away from him. 'Oh, for God's sake, spare me. The thought of you and Ruth in bed together makes me want to throw up.'

'I was going to say Sainsbury's, actually.' He sounded hurt. 'We do the Saturday shop together. She always says she can't trust me to get the right things.'

'Sounds really cosy.' She leapt to her feet and drank some wine. 'Look, either do it or don't do it. Just stop messing me around.'

'Messing you around?'

Anna banged the glass down on the table. 'It wasn't me who asked you to leave – you told *me* your marriage was finished, that it'd been over for years before you met me. That you'd been wanting to leave sodding Ruth ever since she laughed when you told her you wanted to write a play.'

'Or a film script. You know I've often thought that's where my true vocation –'

'That you … that I … that *we* …' Her voice broke.

'Anna, darling, please.' He was trying to pull up his corduroys. Anna could see that his underpants had got caught in the zip; she made no move to help him. Her eyes filled with tears.

11

'It's the second time, Jack – the second bloody time you've chickened out! Why didn't you have the guts to tell me when you came?'

His underpants came free. Zipping up his trousers he got to his feet and reached for his shirt. 'Came?' He glanced at her from under his eyelashes and attempted a rueful smile. Anna could tell someone – sodding Ruth, probably – had once told him it made him look like a little boy. 'Well, chance would have been a fine thing.'

'You cheap bastard, Jack.' She picked up his shirt and hurled it at him. 'Get out.'

'Anna –'

'Just go, Jack.'

He was buttoning up his shirt. 'I'll tell her tonight, I promise. Maybe she'll be in a better mood.'

She threw his jacket at him. '*Now*!'

He took a hesitant step towards her. 'Please, Anna, be reasonable –'

'*Reasonable*?' She backed away from him.

His shoulders slumped; he passed his hand over his eyes in a gesture of defeat and picked up his briefcase. 'I'll ring you tonight. Well, if I can, Ruth –'

He was already at the kitchen door. Anna picked up the corkscrew and threw it with all the force she could. It bounced harmlessly off the pine panelling. After a moment, she heard the front door close quietly. For a second, she stood motionless. Then she poured the wine down the sink, threw the bottle in the bin and hurled the glasses and plates of sandwiches after it. The glasses shattered and the plates broke with a satisfying crack. Good – she'd never liked them. In fact, come to think of it, she completely and absolutely loathed them.

She slumped to the floor and burst into tears. *Bastard* – she must have been mad to have believed he'd really go through with it. Yet on Tuesday night he'd seemed so certain, so sure. In the three years they'd been together she couldn't remember a single disagreement. It had been bliss. Well, all right, they hadn't been *together*, exactly. You couldn't call two evenings a week and one lunch hour (when he could skive off school dinner duties) being *together*, but that was the whole point, that was why he'd made up his mind to finally make the break with Ruth. Their relationship was nothing like his married life – hell on wheels, he called it. Meeting Anna had opened his eyes to what love *should* be. She rubbed at her eyes, not caring if her eyeshadow smeared and her mascara ran.

It had all been so perfect at first. She'd never forget his startled look that day three years ago when he literally bumped into her in HMV. He was turning away from the counter having just paid for his goods; she was approaching with a stack of CDs she was planning to give as Christmas presents. Their purchases had fallen to the floor with a crash, and since several of their choices were identical, it had taken some time to sort them out. While they did so, a mutual attraction had manifested itself, helped on by their shared taste in music. When he'd asked hesitantly if she had time for a quick coffee so that they could continue their discussion of Ella Fitzgerald, her first thought had been to refuse – what kind of person let themselves be picked up in a chain store? And anyway, she still had loads of shopping to do … He'd picked up her reluctance and, apologising, turned away: a tall man with dark hair that kept falling into his eyes and a wide mouth that looked as if it hadn't smiled for a long time. He'd been wearing ancient jeans and a grey tweed jacket. That night as she lay in bed she thought to herself that if anybody had told her she'd find grey tweed with leather patches on the elbows sexy, she'd have said they were mad.

Her nose was running; she wiped at it angrily with her forearm. She probably *had* been mad, sod it – mad to have changed her mind and gone to Starbucks with him. Mad to have accepted a second tall latte. Mad not to have left the moment he told her he was married, no matter how unhappy he was with sodding Ruth …

She was still weeping five minutes later when she heard the sound of the front door opening. Anna froze. It couldn't be Jack – he had to be back for 'Time for Self-expression' with the third year. The front door closed quietly. Simultaneously overcome with joy (he'd come back!) – and panic (her eye make-up had run, her face must be a mess of tear stains and snot) she leapt to her feet, grabbed a handful of tissues from a box on the dresser and dabbed frantically at her cheeks. It took three seconds to pull her underwear back on. She'd throw herself into his arms, tell him she forgave him. Of course he'd tell Ruth tonight, she was a cow ever to have doubted him.

The kitchen door opened.

Arms outstretched, Anna ran forward.

And stopped dead in her tracks.

'*Mum*?'

Anna had read about people wishing the ground would open beneath their feet and swallow them. She had always assumed this was wild exaggeration; she knew now it was not.

'Sam!' Her voice was high and thin as a bat squeak.

Her son stood in the doorway, regarding her with horrified amazement.

Behind him – which made things even worse, if it were possible – stood Lucy, his girlfriend.

CHAPTER TWO

'Mum, what the hell's going on? Why aren't you wearing any clothes?'

Even as a small boy, Sam had been a stickler for niceties. Conformist at the age of five – 'Mum, my Mr Man mug doesn't match my plate'; by eleven he'd become positively strict – 'Mum, you must never, ever come to meet me wearing your stripy socks.' At eighteen, she had a strong suspicion he told his friends he'd been recently bereaved – 'Sam's mother? Weird; he's never mentioned you.' Now, at the ripe old age of twenty-five, he stood in the doorway clad in his idea of leisurewear (butter-soft caramel suede Ralph Lauren bomber jacket, moss green moleskins and checked wool Paul Smith shirt) regarding her with a disapproving frown not dissimilar, Anna imagined, to the look God bestowed on the naked Eve after the apple episode.

She strove for calm. 'Sam! Lucy! How lovely to see you!'

The corkscrew glinted a couple of feet away from his chocolate brown loafers. Under cover of giving them both a swift hug, she deftly kicked it out of sight beneath the dresser.

'And you've been crying!' His tone was accusing.

Anna gave what she hoped was a light laugh and headed for her blouse. Inspiration struck as she bent to pick it up and caught sight of the fat ceramic pepper pot on the table.

'I know, darling.' She slipped the blouse on gratefully, and fastened the buttons. 'It's just that I was trying on some new underwear and it's too small, dammit. I suppose I was crying because I'm disappointed my diet isn't working.'

'You can say that again. And what on earth are you doing wearing red, Mum? You know you always wear grey stuff.'

15

Grey? OK, so she tended to wear underwear – well, everything, come to think of it – till it was so old it was ready to fall apart, but describing it as grey was a bit much. Anna stepped into her jeans and yanked them up. 'I know, hideous, isn't it? But it was the only colour they had in what I thought was my size.'

'Oh well, it's not as if anyone's going to see it, is it?' He smiled kindly at her.

Lucy stepped forward and pressed a large bunch of tulips into Anna's arms. 'I thought the colour looked rather good on you, actually, Anna. Goes with your skin tone.'

'Honestly? Thanks, Lucy, that's –'

'By the way, Mum, I thought your half day was Wednesday? We stopped by the gallery first. The plan was to take you out for a swift drink in your lunch hour. Roxanne said you'd changed to Thursdays.'

Yes, because old Jennings had practically forced Jack to supervise the first-year Remedial Reading group in Wednesday lunch hours.

'The shopping centre's so much quieter on Thursdays, darling. Makes it so much nicer for, er, shopping.' Change the subject, quickly. 'So how were things at the coffee bar? Busy?'

'God yes, heaving, weren't they, Lucy? Don't know how you stand it, Mum.'

'It was pretty busy,' Lucy laughed. 'Trish was trying to cope with some woman who was complaining about the colour of the paper napkins. I loved the exhibition.'

'Yes? It sounds awful, but I never have time to look at what's on the walls.'

Lucy looked shocked. 'Oh, Anna, you should. They're photographs, black and white, by some Irish photographer I've never heard of.'

Anna grinned. That wasn't surprising; Alastair prided himself on spotting new talent. 'I'll make a point of taking a look. What sort of photographs are they – landscapes? Portraits?'

'That's just the point, it's hard to –'

'Mum?' Sam was advancing into the kitchen. 'What the hell's that godawful smell?'

Anna froze. Surely even Sam couldn't detect ... Anyway, she and Jack hadn't –

'I think something's burning.' Lucy made for the oven, and opened it. Clouds of dense black smoke billowed out: the pecan pie.

'Bugger. I meant to lower the regulo –'

'Stand clear, you two; I'll deal with this.' Sam grabbed a tea cloth, grasped the offending confection and dropped it in the sink. 'God, Mum, you really want to watch it. Can't have you getting forgetful as well as fat.' He bent and examined the charred remains of the pie. 'Isn't this a pecan pie?' He frowned. 'No wonder that diet's not working, Mum. You really will have to take it a bit more seriously if you want to see results. Still, at least nobody could say it was undercooked – at least there's no chance of it giving anyone E-coli.' He roared with laughter.

Anna gritted her teeth. Much more of this and she'd tell Lucy about the problems she'd had getting her darling boyfriend potty trained.

'Oh, isn't this absolutely *dear*!'

She turned. Lucy was holding out a slender arm and Jack's tie dangled at the end of her French-manicured fingernails. Anna concentrated hard on not screaming.

'Mum, tell me that's not my birthday present.' Sam stared in horror at the ochre ribbon patterned with rows of little panda bears. The logo of the World Wildlife Fund was emblazoned at the bottom.

Think. Present ...

'Your birthday present? Good heavens, no.' She retrieved the tie and folded it carefully. 'No, this is for Mr Simwak-Kim.'

From what she'd gleaned of her Thai lodger's eating habits he was more likely to stir-fry bits of panda than have them decorating his ties, but now wasn't the moment to share that information with Sam.

'Phew, right. It's not really my style.' He rolled his eyes at Lucy.

Anna restrained herself from slapping him. 'Why don't you put the kettle on, darling. I'll just pop upstairs and –' scream into a pillow for half an hour or so '– freshen up. Can you stay long?'

'Only a couple of hours. Lucy wants to nip up to Kemp Town to see a friend while we're here, then we'll have to be getting back. Just thought we'd take the opportunity to get out of town while the pressure's off for a bit. I told you I'm up for the Zircon contract, didn't I?'

Anna nodded, smiling enthusiastically. 'Yes, that's –'

'And I'm on the team for the Goldstein Bloom deal.' Lucy smiled up at him adoringly.

'Sam! That's terrific –'

'And Lucy's just finished up on the Lavglo account, so –'

'So...' Lucy rubbed her head against his shoulder. She and Sam smiled at each other conspiratorially.

She would not think about Jack. 'So, here you are. And I can't tell you how lovely it is to see you both. Get that kettle on, Sam – I'll be back in a jiff.'

In the safety of her bedroom she dragged a brush through her hair and repaired the worst of the ravages to her face, reflecting on the fact that the sight of her thoroughly grown-up son never ceased to surprise her. Did all mothers of grown-up children feel the same? She must remember to ask Roxy tomorrow. One minute Sam had been a toddler and the next he'd somehow metamorphosed into a sophisticated adult. She still thought it was incredible that at the age twenty-five – *twenty-five? How was it possible?* – he was consultant – *consultant!* – to one of Europe's biggest IT companies, lived in a huge flat in Muswell Hill, drove an Audi TT and probably earned more money in a year than Anna had earned in her entire life.

After a string of girlfriends while he was at university (most of whom he'd kept well away from Brighton) he'd met Lucy O'Shaughnessy, who was pursuing an equally brilliant career in advertising. They'd 'clicked' straight away, apparently, and she'd been living with him for some while now. A beautiful girl, all milky Irish skin and auburn hair; she and Anna, though

18

hardly soulmates, got on extremely well, sharing a fascination with cheap horror films, a loathing of animal cruelty and a terminal fear of dentists.

She could just about accept all these changes when Sam was visible in the flesh, thought Anna, as she touched up her mascara. The problem was that when he wasn't, which of course these days was almost all of the time, he reverted in her memory to toddlerhood. She frequently saw small boys in town while she was out shopping that for brief but heart-stopping moments she thought were Sam; and although she laughed at herself for her foolishness, a painful wrench always accompanied the realisation that she'd been mistaken.

She returned to the kitchen. Sam had forgotten to put the kettle on. Restraining herself from ruffling his carefully styled and gelled hair as she passed, she went to the sink to fill it. As she took the tea caddy from the dresser, she saw Sam exchange a meaningful look with Lucy. What now, for heaven's sake? Had they discovered Jack's underpants dangling from the lampshade? Unearthed the copy of *Hot Sex and How to Do It* she kept stashed behind the cookery books? Suddenly she clicked. Of course – she should have thought to ask. Lucy didn't drink tea. 'Sorry, Lucy, I didn't think to ask. Coffee's no trouble, if you'd –'

Sam cleared his throat. 'Actually, Mum, we've got something to tell you.'

Lucy nodded.

He'd lost his job, and – no, he'd just told her about the Zenith thing, and the Goldman Bloom whatsit, it couldn't be that. Oh, dear god. Perhaps he was seriously ill and he'd decided to come down and tell her personally instead of giving her the news by phone.

He and Lucy stood close together, holding hands. 'Mum …'

Whatever happened, she wouldn't cry. She'd take it on the chin, the way she'd always taken everything in life, and she'd deal with it.

'… Lucy and I – we're getting married.'

Anna burst into tears.

19

It was some time before she could convince them both that her reaction was simply one of amazed pleasure. She hugged them both, offering her warmest congratulations and heartfelt good wishes for a long and joyous future, which – she smiled at Lucy – she was absolutely certain would be in store for them. As Anna spoke, looking at her much-loved son and his bride-to-be, she realised that she meant it. Her words precipitated a flood of tears from Lucy; they cried pleasurably in one another's arms for some minutes while Sam looked on with lofty embarrassment. At last Anna disengaged herself, laughing, and wiped her eyes. 'I think a toast's in order, isn't it?'

Sam eyed the wine box on the dresser warily. 'Actually, Mum –'

Lucy hiccuped, took her calfskin bag from the table and produced a bottle of champagne. 'Ta da!'

Anna blinked. Wow, Moët – she'd had champagne several times in her life, but rarely one as expensive as this. When she'd rustled up glasses, and filled a couple of bowls with nuts and crisps, they repaired to the living room. Sam prised the cork from the bottle with a pleasingly loud pop, and Lucy applauded as he poured it, foaming wildly, into their waiting glasses.

Anna raised her glass. 'To Sam, my beloved son, and to Lucy, his beautiful fiancée.' Fiancée? Dear lord – that meant daughter-in-law would come next. How could this possibly be? She wasn't old enough for this, she wasn't ready. Please God it would be a long engagement. Oh, why wasn't Jack here to help her make sense of everything? Sam smiled at her approvingly; Lucy kissed her again. Anna noticed she wasn't wearing a ring. Struck by a thought, she turned to Sam. 'Darling, why don't you take Lucy to the Lanes to find a ring? There are some fabulous antique shops there with really beautiful things, you know, Georgian garnets, Victorian sapphires in those sort of twisty settings…'

She'd been looking for a present for her mother's birthday a few weeks ago in the area of Brighton known as the Lanes. The winding, cobbled streets boasted several shops selling antique jewellery; she'd found the little silver creamer she'd bought for her mother beside a locked case with row upon row of exquisite rings. She'd stood for ages gazing at a square-cut amethyst surrounded by tiny seed pearls, hoping that one day Jack would …

She swallowed hard, and smiled brightly at Lucy. 'Though I expect you'd probably prefer to look for something in London.'

'Actually, Mum –'

'What about Portobello?'

'Mum.'

'Though from what I've read, it is incredibly expensive there now. Apparently the Americans –'

'Mum, I've bought Lucy a stone – a rather special stone.' He grinned. 'I think you're going to be surprised.'

'And when he says stone, he means *stone*.' Lucy looked serious. 'It has *meaning*, you know?'

Anna tried not to look surprised. Lucy looked far too – well, *worldly* – for esoteric tokens. Her cashmere jacket and knee-high boots must have cost more than Anna's entire wardrobe. Still, maybe she was a secret Druidess or something. Anna had read an article in one of the Sundays on the way stress was taking its toll on female high-flyers; apparently they were taking up yoga and meditation in droves. If Lavaglo was as repellent as it sounded, working on its account would surely tax the staunchest constitution. Druidism was probably the latest stress-buster for top female advertising executives – Lucy would certainly look good in the flowing robes, and those twig crowns they went in for would look great on her auburn hair. And all that chanting and prancing around in the open air must be doing her the world of good.

'I think that's fantastic.' She put her arms round Lucy and hugged her. 'What kind of stone?' She put her hand to her mouth. It would doubtless have some obscure meaning that was none of her business, like runes or something. 'Sorry, Lucy. Honestly, I don't mean to pry –'

'For heaven's sake, Mum, it's not exactly a state secret.' Sam looked impatient. 'I got it last week in London.'

Must have been at one of those weird little shops near the British Museum.

'It was from a jewellers in Hatton Gardens. A two-carat diamond. Pricey, but what the hell – frankly, we look at it as an investment.'

Well, OK! It was definitely one way of looking at 'meaning'.

Lucy smiled at her. 'We're having it set in platinum.'

Platinum?

'Mum. You're spilling your champagne.'

Anna resolutely banished memories of a small boy earnestly counting pennies from his china pig to buy her a tube of Love Hearts on Mothers' Day. 'So I am. Well, I must say it sounds as if it'll be absolutely fantastic – can't wait to see it.' She drained her glass. 'So, when's the big day? And where's it to be?'

She knew Lucy came from a big right-wing middle-class family. More to the point, perhaps, she knew they were staunch Catholics. But Lucy herself no longer attended church, and as far as Anna was aware, Sam had held no religious convictions since he was a small boy. Obviously Sam and Lucy would do what most young couples did these days – those that got married at all, that is – and opt for a simple civil service at a registry office. In London, presumably, since that was where most of their friends lived, to be followed by a party of some kind later in their flat, perhaps.

'... so that will mean about two hundred and fifty people at the church ...'

Church?

'... I rather thought a buffet at the reception, actually, but Mummy – oh, her name's Tina, by the way, she's absolutely dying to meet you – insists it should be sit-down. She says ...'

Two hundred and fifty?

'... in September. Probably the second week ...'

Carricktown? Wasn't that somewhere in Ireland? Still, be grateful for small mercies; at least it wasn't to be for another eighteen months. Anna murmured something jolly about leprechauns and shamrock, and let Sam refill her glass.

22

'... or roses and gypsophila. – Mummy hasn't decided yet. And I'm going to have page boys as well as bridesmaids. Well, Mummy says we've got to, most of her brothers have got sons and obviously they'll be terribly offended if they aren't included...'

Page boys? Anna risked a glance at her son. He was sitting in the velvet-covered armchair she always used to find him curled up in when she got home from work, devouring the peanut butter sandwiches she'd left for him while he did his homework ('it's easy-peasy, Mum') and watched *Blue Peter* ... *Grange Hill* ... *Star Trek* ... She looked away quickly, but he'd caught her glance.

He grinned. 'Got the message, Mum.' Getting up, he refilled the glasses, giving Lucy a kiss on the top of her head as he reached across her.

'... and probably The Trumpet Voluntary at the end, you know, when we come down the aisle.' She burst out laughing. 'Daddy says we ought to have Fight the Good Fight. I don't know, he's awful, Dads.'

Anna thought she didn't like the sound of Mummy too much, either.

'They're being absolutely fantastic about Sam not being a Catholic, aren't they, darling?' Lucy put her hand over Sam's. He nodded earnestly. 'So's Father O'Malley – he's known me forever. He baptised me, served my first communion and everything. He's grand.'

Anna thought of *Father Ted*, one of her all-time favourite television programmes, and the dissolute, drunken old priest who was one of the most popular characters, and repressed a desire to laugh hysterically.

'... children, of course – but he says as long as Sam attends the full course of marriage training all his engaged couples attend, it's fine with him.'

Marriage training? Sam? With his flash car and Alexander McQueen suits? Or maybe Lucy was joking? Yes, surely that must be it. Anna shifted slightly against the sofa cushions and looked at Sam. He was frowning at his clasped hands and

23

nodding earnestly. So it wasn't a joke, then. Oh, well. Best not go there. She must think of something intelligent to ask Lucy.

'Cake. I expect there'll be a cake, will there?'

Lucy beamed. 'Oh, yes, Mummy says she'll …'

Anna gripped the stem of her glass. Saw Sam notice, and twirled it lightly, smiling at Lucy and nodding in what +-

Smiling cheerfully, Anna raised her glass to her lips.

'… on the top tier, and pale pink rosebuds trailing round the rest …'

How many sodding tiers were there going to be? Hundreds, probably – after all, they were going to be feeding the five thousand …

'… and ivy twining round the bottom one, though Mummy may change her mind about that.' Lucy glanced at her watch. 'Lord, I can't believe it's nearly half-two! I'm sorry, Anna, I'm afraid you'll think me terribly rude, but I'm going to have to go.'

Anna was already on her feet. 'No, honestly, Lucy, I quite understand –'

'It's just that while we're down I want to see Kate. We were at uni together, best friends. She and Ben have just moved down to Kemp Town and their flat sounds to die for. They design company websites and honestly, they've made an absolute fortune. I'm going to ask her to be my matron of honour, and with time so short to get a dress made …'

What did she mean, with time so short? Anna laughed. 'It won't take eighteen months to make, surely?' Though come to think of it, Lucy's gown almost certainly would. Her mother was probably hiring the royal dressmakers, God help them; Kate Middleton's lacy gown with its semi-bustle and exquisite veil would seem like a mere practice run.

'For god's sake, Mum.' Sam hugged Anna affectionately 'It's April now, OK? Wedding's in September, right?' He counted on his fingers with exaggerated care. 'Yup, I still make that five.' He rolled his eyes at Lucy. 'Her maths always were lousy.'

Five months?

Anna set her glass down carefully. 'But?'

Five months?

Sam shrugged. 'No point in waiting to implement a decision once it's been made. First rule of management, right?'

Lucy gazed at him adoringly. 'Right, darling.'

Anna clutched weakly at a frail straw, knowing that it would snap even as she spoke. 'But how on earth will your mother get everything …?'

'You don't know Mummy.' Lucy laughed. 'She always says she works best under pressure.'

'But what about your dress? If five months is barely long enough to make one for the matron of honour –'

'Oh, that's no problem. Mummy wants me to wear hers.'

Anna made a sound that even to her own ears sounded like a chicken being strangled. Sam nudged her affectionately. 'You girls – I dunno. Talk about excited.' He turned to Lucy. 'Look, you really ought to be going, darling.'

'Bye, Anna.' Lucy beamed at her radiantly. 'I can't tell you how glad I am you're so thrilled about everything.' She turned to Sam. 'Back in about an hour to pick you up, OK, Samipops?'

Anna blinked. The champagne must be affecting her hearing. She couldn't have called him that.

'Sure, Lucykins –'

Anna picked up Lucy's still half-full glass, and drained it.

Kisses were exchanged; Sam went out into the hall with Lucy. Anna sat down again, and concentrated hard on staying calm. At least she'd have Sam to herself for a bit. Maybe once they were alone he'd feel safe to express his true feelings about the ridiculously grand scale of the wedding plans, and this marriage-training guff with Father O'Whatever-his-name-was.

'OK, Mum?'

Sam was back, and pouring more champagne into their glasses.

'You are happy about the news, aren't you? Lucy, she …' He beamed at her.

Anna thought with a pang that it was exactly the same expression he'd had when he'd rushed home from school to tell her he'd been picked for the first-year swimming team. Or the day he'd heard he'd got straight As in physics, maths and chemistry. Or the time he'd –

'She really is the one, you know.'

Anna felt a rush of love for her son so intense it required a major effort not to jump up and throw her arms round him. Instead, she picked up her glass. 'I'm happier than I can say for you, darling. And for what it's worth, I've never seen a couple better suited in my life.' It was true. Lucy and Sam *fitted.* And she'd get used to Lucy's mother's wedding with its poxy page boys and its festering Father O'Malley and its trillion-tiered cake being only five months away if it killed her. She raised her glass. 'Here's to you both.' They clinked glasses. Anna settled back comfortably amongst the cushions. 'Certainly sounds as if it's going to be quite a wedding. So many people – I'd no idea you had so many friends.'

'Oh, it's not only our friends, Mum. Tina and Eamonn are inviting all their friends, too. And everyone from the firm, of course – and their most important clients.'

Anna blinked.

The firm?

Clients? Lucy had mentioned something once about her father's company; something to do with steel imports. Sam must be furious, having his wedding turned into some sort of public relations jamboree. Hell, if it was her and Jack, she'd ... No. Definitely mustn't go there. She drank some more champagne. She'd have to find a way to drop a discreet hint to Lucy.

'Makes a lot of sense – there's always plenty of opportunity for networking at these occasions. There'll be some useful contacts there; in fact one or two who could prove to be very helpful in the future.'

'And you're OK with it being in church?'

He looked puzzled. 'Why wouldn't I be? Always think there's no sense of occasion in a registry office. We went to

Jules and Ozzie's do at Hampstead a couple of weeks ago. Frankly, they might as well have been nipping in to pay their council tax. No, if you want a sense of occasion, if you really want to make a bit of a splash, it's got to be a church. You get that sense of grandeur, of – I don't know – splendor, of –'

'So you've got no problems with the page boys, then.'

'Hell, no.' Sam drained his glass. 'There'd be a civil war in Fergustown if we veto page boys.'

'Right … Sam?'

'Gotcha.' He tipped the rest of the champagne into Anna's glass.

'No, I mean … Thank you, darling.' She took a sip. 'I … I'm sure you don't have to go through with this …' She imagined the dissolute old priest from *Father Ted* drunkenly effing and blinding his way through a lecture on the sanctity of holy wedlock. A giggle bubbled up in her throat. '… this marriage-training business, if you don't want to.'

Sam set down the empty bottle. 'I think it really is a very sound idea, you know. Consolidates one's sense of … things. Confirms one's idea of various … other things. Matter of fact, Tina's made it a condition of the union; she and Father O'Malley are very close. In fact you know, Mum, I sometimes wonder –' He gazed into space, frowning, then pulled himself together. 'And Eamonn –' He spread his hands comically. 'Well, you know Eamonn –'

'We've never met, darling –'

'No sorry, I keep forgetting. Don't worry, you soon will. Tina's planning to ring you – '

Oh god.

'And Lucy's keen to get things sorted out, so …'

'So?'

'It's just … I mean … no sense in rocking the boat.' He looked at her intently for a moment, then got up and moved to stand in front of the fireplace. 'Mum?'

He was hungry. Anna realised she was ravenous herself; she'd eaten hardly anything all day. She stood up, swaying slightly as the champagne made itself felt.

27

'Let me fix you something to eat, darling, you must be starving. There's loads of pasta, and I've got a pot of that sauce you like in the freezer. If I stick it on now, it'll be ready by the time Lucy gets back.'

'Mum?'

'Or there's some quiche, if you'd prefer – mushroom, I think, or is it spinach?'

'*Mum*? About Lucy's family. I don't just mean Tina and Eamonn – there are two sets of grandparents, and several aunts, and loads of great aunts, too. Plus all the uncles and their wives –'

She giggled. 'Going to be heavy on bath salts at Christmas.'

'The point is they're a very traditional lot. Conventional. Like things done a certain way.'

Anna smiled fondly at him. She knew exactly what he was trying to get up the courage to say: he wanted her to wear a hat. She'd never possessed a hat in her life, other than the despised berets and Panamas she'd been forced to wear at grammar school. Not surprisingly, they'd instilled a lifelong loathing of head gear of any kind. Still … maybe it was time to change her attitude. Look on hats as *fun*, a means of self-expression. Think of Andie McDowell in that film with Hugh Grant – she'd looked fabulous in that black and white cartwheel thing. And what about Audrey Hepburn in *My Fair Lady*? She'd worn some amazing creations …

'… and Grandma Taylor and Aunt Gwen. Of course, I don't know if Barbara and Don will be able to make it …'

Not that she'd want anything so conspicuous. Flowers might be nice, with the merest wisp of black veiling. The sort with tiny velvet dots, she'd always thought they were fabulous.

'… Uncle Mark, and obviously all my friends will be there, and the guys from work. I'm thinking of asking J.T. to be my best man. You remember him, Mum? Same year at Oxford, just been made head honcho at Gunter Prote –'

'Sam, it's going to be lovely. You know, I'm beginning to feel quite excited.'

28

'So there's no problem there.' He put his hands in his pockets. Took them out again. Cleared his throat. 'The thing is, Mum –'

'Darling, you're starving – what am I thinking of? Come and talk to me in the kitchen and I'll organise the food.'

'Mum?' He shoved his hands in his pockets again. 'Going back to Lucy's family …'

Smiling, Anna began to put the empty glasses on the tray. 'Don't worry, angel, I promise to wear a hat. Now, how about some garlic bread? And I'll throw together a green salad. Or maybe tomato and basil would be nice?'

'As I said, they've got very old-fashioned values. Lucy's father's just been made chief warden of St Aloysius. Tina's a pillar of the Mothers' Union. They donate God knows how much to the church every year, and at least three of the great-aunts are nuns. Father O'Malley's always holding them up as the perfect example of the ideal Catholic family, and I …' He put the half-empty bowl of nuts on the tray. 'I don't want to look different.'

'Different? But Don's doing fine now Barbara's finally managed to get him to AA, and ever since Grandpa Taylor passed on, Grandma's been much better behaved.'

Sam placed the bottle on the tray. Took a nut from the bowl, lifted it to his mouth, put it back again and slowly straightened up. Anna noticed that his hands were shaking.

'Sam? What on earth …?'

'I want to invite my father to the wedding.'

Anna was suddenly aware of the deep pink of the lilies in their tall vase in front of the fireplace, the sound of a car backfiring in the street, a trail of biscuit crumbs – biscuit crumbs? No, they must be from the crisps – on the polished wood of the coffee table. She bent down slowly. Grasped the handles of the tray.

When she straightened up, she was smiling. 'No problem, darling. In fact I'm sure he'll be thrilled to be invited.' Her reward was the look of pure relief on her son's face.

She handed him the tray. 'Come on, let's get that pasta on the go. Lucy'll be back soon.'

'Sure thing. I'll grate the parmesan, if you like. Hey, I might even lay the table!'

He led the way out into the hall. Anna followed him. For now, she'd concentrate on making sure the rest of Sam and Lucy's visit passed off successfully, and the tomato and garlic sauce didn't burn.

Now wasn't the time to worry about how she was going to cope with Tony, the ex-husband neither she nor Sam had seen or heard from for the past seventeen years.

There'd be plenty of time for that later.

CHAPTER THREE

Jack strode purposefully down Beech Avenue in the early evening sunshine, heading for home. Tonight he was definitely going to sort things out: call a spade a spade; put his money where his mouth was; kick ass, and so on. He'd show Anna he could cut it, oh yes. He felt terrible that she'd been so upset at lunchtime. Christ knows, it had been hard enough to get to see her at all – bloody Jennings had tried to force him to take library duty, the old bastard. It had taken all his ingenuity to get out of it. Still, he was pretty proud of the excuse he'd come up with. Not everyone would have thought to say they had an appointment with the chiropodist. Doctor, yes. Dentist, even. But to come up with *chiropodist* took a pretty cool head, if he did say so himself. He must remember to limp a bit if he bumped into the old buzzard tomorrow.

After all that to have things go so hideously wrong! Jesus, he hadn't even got to first base. And she'd been looking more amazing than ever. In fact, just thinking about Anna in that red underwear made him – he groaned aloud. Christ, he could hardly walk. Quick, think about something unpleasant, Jack Teale, and fast.

Ruth.

That had done the trick all right. He hoped she wouldn't be in one of her moods when he got in. If she was, he didn't stand a hope in hell of getting through. In fact now he came to think of it, wasn't Thursday one of her teaching nights? Christ, she'd be unbearable. He'd have to put things off till tomorrow. But then what would he tell Anna if she rang in the lunch hour? Maybe he could leave his mobile at home by mistake so she couldn't get through. No, she'd know – bloody women always had a nose for that sort of thing.

His step slowed; in a couple of minutes he'd be home. Hell and damnation, he'd been feeling fine until a couple of minutes ago – that Red Bull Geoff had recommended had really done the trick. He'd been buzzing with energy. Maybe he should have another can? Geoff said he often sank a second swift one at half-time when he was coaching the fifth-year rugger buggers. The poor sod could barely stay awake these days what with his new sprog screaming its head off till dawn and his wife refusing to do night feeds.

Glancing round furtively, he set down his briefcase and pulled the red-and-blue striped can from his pocket. The street was empty apart from some old girl tottering along on her walker on the other side of the street. Ripping off the tab he downed the contents in one long pull, wiped his mouth on the back of his hand and settled his spectacles more comfortably on the bridge of his nose.

That was more like it! That had got the blood coursing pretty smartly round the old veins again. In fact he felt like a million dollars. He'd take Geoff out for a quick one at lunchtime tomorrow to say thanks, and to hell with Sixth Form Chess Club! Now to show Ruth who was boss. Picking up his briefcase, he strode on, humming the theme from *Superman*. As he passed the postbox (nearly at No 58, now) he gave a fearless laugh and chucked the empty can into the gutter. *Da DEE! Da da da DEE da!* Put things off? What on earth could he have been thinking of?

'Young man!'

He'd go straight in the kitchen and say his piece right away. Force bloody Ruth to listen.

'Vandal! Hooligan! Pick that up at once, or I shall report you.'

The old lady – who must have been moving with astonishing speed, he reflected later – had drawn abreast on the opposite side of the road and stood leaning on her walker beneath a sparsely blossomed cherry tree, waving a palsied fist at him.

He jumped. Dear God, please don't let any of the neighbours be looking out of their windows.

'Right away, ma'am, didn't mean for a moment to … Darn thing just slipped out of my hand –'

She stood watching him closely as he retrieved the offending can and stuffed it into his pocket.

'Won't happen again, I assure you, ma'am.'

What if she reported him to Neighbourhood Watch? Bound to give a good description, old bat obviously had twenty-twenty vision under those inch-thick bifocals. What if it got back to Jennings? He flashed her a placatory smile. 'Good heavens, look – somebody's dropped a nasty old burger box, ooh yuck, ugh.' He picked it up and thrust it in his pocket.

'That's better, young man. And remember, I've got my eye on you.'

His hand was shaking as he opened his front gate. Hell, this was no good. He was going to have to down another booster if he was going to say his piece to Ruth. Lucky he had more left.

He hurried up the path and round the side of the house, tripping over his son's tricycle as he foraged in his briefcase for another can. Old bitch – he'd keep an eye out for her next time he was in the car and sound the horn so loudly the old bat would drop dead of a heart attack. He ripped off the tag, and drank deeply. It would probably take a nuclear explosion to see her off, but it would at least give her a fright, which would certainly make him feel a whole lot better. He polished off the rest of the can's contents. Wow. That felt great! *Da DEE*! *Da da da DEE da*!

Chucking the empty can and burger box into Spike's kennel (checking casually to see if it was empty first, of course – no sense in buying trouble), he went round to the front of the house, opened the front door with a masterful air and went inside, wincing as a wall of sound hit him. From upstairs came the thudding backbeat of whichever group the twins currently favoured; from the living room the soundtrack of some American cartoon blared, accompanied by Spike's frenzied barking. As he dropped his keys in the cracked ceramic bowl on the Spanish pine chest, he noted fresh scratch marks gouged into the delicately carved lower panel. Why the hell had they bought Charlie that mini-scooter for Christmas? Because he'd have screamed blue murder whenever the ruddy advert came on if they hadn't, that was why, and because he'd have soiled his *Finding Nemo* duvet cover every night for the next six months to teach them a lesson. As soon as he'd informed Ruth of his intentions, he'd sort Charlie out, starting with getting him to bring in his tricycle when he'd finished playing – he could have broken his leg. Hell, he could have broken both legs.

OK. He stripped off his mac and headed for the coat stand, his progress impeded by the litter of sequinned bomber jackets (the twins) and small brown and navy padded anorak from Mini Boden (Charlie) strewn over the carpet. As he kicked aside a pink PVC garment with 'SLITS RULE OK' picked out in glitter on the back, he reflected that a casual visitor might have supposed the house to be inhabited by prostitutes and midget workmen. It simply wasn't good enough. Before he gave Ruth the news about his imminent departure, he'd give her a piece of his mind about the mess in the hall. And everywhere else in the house, for that matter. And as for the noise! He strode to the bottom of the stairs and yelled the twins' names. No reply. Hardly surprising, they'd probably both gone completely deaf by now. He'd wait till they came down for supper, then by God he'd let them have it. As for Charlie, he could turn that racket down *right now*, and stop whatever he was doing to the bloody dog. Picking up his briefcase, he headed for the living room and pushed open the door.

His small son was crouched on the floor, his back to the television, gripping the writhing Spike tightly with one hand and doing something in the region of the dog's muzzle with the other. With one stride Jack was at the television. Switching it off, he turned to Charlie. 'Just what the hell is going on in here? Either keep the sound down or it stays off, right, Charlie? And stop whatever it is you're doing to Spike, you can see he doesn't –' At once his son burst into furious tears, saying, or rather babbling, in Jack's opinion no five-year-old could be said to talk, that a) he *had* been watching, it was his favourite and it wasn't fair, and b) he and Spike were playing a *game*, and that wasn't fair either, and c) he hated his father. To back up this information he threw himself flat on his back and began to scream at a pitch Jack had hitherto assumed only bats could hear, simultaneously drumming his heels hard on the floor.

Spike shot behind the sofa, barking louder than ever.

Right. Maybe this wasn't the best moment; the boy was probably hungry. Or thirsty. Or tired, yes, that could be it. He'd speak firmly to him later about the tricycle – very firmly, no question about that. Meanwhile, he'd switch the television on again, though not too loudly, one had to take a stand – and give Spike a stern warning. As he left the room and set off down the passage to the kitchen, he tried not to notice that the television sound had been turned up again to full volume, and that Spike's barks had not diminished.

Now for Ruth. After the little contretemps with Charlie, he was in no mood to be trifled with, as she'd certainly find to her cost if she gave him any trouble. *Da DEE! Da da da* – how did the rest go? No matter; he was already at the kitchen door. Deep breath. Push it open with a manly gesture, and –

'Where the hell have you been? Christ, can't you *ever* get home on time?' His wife bent over the dishwasher, tugging irritably at a dangerously overloaded wire tray. She didn't look up.

He slammed his briefcase down on the nearest chair, not noticing the heap of DVD's already in occupation. Several slid to the floor with a dull thud. Ruth glanced irritably over her shoulder. 'You know those are from the library, I take it? And that any damage has to be paid for?'

He started to pick them up, then stopped himself; he had more weighty matters to address. He folded his arms magisterially. 'There's something I have to say, Ruth –'

With a crash, the tray came loose from its moorings, decanting most of its contents over the floor. Broken crockery awash with an unidentifiable grey liquid spilled over the already greasy tiles.

'Now look what you've made me do!' Ruth swung round to face him, her face tight with anger. She ran a hand through her newly cropped black hair. He knew it was fashionable, but it made her look harder, somehow, and gave her an unnervingly insect-like appearance. For the briefest of moments an image of the way Ruth had been in the early days flashed through his mind: her delicate features and clear, pale skin; her warm brown eyes; her cap of black curls; her interest in everything, her delightful laugh. The image of Audrey Hepburn, his father used to say, with a grin that said *lucky chap*. Where had it all gone? When had it changed? One thing he was damn sure of – it wasn't down to *him*, no sirree.

'I *told* you we should have bought the Zanussi – it's bloody useless, this.'

Hell, she was still rabbiting on. He was pretty sure of something else – if his father was still alive he wouldn't be grinning at him now. Forget Kay Kendall – one of the warders in *Prisoner Cell Block H* was more the mark these days …

'Just because it was a few quid cheaper! Bloody typical. Well, you can clean this lot up yourself, I'm off in twenty minutes and I haven't even planned the little bastard's lesson yet.'

Time to get a grip. Let's see … *DEE da*! Yup, that was it. Now, where had he got to?

'– something very important.'

'Important? I'll tell you what's important.' She crouched down and foraged in the cupboard under the sink. Jack tried not to notice the way her green wool skirt emphasised her boyish shape, her lack of curves, so different from Anna's body, though he mustn't think about that now. Too late – the old trouser-snake was already reacting … He edged behind the table.

'What's important is that I'm not late to teach Quentin Wetherby-bloody-Smythe compound fractions in the hope that with the grace of God and a fair following wind the little shit will pass his GCSE in a couple of months and his grateful parents will give his bloody tutor a bonus.' She backed out from under the sink and hurled a pungent floor cloth at Jack. 'So that said tutor will be able to shell out for the next electricity bill. Got it?'

He knelt, with difficulty, and began to clean up the mess. 'Look Ruth, this can't wait.'

She turned away, and began taking packets of food from the fridge and throwing them down on the table. 'Neither can the kids' tea.'

He cleared his throat and ran a finger round the back of his collar. '*Onward, onward into the shadow of death rode the six hundred.*'

'I've decided I'm leav –'

As she dumped a packet of oven chips on the table, she glanced up. Her eyes narrowed. 'What the hell have you done with your tie?'

Tie? What was she talking about? Suddenly he had a mental picture of himself in Anna's kitchen, pulling off his tie as she … He closed his eyes briefly. When he opened them again he saw with a sudden loosening of the bowels that Ruth was standing over him, so close he could see the whiteheads on her chin.

'My mother gave you that tie, Jack. I know you were wearing it when you left this morning because I noticed the egg stain on it, so *where is it now*?'

He could feel the blood drain from his cheeks. Think. Head bent, he scooped the broken fragments of glass and china into an untidy pile. Think! Christ, if only he had another Red Bull in his briefcase …

'Er … yes. Afraid I had to lend it to Geoff.'

'Geoff?'

'One of the games staff.'

'Why, pray?'

'Because he had to er … go to a funeral. Yes. Of a friend.'

'But it's not a black tie.'

'Er … no. They weren't very close friends.'

'But –'

There was the sound of pounding feet in the passage and the kitchen door was thrown open. It banged against the faded yellow wall behind it, deepening the already sizeable hole in the plaster. Charlie hurtled in, followed by the maniacally barking dog. He threw himself at his mother's legs, wailing something entirely incomprehensible to Jack. Really, it was too much; he was going to have to assert himself here. 'Charlie, your mother and I are trying to have a little talk here, and I'd appreciate it if –'

Ruth scowled at him. 'Oh, for God's sake, Jack –' The door shot open again and the twins erupted into the kitchen, identical expressions of outrage on their heavily made-up fifteen-year-old faces. They threw themselves down at the table. At least he could sort *them* out. He got to his feet. 'Right girls. I've said this before and I'm saying it again; the noise from your bedroom is entirely unacc –'

Ignoring him, Jess turned to Ruth. 'Mum, tell the little shite we'll kill him –'

'Language, girls, *please*.' Ruth frowned. 'I've told you before, it's not big –'

'Yeah, too right, kill him –' Poppy drew a forefinger sharply across her throat.

'If he goes into our room again.'

'Too right.' The younger by ten minutes, Poppy always acted as support act to her sister.

'... and it's not clever.'

A noisy exchange ensued between Ruth and the twins from which it became apparent that Charlie had filched the girls' new gold eyeliner, sneaked it downstairs and applied it liberally to Spike's eyelids, or as close to Spike's eyelids as the frantic dog would allow him to get.

With a sigh, Jack got to his feet, fished a yellowing *Guardian* from the pile of old newspapers on top of the fridge, bundled the dripping shards of china and glass into it and dropped the whole mess in the bin. The crash as it hit the horrors already lurking within caused his entire family to swing round and glare wordlessly at him before returning to the row. While Ruth's attention was diverted he took the opportunity to slip a Budweiser from the fridge. With a bit of luck things would run their course and the twins would bugger off upstairs, taking Charlie with them to teach him a short, sharp lesson, and he'd have a chance to finish sorting Ruth out. He took a long pull at the beer. He'd definitely make his point this time, oh yes, and in no uncertain terms, either.

'Everybody happy again?' Ruth hugged the girls briskly, kissed Charlie and patted the dog. 'There's sausage and chips, and those breaded onion rings you like. Pack of family fruit trifles in the fridge for afters. Make sure your father –'

'Oh Mum, he's not *cooking*, is he?' Poppy and Jess regarded him balefully. '*Gross*.'

'OK, Jack? Instructions on the packets not too difficult for an M.A. Hons in English Literature to follow, I hope?'

She was at the door.

Christ, she wasn't going already, was she? But he hadn't had a chance to finish what he had to say! And what was that about breaded onion rings? Surely she didn't expect him to *cook*? That was *her* job, like bringing up the children was supposed to be.

'But Ruth – I've got a pile of essays to mark, and I still haven't finished my report on last term's percentages for old Jennings –'

'And I've got a pile of bloody tutoring to do.'

The twins, who'd been drawing lewd diagrams in the spill of brown sugar they'd tipped from the sugar bowl, smirked at him. 'Call up or text us when it's ready, OK? And cook the bloody sausages right through this time, or me and Poppy'll report you to Childline for giving us worms, OK?'

'Yeah, Childline.' Poppy narrowed her eyes, looking terrifyingly like Ruth. 'And we'll tell them the address.'

Charlie began to cry. Ruth blew him a kiss and told him that if he was very, very good, Daddy would let him help.

Last time she'd made him cook, the fish fingers had still been frozen in the middle when he served them. The twins' silence had cost him twenty-five pounds apiece.

'But you're so much better at it than I am, poppet – and I really am snowed under with work.' He gestured at his

39

briefcase. 'Couldn't you call the Wetherby-Smythes and say you'll be half an hour late?'

'Bloody hell, d'you think I *want* to go out at this time of the evening and bore myself to death for two hours trying to explain basic mathematics to a fourteen-year-old with a brain the size of a dried pea?' She snatched her bag from the hook on the back of the door. 'Jesus, Jack – if you'd applied for Head of English at Dulverton High last year I wouldn't *need* to be bloody tutoring.'

Jack looked away. The reason he hadn't applied was because he didn't want to move away from Anna. He thought of her face – her expression when she was coming, the way she arched her back as she called his name, the way she ... He set the Budweiser down forcefully on the table. *Da DEE!*

'Look, the reason I didn't apply –'

Ruth was watching him through narrowed eyes.

Da da da DEE da! 'I've been trying to say this for a while now. Come into the living room and I'll –'

There was a crash and a screech from Charlie as he reached for the packet of cereal still on the table from breakfast and knocked over Jack's bottle of beer. Before he could get to it, Spike had shot out of his basket, where he had retreated to sulk, and was lapping up Budweiser like a desperate alcoholic, egged on by the delighted twins.

'For God's sake, Jack!' Ruth dropped her bag, shot over to the dog and grabbed his collar. 'Can't you even be trusted with a bloody –'

The girls clapped and whistled as she tried to drag Spike away from the pool of beer. Head down and legs stiffly splayed, he resisted, lapping faster as she tugged.

'Sorry ... sorry ...' He opened the back door, seized Spike and chucked him out into the garden.

Charlie burst into tears again, the twins booed. Ruth washed her hands in the sink. She shot him a furious glance over her shoulder. 'How the hell could you be so stupid as to leave it there? And then not to make the smallest, slightest effort to stop him drinking it! Can't you do *anything* right, Jack?' She hugged

Charlie and reminded him about helping Daddy cook. Jack repressed a groan. Muttering something about 'things to do', the twins slid out of the room, nudging each other and giggling.

What was it the Duke of Wellington had said? '*To know when to retreat – and to dare to do it.*' Poor blighter must have been married to a bitch like Ruth. With a sigh, he took off his jacket, hung it over the chair and rolled up his sleeves. The chipolatas lay like somnolent slugs in their clouded cellophane; they reminded him horribly of limp penises. Taking a knife from the table drawer, he started to slit open the slippery bag of oven chips. With a crow of delight, Charlie grabbed the bag and upended it onto the floor.

'By the way, Jack,' Ruth stood by the kitchen door. 'I know why you didn't apply to Dulverton.'

He went quite cold; the knife slipped from his nerveless fingers. He turned his head slowly.

'Because you were *too bloody chicken.*' Her lip curled. 'You just couldn't face up to the challenge, could you?'

She left the room, slamming the door hard behind her.

He knew it had been a mistake, trying to tell her on one of her teaching nights.

He'd try again tomorrow.

CHAPTER FOUR

Anna peered at her reflection in the tiny mirror in the coffee bar loo, trying to decide whether make-up would improve things. Probably not; it would take more than a dab of mascara and a slick of lip gloss to repair the ravages wrought by too much alcohol and too little sleep. Best leave well alone. Sighing, she scooped the tubes and brushes back into her bag, retied her navy-and-white striped apron and headed back behind the serving counter.

Working fast so that she wouldn't have time to think about anything except the task in hand, she got the coffee makers started, set out the stacks of crockery, baskets of cutlery and piles of napkins, and put the fruit and vegetables for the salads beside the chopping boards. She was placing an earthenware jug of daffodils beside the till when Trish and Susie, her part-time assistants, strolled in.

'Blimey, Anna – early bird or what?' Trish, a plump, shaven-headed graphics student at the local art college, grinned as she hung up her donkey jacket and rolled up her sleeves.

Anna shrugged in what she hoped was a casual manner. 'I caught the early bus by mistake, think my watch must be fast.' In fact, she'd left home at half past eight because she couldn't bear to sit in the kitchen nursing a cold cup of tea and brooding any longer.

'Oh, it's awful when that happens, isn't it?' Susie, another graphics student, rolled her eyes. Her blonde prettiness was all but obliterated this morning by a thick layer of what appeared to be white undercoat and rings of purple eyeshadow that made her look as if she'd just gone a couple of rounds with Mike Tyson. 'Much worse than being late.'

Anna laughed. 'Definitely. OK, could you make a start on the stuff for the fruit salad, Susie? And Trish, today there's onion tart, parsnip soup and rice salad.' Trish had a reputation for her witty culinary illustrations, and her first task every morning was to chalk up the specials on the blackboard. While the girls set to work, discussing the shortcomings of the head of the graphics department and musing on painful methods of despatching him, Anna hauled the enormous bowl of rice she'd cooked the previous morning from the industrial-sized fridge and began to prepare the rest of the ingredients.

It was harder not to think about yesterday when she was standing still; no matter how fast she chopped onions and peppers. Images – in technicolour, with a sinister accompaniment reminiscent of the soundtrack from *Jaws* – kept popping into her mind. Sam, gazing in horror at her red underwear. Lucy, smiling as she handed her a bunch of tulips. And oh, God, Sam clearing his throat, and saying, 'Mum, we've got something to tell you.'

She picked up another pepper. This one wasn't as fresh as the others she'd used; she must have missed it yesterday when she made her daily cull of the fridge for any produce past its sell-by date. She was about to throw it in the bin when she looked at it more closely. It was an almost perfect heart shape, a deep crimson colour, rather than the bright scarlet of the other fruit. After a moment she took the knife and cut it in half. A trickle of dark red juice began to seep onto the wooden chopping board. Anna gazed at it for a while; at the seeds clinging to the ventricles of yellowing flesh, like little clusters of withered hopes. Then, digging in her apron pocket, she found a crumpled bill and a stub of pencil and began to write.

She jumped as an elbow dug her sharply in the ribs.

'Hi, Anna! Sorry I'm late, only Ron let Damien stay up 'til gone one to watch the horror even though it was a bleedin' school night, so he couldn't get up this morning could he? Little sod was only tryin' to make out he had meningitis, wasn't he? I can tell you he really had me goin' for a minute there. Then Jade screamed blue murder all the way to play school 'cos I wouldn't let her take the dead pigeon she found in the gutter for Show and Tell, so we had to stop off at McDonald's for one of them ice-cream doodahs to shut her up ... '

Roxy, who'd worked for Anna for almost two years and so far hadn't once arrived on time, shucked off her fun-fur coat, flung it in the direction of the row of coat pegs, fished an apron from beneath a pile of tea cloths, threw a stack of baguettes she'd collected on her way to work onto a chopping board and set to work. Anna never complained about Roxy's erratic timekeeping, knowing that she always made up for her late starts by doing extra time at the end of her shifts and never refused to work Saturdays. 'To be honest I prefer it, duck, I'd work Sundays too to if we was open, I mean the kids and Ron under me feet all day? I tell you, the lounge, it's like a scene from *Gladiator* by the time *Casualty* comes on.'

'Hi, Roxy.' Anna scooped slices of red pepper into the bowl of rice salad, and tried to smile. 'A dead pigeon, eh? Still, you've got to admit it'd make a change from teddy bears and Sindy dolls.'

'Teddy bears and ...?' Roxy eyed her incredulously and chopped a baguette into three uneven portions with a flourish. 'You got to be kidding. It's all mobiles and tablets these days, love. I said to Ron – Yes, love?' She hurried to the counter to serve an early customer needing coffee.

Anna gave the rice salad a final stir, covered it with a clean tea cloth and returned it to the fridge. Then she lit the ancient gas oven and drew the trays of onion tarts from the freezer, counting them aloud in a vain attempt to keep the memory of the dread words, 'I want to invite my father' at bay.

'Anna?' Roxy had given the customer her change and was looking at her curiously. 'You all right?'

'Me? Yes, course I am.' As Anna energetically wiped over the area where she'd been working, the vegetable knife fell to the floor with a clatter, narrowly missing her sandalled foot. She burst into tears.

'Blimey, what's up love?'

'Nothing, I –' She scrubbed at her eyes with the hem of her apron.

'Don't do that, love, you'll give yourself conjunctivitis.' Roxy poured coffee into a mug and pressed it into Anna's hand. 'Time of the month, is it?'

Anna shook her head.

'Come on, you know you can tell your Auntie Roxy. Trouble shared is a trouble halved, and that.' She poked a bright red comb that was threatening to become dislodged firmly into place at the back of her blonde beehive. 'I felt shitloads better after I told you about Ron's rash on his dingle that time. I was dead certain it was one of them sexually transmuted things, but you were right on track about changing the washing powder.'

Roxy took a lipstick-smeared tissue from her apron pocket and thrust it at Anna. She took it gratefully and blew her nose.

'It's … Sam.'

'Oh yeah, meant to say; he was in lunchtime yesterday lookin' for you. Dead flash clobber, and not cheap, neither – I seen that jacket in Topman's window last week, it was nearly eighty quid. Find you all right, did he? Said him and his girlfriend wanted to take you out for a drink. His birthday, was it?'

'No. He's …' Anna scrubbed hard at her wet eyes. '… He's getting married.'

'But that's *good* news, innit, love?' Roxy hugged her enthusiastically. 'I mean 's'not as if it was a daughter, where you'd be run off your feet trailing round up town looking for a dress and forced to work all the hours God sends makin' sardine vol au vents and that for the reception.'

Anna managed a watery smile.

'Get on all right with the girlfriend, do you? Must say she seemed nice enough, though I got to admit I've never been a one for gingernuts.'

'She's lovely. And Sam adores her –'

'Just you feel like you're losin' a son, not gainin' a daughter. Don't worry, love, you're bound to feel a bit wonky for a few days. Though like I said to Ron the other night after I caught

Dean tryin' to shave his hamster with my Ladyshave, my two can't leave home fast enough for me.' She bent and picked up the knife Anna had dropped and exchanged it for a clean one. 'Tell you what, try lookin' on it as an excuse for a new outfit. If you like, we could –'

'Excuse me, I assume the coffee's decaffeinated?'

A thin, fair-haired woman in a green anorak and floral leggings was staring at the row of steaming Conas accusingly. 'If not, allow me to tell you precisely why it should be. I've just read a most alarming article in the current issue of *Nature's Way*. It's on the same page as the excellent recipe for fig-and-prune smoothie, if memory serves me right, and believe me –'

Roxy rolled her eyes at Anna. 'Back in a jiff.' She turned towards the counter with a look of exaggerated interest.

Anna got Trish to scrub down the draining boards, and asked Susie to go out for more supplies of the peppermint teabags there'd been a run on in the afternoons recently. She was sliding the last of the onion tarts into the oven by the time Roxy finally got rid of the woman.

'Silly bitch. What's the point of having a coffee if it don't give you a bit of a buzz?' She wiped her hands on her apron. 'Make a start on filling the French things, shall I?'

'Thanks, Roxy.'

'So, where was I? Yeah, shopping. We could go round the shops together, if you want. The way I see it, being the bridegroom's mother's an opportunity to really go to town.' She began to smear butter on the baguettes. 'What d'you want in 'em today, love? Bit of cheese and salad? Few tunas? Couple with that hummus muck for the weirdos?'

'Great.'

'I seen a fab leopard-skin coat up the market last weekend. I said to Ron, you'd never know it was fake if it wasn't electric blue. And there was a hat went with it, like them Russians wear, it'd look dead good with big glittery earrings. I could lend you some if you want, I got hundreds. Crocodile stilettos, and a big matching bag – your boy'll wet himself he'll be so proud.'

She squeezed past Anna to get to the fridge, and saw her miserable expression. 'Hey, it don't have to be leopard skin if you don't fancy it, love. They got all sorts – '

'No, it's not that, honestly. It's just … just …'

'Come on, love, spit it out.' Roxy opened the fridge and peered inside. 'I know, it's the present, isn't it? Not to worry, I got an idea for that, too.' She took out several plastic containers, stacked them on top of each other, balanced a couple of lettuces and a cucumber on the summit of the pile, kicked the fridge door shut and stood regarding Anna triumphantly. 'A Ruby Red Venetian Glass Punch Set with Gilt Effect Engraving, that's what you want.'

'Punch set?' Anna lifted the lettuces and cucumber from their shaky perch and began to prepare them.

'Yeah. The Perfect Gift for that Auspicious Occasion. Or you could go for the Lime Green, that's the one we gave Ron's mum and dad for their Golden. Talking point or what – you'll never hear the end of it, once they work out what it is.' She cut a corner off a piece of Emmenthal and stuffed it in her mouth. 'Tell you what, I'll bring the catalogue in tomorrow.'

'Catalogue?'

'Argos.'

'OK. Um … thanks.'

Roxy watched Anna chop a lettuce into smaller and smaller shreds. 'Present's not it either, is it love?'

'No, really, that's a great idea –'

'Then how come you're still lookin' like you lost a tenner and found five p?'

'It's just …' Anna shoved the pile of almost puréed lettuce to the side of the chopping board and ran a hand through her hair. 'Oh God, Roxy. Sam wants to invite Tony to the wedding.'

'Druggie, is he? Still, you can't stop Sam inviting his friends, love –'

'He's not a friend. He's his father.' She peeled the cucumber. 'My ex.'

'Blimey, you never mentioned an ex before.'

'I try not to think about him.'

'Live in Brighton, does he?'

Anna shook her head.

Roxy added slices of cucumber to the tuna-filled baguettes. 'Sam's close to him though, I s'pect. My sister Renee's divorced and she says her kids think their dad's the bleedin' tops, what with all them visits up Alton Parks and that every weekend. Stands to reason he'd want to invite him, if you think, love. Probably got up to all sorts together in the last few years, ten pin bowlin' … go-kartin' …'

'Roxy.'

'Course, age your Sam is it'd be more like paint-ballin' weekends and that.'

'Afraid not.' Anna began to purée the second lettuce. 'He emigrated when Sam was five.'

Roxy stared at her. 'He never.'

'Said he needed to find himself.'

'Come again?'

'He liked to think of himself as an Artist. Unfortunately, a third-class degree in graphic design isn't really adequate qualification for acceptance into the higher echelons of the art world.' She grinned. 'Or even the lower echelons, come to that. Anyway, after he'd failed to get an offer from a single gallery he had a string of jobs in crappy design agencies. Got "let go" by all of them, and after that, things at home went from bad to worse. I woke up one morning to find a note on his pillow saying he'd gone to Australia "a country where his talent would be appreciated", to "follow his destiny" without "the shackles of family life" holding him back.'

'Been watchin' too much of that *Crocodile Dundee*, by the sound of it.'

'Anyway, we haven't seen or heard from him since. Unless you count a postcard a year or so after he left. Since then, zilch.'

The postcard hadn't even said 'wish you were here'. Anna turned away and pulled a couple of large tins from a cupboard. 'Stick the baguettes in a basket and put them on the counter, would you, Roxy? Thanks.' She removed several cakes from the tins and began to slice them.

'Blimey.' Roxy was silent for a while as she fought the baguettes into an untidy heap and transferred them to a basket. 'But if he was such a doober, why did you …?'

'Usual story. We were at the same art college – I was studying fabric design. I got pregnant after a party.' She shrugged. 'We just sort of drifted into getting married. Our parents encouraged it, Tony was handsome … '

'Yeah, Ron was a looker when I met him, dead ringer for Elvis.'

'It was OK at first, I suppose, except he wouldn't let me take any of the jobs I was offered.'

'Ooh, you got your certificate, then, did you?'

Anna nodded. She'd got a starred first, and been deluged with offers of work from top-level design companies, all of whom would have been happy to continue to employ her on a part-time basis after the baby was born. Tony had refused point blank to let her take up any of them; no child of his was going to have an absentee mother. Or, Anna had thought, but restrained herself from saying, a child whose mother was more successful than his father.

'Somehow things just went from bad to worse.'

The rows escalated; in the end Anna gave in. The next five years were a nightmare. Sam was a sickly child, suffering from a series of infections that made him scream non-stop; Tony was incapable of holding down a job for more than a week and made it crystal clear that he blamed his failure on his wife and child. Apparently he was under so much stress that it was simply impossible for him to *create*.

'In the end, it was almost a relief when he went.'

'I can imagine. So how'd you manage?'

'It was too late by then to get back into design. There was too much new technology I'd missed out on. Still, we had to eat, and the bills were piling up –'

'The bugger never sent you no money, then?'

'No.'

'Rotten bastard. Still, bears out what I always say, dunnit?'

Anna looked enquiring – there were a lot of things Roxy always said.

'Shits, the lot of 'em. I mean look at Ron, useless bugger. Soon as I've saved enough from me wages here, I'll be off.'

Anna tried not to smile. Despite Roxy's constant denigration of the hapless Ron, it was clear from the affectionate remarks that occasionally slipped out that she could no more have lived without him than without her three equally maligned offspring.

'Anyway, a couple of weeks after he'd gone I saw an advert for a coffee-bar assistant in the *Evening Argus*. Sam was back at school by then. For some reason his health cleared up like magic as soon as Tony left. So …'

'Excuse me, miss. Is anyone actually serving here?' An elderly clergyman with a face like a malevolent rat stood tapping a copy of the *Church Times* impatiently on the counter.

Roxy grinned at Anna. 'And from there it was straight to the top, eh?' She turned to the clergyman, looking serious. 'So sorry, your worship. My colleague and me was just discussing the relevance of religion, if any, to modern life. I don't know, the Ten Commandments …' She slapped her thigh. 'Don't you just love 'em?' She resumed her serious look again. 'Now, what can I help you with?' She started to list the entire menu, ignoring him whenever he tried to interrupt.

Anna concentrated hard on cutting up a ginger cake, and let her thoughts drift back to Life After Tony. It had been tough, but at least she had the satisfaction of knowing she'd brought her son up single-handed without so much as a Good Luck card from his father, let alone regular child support. Somehow she'd always managed to scrimp together enough for Christmas and birthday presents, and once she'd even managed to send Sam on a school trip to France. True, she could rarely afford to buy new clothes for herself, and the nearest she ever got to a holiday was the day trip to London she allowed herself once every summer, when she visited all the free exhibitions and bought a cheap ticket for the Proms. But she'd coped, and she was proud of it.

'That'll teach him.' Roxy watched the clergyman totter off clutching a tray. 'Them flapjacks ought to give his dentures a serious workout.' She picked a slice of crystallised lemon off the top of a slice of ginger cake and ate it. 'It'll be all right, love. Chances of young Sam managin' to track his father down after all these years must be about zero. Even if he did, there's no way the bugger'd have the brass neck to accept the invitation after the way he's treated you. Speakin' of which, how come young Sam's so keen to make contact if he knows what a tosser his dad is?'

'He doesn't. I never told him what happened. He thinks his father really was a genius, and really did have to go and follow his star. Better that than letting him know what a feckless, irresponsible bastard he was.' She lifted a cake from the other tin.

'Hello hello hello? Is that a cherry gateau I see before me?'

Anna smiled as she saw the man leaning against the counter. 'Hi, Barry. Nice to see you. Coffee?'

'You bet.'

'Slice of cake?'

'You read my mind. Hey, love the photographs.'

'Pardon?'

Barry looked nonplussed. 'The exhibition?' He gestured at the walls.

'Oh, sorry. Good, are they?' She handed him his coffee.

'Well, I certainly think so. Very moody and intense – enormous emotional impact. Hard to tell what the actual subjects are, as a matter of fact. Could be a stone on a beach, could be a woman's … er … flesh, might be abstract, or …' He blushed. 'Not.'

'Sounds interesting. Afraid I haven't had a chance to look properly yet.'

'Oh good heavens, no, yes, well I mean of course …'

Anna grinned. 'Barry, cake. Enjoy.'

'Mmm, yes, scrumptious, looks delish.' He slipped onto one of the counter stools and took an enormous bite. Crumbs cascaded down his navy puffa jacket. 'So, how's the work going? We'll see you at Piers on Sunday night, I hope?'

'You bet. Wouldn't miss it for anything.'

Pier Poets was a group of local writers – a couple of them talented, one already published – who met in the Golden Galleon, a small Victorian pub on the seafront. Every other Sunday night the group got together in the snug to read new work and share information about the latest happenings on the national poetry scene. Criticism and encouragement were offered in equal measure, and in the five years or so in which Anna had been attending her work had achieved a new depth and authority. She remained conscious only of the limitations she had yet to overcome.

'I can't tell you how much I admired the sonnet you read last time. The way you stood the statement in the first quatrain on its head in the final couplet! Brilliant! Quite brilliant! I said to Naomi on the way home – she begged a lift, her Mini's in for new brake shoes, apparently – the use of irony quite dumbfounded me. Put me in mind of Spenser, as a matter of fact. I particularly admired the way you went for images that underlined the point that love –'

Anna poured a coffee and pushed it towards him, grateful for his praise and wishing that she found him more attractive. Recently divorced (rumour had it at Pier Poets that his wife had run off with her Pilates instructor), kind, solvent – he owned one of the town's best bookshops – he possessed excellent critical faculties and was one of the group's founders. The trouble was, thought Anna, as she pushed the sugar bowl towards him, thinning red hair and freckles just weren't sexy. The out-sized quilted jackets he favoured didn't help much, either. She considered him now, narrowing her eyes so that his shape blurred, wondering whether a grey tweed jacket with leather patches would help matters. Tears suddenly threatened, and she stopped herself quickly.

'... increasingly wide range. Such a contrast to the yearning tones of last week's sestina –' He broke off and stood staring at her, a slow tide of blood suffusing his pale features.

What on earth was the matter with him? Was he having a hot flush? Maybe he was trying to give up sugar, and the sight of the sugar bowl upset him. She removed it and placed it firmly behind the milk jug. That was better, he was smiling at her now. He took a sip of coffee, and glanced at his watch. Anna noticed that his hand was shaking slightly. God, maybe he should keep off caffeine, too.

'Well, I must be going – things to do, things to do.' He slid three pound coins onto the counter. 'So we'll see you on Sunday, then – can't tell you how much I'm looking forward to hearing your latest. And don't forget, be sure to bring copies.'

He backed away, almost tripping over a pushchair, and waved a hand skittishly. '*À bientôt*!'

Roxy handed change to a customer, put her hands on her hips and raised an eyebrow at Anna. 'Blimey, he's got it bad.'

'Think it's stress, they say it can cause –'

'Duh. He fancies you, anyone could see that. And talk about leadin' the poor sod on!' She batted her mascara-caked eyelashes and pouted languorously at the baguettes. 'I thought he was goin' to pass out. Still, s'pose the jacket would've cushioned the fall.'

'Leading him …? But I wasn't! I was just wondering if he'd look any better in –' She swallowed hard.

'Goin' back to the weddin'. Seein' as you got no man in your life –'

For a brief moment, Anna thought of telling Roxy about Jack, then rejected the idea. Roxy was an incurable gossip, and it would be all over Brighton by Sunday.

Anyway, Jack wasn't in her life any more.

'Seems to me you could do worse than take Mr Michelin along.'

'Mr…?'

Roxy raised her eyebrows and jerked her head in the direction of the departing puffa jacket.

Anna imagined Barry in a hired morning suit a size too small, shaking hands damply with everyone and blushing every time she looked at him. She shook her head.

'No, s'pose not. Still, strikes me you're goin' to feel a right lemon on your own. Tell you what, you could always use Ron to do the honours. Do the bugger good to make himself useful for once. Talk about thick – you'll never guess what he went and let Dean do last night.'

Anna wasn't at all sure she wanted to hear.

'Only let him watch a documentary on bleedin' mummification, didn't he, so he could get on with his model-makin' in peace. I come in from Zumba and what do I find? Young Dean with a chopstick stuck halfway up his nose, that's what.'

'A ...?'

Roxy sniffed darkly. 'Tryin' to drag his brain out through his nostrils, wasn't he, like they done to the Egyptian stiffs.'

Anna fought a strong desire to laugh.

'I'm telling you, another couple of minutes and he'd of succeeded. I said to Ron, it doesn't bear thinkin' about. And it's not just the mess I'm talkin' about – it'd be goodbye to bein' an astronaut, or even a doctor. All because Ron couldn't figure out which way up the cockpit went on his Messerschmidt.'

'Well, I really appreciate the escort offer, Roxy. Maybe I could think about it?'

'Course you can, love. You'd have to watch him at the reception, mind – he's a devil for fishpaste bread rolls.'

'I'll keep that in mind ... OK, hold the fort, will you, Roxy? I'd better start heating up the parsnip soup, and it's time those onion tarts came out of the oven. Give Trish a shout if a queue starts, won't you?'

While she was stirring the soup, she drew the bill she'd scribbled on earlier from her pocket. Thought for a moment and added another couple of lines, then stuffed it back again quickly as Susie returned with the teabags. She'd leave it till her lunch break; try and make a start on the third quatrain then.

That evening Anna knelt on the floor in her living room banging away at the ancient portable Olivetti she'd set up on the coffee table. A glass of white wine sat beside it, Handel poured joyously from the CD player. She'd lit a fire as soon as she got home, telling herself that despite the warmth of the early spring sunshine the evening was chilly, knowing in her heart that the flames would make her feel less lonely.

Still, considering everything, she'd got through the day pretty well. Business had been much as usual at lunchtime, but there'd been a mad rush mid-afternoon on account of the unscheduled arrival of a coachload of French pensioners who were under the impression that Brighton was St Ives and Avant Art was the Tate.

Despite this regrettable misapprehension, a good time appeared to have been had by all. After they'd done the tour of the upper galleries the whole group had descended on the coffee bar, where they'd crowded round the photography exhibition with excited cries of admiration and much enthusiastic waving of bundles of euros. Alastair had had to be called down from his eerie to explain that *non, les photos* were not *à vendre, absolument* not, and *oui,* to be sure they were *vraiment superbes mais, non,* Declan O'Halloran was not a Scottish but an Irish name. The flapjacks and scones were pronounced *étranges* but *magnifiques*, the peppermint tea *délicieux*. By the time they'd left in a flurry of goodwill (though still convinced that they'd visited St Ives) and the clearing up was done, it was gone half past six.

Anna wandered home in a daze of exhaustion, still excited about the poem she'd begun that morning. Every time thoughts of Jack threatened, she stopped and drew the messy wad of scribbled notes (the original crumpled bill had been augmented at lunchtime by several paper napkins) and changed a word, or crossed out a line entirely. By the time she put the key in the front door she had a first draft ready to type up.

A quick shower, an omelette, and now here she was, rattling out the title. Good. Now for –

The phone rang.

Anna jumped so hard she knocked her wine glass over. Jack. She sat motionless, heart thumping, as the ringing went on and on. No way was she going to answer; in fact, she didn't intend to ever speak to him again.

The pool of liquid spread slowly over the wooden surface of the table, magnifying the grain of the amber wood.

Jack.

No. Not *ever* again. It was just that ... OK, if the spilled wine reached the edge of the fruit bowl before the ringing stopped, she'd answer.

The ringing continued. The Frascati halted its slow advance, light years away from the fruit bowl.

Jack.

Suddenly Anna was on her feet and across to the little table under the window, grabbing the phone with a hand that shook so much she almost dropped the receiver. 'Hello?'

'Mrs Hardy?'

Disappointment flooded over her, followed by rage. Nobody ever addressed her as Mrs Hardy except companies who were cold-calling; last week three of them had rung her in one evening and she'd missed all the best bits of the film she'd been watching. Who the hell did they think they were?

'Whatever poxy product it is you're selling I'm not interested, thank you.'

There was a sharp intake of breath at the other end. 'This is Mrs O'Shaughnessy.'

Oh, for God's sake, she didn't know any Mrs O'Shaughnessy. What she did know was that a) the caller wasn't Jack, and b) the only thing that would prevent her bursting into tears and throwing things violently about the room because of this was a speedy return to her poem.

'I'm afraid you've got the wrong –'

'Tina O'Shaughnessy. From Fergustown, in Ireland.'

The voice was hard, with an affected upper-class accent; Anna imagined the speaker crooking her little finger in what she took to be an elegant manner as she held the handset several inches away from her mouth in an attempt to avoid germs.

'Look, why don't you try directory –'

Tina.

Ireland.

Christ.

Her hand flew to her mouth.

'Hello? God, I'm so sorry.' No, no, mustn't say God. 'I mean hi, you must be Lucy's mother! How lovely to hear you. How kind of you to ring!' Lifting the trailing phone cord clear of the table, Anna edged over to the coffee table and grasped the bottle of Frascati she'd left on the floor beside it by the neck. Raising it to her lips, she drank deeply.

'... about the wedding.'

'The wedding! Yes, it's marvellous news, isn't it!'

'Simply wonderful. Now, Eamonn, my husband, and I will be in London in a few weeks visiting relatives –'

So *soon*?

'– and we'd so love it if you could pop up and join us for dinner, if you're free? Lucy and dear Sam will be there too, I'm sure.' Something about Tina's tone suggested she'd want a bloody good reason if they weren't. 'And we can all get to know each other.'

'Gosh, yes!'

'And of course, discuss the wedding plans. I expect Lucy's told you all about my ...'

Anna lifted the bottle to her lips again.

'... *so* much to do, I've got a list here so long you simply wouldn't believe. It's just busy, busy, busy from morning till night. And people can be so unhelpful! I've just called the chief bell ringer at St Aloysius – you absolutely wouldn't *credit* how rude the fellow was when I said I wanted the team to wear violet satin cassocks to tone with the page boys' lilac trousers, instead of their usual mauve cloth.'

Bell ringers? Violet *satin*?

'"What's the feckin difference? Who's going to feckin see?" is what he had the impertinence to ask me. Can you credit it?' A strong Irish accent had begun to edge its way into her vowels. 'I said to him in no uncertain terms, "*God* will see, Mr Heaney. And I'm quite sure that God can tell the difference between violet and mauve, even if you can*not*."' There was a sharp

58

rustle of paper down the line. 'Well, I must get on, I have to ring the photographer next.'

Poor guy.

'He did the photos for the daughter of a friend of mine's wedding, not that it was a patch on this do, of course. No, Annabel's was a very paltry affair; only four bridesmaids and a mere three tiers to the cake. Still, the photographs were frightfully good. I shall tell him to model the groups on Royal weddings, and I do think it's so important to have a really good portrait of the bride's mother to mark the occasion. Hello? ... Mrs Hardy?'

Anna put the bottle down very carefully. 'Yes. Gosh.'

'Now, let's set a date. How about the last Wednesday in June, the twenty-seventh?'

'Yes, that would be –'

'Let's say seven-thirty then.'

Where? The Waldorf? The Ritz?

'At Chez Gaston, in Covent Garden. Do you know it?'

Well, she didn't *know* it exactly – she'd walked past it occasionally on trips to London and caught a glimpse of the pink-shaded table lamps and lavish flower arrangements lurking in the gloom beyond the supercilious doorman's epauletted shoulder.

'Gosh ... Yes. Lovely, I'll look forward to it.'

'So shall I, if I haven't died of comp*lete* exhaustion by then.' A venomous sigh hissed down the line. 'Well, I must get on. Goodbye, Mrs Hardy.'

'Bye – and thank –'

The phone buzzed in her hand.

After a while, she put another log on the fire, cleared up the sticky mess on the table and made herself some coffee.

Then, with a sigh of relief, she knelt down at the typewriter again and got back to the red peppers.

CHAPTER FIVE

Declan O'Halloran shifted slightly, trying to accommodate his right knee where a particularly sharp piece of flint was digging into his flesh so hard it had pierced the worn denim of his trouser leg. The ground was littered with jagged stones and fragments of shale marking the area in front of the wayside shrine as separate from the weed-choked turf that surrounded it. Gritting his teeth, he pressed his hands harder together and tried to pray. Any passerby – though there was little chance of one in such a remote area of Connemara – would have seen a spare, wiry figure in jeans and an ancient fisherman's sweater, with black hair, a two-day stubble shadowing his angular jaw and intense brown eyes. Indeed the passerby, had he or she stopped for a chat, would very likely have enquired whether Declan might not be Gabriel Byrne's brother. Declan, who was tired of being asked this question, and had no idea who Gabriel Byrne was, always assumed it to be some thinly veiled insult and would gaze into the distance until his interrogator, embarrassed, moved away.

The afternoon light was fading fast now, but it was half an hour before he opened his eyes. Rising to his feet he stood, head bowed. Tears streaming down his face, he picked up the daisies wrapped in Queen Anne's lace he'd placed at the foot of the shrine the previous Thursday and replaced them with his new offering. Meadowsweet, candytuft and clover glowed like jewels among the dark green ferns in which he'd carefully wrapped them; he'd wanted to add buttercups but he couldn't remember if Maura had liked them.

He said a final prayer, made the sign of the Cross and stepped back, gazing at the shrine. It was recessed deep into the grey drystone wall, veined and threaded with ochre-coloured lichen and exuberantly patterned with shockingly white bird shit. Declan hated the bird shit – it spoke too strongly of life. He looked away.

Today he'd decided he was going to do something about the desiccated remains of the floral offerings others had left for loved ones, years ago, by the look of some of them – a few in stained and cracked jam jars, a couple in empty Guinness bottles. He couldn't leave them; Maura must hate it. She'd always been a stickler for tidiness, what with being a nurse and all. She had nagged for months after they were married to get him to pick up his socks and put them in the basket instead of dropping them on the floor beside the bed. Their bed, with its crisp white cotton sheets ... Bed linen had been Maura's one extravagance; she couldn't abide nylon, or polyester, or any of that stuff. He hadn't known the difference himself until she showed him. He closed his eyes. There were a lot of things he hadn't known till Maura showed him. Gently teasing him, with laughter in her eyes, she'd given him lessons in parts of the female anatomy he hadn't even known existed. He'd been a more than willing pupil; some nights they'd still been making love when the first buses could be heard rumbling down Cobb Street. Now the only sound he heard at dawn was his own breathing as he stared into the darkness, and these days he didn't bother with sheets at all.

Bowing his head to show he meant no disrespect, he added the withered flowers to the decaying heap and turned away, 'Till next week, darlin'.'

He stepped back onto the muddy track, and headed for the tiny whitewashed cottage he had called home for the last three years. The Virgin Mary stood smiling sadly after him, watching him walk away.

As he trudged down the track in the gathering dusk and took the fork that led to the cottage his eye was drawn to the setting sun as it slipped behind the Maumturk mountains. The sky glowed in a blaze of fiery orange, shading to a deeper red that in turn faded to a wash of translucent pink. It was a long time since a sunset had reminded him of anything but blood.

Pushing through the thicket of nettles that threatened to block the front entrance to the cottage, he almost slipped in the mud. Damned weather – last week the track leading to the main road to Galway, where he worked on the *Gazette* as a part-time staff photographer, had been so muddy as to be almost unnavigable. As he passed the rain butt, he saw that it was almost full. At least he'd have enough water to wash his clothes tonight. As soon as he'd got the fire going, he'd cover the range with enough pans of water to fill the tin bath. He'd wash the clothes and then himself, then heat a pot of soup and get down to work.

As he pushed open the door and entered the dark living room, with its flagstones and sparse furniture, he realised with a rush of shame that he felt almost happy.

It was late that evening before he'd finally completed his chores. It had taken an age to get the range going – the slabs of peat he burned for fuel were stored in a lean-to at the side of the cottage and they'd become damp. He went out with a torch and saw that last night's gale had created a gap the width of his spread fingers between two of the galvanized tin sheets that formed the roof. Thank God the generator that was the cottage's sole source of electricity, and vital to his work, hadn't suffered.

Eventually he'd hung the last shirt over the wooden rack to dry, given himself a perfunctory scrub in the unpleasantly gritty water, eaten his soup and soda bread and stashed in his camera case everything he might need for whatever jaunt Andy McGinty, the *Gazette*'s editor, was planning to spring on him the following morning. Please God it wouldn't be another dog show. Slipping into his dark room, he closed the door behind him and pulled gently on a string.

The safe light came on, bathing the jars and trays on the wooden trestle table in a warm red glow. On another table was an ancient enlarger and a small metal shelf unit cluttered with photographic equipment. Pegged neatly by their corners from a line strung wall to wall just below the ceiling hung several contact sheets, their subjects unclear in the rosy gloom. Equally indistinct was the framed poster announcing an exhibition of photographs on the wall opposite the door.

Declan picked up the camera from the end of the trestle table, flipped up the cover at the back of the case and removed the film.

Smiling for the first time that day, he began to work.

CHAPTER SIX

All things considered, Anna reckoned she'd got through the weekend pretty well. Saturday was always the coffee bar's busiest day, and she'd had almost no time to think about Jack. The Tony nightmare and the Tina horror had only one benefit – that they could take the place of her feelings for Jack in her mind. Every time thoughts threatened of Jack's hands, his voice, the defeated look on his face as he was leaving, she banished them by worrying about the approaching reunion with her ex-husband (what would he say? How would he look?) or the forthcoming dinner at Chez Gaston (what shouldn't she say? How shouldn't she look?). Of course it was silly to worry – Roxy was right, Sam would never manage to track his father down, and even if he did, Tony would refuse to come to the wedding. And Tina was probably really nice when you met her, she just wasn't at her best on the phone. The poor woman had a lot on her plate. Anna wouldn't want to be organising a wedding for three-hundred people. Or was it five hundred? No, that was the reception, wasn't it? Or possibly the number of bell ringers ...

She spent Saturday night working on the fourth draft of the new poem, anxious to have something worth taking to Piers Poets the following evening. By the early hours she'd achieved her aim; exhausted, she fell asleep on the sofa as the last log collapsed into ashes in the grate and didn't wake until late afternoon. After she'd spent a couple of hours on cleaning and laundry, she bathed, ate a bacon sandwich and set off for The Vines.

The group's reaction to her work cheered her enormously; the praise was heartening and the criticism constructive. Barry took her aside during the break and begged to be allowed to keep his copy of the new poem. She was touched by his enthusiasm and agreed, though she wriggled out of accepting his offer of a lift home by saying she planned to walk on the beach for a while to ponder another poem she'd begun to make notes for. This, apart from being an excuse she knew Barry would readily accept, was true: as she'd been walking along the promenade en route to the pub, she'd passed a young couple entwined in one of the glass-sided bus shelters. Something about the girl (the dark curls tumbling over her shoulders, her air of intensity) reminded Anna of her younger self. The boy (blond and handsome, idly scanning the passing women over the girl's shoulder despite the apparent passion of his kiss) reminded her of Tony. As Anna walked on, she wondered what future lay in store for the couple. Before she knew it, she'd whipped her notebook from her pocket and was scribbling as she walked.

After the meeting broke up, she set off along the beach, but she was too tired to add more than a couple of ideas to her notes. She went straight to bed when she got home and as she spiralled down into sleep, Jack drifted into her mind, naked except for his tie, gazing at her with an expression of despair – 'the only one who'd even heard of pecan pie was Hayley'. His image was replaced by Lucy's, encased in a wedding dress made of delicately browned meringue, a whirl of piped cream topping her immaculate chignon – 'I think that poem looks rather good on you, actually, Anna'. And then Anna was on the beach, kneeling in front of a coffee table and gazing into a golden pool of spilled wine that surrounded a Lilliputian couple as they embraced in a tiny bus shelter, laughing – 'frankly, we look on it as an investment' – breaking apart in alarm as church bells began to peal discordantly …

Anna stirred, and woke. She rolled over, reaching for the glass of water on her bedside table. She'd been dreaming – something about church bells …? No, it couldn't have been a dream – she could still hear them. Alarm clock? She checked the time – no, it wasn't that, it was only seven twenty-two, there were still eight minutes to go before the bloody thing was due to go off, so what on earth …? Of course – *the phone*. She slid out of bed, cursing. Who the hell would be ringing at this hour? She pulled on her dressing gown and blearily made her way downstairs, glad that at least Sam couldn't see her and a) criticise her for not having an extension by the bed b) make fun of her for being the last person in the Western world to refuse to have a mobile phone and c) mock her ancient candlewick dressing gown.

Stumbling into the living room, she almost fell over a can of furniture polish she had forgotten to put away. More annoyed than ever, she snatched up the receiver.

'Anna?'

Suddenly it was hard to breathe. 'Jack?'

'Anna. *Anna* …'

She clutched the lapels of her dressing gown tightly together.

'Anna – look, I've got to see you. I miss you, I can't –'

She could hear birds singing faintly in the background. 'Jack? Where are you? … Jack?'

'Back garden. Look, I've only got five minutes – the twins could spot me from their window any minute. Darling, can I come tonight?'

Of course – it was Monday, and Monday was one of their regular nights. But hadn't she decided she wasn't going to see him any more? Unless –

'Jack? Have you told her?'

A pause. She could hear a dog yapping frantically somewhere. 'No, not yet – I tried again last night, honestly, but just as I got started there was an accident with the bloody dog, and I couldn't –'

Suddenly there was a crash, as if a door had burst open suddenly nearby. The yapping increased, punctuated by shrill childish screams of joy. 'Down, Spike, down! Charlie, for Christ's sake – get those Wellington boots off him this minute!'

The uproar increased, almost drowning out Jack's whispered, anguished plea. 'Anna? *Please*, darling – please say I can come.'

67

She thought of his hands, his voice, the defeated look on his face as he was leaving … 'Oh god, Jack, I miss you too. Seven o'clock?'

'Anna, thank you. *Thank* you, darling. I can't tell you how –'

He gave a sudden hoarse shout – there was a loud thump, as if he'd fallen, and the line went dead.

Anna went into the kitchen to put on the kettle for tea. As she reached into the fridge for the milk jug she realised she was singing.

The day sped past. She rushed out at lunchtime and bought pesto and homemade pasta from the little Italian delicatessen in Monmouth Street, and was halfway back to Avant Art when she realised she was almost out of fresh parmesan and ran all the way back again. She added garlic breadsticks, plus a bunch of daffodils from the red enamel bucket full of spring flowers beside the chilled cabinet, and just made it back in time to let Trish and Susie go for their break. Roxy grinned when she saw her pink cheeks.

'Lookin' a bit happier than last week, I'm glad to see; been mullin' over your Aunty Roxy's words of wisdom, I expect.' She stuffed a flapjack in her mouth. 'You take my word for it, girl, there's no way that scumbag'll dare show his face at the wedding.'

Anna thought of telling her about Tina's phone call, but it would be disloyal to Sam to start criticising his future mother-in-law before she'd even met her, and anyway, if – no, *when* – Tina turned out to be lovely, she'd feel terrible. She spent the rest of the afternoon baking supplies for the week ahead while the girls served the customers and Roxy scrubbed out the fridge, regaling Anna with horror stories about the weddings of her apparently limitless relatives.

By six o'clock she was home. By twenty past she'd changed the white sheets already on her bed for Jack's favourite dark green set, sprayed them liberally with the Body Shop's vanilla perfume and arranged the daffodils in a blue jug on the bedside table. By six thirty-five she'd lit the fire in the living room, switched on the lamps, replaced the fading lilies in the fireplace with Sam and Lucy's tulips and put Dave Brubeck on the CD player, turned low. By five to seven she was out of the bathroom and in the kitchen, wearing her peacock blue silk shirt (Jack's favourite) and black trousers, her hair pinned up (so that he could unpin it again later) her make-up carefully renewed, her pulse points sprayed with more vanilla. She'd washed the rocket and watercress for the salad and the water for the pasta was just coming to the boil when she heard a key turn in the lock. She stood quite still for a moment, letting pleasure and anticipation wash over her. She was transferring the salad greens to the shaker when the kitchen door opened. She turned. Jack stood in the doorway, gazing at her anxiously, clasping an enormous papier-mâché ass's head to his chest. 'Anna ... I'm so, so sorry, darling.'

He looked if anything even more exhausted than the last time she'd seen him, and noticed with a pang how badly his hair needed cutting. She turned off the gas. The last thing she saw as they rushed towards each other was that the button that had been hanging by a thread last Thursday had now fallen off entirely, and then she was in his arms, the ass's head crushed between them.

'Oh God, I'm sorry too, Jack. I should have been more understanding. Of *course* I realise how difficult it must be for you to tell her –'

'No, no, it was all my fault. I should have been more sensitive to your feelings. I know how badly you want –'

'No, I was horrible – totally unreasonable, you were right. Oh God, I've missed you –'

'Missed you too, darling. Angel –'

It was some time before they stopped kissing. When Jack finally held her away from him so that he could look at her better, the ass's head fell to the floor with a dull thud and lay staring up at them accusingly.

Anna grinned. 'Afraid he's looking a bit cross-eyed.'

'Jealous, probably.' He kissed her again.

'Still, ought to do the trick, I should think.'

'God, I hope so. Don't want to go through last week again.'

Jack had managed to wangle every Monday evening with Anna this term by telling Ruth he was directing the school Drama Society's production of *A Midsummer Night's Dream*. Monday night was the putative rehearsal night. He strengthened his alibi by returning home each week casually clasping some prop relevant to the play. Last week he'd been running late, detained by a staff meeting that had gone on longer than scheduled. He'd been so desperate to get to Anna's that he'd grabbed the nearest object from the props cupboard without bothering to check what it was and it wasn't until he was leaving her house that he realised he'd taken an alarmingly life-like Baby Jesus used in the first year's Nativity play. Fortunately, Jack had had plenty of time to come up with an explanation as he cycled home. 'You can't see where a baby fits into the plot of *The Dream*, dear?'

Ruth glared at him suspiciously.

'You know that's exactly what I thought, at first.'

'And?' She folded her arms. 'I'm waiting, Jack.'

'Very interesting concept – came up in a class discussion of the play's relevance to today's society.' He laid the rubbery baby on the table, hoping she wouldn't notice the three-day stubble some WAG had pencilled on its pink chin. 'Sharon's idea, actually.' He allowed himself to savour a brief pause before going for the *coup de grâce*. 'She suggested Oberon and Titania should have a love child.'

'Oh, spare me!' she said. 'I don't know, you'll be telling me next they want all the fairies snorting coke. Really, Jack, I don't understand why on earth you can't stick to good old-fashioned –'

She was off, as he'd known she would be, on one of her favourite hobby horses. She was still at it an hour later, when he switched off his bedside lamp …

Anna was laughing. 'Nearly as bad as the week you turned up carrying that huge sparkly wand.'

'God, don't remind me. Simwak-Kim's been giving me funny looks ever since.'

And then they were kissing again.

Anna told Jack about Sam's impending wedding, and that he wanted his father to come, as they lay naked on the rug in front of the fire after making love, sipping wine and nibbling the fat Greek olives Jack always brought. He listened sleepily, stroking her back and trying to comfort her. He knew about Tony's abrupt departure, leaving his wife and son with no means of support or any way of contacting him. He'd been shocked when Anna told him. Desperate as he was to leave Ruth, it would never have occurred to him to abandon her, or to leave her unprovided for. After a while Anna changed the subject, not wanting to spoil the evening by dwelling on her ex-husband's shortcomings. She made Jack laugh as she recounted her stupidity over the stone in Lucy's ring; he laughed even harder when she gave him a blow-by-blow account of Tina's phone call.

At last they got dressed and went back to the kitchen to finish preparing supper. They'd finished the pasta and begun on the goat's cheese and grapes Jack had brought, when Anna frowned and put down the cream cracker she'd been about to eat.

'God, suddenly everything little thing reminds me of him.'

'Who, angel?'

She sat back in her chair. 'Tony, the bastard. There were a couple of Australian students in the coffee bar this morning, perfectly nice guys, but I just couldn't face serving them. I made an excuse and got Trish do it. She went around for the rest of her shift saying "fair dinkum, cobber" every time I asked her to do something, so I lived to regret it.'

He laughed, saw the look on her face and stopped. 'So what's the problem with the cheese, angel?'

'I just remembered goat's cheese always used to be his favourite.' She pushed her plate away.

'Look, try to forget about him, sweetheart.' Jack leaned forward and poured the last of the wine into her glass.

'Anyway, I bet Roxy's right – the bugger'll never dare show up. Everything'll be fine, you wait and see.'

Anna got up and began to clear the plates. 'It's not just Tony I'm worried about. From what Lucy was saying, it's going to be a seriously grand occasion – page boys, twenty-five-tier cake, slimy photographer, that sort of thing. All Lucy's relatives are going to be there – believe me, there are hundreds, and that's just the maiden great-aunts – and there's the priest. Apparently this priest, Father O'Wally or somesuch, is going to give Sam instructions about –' She began to laugh.

'Jesus.' Jack joined her at the sink and put his arms round her. 'Well, at least nobody needed to give *us* instructions, angel.'

Anna stopped laughing and leant her head against his shoulder, suddenly sad. She rubbed her cheek against his soft shirt sleeve. 'I'll miss him.'

'Miss who?'

She pulled away, irritated with him for not understanding, and began to fill the percolator. 'Sam, of course.'

'But –'

'I know he doesn't live hear any more – in fact, I hardly see him from one month's end to another, but … Oh, I don't know, Jack. It seems only yesterday I was slipping pound coins under his pillow when he lost his milk teeth and teaching him to tie his shoelaces. It took him weeks to get the hang of it – I had to draw coloured diagrams in the end. Testing his French verbs.' She sighed. 'He just doesn't seem old enough to be getting married.'

'Look on the bright side. At least you aren't going to be landed with the bill for this shindig. God knows how I'm going to cope when it comes to Poppy and Jess.' He went to his briefcase, pulled out a second bottle of claret and began to open it. 'Ruth's sure to want to push the bloody boat out.'

Anna stiffened.

'She'll probably insist on trussing me up in morning dress – she's got a thing about it for some reason. And uniforms, come to think of it – her first boyfriend was a police cadet. Or was it a traffic warden? Anyway, as soon as we were safely aboard the horse and carriage her parents insisted we travel to the reception in – did I ever tell you about that? Her mother's a big fan of Jane Austen, apparently – Ruth absolutely fell on me.' He extracted the cork from the bottle and examined it, frowning. 'Next thing I knew she'd got her hand –' He glanced up, and saw Anna's expression. 'God sorry, darling, don't know why on earth I'm rabbiting on about all that. Believe me, the whole day was an absolute nightmare. The wedding breakfast took hours and the speeches seemed to go on for days. Honestly, we thought we'd never get to –' He struck his forehead with the heel of his hand. 'I'm making it worse, aren't I?'

'It's not that.'

'It's not?'

'It's what you said about the twins.' Anna had never met them, but she'd seen a photograph. In her opinion only a blind, deaf mute with an IQ of minus ten would even consider marriage to either of them, but that wasn't the point here. 'And Ruth being sure to want to push the –' She shivered. 'You sounded as if you thought you'd still be –'

'No! *Christ* no, darling, you couldn't be more wrong. It's just that … Well, you know how it is … When you've been together for ages, you just sort of get into the habit of –'

'Oh, for God's sake, Jack. I don't want to hear.'

Turning her back, she dumped the empty wine bottle noisily in the bin.

'Please, angel, you know we'll be together by then. Hell, I almost got her to listen last night – next time I'll get through even if I have to truss her up and gag her first.'

Anna rather liked the sound of that. She turned to him again.

He was gazing at her with the hang-dog expression he always wore when he knew he'd put his foot in it, and she was struck with remorse. She really must stop being so touchy; after all, it wasn't his fault he'd been married for twenty years to the wrong person. If she really loved him she'd try and be more understanding when he accidentally let slip details of his past that she'd rather not know about – for heaven's sake, he already got more than enough bitching at home. She put her arms round his neck. 'Let's forget about coffee, shall we, and take the wine upstairs with us?'

He picked up the bottle and glasses, then covered her mouth with his.

After a while she pulled away slightly. 'Didn't you say something about binding and gagging?'

He blinked.

'Hmmm. I was thinking more about ...' She bit his earlobe. 'I always say actions speak louder than words.' He swallowed and watched as she went to the fridge and filled a bowl with ice cubes.

As she shut the fridge door, the phone began to ring in the living room. Anna ignored it.

Jack looked nervously at the ice cubes. 'Don't mind me if you want to answer that, darling.'

'No way. It's bound to be Alastair, banging on about yesterday's *fantashtically* high visitor quota, and would I like to *fink* again about opening the coffee bar on Sundays. He usually has a go about it on Monday afternoons before I leave – I was gone before he could catch me today.'

Smiling, Anna ran a finger lightly down the front of his shirt. Then, taking his tie between her finger and thumb, she led him out of the kitchen.

Anna closed the bedroom door, drew the curtains and lit the beeswax candle on the bedside table. She set the bowl of ice beside it. Smiling, Jack set the bottle and glasses down beside the bed, and tried to take her in his arms. She pushed him away. 'OK, strip.'

'Anna?' He sounded worried.

'Look, I'm not supposed to smile, OK?' She put her hands on her hips and tried to look stern.

Suddenly Jack caught on. '*OK* ...' He began to take off his clothes. At least she'd finally taught him to take off his socks before his trousers; there was nothing less sexy than a man in his socks and underpants. Thank god he wasn't a man for vests.

When he was finally naked, he stood at the foot of the bed, waiting. 'Er ... all right?'

Very much all right, from where she was standing.

She gave him a gentle push, so that he collapsed backwards onto the duvet. 'Don't move.' Going to the chest of drawers, she pulled open the top drawer and removed a black chiffon scarf (it had come free with a bottle of conditioning shampoo, but Jack didn't need to know that). She turned back to the bed. Jack lay on his back, his expression a mixture of fear and pleasurable expectation. '... Anna?'

'Lift your head.'

He did as he was told. Swiftly, she blindfolded him with the scarf, and pushed him down again. He cleared his throat. 'Anna, are you sure this is a good –'

She poured some claret into one of the glasses, dipped her little finger into the dark red wine then inserted it into his mouth. He groaned, and sucked greedily. 'More.'

'Wait.'

'Oh, come on, Anna –' He began to sit up.

She pushed him down again hard. 'So you're going to give me trouble, are you, big boy? In that case...' She went to the chest of drawers again and took out a pair of stockings. Returned to the bed and trailed one very slowly across his chest. '... I'm afraid I'm going to have to tie you to the bed.'

A smile spread across his face beneath the blindfold. 'Hmmm. Well. If you absolutely *must* ...'

Resisting the temptation to kiss him, she tied his wrists securely to the carved antique pine bed posts.

'And now ...' She began to take off her clothes, making sure he could hear the susurration of the silk as she slipped her blouse from her shoulders. '*Now*, Mr Teale, you are completely in my power.'

It was clear from his reaction that he didn't object to that at all.

Some time later, Anna climbed off her recumbent lover and collapsed beside him, her cheeks flushed, damp with perspiration. Jack lay on his back, still panting. After a while, she rolled over and poured more wine into a glass. She swallowed some, then took another mouthful and trickled it over Jack's chest. 'Anna …?'

'Right here, honey.' Funny how this sort of thing seemed to lend itself to an American accent. And she hadn't even begun – by the time the next couple of hours were up she'd be sounding like Mae West. She took another mouthful of wine and dribbled it into Jack's eager mouth. 'So. You ready for … more?'

He sighed luxuriously. 'You bet, babe.'

She smiled affectionately, safe in the knowledge that he couldn't see her, and reached for the bowl of ice.

The next half hour or so should take him to seventh heaven.

She scooped up a couple of ice cubes. God, they were cold. Not to mention slippery …

She was just about to pop them in her mouth when she heard the sound of the front door opening.

With a gasp of horror she leapt off the bed, unaware that she'd spilled the bowl of ice all over Jack's stomach. Ignoring his frantic yell, she flew to the door and opened it a fraction, as a voice called from downstairs.

'Mum?'

Sam? It couldn't be – she must be hallucinating.

'Mum?'

She closed the door again. 'It's Sam! Christ, Jack, it's Sam!' She cast frantically round the bedroom, caught sight of her dressing gown hanging on the back of the door, yanked it on and ran back to the writhing figure on the bed. 'Shut *up*, Jack, for Christ's sake – he'll hear you!'

The yells diminished to agonised, indistinct entreaties.

'For God's sake, Jack, there's no time for sex now! Stay here and shut up – maybe we can try again when I've got rid of Sam, OK?'

She tied her belt in a tight double bow. Thank heavens for candlewick, Sam would never guess she didn't have anything on underneath. Pasting a delighted smile into place she hurried out on to the landing, closing the bedroom door behind her.

76

The living room was empty. Grateful that at least they hadn't been discovered making love on the rug in front of the fire, or doing inventive things in one of the armchairs, Anna headed for the kitchen. Sam was leaning over the table, frowning.

'Darling! What a lovely surprise! And Lucy's with you too, I hope?' Brilliant. She should have been an actress. 'Just going to get in the bath when I heard you calling.'

'Oh. I wondered why you didn't answer the phone.'

Bugger. She'd never ignore a ringing phone again. She smiled brightly. 'So, what brings you –'

'We nipped down so Lucy can have a quick chinwag with Kate about her dress. I've just dropped her off in Kemp Town. Tina's sent a couple of brocade samples, and she wants a decision by tomorrow. I'm off to collect her in an hour then it's straight back to town; we've both got breakfast meetings in the morning ... Mum, what the hell's this?'

What was *what,* for Christ's sake? Neither she nor Jack had started to undress till they got upstairs, the kitchen wasn't exactly littered with sex aids unless you counted the weird Portuguese ceramic oil and vinegar containers on the dresser or the rather brown banana in the fruit bowl, and there was no evidence that two people rather than one had recently eaten there, since she'd put their plates in the sink.

Sam pointed at the dish of cheese and grapes.

'Cheese, of course, darling.' Suddenly she remembered – goat's cheese was Sam's favourite as well as Tony's. Good heavens, there must be something in this genes business, she'd simply never made the connection before.

He sighed heavily. 'I can see that, Mum.' He scooped a piece and spread it on a cracker. 'My point is this.' He took a bite. 'You're supposed to be on a diet.'

'And so I am. Except for Mondays. On this particular regime – Susie told me about it, you know, she works in the coffee bar? Her mother's a top nutritionist –' She was a school dinner lady, actually, but sometimes one was forced by circumstance to elaborate a bit '– on this regime it's essential to eat normally

77

once a week. Shakes your metabolism up so it works even more efficiently getting rid of – er – things when the diet kicks in again. On the other days, of course, the menu's a nightmare.' She kissed him lightly on the cheek, moved away quickly and switched on the kettle. 'Strictly nothing but water and the odd cup of cabbage soup.'

He brushed crumbs from the lapels of his superbly cut pinstriped jacket and cast a disapproving eye at her dressing gown. He was opening his mouth to speak (about to order her to take it out in the garden and burn it there and then, no doubt) when his eyes widened.

What? *What*? Were there unseemly stains on the candlewick? Had she –

Sam was pointing at the floor. Anna followed his gaze. The papier-mâché ass's head glared back at her. 'Ah. I expect you're wondering what on earth an ass's head is doing on the kitchen floor. Well, the thing is …' She cast round wildly for inspiration and caught sight through the kitchen window of a pigeon alighting on next door's guttering in the evening light. It reminded her of something … Hey, Jade's Show 'n' Tell! Thanks, kid.

'The thing is Roxy's daughter is in the school play, and Roxy's helping with the props. She's having a bit of trouble with the ass – see, it's all sort of dented –'

'I'll say.' He snorted with laughter. 'Looks more like a crocodile with toothache, if you ask me.'

'– so I said I'd give her a hand.' She hurried on. 'Anyway, tea or coffee, darling?'

'Coffee ought to hit the spot. By the way, Tina said she'd been in touch about everyone meeting up. Wednesday the twenty-seventh, isn't it? Great. Couple of things I thought I'd better mention while I'm here. Just off for a quick slash first. Be right back.'

Still chortling, he strode out. After a moment, the door to the downstairs loo next to the kitchen shut with a bang.

Anna closed her eyes, took a deep breath and exhaled slowly in the manner recommended by an elderly Indian healer she'd seen expounding on Inner Calm on breakfast TV that morning.

As she made the coffee and got out the cake tin, she pondered previous relationships she'd had that had foundered on Sam's unexpected arrival home. She'd avoided getting seriously involved with anyone since he'd come home from school one afternoon when he was eleven and burst into the kitchen where she and Mark, at that time a colleague at Avant Art, were about to make love. They had been on the verge of an affair for months and that Thursday afternoon was to have seen its beginning while Sam went to tea with a friend. Unfortunately, the mother of this friend had lost the crown from a tooth that lunchtime and gone for an emergency dental appointment.. Sam's friend had gone with her, and Sam had returned home. The only consolation Anna could take from the ensuing farce was that it could have been worse. Her explanation for lying on the kitchen floor with one of her colleagues who had removed his shirt was ingenious. She said, as Sam stood regarding her beadily, looking alarmingly like his father, that the U-bend under the sink was blocked and Mark had very kindly offered to fix it. The offending blockage also took the blame for the pungent smell of the joint Mark had lit a few moments before.

After this her memory of her prospective lover's departure was hazy. Relations between them were somewhat strained the next day. By tacit consent the incident wasn't referred to directly and Anna felt nothing but relief when he left soon after to take up a position at the Hayward Gallery.

She resolved to put sex on hold till Sam left home for university. The risk of causing distress to herself and to her son had simply been too great. He relied on her to provide a stable emotional background and a secure environment. Once he'd gone away to university, however, she felt that at last she had the right to a private life, and had casually dated a couple of men she found attractive. In the event, neither developed into anything long term, but things changed when Sam was in his third term at Oxford and she met Luke, a lecturer in art history at the Slade, at Alastair's annual Christmas party. Quiet and good looking, he had two grown-up daughters, and had been widowed five years previously when his wife died of ovarian cancer. They'd hit it off immediately. After a couple of meals out and a visit to the Royal Court to see *Jumpers* it was clear that they had a lot in common, not least a shared sense of humour; soon they were meeting most Sundays in London and he was phoning her nearly every night.

The relationship moved onto a new footing when he visited Brighton to speak at a conference on Dadaism and arranged to stay the night, ostensibly to avoid driving back to Cambridge in the early hours. After a companionable biryani (he'd chosen prawn, Anna went for mushroom; they shared automatically without even discussing it) at the Star of India, they'd gone to see a late-night showing of *The Blair Witch Project*. By the end of the film, most of which Anna spent with her head burrowed inside Luke's linen jacket (for the rest of her life the smell of warm fabric conditioner would remind her of that night) she was too frightened to speak. As they walked home Luke re-enacted the most frightening bits with a terse running commentary delivered Groucho Marx style, complete with appropriate crouching walk. By the time she opened the front door she was helpless with laughter.

Ten minutes later, they were in bed.

The affair had developed fast. By the end of June, he was spending every weekend in Brighton. All was well until Sam turned up unexpectedly late one Friday night a few days before the scheduled end of term following a mumps scare in his college. Anna and Luke had been lying in bed feeding each other strawberries dipped in champagne and listening to Brahms after a lengthy love-making session, their passage from living room to bedroom marked by a trail of discarded garments. If Sam hadn't uncharacteristically forgotten his key and been obliged to ring the front doorbell he would almost certainly have surprised his mother and her lover in bed.

Anna practically fainted when she peered out of the window and saw her son standing on the doorstep, looking impatient and pulling leaves off the potted bay tree. Hissing at Luke to be quiet, she turned off the music, yanked her clothes back on (when she undressed again that night she discovered she was wearing Luke's underpants) and shot out of the room. She thought she'd collected everything as she hurried to answer the door, thrusting the whole bundle hastily into the hall cupboard as she passed, but Sam spotted a stocking dangling from the Japanese lampshade the minute he walked into the living room. His expression made it clear that her explanation that she'd run out of drying space cut no ice, and as he turned away she was pretty certain he was grinning. Luke had been very decent about hiding in her bedroom reading old copies of *Hello* magazine until Sam went to bed, before creeping downstairs and driving back to Cambridge. But following this, their relationship had cooled. A few months later, Alastair mentioned that Luke had become engaged to one of the secretaries at The Slade.

Upset at her inability to combine single parenthood with anything remotely approaching a satisfactory sex life, Anna asked the advice of her neighbour Beth, a sixty-something alternative therapist. Beth polished her rimless spectacles on a fold of her ankle-length dirndl and looked thoughtful as Anna related her tale over thimbles of green tea and organic oatcakes. Maybe Anna needed to think about whom she was *really* protecting, instead of worrying about Samuel, who seemed from Beth's observations to be a young man with a more than adequately developed ego and sense of – how could she put it – *self*. Was there perhaps some dark interlude in Anna's own childhood that needed to be brought into the light of day and examined? Beth lit a small black cheroot and leaned forward, looking intense. Anna tried hard to come up with something, but other than the untimely death of her guinea pig from overeating when she was eight she couldn't think of anything particularly distressing.

Roxy was more helpful; she roared with laughter when Anna described Luke creeping downstairs in the dark in the small hours, and reckoned it had probably done Sam a power of good to know his mother was on the pull, especially since the little bugger was probably permanently shagging himself senseless up college.

This, Anna decided, was probably true. By the time Sam was in his third year he was spending all his vacations abroad, teaching English in locations so far-flung that his neatly written and informative postcards (*'Group 2 having the usual difficulties with the subjunctive, although their use of vocabulary is improving. Planning to make the climb to an abandoned lamasery on the northern outskirts of Lhasa tomorrow, should the guide deem the weather to be suitably clement.'*) arrived several months after he'd returned to England. The morning she bumped into Jack in HMV, Sam had phoned just before she left the house to say he'd arrived safely in Caracas, where he was to spend Christmas teaching Business English to trainee IT sales managers. And since circumstances dictated that she and Jack never met at weekends, which was the only time Sam descended unannounced, their assignations continued to take place undisturbed. Things had continued in this relaxed vein. After Sam left Oxford and moved to London, she rarely saw him; once Lucy moved in notice of a visit had always been politely given (at Lucy's prompting, Anna suspected).

Until today ...

She splashed milk into a jug and dumped more demerara in the sugar bowl. Hell, maybe she *should* tell Sam about Jack. After all, he wasn't exactly a child any more; it really was ridiculous to keep creeping about like this, as if she was some sort of criminal and he was the secret police. Sam wasn't exactly liberal in his outlook: he thought anyone who voted Labour should be undergo psychiatric treatment and he was probably the only male in the Western world under the age of eighty who'd never owned a pair of jeans, but hey, this was the twenty-first century, wasn't it? Anyway, now he was so happily settled with Lucy, his mother didn't have the same significance in his life – he probably wouldn't care if she shacked up with a serial killer. Provided he voted Conservative, of course ... Right. As soon as he came back, she'd tell him. She heard the sound of the loo flushing, followed by the sound of running water. A moment later, Sam appeared in the doorway, looking disapproving. He held the copy of *Private Eye* she'd been reading in the loo this morning between finger and thumb.

'Honestly, Mum, you really shouldn't leave this sort of thing lying around. Anyone might see it. God, *Lucy* might have gone in there.'

Anna took the offending publication, slipped it behind the cushion on the rocking chair and pretended to check that no errant corners were protruding. Sam didn't laugh. Oh well, things might have been worse – it could have been a copy of the *Socialist Worker,* or *Toyboy Today*.

'Cake, darling?'

'Please.' He sat down at the table, cut himself a slice of date loaf and took a huge bite.

Anna poured the coffee and slipped onto the chair beside him. Right, go for it.

'Sam, darling, there's something I –'

'Mmm. Delicious.' He stirred sugar vigorously into his brimming mug. 'Look Mum, about meeting the O'Shaughnessys. As I said before, Lucy's family are very conventional, very traditional.' He took another bite of date loaf. 'Thing is, Tina's always done up to the nines, prides herself on looking her best. Must spend a fortune on clothes, actually; she'd rather die than be seen wearing the same outfit twice.' He shook his head admiringly. 'Keeps the Irish charity shops going singlehandedly with her donations, according to Eamonn.'

Anna busied herself with the percolator. All her favourite garments – velvet jackets, Edwardian lace blouses, floral tea gowns – came from Brighton's second-hand clothes shops.

'So I just wanted to say, don't wear anything too weird, OK?'

Pity he was too old for a good cuff round the head.

'But absolutely *not*. In fact, in view of the occasion, I was planning on going for the formal look.' She looked serious. 'I thought my Russian hussar's jacket – I know it's old, but all that gold braid really is to die for – teamed with a terrific little ruffled ra-ra skirt I saw in Topshop last week. It's bright green, in fact I'd almost call it *shamrock* green, come to think of it, with white polka dots – I thought it would hit the spot. Haven't decided about shoes yet, but I'm pretty sure I could get Roxy to lend me her cowboy boots, the ones with all the punching and the little spurs.'

Sam's mouth had dropped open as she spoke; his eyes were wide with alarm. Several crumbs of date loaf had fallen on his perfectly cut lapel; she reached out and brushed them off. She allowed herself the luxury of a few seconds more silence before putting him out of his misery.

'Only kidding, darling.'

By the time he'd stopped coughing and downed a glass of water, she felt better.

'OK, very amusing. Look, Mum, just keep it low key and you'll be fine. Now, I've been giving some thought as to how you should describe your job. I mean you can't exactly tell them you run a coffee bar, can you?'

She couldn't?

'So I think the best thing would be to say you're in the Art World in a culinary-advisory capacity.' He glanced at his watch, and sprang to his feet. 'Must dash, Lucy'll be waiting.'

Not sure whether to laugh or cry, Anna followed him out into the hall.

'Oh yes. One last point.. About … stuff. Differences of … *you* know … Though if you ask me, it's really rather moving to hear Tina talking about the trip to Lourdes she encouraged her daily help to take when she wanted to give in her notice on account of her arthritis. Anyway, what I'm trying to say is *please*, Mum, no swearing and none of your religious jokes, OK?' He hugged her briefly and flung open the front door. 'Great. See you on the twenty-seventh at Chez Gaston. Look forward it.'

Anna stood waving until the tail lights of the Audi disappeared from view. Then she shut the door very quietly, and screamed all the most offensive swear words she knew as

84

loudly as she could. She was drawing breath to repeat the exercise, reflecting that someone really should tell the Indian healer about this – it sure as hell was a lot more satisfying than all that deep breathing – when she became aware of a muffled thumping coming from upstairs.

She froze.

Great god in heaven – *Jack*! Her married, blindfolded, bound-to-the-bedposts lover!

Thank Christ she hadn't mentioned him to Sam – he'd probably get Father Thing to come round and give her a good talking to about her moral infirmity, or exorcise her, or something.

The thumping intensified, accompanied now by muffled shouts.

As Anna took the stairs two at a time, she was laughing.

CHAPTER SEVEN

'Well, I certainly feel much better for your words of advice, Declan. I'll ask her on Friday, so I will. Now, will you be having another, then?'

Declan hesitated. He'd already had several whiskies, and he'd have to be up early next morning if he was to be in Galway by half past ten; McGinty had rung him earlier in the week with orders to photograph the opening of a new supermarket by a rising young soap star who'd just bought a holiday home on the bay. But hell, his camera bag was packed, his good work shirt was ironed, and the thought of the cold, damp cottage waiting for his return was not an inviting one. With an effort, he smiled at Finn as he sprawled across settle on the opposite side of the stone hearth. The flickering of the peat fire cast shadows on his friend's craggy features, picking out the gold rim of his glasses and the edge of his signet ring. Noting subconsciously the dramatic contrasts in tonal values he downed the last of his Jameson's. 'You know I think I might, at that.'

Finn grinned, collected their empty glasses and set off for refills.

Declan sank lower in the rickety carver chair. He'd come across Finn during one of his solitary weekend hikes some months after he moved into the cottage. Finn had set up his easel in the middle of a field and, oblivious to the weather, and the attentions of an aggressive sheep, was wildly slashing oil paint at a Turner-esque depiction of the nearby mountains. The two men had taken to each other at once, and frequently passed their evenings at the tiny pub in the nearby village where Finn lived. What the pub lacked in amenities – the flagstoned floor was rarely swept, on stormy nights the air was thick with smoke from the fire, and often the only other customer was an old man who sat at the bar quaffing Guinness and playing mournful dirges on his fiddle – it more than made up for in the low price of the drinks, and the fact that the landlord, an ancient of jovial disposition who tended to break into songs from pre-war musicals in a vain attempt to persuade the fiddler to play something more cheerful, had apparently never heard of closing time.

Declan and Finn spent most of their time arguing about painting and photography; very occasionally, they would stray on to something more personal. Tonight Finn, who was divorced, had been telling Declan about a student at the art class he taught in Cork twice a week, and who he had a mind to invite to the cinema. Declan offered encouragement, with the result that Finn, who considered himself out of practice in these matters, had resolved to go for it the following Friday.

As Finn chatted to the barman, nodding cheerily at the fiddler, who responded by breaking into a tragic rendition of 'Molly Malone', Declan tried to take pleasure in his friend's prospective happiness. He tried not to feel blank misery as he caught sight of the night pressing against the grimy window set deep in the thick whitewashed wall.

Tried to forget the fact that today would have been Maura's thirty-fifth birthday.

Three years since …

Since …

First thing that morning he'd laid a bunch of wild hyacinths at the shrine. He found them growing at the edge of the loch beyond the fields at the back of the cottage, tiny flowers with variegated blue petals that reminded him of the colour of Maura's eyes. He made things looks as tidy as he could, but it wasn't easy; a bank of cloud had swept in suddenly from the mountains, and gusts of wind kept blowing his offering off-centre. It started to rain as he left, increasing his sense of desolation. If only there was a grave he could visit – somewhere he could feel he was near her. Where he could *talk* to her – tell her how sorry, how indescribably, unutterably sorry he was, and ask her forgiveness …

Still and all, he was grateful for the shrine. Maura's parents had insisted on taking their daughter's ashes back to their bungalow in County Antrim, where he imagined they were kept in an elaborate Wedgwood urn among garish china figures and bubbled-glass specimen vases on the mantelpiece above the log-effect gas fire. At the funeral, her parents had refused to look at him, let alone speak to him. Immediately after it, he'd packed up and left the flat on the outskirts of Dublin with no idea where he was going. He'd driven for three days, instinctively heading west towards the Connemara mountains where they'd spent their honeymoon. He slept in the van, stopping twice to buy more whiskey. On the third morning, after being forced to drive at a snail's pace behind a lorry loaded with farm manure for almost thirty miles, he'd taken an unmarked left turn on the spur of the moment. After a while, the road narrowed, then dwindled to a track. He was about to turn back, when he caught sight of the shrine, half hidden by the overgrown hedgerow.

He stopped the van, and got out. Until then he hadn't been able to cry, but the sight of a little bunch of daisies carefully arranged in a cracked green plastic egg cup at the Virgin Mary's feet undid him entirely; it was as if it was a sign. Maura had made a daisy chain and hung it round her slender neck the first time he'd taken her to visit his parents. He'd taken a photograph of her, sitting on their lawn, head thrown back, laughing at some foolish joke his father had made ...

At first he thought some trapped wild animal must be making the dreadful sounds; he'd been stumbling to his feet, about to set out to look for it, to rescue it, or put it out of its misery – anything to stop the noise – when he realised they were coming from him.

He stayed at the shrine until it began to grow dark. At last he got himself back into the van, his whole body numb and his eyes so swollen he could hardly see. He'd barely driven a mile or so when he saw the sign, 'Cottage To Let', with a scrawled telephone number beneath. The numbers added up to the date of

Maura's birthday, if you left off the 62 at the end and didn't count the code in; it had to be another sign.

He moved in the following day.

'There you go, wrap yourself round this.' Finn was standing beside him, handing him a glass and Declan took it gratefully. Finn sat himself down in the corner of the settle again, and they drank in companionable silence for a while. Suddenly a turf at the back of the fire settled deeper in the grate, sending up a shower of sparks. Finn stirred, shot a sideways glance at Declan, took a gulp of whiskey and cleared his throat.

'Declan, don't mind me saying this, now, but …' He took another gulp of whiskey. 'Is it not time you were maybe thinking of moving on yourself?'

'Movin on?' Declan frowned. 'And why would that be?'

'You'll excuse me for mentioning it, but you said yourself it's been three years now since –' He gestured mutely with the hand that held the glass.

Fury sparked in Declan's dark brown eyes and died as he saw the concern in Finn's anxious gaze. After a while he leaned forward, his elbows on his knees, and gazed unseeingly into the fire. 'I can't, Finn.'

'But d'ye not think –'

'No.'

'But –'

'No.'

'So ye're planning to stay unhappy for ever, is that it? Ye'll pardon me for saying so, but I can't help seeing that as a very negative attitude to life.'

Declan drained his whiskey. 'I don't deserve to be happy, Finn.'

Astonished, Finn leaned forward and hit him smartly on the shoulder. 'Course ye do, man – course ye do!' He sprang to his feet. 'What kind o' thinking's that?

The ancient fiddler set his glass tankard on the counter, closed his eyes and began to play 'She Walked Through the Fair' with great feeling in an affecting minor key. Declan noted idly how the firelight diffused a reddish glow through the dregs in the bottom of the tankard, so the liquid looked like diluted blood in some sort of medical receptacle.

He smiled mirthlessly at Finn. 'I've got to pay the price for not being dead too.'

Getting to his feet, he took their empty glasses and headed for the bar.

CHAPTER EIGHT

A shower of coins spewed from a nearby fruit machine to shouts of triumph from the youths around it as Anna left the Ladies and pushed her way through the Sunday night throng towards the bar. The Golden Galleon was packed, as usual. The other members of Pier Poets were crammed between a grandfather clock and a peeling ship's figurehead of Aphrodite, engaged in a heated discussion about the latest publication by the Poet Laureate. Some excellent poems had been workshopped during the first half of the session, and she tried not to feel nervous about the fact that she was scheduled to read next. Despite the fact that her work invariably received favourable comment – 'Red Peppers' had met with almost unanimous praise at the last meeting – she always dreaded the moment when she'd have to stand up and expose her innermost thoughts to public scrutiny. The poem she planned to read tonight was a melancholy piece about the young couple she'd seen in the bus shelter who reminded her of herself and Tony at that age; she'd spent every free moment of the last week or so working on it, and she was pleased with the way it was shaping up.

Things had generally been pretty peaceful lately. She'd resolved not to mention the 'Ruth situation' to Jack again, reasoning that the more pressure he was under to take action the more likely he was to handle things badly. Though that didn't stop her secretly worrying … Still, for the moment she'd forget about the vagaries of her love life and enjoy her esoteric surroundings. She was just admiring the fairy lights draped incongruously among the fans of dried coral which bore an unpleasant resemblance to skeletal fingers on the shelves at the back of the bar when her elbow was jogged familiarly. 'Hey, Anna – how's it going? Drink?'

Sonia, one of the older members of the group, leaned against the bar waving a twenty pound note at the harassed barman. Anna smiled. She was extremely fond of Sonia, who at around sixty-five wore her long silver hair waist-length, favoured clothes that made Vivienne Westwood look positively restrained and was outspoken but constructive in her criticism of her fellow members' work. In another life she had taught English Literature in Rome; since retiring she'd made her home in Brighton and now devoted all her time to writing. Anna admired her work more than that of almost anyone else in the group. 'Thanks – a glass of red would be great.'

Sonia yelled the addition to her order to the barman, and turned to Anna. 'Up next, are you? I can tell by that hunted look.' She smiled at her kindly. 'Don't worry, you'll be fine. Anyway, you and I know there are a hell of a lot of things in life more important than poetry. Did you see *Men in Black* last night? I'm not kidding, I laughed so much I nearly threw up.'

Anna cheered up immediately. She too had watched *Men in Black*, and she too had laughed so hard and so often that by the end her stomach hurt. She and Sonia reprised their favourite scenes. (Sonia turned out to have an unexpected talent for mimicry and could imitate the terse little bulldog's voice perfectly.) They were soon in fits over Will Smith being savaged by the octopus from outer space as it gave birth in the back of a car and were still laughing when their drinks arrived. Anna was passing Sonia her vodka and tonic when Barry pushed into the space beside her. He beamed at her. 'Anna! I can't tell you what a pleasure it is to see you laughing!' He gazed at her for a moment, blushing. 'And you too, of course, Sonia.'

Sonia grinned, and ate an ice cube.

'Do tell me what the joke is!' said Barry.

Anna took a sip of her wine. 'It's just that we both watched *Men in Black* last night. Have you seen it?'

'Let me see … no, I haven't. Last night I was watching a documentary on Ancient Norse dialect. Most thought-provoking.' He consulted the elaborate multi-faced watch on his bony wrist. 'Time's getting on, I see. May I offer you ladies a top-up?'

He tried to attract the barman's attention. By the time he'd succeeded, Sonia and Anna were in fits again about the film's mortuary scene. He eyed them wistfully as he handed them fresh drinks. 'I must say it does sound the most tremendous fun – I almost wish I'd foregone Norse semantics.' He broke off as a figure elbowed its way past Anna to stand beside him. 'Ah – Helena.'

Helena, a dour woman with a thicket of straight black hair, a large mole on her upper lip and the furriest legs Anna had ever seen on a woman, simpered up at him. 'I saw the programme about Norse dialect too. Riveting, simply riveting.' She narrowed her eyes at Anna. 'I'm surprised you weren't watching it, Anna – I'd have thought any *serious* poet would be.' She slurped at her bitter lemon.

Sonia shot Helena a look. 'Actually, I'd say the more serious the poet, the more fun she's going to need to balance the angst if she's going to stay anything like sane.' She winked at Anna. 'In fact I've often asked myself the question: *would* Sylvia Plath have put her head in the gas oven that January night if she could have taken her mind off things with a vindaloo, a couple of cans and *Pure Hell at St Trinian's* on the telly?'

Helena frowned. 'Hmmm. Speaking as a music therapist –'

Barry edged furtively towards Anna and touched her elbow. 'Anna, I wonder if I might have a word?'

Oh God, he was going to ask her out.

'It won't take a moment.' He drew her away from the others into a corner by the window; Anna was aware of Helena eyeing her jealously as she enlightened Sonia with her views on the true cause of Sylvia Plath's suicide. 'The thing is –' Barry glanced round furtively.

Would he invite her to Amsterdam for a quick frolic?

'– I do hope you don't mind …' He frowned at his half pint of shandy. 'And perhaps I should have discussed it with you first, but I know how diffident you are about your work, despite your extraordinary talent …'

Or would it be a weekend doing the rounds at the Reeperbahn?

'In fact, if I may say so I remain of the opinion that you should have entered "Rip Tide" for the National Poetry Competition. It was tremendous: the innovative use of layout as the words spill down the page like a *tsunami*, the analogy of the destructive power of love with the savage power of the sea … Though us chaps aren't all as badly behaved as the bounder in the poem, you know, ha ha –' He wagged his finger roguishly at Anna, spilling shandy on the hectically patterned carpet. …'

Anna was distracted by the painted bust of Britannia on a shelf above Barry's head which bore an uncanny resemblance to Margaret Thatcher.

'… Leaving the poor girl lying like so much detritus on the darkening shore …' He took an emotional pull at the remains of his shandy. 'Marvellous. Then I began to think about all the other fine work you've read here.'

Although it was hard to imagine Mrs Thatcher going out without a top on.

'"Lessons", "Glass House", and not to mention …'

Anna mentally added a flesh-pink bra to the figurehead.

'It struck me that it's high time you reached a wider audience, and that your work got the recognition it so richly deserves.'

She changed flesh-pink to electric-blue leopardskin.

'And so I took it upon myself to submit twenty-five of your poems to Wild Horses, the poetry press.' He flashed her a roguish grin. 'Ah! I see from your expression that you are not entirely displeased.'

Great, that was much more –

Wild Horses.

The poetry press.

Anna's smile slowly faded.

Twenty-five of your poems.

She stared at him, dumbstruck. 'But … you *can't*! I mean it's very kind of you and everything, but for God's sake, Barry – Wild Horses?' She downed the remainder of her wine, and laughed. 'Honestly, you know I don't stand a snowball's chance in hell of them wanting to publish me.'

The rest of the group were beginning to straggle back to the snug for the second half of the workshop and Anna tensed as she realised it was almost time for her to read.

She ran a hand through her hair. 'I mean … they published Andrew Hoskins last year.'

'Precisely.' Barry set his empty glass down carefully on the bar. 'They know talent when they see it.'

'But –'

Barry looked at her sternly. 'And so do I.'

Conscious at last of the compliment he was paying her work, and that further protestations would be churlish, Anna stepped forward and kissed him quickly on the cheek. 'Thank you.'

'Golly!' Barry cleared his throat and busied himself with his papers. Anna tried not to notice that he was beetroot red, or that Helena, now arguing with Sonia about the therapeutic effects of vindaloo, was glaring balefully at her. Barry puffed out his chest, adjusted his tie and gestured with a beaming smile towards the snug. 'Well! It's on with the show, if you're ready!' Unfortunately he knocked his papers to the floor, spewing dog-eared poems, notes and flyers for forthcoming readings everywhere.

Anna helped him gather them up, reassuring him that it could have happened to anyone and that she didn't think the old man who'd received a direct hit from Barry's notebook had suffered permanent damage. It took longer to gather up the coins that he'd knocked from the charity collection box on the bar and separate them (under the barman's scornful eye) from the cashew nuts next to it.

Social embarrassment had its advantages she reflected, as she followed Barry into the snug to join the rest of the group.

She'd entirely forgotten her nervousness about being the next to read.

CHAPTER NINE

Declan left the pub that evening earlier than usual. Depressed at his failure to explain his feelings to Finn, he'd told him he had to get back to develop some film he'd shot earlier that day. It wasn't entirely untrue; unable to sleep, he'd risen with the dawn and taken shot after shot of a dead sheep he discovered on his walk. The creature had got itself trapped in a barbed-wire fence, and had clearly been there for several days. Its matted coat hung in ragged clumps and maggots were already infesting its rump, festooned with dangling clumps of greenish faecal matter. But it wasn't the carcass Declan was interested in: it was the pale coin of early morning sun reflected in the pupil of the sheep's eye.

Finn had ordered himself another whiskey, and wished him godspeed. As Declan left, Finn was discussing the plans for his date: the landlord recommended Finn cast all thought of a visit to the cinema from his mind. He knew women, and strongly recommended that Finn impress the young lady with a visit to a French restaurant he could recommend in Limerick if he was hoping to make touchdown in the back of the car that night.

A fine rain was falling as Declan set off into the darkness; the air was heady with the scent of hawthorn and cow parsley; small creatures burrowed and scuttered in the hedgerows; a bat skittered silently past inches from his face. As he walked he began to feel better, and realised that he had spoken the truth to his friend unwittingly. The thought of getting to work on developing a first set of prints from the morning was increasingly compelling. As he neared the cottage he began to increase his pace, pondering different developing techniques he might experiment with and which grades of paper might be best. The blue gate to the cottage hung from its hinges like a rotting tooth but as he pushed it open he heard the phone was ringing inside. His heart leapt – before the realization hit him that it would never be her.

When will you get it straight, you stupid bastard, you useless, worthless piece of shit? Dead people don't make phone calls.

He crushed the nettles at the front door with his hand, enjoying the pain, until at last, the ringing stopped. He turned and leant against the rain butt, letting the drizzle mingle with his tears. The silhouetted branches of the apple trees seemed to have trapped the moon, like the sheep tangled in the wire that morning. He looked away. There was nothing he could do to help it. There was nothing he could do to help anyone …

Dimly he became aware that the phone was ringing again. Hell and damnation, it must be McGinty with new instructions about tomorrow. He'd probably got another assignment for him after the supermarket. Please God not another one involving kids.

Last week he'd been sent to photograph a swimming gala at McGinty's daughter's school. Everything had gone fine at first – swimmingly, you might say, if you were of a humorous turn of mind. In fact he'd even go so far as to say he was enjoying himself, what with the excitement of the kids and the proud expressions on their parents' faces, not to mention that daft bugger of a monsignor nearly going arse over tit as he mounted the podium to present the cups and looking daggers when the audience laughed. He'd got a great shot of that; you didn't need one of those thought bubbles drawn in to tell you the kind of language that was going through His Grace's mind. Sure, he'd been having a fine time of it until he saw the child.

She was one of the youngest – not more than eight or nine – waiting, shivering on the edge of the pool to take her turn in the relay team, giggling and chattering with her friends, clutching some little stuffed animal for luck. It might have been a rabbit; he couldn't tell for sure. But the thing of it … sweet Jesus, the thing of it was she was the image, the spitting god-given image of Maura: same colour eyes, same wicked grin, same ragged, smoky hair, same slightly knock knees. His mouth twitched briefly: Maura had hit him with a pillow when he'd made a joke about them once and refused to believe that he adored them ...

He'd looked at the little girl. She wore a silver cross round her neck and a bracelet of bright pink plastic beads hung around her bird-bone wrist. He pictured her threading the cheap gewgaws onto the elastic, effortfully tying a double knot, the tip of her tongue protruding from the corner of her mouth as she concentrated. The kid he and Maura might have had one day, given luck and a fair wind following ...

Except there hadn't been a fair wind following, only driving rain, and it wasn't luck that had been powering down the Glencree road to meet them, it was ...

He opened his eyes. The moon gazed at him through the tangle of black branches, the cold night air chilled him to the bone through his damp clothes, his stinging palms throbbed.

The phone was still ringing.

Fumbling with the latch (the rust was getting worse, he must remember to get some oil to it) he got the door open and picked up the phone.

'... Mr O'Halloran?' Not McGinty: a woman's sharp, insistent voice. Suddenly he became aware of the lateness of the hour. Sweet Jesus, it must be some kind of emergency. His father? When he last phoned his mother had said that his blood pressure was causing serious concern, and a bypass couldn't be ruled out. His throat went dry.

'Mr O'Halloran?' She sounded impatient – probably anxious to get the bad news over with. They were trained to sound professional, weren't they?

The older policeman firmly gripping his shoulder as he sat next to him by the side of the road. The policewoman handing him a mug of hot sweet tea and holding his head when he threw up seconds later. The younger policeman crossing himself before beginning to write in his notebook.

'... Yes?'

'At last! I've been trying to get hold of you for ages! Now, you don't know me, but –'

'It's my dad, isn't it?' His throat was dry.

'I believe you know a friend of mine.' There was a pause, followed by an affected little laugh. 'Well, more of an acquaintance, really. We don't move in quite the same social circles, if you know what I mean. Anyway, somehow – and it's my opinion the grandparents must have chipped in – they managed a really quite pleasant little wedding for their daughter …'

It was a wrong fucking number, for Christ's fucking sake. He drew a shuddering breath.

'… and only three bridesmaids! All dressed, I may say, in the most …'

Thank God it wasn't his father. Still, he'd ring home tomorrow, just to check everything was OK.

'Look, sorry but you've got the wrong –'

'– sweet peas! I mean I don't need to tell you, the colours clashed frightfully with their frocks …'

He felt in his pocket for matches; he'd feel better if the lamp was lit.

'And then of course the cake! Well, for a start, there were only –'

Maybe if he just replaced the receiver?

'… really quite embarrassing. But the one thing that was an absolute triumph – and I remember saying to Eamonn when Dolly suddenly produced the album at the Rotary dinner last month, well, thank heaven at least she managed to get *something* right – was the photographs.'

Photographs?

'And the close-ups of the happy couple, too – though I do think somebody should have had a word with Cameron about his choice of waistcoat. There was a splendid group taken by the fountain …'

Declan closed his eyes. He hardly ever did weddings, it was just too painful, but now and again he'd take a booking if he really needed the money. He'd been offered this one over a lunchtime drink by a journalist at the *Gazette* whose girlfriend was a friend of the bride.

'Of course, this wedding will be a much grander affair than poor Dolly's.'

At first Declan had turned it down flat, but the very next day his van had hit a fucking great pothole when he'd swerved to avoid a rabbit in the lane on his way back from a dawn foray into the mountains. There'd been a hell of a crash, and for a while he'd just sat there gripping the steering wheel, sweating and shaking as the memories engulfed him.

'There'll be two hundred and fifty at the reception ...'

After a while he'd wiped his face on his coat sleeve and driven on, but the engine was making a hell of a racket and he knew he'd done some serious damage. Next morning he'd driven very slowly to a garage on the main road a few miles from the cottage, where he'd learnt that the roll bar was badly bent and it would cost a couple of hundred euros to fix it.

'... and six page boys in shades of purple and lavender. I always say there's nothing like ...'

The mechanic had grinned and kicked the side of the van when he'd finally crawled out from underneath the chassis. If he was Declan he'd jack this heap of junk in, so he would. Would he not be better off with something that would pull a few girls, now?

'... mauve satin knickerbockers ...'

Declan stiffened, and thrust a clenched fist deep in his jacket pocket. He'd bought the van the week before he met Maura, and they'd gone everywhere in it together; shopping, picnics, holidays. Jesus, they'd toured Connemara in it on their honeymoon. Sometimes, he thought he could still smell the faintest hint of her perfume when he was driving. In fact, he always thought if it had been the van he'd been driving that day ...

Brusquely he'd told the bloke to just get it fixed, and strode away. He was almost home when he realised he didn't *have* a spare couple of hundred euros. He was on the phone to his journalist mate and getting a phone number for the bride's parents the minute he got inside the cottage.

'... to match the bridesmaids' sashes ...'

The wedding really hadn't been that bad. He had blocked out all feeling and concentrated on doing the job. The sky had been heavily overcast, and he'd had his work cut out sorting the lighting and finding the best shooting angles. But the young couple had been great, and if it hadn't been for the nature of the occasion he would have accepted the drinks that friendly guests kept pressing on him and joined in the spirit of things instead of remaining silent and aloof as he went about his work.

'… and the bridegroom is something *very* important in the City. Now, September the twenty-fifth is the date I've chosen. *Do* tell me you'll be free then, Mr O'Halloran!'

He was about to refuse when he thought of the negatives of the sheep's eye hanging in the darkroom. He was already pretty sure they were good; but he knew too that the pin-sharp definition essential in such detailed work – in essence a series of exquisitely abstract miniatures – would have been even crisper if he'd been using one of the ruthlessly effective but prohibitively expensive new Hasselblads.

'Mr O'Halloran?'

If McGinty wanted him to work that day, he'd plead an important prior engagement. He never had anything but work to do on a Saturday. McGinty couldn't exactly complain – it would be the first time he would have been unavailable in all his years at the paper. 'Yes. Yes, I'll be free then, Mrs …?'

He winced, and held the receiver away from his ear as she squealed with girlish delight.

'With family groups posed along lines similarly formal lines. And, of course, several portraits of myself?'

Declan located the matches at last among the jumble of lens caps and marker pens in his pocket.

'… thigh-length lime-green brocade, though I haven't finally decided on my jewellery yet …'

He laid the receiver down on the table and felt his way across the room in the darkness towards the round table where the oil lamp stood. Lifting off the glass bowl of the oil lamp – it was engraved with lilies, their once golden outlines now stained and tarnished with age and neglect. – he lit a match and touched it to the wick. The flame flared a brief, startling blue for a moment, then settled to a steady yellow glow. He replaced the bowl, found a discarded bill and a stub of pencil amid the detritus of newspapers and dirty dishes and returned to the phone. Shrill squawks were still issuing from the receiver as he picked it up.

'… elbow-length gloves. Suede, I think, if I can find a tangerine bright enough. Hello …?' Her tone sharpened; the cut-glass vowels flattened slightly, allowing a Northern Irish accent to slip through momentarily. 'Mr O'Halloran?'

He repressed a grin. 'Hello, Mrs –? I'm sorry, I'm afraid I didn't catch your –'

'O'Shaughnessy. But do call me Tina.' The sharpness was coated with honey once more. 'Now. The wedding is at two thirty at St Aloysius, an absolutely *charming* little church in the countryside near Fergustown, followed by the reception at the Grand Hotel. I expect you've read about it in the nationals. It was featured very prominently on *Holiday!* on TV recently. It's frightfully old, and the chef trained in Paris at the George Cinq, so he's obviously the absolute *top* of his tree. As I said to poor Dolly, where else could one possibly have one's reception?'

Declan scribbled down the information. He spent the next few minutes thinking about the various papers he was planning to experiment with when he printed the sheep's eye miniatures while she told him a lot more about the wonders of the cuisine at the Grand Hotel.

'And I'm planning to ask chef to devise a special dessert just for me. I mean for Lucy and dear Sam.' She sighed. 'Well, I'd love to go on chatting to you, Mr O'Halloran, but if you could *see* the list I have in front of me! I'm about to ring the florist to tell her all about a delightful new rose I saw on *Gardening Gems* last night – it would be perfect for the buttonholes.'

Declan blinked. 'But won't the shop be closed at this time of night?'

'Well, naturally. But fortunately I've just found her home number in the directory. I'll be in touch again shortly, Mr O'Halloran, to discuss things in more detail – and let me just say I look forward to the superb record I just know you're going to make of what's going to be a simply wonderful, *wonderful* day.'

As Declan headed for the kitchen to put the kettle on, desperate for coffee, tea, cocoa – Jesus, *anything* – he glanced out of the window. The rain had stopped and the sky was clear now, a gentle ultramarine shading to a deep purple over the distant mountains.

Purple.

Page boys.

Satin knickerbockers.

Holy Mother of God. Despite himself, he grinned. His attention was soon diverted by a new patch of fungus pushing through the crack in the plastered wall, and he moved away from the window without noticing that the moon had unfettered herself from the dark embrace of the apple tree and was sailing once more free and clear across the unclouded sky.

CHAPTER TEN

Anna set her glass of wine down carefully on the coffee table, kicked off her sandals, chucked her bag on the sofa and threw herself down after it with a sigh of relief. Ten past six. Great, she had nearly an hour before Jack arrived; time to put her feet up for five minutes before she made herself presentable and got supper started. She closed her eyes and rested her aching head against a cushion. Just for a moment she allowed herself to imagine how delightful it would to arrive home just once and find Jack there before her, newly showered and freshly shaved, smelling deliciously of some exotic aftershave. She'd never liked to tell him but she actually couldn't stand whatever it was he wore. She bet sodding Ruth bought him a bloody great keg of it every Christmas and forced him to use it …

Anyway, he'd be standing in the kitchen with a welcoming smile, and delicious smells would be wafting from the oven behind him. He'd have made some sort of chicken dish, maybe baked tandoori-style in one of those Indian clay whatsits. With all the trimmings, of course, and there'd be some chilled beers to go with it … Yes, and pigs might fly. She couldn't recall Jack as much as making a piece of toast for her, now she came to think of it.

This wouldn't do – what on earth was the matter with her? She took a sip of wine, drew her feet up and massaged her left heel where the strap of her sandal had been rubbing all day. Anyone would have thought she wasn't desperate to see him. And she was, she really, really was – it was an age since last Thursday. It was just that today had been a bugger of a day, worse even than Mondays usually were. Both Trish and Susie had called in sick first thing, ostensibly with flu but in fact because they were behind with their graphics coursework.

107

She'd overheard them discussing it on Saturday – they only had one day left to complete a 3D scale model of the Pompidou Centre which they were supposed to have spent the last three months toiling over, but hadn't even yet begun.

Anna was secretly sympathetic to their plight, and accepted their excuses graciously. She felt a lot less understanding when the impatient lunchtime queue reached almost as far as the entrance, and there was nobody to keep the coffee machines going or make extra baguettes. She and Roxy had been recovering with a cup of tea and the remains of the cauliflower and walnut quiche when the first of the two school parties Alastair had forgotten to inform her were coming arrived. They made a beeline straight for the coffee bar like junkies drawn to an opium den and immediately complained about the shortage of orange juice and brownies. She'd managed to quell the incipient riot by whipping up a triple batch of chocolate shortbread, but by the time she'd finished she was exhausted and still had the teatime rush to come.

Ten minutes before closing time she'd been putting the batter she'd made for tomorrow's drop scones in the fridge when she became aware of a steady dripping coming from the freezer, which had become a near-solid block of ice. Since Anna never used frozen products in any of the dishes this wasn't a problem, but she knew she was in for trouble if she ignored the warning signs, which meant, sod it, that she'd have to switch the entire fridge off on Saturday when she shut up shop and spend Sunday – *Sunday*, for God's sake! – at work, defrosting and cleaning.

To top it all, Alastair had waylaid her as she was leaving and, far from apologising for forgetting to tell her about the school parties, had pressingly reprised his regular Monday request that she *sherioushly conshider* opening on Sundays. Forbearing to take Roxy's whispered advice to tell him to stuff his bleeding request where the sun don't shine, she'd promised to think about it and stalked off, trying not to limp on account of her painful heel.

She'd felt too exhausted even to contemplate walking home. While she was standing at the bus stop, a rack of magazines on a nearby newsstand caught her eye. Maybe she'd splash out on the current edition of *Hello!* She deserved it after the day she'd had. No bus was in sight. Hurrying over, she was about to hand over the money to the dour old man in charge when she spotted a glossy magazine on the end of the row. On the cover was a girl she had to assume to be a bride, since the magazine bore the title in giant embossed gold letters. Without this clue, one might have been forgiven for assuming the creature to be a homeless drug addict, since she was stick thin, nearly bald and wearing glistening black lipstick which rendered her pallid skin even paler. The wedding gown seemed to consist of a couple of paper tissues held together by safety pins. Anna grinned, imagining Tina's reaction should Lucy discover a rebellious streak and hold out for what the caption proclaimed to be 'The Now Look!' Below the caption was a list of articles - all surprisingly traditional, considering the cover. She was smirking at 'Make-up Magic for your Special Day', and 'Twenty Top Tips for Honeymoon Happiness' when her smile faded. At the bottom of the list, in slightly smaller type beside the bride's bright green Doc Martens, it read 'So You're the Mother of the Groom'. Anna's jaw dropped.

She was about to be the Mother of a Groom!

They were talking about *her*!

She shivered, and pulled her denim jacket tightly round her. It wasn't fair. She just wasn't ready for this. 'Mother' was fine. But 'Mother of the Groom'? It had a hideously formal sound, a smell of violets and dusty lace hung about it. Quite possibly more than a whiff of incontinence pads too.

She was about to turn away when the model on the cover caught her eye again. Wait a minute – maybe things weren't as bad as she thought. Maybe people still stuck to the same old-fashioned titles where weddings were concerned – Lucy was having a matron of honour, for God's sake – but that didn't mean they were still expected to fulfill old-fashioned stereotypes. Look at the 'bride' on the cover – hell, she was so

'Now!' she was practically 'Tomorrow!' Alastair would probably 'fanshy her somefing crool'. She'd buy it and pick up a few tips on the latest trends. Maybe there'd be something delightfully Biba-esque recommended for M's of the G ... As she dug into her bag to find her purse her bus heaved into view. The queue for it was now depressingly long.

She had to stand nearly all the way home, hemmed in by a press of shoppers and their outsize bags. She had just managed to extract her copy of *Bride* from her bag and was about to open it when she caught sight of a pair of rheumy eyes boring into her from behind a pair of rakishly diamantéed spectacles. Dear God, it was the old crone she'd tried to hurry the day she bought her scarlet underwear – worse, she was determinedly elbowing her way towards her.

Mercifully, the bus was spluttering to a halt. Muttering apologies, Anna pushed her way to the exit and jumped off, not looking back as she crossed the road and hurried along the Steine and up the hill. She didn't stop until she'd closed the front door behind her.

Anna sighed. A perfect end to a perfect day. Except it wasn't the end of the day – Jack was coming, and the best was ahead. She smiled, and took a sip of wine. She didn't really mind cooking; she'd just had a lousy day, that was all. She'd have a quick glance at *Bride* while she finished her drink, then make a start. Taking the magazine from her bag, she began to leaf through it. The first thing that struck her was the hedonism of the advertisements: staggeringly beautiful girls wearing wedding dresses so fragile, so exquisite, it was impossible to imagine them being worn outside the photographer's studio, let alone surviving the ceremony (potential hazard: tiny bridesmaids stepping on train), the reception (potential hazard: new husband's ex-girlfriend accidentally spilling large glass of red wine down front), or quickie with new husband in hotel broom cupboard before changing to leave for honeymoon (potential hazards: too numerous not here to mention). Then there were the veils, delicate wisps of gossamer, pearl studded, flower embroidered, and one with pale pink sequins tossed seemingly at random over the transparent gauze, and so beautiful it brought tears to Anna's eyes.

She turned the page to an article on bridal tiaras and gazed at them for a while, trying to decide which one she'd have if her fairy godmother absolutely *forced* her to choose, finally settling on a diadem with diamonds in the shape of wild roses mounted on gold and set in silver. Hold on a minute, though – apparently the flowers were set *en tremblant*, and would be animated by the slightest movement of the head. What would happen if she nodded too vigorously when the registrar asked if she 'took this man'? Or laughed too hard at some risqué joke in the best man's speech? Actually, she was pretty sold on the pierced gold tiara with brilliant-cut diamonds in the form of twining lilies to which clung moonstone drops, now she came to think about it …

This was ridiculous – she didn't have time for such fantasies. She'd just take a quick peek at the gear for mothers-of-the-groom, then she'd get on. Taking a fortifying sip of wine, she leafed past the magic make-up tips and honeymoon-happiness advice, and almost choked on her wine. Instead of the trendy, slightly kooky look she'd been hoping for, she was faced by two sombre-looking matrons. One was draped in mushroom calf-length pleats topped by a jacket with outsize lapels, and seemed to be wearing a matching standard lampshade on her head. The second had calf-length pleats in navy, topped by a jacket that featured a collar that was presumably meant to convey an insouciant nautical air but looked worryingly like a bib that had been attached by a social-services carer to catch embarrassing geriatric dribbles. Her hat was a navy and white sailor-type cap tilted at what was no doubt intended to be a jaunty angle but merely looked as if it had slipped from the wearer's tremulous grasp when she put it on. Both women carried immaculate white gloves and little clutch bags in – predictably – mushroom and navy.

Why was the cover so way-out if the contents were so bloody conservative? Come to think of it, the brides' dresses, lovely as they were, were as traditional as confetti and choir boys, not a paper handkerchief or safety pin in sight. None of the articles sounded exactly ground-breaking – unless 'magic make-up tips' gave hints on how to achieve the Goth Look on your special day, and 'honeymoon happiness' gave tips on making love in a diving suit while swinging from the hotel chandelier. She checked. They didn't. She flipped back to the cover again. And noticed for the first time the caption below the bride's other Doc Martened foot: 'Winner of Last Month's Fashion Students' Competition'. She thought of Susie and Trish's sometimes alarming outfits. That explained it, then.

With a sigh, she drank the rest of her wine and, like someone probing an aching tooth with her tongue just to make sure it really was agony, examined the mothers-of-the-groom outfits again. They still looked just as unappetising; her *grandmother* wouldn't be seen dead in these clothes. If she was alive, that is. Anna was about to chuck the magazine in the wastepaper basket when she noticed the article at the bottom of the page. 'Make Him Proud to Introduce His Mother'. She didn't need to read rubbish like that. Though what was that bit about a total skincare programme? She had to admit, her beauty regime really was pretty slapdash … She read on. Oh dear, it was true, her nails were hideously neglected, and she was going to have to shake hands with all Lucy's relatives … The 'before' and 'after' the 'Special Low-Fat Diet' photos certainly did make you think. She took another look at the models sporting the M-of-the-G fashions. They were slim, with glowing skin and immaculate hair. She had to admit they seemed pretty damn *soignée*, even if they were looking daggers at each other. You could bet your life Sam would be proud of *them* …

Anna read the rest of the article; 'elegant' and 'toned' were adjectives that recurred. She took a last look at the pleats. Maybe they weren't so bad after all, once you got used to them. And you could always take the shoulder pads out of the mushroom thing, or trim the collar down a bit on the navy affair – she'd worry about the white gloves and clutch bags later. Riffling through the bowl of odds and ends on the coffee table beside her empty glass she found the red pen she always used to edit poems, circled the article heavily, underlining the title twice. She laid the magazine carefully in the centre of the coffee table, resisting the urge to shove it out of sight under the sofa. If she kept it in view, sheer terror would make her stick to her new regime – and she was going to have her work cut out if she was going to Make Sam Proud of Her. She glanced at the clock on the mantelpiece and jumped to her feet. Better get a move on – she hadn't even started getting ready for Jack yet. Still, no time like the present; before he arrived, she was going to put step one of the Total Skin Care programme into operation.

'So I said to them, one more peep out of you, you little bastards, and I will personally wring your collective necks. Well, that showed them. Still had to read the whole thing aloud myself, of course – every time I tried to get one of the kids to do it they'd put on a silly voice, you know: the Queen, some rubbish foreign football star or what have you.' He frowned. 'I can't tell you how weird the beginning of Henry the Fifth's speech sounds done in the style of Julian Clary – "Once more unto the breach ..." Mmm, you smell good. Ylang ylang, would that be?' Jack nuzzled the back of Anna's neck.

Anna pulled away. 'Don't, Jack, I need to check the recipe for the salad dressing.'

He looked puzzled. 'But you said on the phone this morning we were having spaghetti carbonara?'

'I know. That was then.' Before she'd rushed upstairs and taken a long hard look at herself in the harsh light of the bathroom mirror, as the article in *Bride* suggested. Before she realised she possessed in abundance the three major no-nos listed: freckles on her nose, ragged cuticles and most heinous of all – *an hourglass shape*. 'I changed my mind. I thought I'd just do a simple salad.'

'Oh.'

'Yes. Tomato and herbs with a balsamic vinegar dressing.'

'But what about –'

113

'Oh, for God's sake, Jack, do you have to criticise every little thing I do?' She pushed past him irritably. 'Now I've forgotten to add the black pepper.'

Christ, women. He tried to remember where she was in her cycle, and failed – that sort of thing was always impossible to keep track of when you had really important stuff to think about. Still, had to be hormones of some sort – Anna was normally so easygoing. Perhaps he should have brought her flowers, but he'd pushed the boat out on tulips from the garage for Ruth at the weekend, hoping he'd soften her up enough to get her to let him talk. No joy, though – she'd gone on about the scandal of flower-picking gangs of immigrant labourers paid a mere pittance, and when he'd tried to raise the topic of his impending departure she'd shushed him because some bloody programme about the Euro was coming on. He backed away from Anna, holding his hands up in mock defeat. 'Sorry, darling, you're the boss. It's just that carbonara's my favourite.'

'I know.' She sighed, and turned to face him. 'I can't say I'm entirely averse to it myself. It's just that I think it's time I – we – started to go a bit easy on the butter and cream, and this salad has practically no calories.'

Definitely not the time to argue. Damn. He'd been looking forward to supper all day. 'Whatever you say, angel. And I'm sure it'll be delicious.' Oh well. At least there was always sex. He held out his arms. 'Come here, angel.'

She gave the dressing a final stir, and turned into his embrace. 'I'm sorry, Jack. I just –'

He held her close. 'It's all right, sweetheart, I understand.' He rubbed his face against hers, then held her away from him slightly. There was a sharp odour coming from somewhere, and his cheek felt unpleasantly sticky. 'Anna? There seems to be something odd about your …' He rubbed his hand surreptitiously against his trouser leg.

She stared at him for a minute, then clapped a hand to her mouth. 'Oh no! Bugger, now I'll have to start all over again.'

'But what on earth …?'

She was rummaging in the fridge. 'Lemon juice.'

He must have misheard. He smiled fondly as she hurried to the sink. 'For a moment there, angel, I thought you said lemon juice.'

'I did.' Tilting her head back, she started to rub something on her nose. It was half a lemon.

'Anna, what on earth …?'

'Freckles. Gets rid of them.'

'But what on earth's wrong with your freckles? I love your freckles, they're sweet –'

'Sweet?' She whirled round. 'I don't want to look *sweet*, Jack. In fact, *sweet* is precisely what I do not want to look. *Soignée* is the look I'm going for. Plus *elegant* and *toned*.'

Toned? What the hell was she on about?

Suddenly she was at his side, adding the dressing to the salad and irritably tossing the whole revolting mess together. Christ, she was in a mood. It was nearly as bad as being at home. No, cancel that. Of course he didn't mean that. It was just … Maybe he should get her some evening primrose oil or whatever that stuff was Ruth kept on the bathroom shelf. Not that it seemed to improve Ruth much … He'd open the wine, yes, that should help things along a bit. He started to hunt in the drawer for the corkscrew.

'I'm only having one glass, OK?'

'*No problemo*. Tell you what – music, that's what you need, angel. I know a quick burst of Rach Two – especially that lovely quiet smoochy bit in the middle – works wonders for me when I'm a bit down. Soothes the savage breast, and all that. You serve up and light the candle. Back in a jiff.'

He headed for the living room. Phew. Full marks, Teale … Now, let's see. If only Anna kept her CDs in some sort of order instead of lying about all over the place, several of them not even in their boxes, it would be easier to find what he was looking for. Chuck Berry's *Greatest Hits* and Meat Loaf's *Bat Out of Hell* lay on the coffee table; somehow he didn't think they were going to fit the bill. What was that magazine beside them? Curious, he picked it up – and dropped it again as he saw the title, *Bride*.

Christ on a rusty unicycle!

Panic gripped him, turning the contents of his bowels to molten lava as if he'd just forced down one of Ruth's lamb curries.

Surely Anna didn't … wasn't …

He sat down heavily on the sofa. Could he persuade her he had suddenly developed a killer headache and had to get home and lie in a darkened room for a couple of hours? Or should he just make a run for it? As he tried to decide between the options, he caught sight of the page at which *Bride* had fallen open when it fell from his nerveless grasp. Dear God! She'd already started annotating the articles – tips on where to buy the dress, and have the reception! Feverishly snatching up the magazine, he started to read.

Anna set the bowl of salad on the table, wishing she could at least sprinkle it with croutons. Damn, she wasn't allowed sodding croutons. Croutons were the devil's work, along with cream and butter and chocolate and ice cream – best not go on with the list. Still, there was no gain without pain, and she'd feel fantastic once she began to see the results. She lit the candle in the middle of the table, alongside the bottle of burgundy, and resolved to pull herself together. After all, it wasn't Jack's fault she had a bum the size of a house, hideous cuticles and a nose so revoltingly freckled she had probably been frightening small children all her life without knowing it. And anyway, the poor love was stressed enough already, what with trying to find a way to tell sodding Ruth he was leaving, and the fourth year taking the piss about Henry's speech. Though actually, come to think of it she'd rather enjoy hearing it declaimed à la Julian Clary … She set her favourite red gingham napkins beside their plates, and sat down to wait. It was lovely of him to go and find some soothing music – he'd looked so sweet when he ambled out. She hoped he wouldn't be long, the salad was already looking less than inviting. Ah, she could hear him coming now …

'Mother of the Groom?' Jack practically fell into the kitchen, he was laughing so hard. He dropped *Bride* on the table, and collapsed into his chair, weak with relief. 'Make Him Proud?' He felt like a condemned man who'd been reprieved at the eleventh hour. He wiped tears of laughter from his eyes. 'Make Him Wet Himself with Fright, I should think, if his mum turned up looking like one of these old bags.' He gurgled with delight. 'Got to hand it to you, angel – beats *Private Eye* any day.' He began to pour the wine.

Anna burst into tears.

Jack got clumsily to his feet, gazing at her in consternation. 'Anna? Anna, sweetheart … angel …'

She cried harder. After a moment Jack came round the table and knelt beside her. 'Darling, come on, now …' An awful thought struck him. Surely she wasn't taking the bloody article seriously?

Anna seized a napkin and buried her face in it. Her voice came out in muffled snatches; he had to strain to hear her. '… *Elegant* … *never* get thin enough in time … *Toned* … cellulite … sleek … hips… French manicure … *elegant*… strengthening polish …*toned* … freckles … bleach … juice …'

Jack's stomach rumbled; he cast a furtive look at the salad bowl. Christ, the things he had to put up with … Gritting his teeth, he put his arms round Anna. She clung on to him as if he was a life raft.

'I can't do it on my own Jack – it's too hard!' She started to sob again. 'Even if I do manage to lose a couple of stone …'

Lose a couple of *stone*?

'… get rid of my boobs and bum and things …'

Get rid of her …?

'… bleach out my bloody freckles …'

But he loved her bloody –

'Buy one of those sodding awful frocks …'

117

She couldn't be serious. He'd never seen her in anything as ordinary – or let's call a spade a spade here, so bloody hideous, so unremittingly sexless, as those …

'Everyone will be staring at me! Pointing and laughing! Saying that's the Mother of the Groom, and can't you tell she's simply not up to the job? Her poor son, he must be *so* ashamed of her!' The tears became wrenching sobs. 'I can't do it on my own, Jack – I can't!' She clutched at his jacket. 'Please, *please* say you'll come with me …'

For a moment, he thought she meant she wanted him to go with her to buy one of those hideous frocks the crones in the article were sporting. Why were they wearing headgear that would send rhinoceroses stampeding in terror? Why were they carrying those damn silly gloves instead of wearing them? And what did they keep in those ridiculous purses? Suicide pills? If that was the form and Anna was hell bent on combing the department stores until she found such a repugnant garment and wanted him along for moral support he supposed he was going to have to do the decent thing – though obviously they'd have to go further afield than Brighton, for heaven's sake, anyone might see them – somewhere like Shoreham, say, no one in their right mind ever went there, and there was bound to be some sort of women's shop. He wiped his forehead. It couldn't be any worse than last year when Ruth dragged him along to find a suitable dress to wear to her niece's christening. At least that little episode had taught him never to tell the truth when a female asked if yellow made her skin look sallow, or if the frill things on the hem of the skirt were too young for her. The get-up had made her look like a superannuated mermaid with a bad case of jaundice, but it turned out that hadn't been the right thing to say.

He ran a finger round the inside of his collar as he recalled the scene that had followed, then pushed it firmly from his mind and squared his shoulders in a manly sort of way. Of course he'd be there if Anna needed him. However badly things went he was pretty sure he could count on her not to punch him in the teeth or set about him with the chair from the cubicle. He was just opening his mouth to say of course he would, angel, and they could go and have a nice lunch in a nice café afterwards, when his mouth went dry and a chill slithered through his gut. It wasn't a shopping trip she wanted him to accompany her on – *it was the bloody wedding*!

He went rigid. It was impossible. Totally and utterly, nuke-me-now-lord-if-I-tell-a-word-of-a-lie completely im-fucking-possible. He nuzzled into Anna's neck.

'Angel, that's a wonderful idea.' He patted her back. 'Brilliant. And honestly, there's absolutely nothing I'd like better …' She was pulling away from him, gazing up at him, eyes alight with hope. Christ. 'The thing is …' The spark flickered. 'I mean the trouble is …' And went out. 'It's just that …' Suddenly she was pulling away from him, struggling to get to her feet. Tears trickled down her cheeks, her nose was running, her curls clung damply to her neck. 'Look, angel, you know I'd love to come. Believe me, there's nothing I'd like more than to go with you to see young Dan get spliced, it's just –'

'It's Sam.'

'Course it is. Sam.' He hit his forehead in what seemed to him to be a rather comical fashion. Anna looked away and blew her nose sadly on her napkin. His eye fell on the bottle of wine. Thank God; a glass of that was sure to lift her spirits. He ripped the cork from the bottle and filled their glasses. Handed Anna hers and touched his own to it. 'To … er …'

She waited.

'The happy couple, Sam and …'

Anna looked at him. After a moment she said very quietly, 'Lucy.'

'Exactly. Sam and Lucy.' He took a huge gulp of wine. Anna sipped hers and stood looking at him. 'So. You were saying; it's just …?'

Oh God, she wasn't going to let it go. 'Sweetheart, it's a marvellous idea, me coming with you. You know there's nothing in the world I want more than –'

'Then why don't you come? It's to be in Ireland –'

Ireland? Why didn't he...? Was she *mad*? *Ireland*? Was he going to have to spell it out? He swallowed down the rest of his wine and gazed at her incredulously. 'Anna, darling. It's impossible – it would mean two days away! Two and a half, quite possibly, with all the travelling. What on earth would I tell Ruth?'

She went white. 'What would you tell *Ruth*?' She took a step towards him. 'What would you tell bloody *Ruth*?' The fingers on the hand holding her glass tightened. 'Why don't you just once, Jack, just fucking, sodding once, worry about what you're going to say to *me*? Doesn't how *I* feel, what *I* want, matter to you at *all*?'

She threw her glass of wine in his face.

Jack's expression of surprise gave way to one of horror as he stared down and saw the enormous dark red stain spreading over the front of his shirt. Bright splashes of scarlet were soaking into the lapels of his jacket and, further down, tracing a delicate pattern over his flies. He gave a gasp as he took in the damage. *Red wine stained, didn't it*? 'Jesus Christ, Anna – help me.' He began to tear off his clothes. 'Salt, that's what we need, lots of salt, quick –'

'Salt? What the hell for?'

'Please, Anna.' He seized the salt cellar, upended it over the biggest stain on his shirt and frantically rubbed it in. 'Great.' He thrust it towards her. 'Now you sponge it with cold water while I fix my jacket.'

He rushed over to the cupboard, found a packet of salt, galloped back and threw the contents over the rest of the stains. Glancing up, he saw that Anna was staring at him, shaking with rage.

'You utter bastard, Jack. You care more about what that silly bitch of a wife of yours is going to say about a couple of wine stains than you do about me.' Reaching across him, she picked up the bottle and refilled her glass. No! No! Please God, no! If she threw any more it would never come out. He hurried round the table and grabbed her arms. 'Anna – angel – you couldn't be more wrong. I want to come with you so much it *hurts* ...'

She stood quite still.

He hurried on. 'The mere thought of you trotting off with your little suitcase all on your ownio with your little ticket and your little map of Dublin –'

'Fergustown.'

'– Fergustown – is simply more than I can bear.'

She softened slightly. 'Oh, Jack – honestly?'

'Honestly, darling.'

She leant against him. He held her tightly, murmuring endearments until he felt her begin to relax; after a while he took the glass from her hand and set it down safely on the table. 'As for the wine stains, hell, I don't give a monkey's cuss what bloody Ruth says about them ...'

Over Anna's shoulder he could see that the livid red patches were already drying in the warmth of the kitchen, the salt crystallizing into crusty rimes. Damn and blast, no point in bothering with cold water now; the damage was done. He closed his eyes briefly, picturing the storm that would break over his head when Ruth saw the state of his clothes; he was going to have his work cut out to come up with anything like an acceptable excuse. Still, one thing at a time; first he had to deal with the present emergency. God, his head ached. Why did women have to make everything so difficult? He nuzzled his chin against the top of Anna's head. Mmm, her hair smelled wonderful, like warm honey. He thought about spending two nights at a hotel with her. OK, so Ireland was the pits as far as he was concerned – his parents had forced him to go on holiday with them once to Cork when he was a child and he'd been sick twice each way on the ferry – but there was bound to be loads of free food and champagne flowing.

Two whole nights ...

He felt the old trouser snake stir. 'Angel, you know how much you mean to me.' He kissed her ear. 'How good you are for me.' He bit her neck gently. 'How well you understand me.' He felt her back arch beneath his hands – that was more like it. He crushed her to him, showering her face with tiny kisses. 'I'll think of something, darling. Trust me.'

Her arms slid round his neck, and she kissed him back.

CHAPTER ELEVEN

And he did think of something. Two things, as it happened, and though he said it himself, they were both pretty damn close to genius.

The first came to him as he was riding home on his bicycle after leaving Anna – feeling a bit shaky, if truth be told, after the intensity of their lovemaking. He really was going to have to stop Anna scratching his back quite so hard; apart from the ever-present danger of Ruth catching sight of the damage – he always wore pyjamas in bed these days, but he'd look bloody silly keeping a T-shirt on in the shower – it was ruddy painful, frankly.

He was pedalling past the Five Bells when he saw a couple of blokes swinging punches at each other in the car park outside. Big chaps, they were hurling abuse at each other as they fought (some altercation about the way one of the blokes had eyed up the other's girlfriend, apparently), egged on by a crowd of jeering onlookers who were all tanked up and still on the beer; a couple of glasses already lay smashed on the pavement. He'd been forced to stop because the traffic lights turned red just as he approached, which quite frankly was pretty worrying. He'd kept his back resolutely turned, making it clear he wasn't taking the slightest interest in the fight. There was no point in looking for trouble; he'd got quite enough of that already, thank you very much … He forced himself not to turn round as he heard another glass smash, followed by a roar of approval from the crowd.

It was then that the first idea came to him.

He'd read somewhere that the best way to succeed with a lie was to stick as closely to the truth as possible – probably the Duke of Wellington again, poor bastard. As the traffic lights went amber, some fool in a BMW started beeping him, which meant he had to get off pretty sharpish as he was in the wrong lane. This was a challenge because someone (what did he mean, *someone*, it had to be the twins paying him back for putting his foot down about their sudden three shower a day habit) had superglued his gear lever so it was permanently stuck in first. He couldn't give his idea the full attention it deserved until he'd got himself safely out of the way. The window on the BMW's nearside was open, and he could hear music as it shot past. It was turned up loud, and was irritatingly familiar. Strauss, was it? Schubert? Suddenly it came to him. Mendelssohn, that was it – *Midsummer Night's Dream*. Quite pretty if you liked that sort of –

The second idea hit him so suddenly, and he was so excited by its sheer brilliance, he nearly fell off his bike.

His adrenaline was up and pumping now, and he positively enjoyed the rest of the ride. As he dismounted outside 58 Beech Avenue he was feeling pretty pleased with himself. By the time he wheeled his bike down the path and round the side of the house (tripping over Charlie's tricycle – oh for Christ's sake, how many more times?) he'd got his excuse off pat.

He didn't break into even the mildest of sweats when the back door was flung open and Ruth stood in the doorway, arms folded, lips tight. He'd known she'd be up. He'd torn himself away from Anna half an hour earlier than usual for a Monday night to get the inevitable confrontation over with: he absolutely *had* to get some sleep tonight. For one thing he had a sixth-form study group on the Lake Poets in the morning, and he was buggered if he could think of a single one at the moment if you didn't count Melvyn Bragg, and for another in his secret heart he wasn't entirely certain his nerve would hold if he left it overnight.

Propping his bike against the wall, he lifted his briefcase from the back basket and turned towards her, wincing – though not too much – and contorting his features into a brave – though not too brave – smile.

She put her hands on her hands on hips as he approached. 'What the hell do you mean by making all that racket? For Christ's sake, Jack, I've only just got Charlie down, he's been crying all evening because Spike's got a bigger willy than he has, and the girls told him …'

He accentuated the limp. Bugger moderation; he'd probably have to point it out to her if he'd just had both legs amputated. He put a bit more wattage into the brave smile as he squeezed past her. As he staggered into the kitchen she gave a shrill cry of horror. Ah, that was more like it. Perhaps now she'd show a bit of …

'You stink to high heaven, what the hell …? And why are you walking in that peculiar way?'

He sat down heavily with a sigh, allowing himself to slump as if suddenly overtaken with exhaustion, the way Tom Hanks did in the good bit at the beginning of *Saving Private Ryan*. Wait till she caught sight of the stains. He leaned back against the chair, allowing the full glare of the kitchen light to fall on him.

She shrieked. 'Blood? For God's sake, Jack – who've you been provoking now?

It wasn't quite the reaction he'd hoped for, but no matter. He smiled wearily, and spread his hands. 'There was a fight outside the Five Bells, Ruth.'

'The Five Bells? What the hell were you doing at the Five Bells? It's not on your way home.'

The one point he'd overlooked. 'I know that, Ruth.'

'And?'

'Ned – you remember, poppet, the art master, he's in charge of … er … scenery for the *Dream* – insisted I went for a swift jar. Just a half, mind, after the rehearsal, to discuss –'

'A swift …?' She slammed the back door and hurtled over to the kettle. 'I always said that man was trouble – I suppose he thinks it's clever to wear red socks. And another thing, I always say …'

Phew. Though what if the stains *had* been blood? He could have haemorrhaged to death by now. He let her rabbit on about the shortcomings of bohemians in red socks/sandals/beards until he got his nerve back, then got her back on track. God, he was tired, it was all right for Anna demanding they always make love twice every time he nipped round; everyone knew it didn't take it out of women like it did men.

'Actually, poppet, it wasn't us doing the fighting. We'd just arrived, and I was explaining to Ned that maybe a swift one wasn't such a good idea after all, it was high time I was getting home to see my beloved lady wife, when all hell broke loose – tiny little bloke rushed out, pursued by this bloody great gang of thugs. Been looking the wrong way at one of the thug's girlfriends, it seems, and these blokes just ...'

He sank lower in his chair, pretending to be Tom Hanks again as he described the fight; he thought he did it rather well. 'Nothing to do with us, of course, but we couldn't just stand by and do nothing, could we, angel? All those huge great brutes setting on one poor little bloke –'

She was pouring hot water into a mug and stirring briskly. Great; he'd never needed a cup of tea more in his life. 'Well, you'd better get those clothes off and start sponging them with cold water right away, it should do the trick if the blood hasn't dried yet. Mind you don't put them in the machine until you've got it all out.'

Thank God.

She picked up the mug and began to hurry past him. 'I'm off to watch *Newsnight*. And remember what I said about not putting anything in the machine until you've got all the stains out. I'll know if you cut corners – there'll be rings when it dries.'

She was almost past when she halted suddenly and wheeled round. 'What *is* that perfectly disgusting smell?' She bent closer, and gave a squeal of disgust. 'That's not blood, Jack, it's wine!' She made 'wine' sound synonymous with leper's pee.

It would be hours before he got to bed now. Back to the original story, fast. 'I know, poppet – that's what I was trying to tell you –'

Ruth's eyes narrowed. Jesus, if the Germans had had Ruth waiting on Omaha beach those poor bloody GIs would have taken one look and turned and run. The war would probably have been over that very same day ... Concentrate, Teale.

'Exactly what I've been trying to tell you, Ruthie. The fight broke up as soon as I made it clear I wasn't going to stand for it – buggers disappeared like snow in June once I came on strong with a couple of the kick-fighting steps I picked up from those Jackie Chan films, and Ned did a sort of Feng Shui thing. (Was that right? Still, Ruth hated all things oriental, with a bit of luck she wouldn't know either.) They could see right away they'd better not mess. Thing is, just as we were strolling back to our bikes –'

Wow, he could see it. He had one of those poncho things thrown over his shoulders, and a cigar stub clenched between his teeth ... (Though he'd always wondered about that, actually. Did Clint have ashtray breath and yellow teeth as a result? And if so, did it put the birds off?) '– when a couple of the thugs chucked their wine over us.' That should do the trick.

'*Wine*?' She was frowning. 'These thugs were drinking *wine*?' Don't crack up now, Teale – think.

'They were foreign.' She bent closer, examining the stain on his shirt suspiciously.

'And what on earth is all *this*?' Christ.

'Salt, dear. From ... er ... perspiration.' He was sweating again now, come to think of it – amazing the effect terror had on one. 'Believe me, it was pretty scary in that car park. Plus I had to cycle home pretty bloody *tout de suite*, I can tell you – wouldn't have put it past the dago in the beret and the striped matelot shirt to hot-foot it after us. Worked up quite a lather.'

She straightened up. 'Well, all I can say is next time come straight home. Understood?'

'Yes, dear.'

'It'll all need a good soak in Bio-Rinse before you machine wash. And see that it's hung out on the line before you go to bed. I don't want it anywhere near my airing cupboard.' She took a peck at whatever poisonous brew she had in the mug.

'Righty-ho, poppet.'

She was making for the door. Should he take a chance and risk the rest of it now? Hell, yes. Go for it, Teale. He got to his feet.

'Still, the rehearsal went very well. Which reminds me …'

She stopped.

Best not to look at her, he'd only lose his nerve. He strolled over to the counter, elaborately casual. 'Er – had a chat with Rodney, the music master, earlier today; he's in charge of the music for *Dream*. Excellent fellow, you'd like him, Ruthie – sings counter tenor in the church madrigal group, wears Hush Puppies …' (If that didn't do it, nothing would.) '… Wife's a GP.' Oh, *superb* touch, Teale. In point of fact, Rod wore a black leather jacket so ancient it was on the verge of falling apart and played bass guitar at weekends in a London band whose sexual exploits (as reported by him in the staffroom on Monday mornings) made the Stones look like choir boys. Notwithstanding, he was also a superb classical musician, and was genuinely engaged in writing an original score for the school play. Jack had only spoken to him once, and that was to ask him to pass the sugar during a staff meeting. '… Anyway, we thought – that is, *Rod* thought – it might be a good idea to pop up to Stratford one weekend in September to see their new production of *Dream*. You know, to get inspiration, throw some ideas around.' He picked up the lurid green box beside the kettle. 'Mmm, nettle. Delicious.' He dropped one of the fetid-smelling bags into a mug and switched on the kettle. 'Thought we'd stay the night and do the whole Elizabethan bit. You know, visit Will's birthplace, Anne Hathaway's cottage – generally soak up the ambience …'

Please God. *Please,* God …

There was silence behind him for a moment before the storm broke. With a shriek, Ruth slammed her mug down on the table and scuttled round to stand directly in front of him. He noticed the whiteheads had got worse.

'Get some inspiration? Soak up the … Do you think I'm a *complete* fool, Jack?'

As she got into her stride, he let his mind wander. What was Anna doing now? ... Why did they always get spotted dick for school dinner on Mondays? ... Why hadn't he made a start on that screenplay yet? ... Should he put some more of that athlete's foot cream between his toes when he went to bed or was he only imagining that the itching had started again ...?

With a rattling bubble and a demented hiss, the kettle (or it might have been Ruth, he certainly wasn't going to risk checking) began to boil. Wearily, he switched it off and began to pour water onto the acrid sachet in his mug.

'I know *exactly* what your little game is.'

She *knew*?

'Do you think I was born yesterday?'

She knew.

Panic turned his knees to jelly. As he turned, palms damp, to face his wife, his grip on the kettle's handle loosened; boiling water splashed agonisingly onto his wrist. He was apologising profusely to the kettle when the kitchen door banged open.

'Mum! *Mum*!' Charlie stood in the doorway, red-faced, his Poisonous Insects of the Tropics pyjamas sagging round his knees, his plastic Kalashnikov cradled in his arms. Jack had never been so glad to see his son. He moved towards him, holding out his arms with a fatherly smile. 'Hey, big guy! What ...?'

Charlie ran to Ruth and buried his face in her skirt, sobbing. 'I had a bad dream, Mummy!' He shot Jack a look of hatred. 'I dreamed Daddy hurted my bikie!'

The little brat must have heard him kicking the living daylights out of his bloody tricycle.

'You see the damage you've done? I'll thank you to save your martial arts skills for the Five Bells in future. I should think you woke up half the street with your disgusting exhibition of mindless violence – and all because the poor little love forgot to put his bike away!' She bent and stroked Charlie's hair. 'It's all right, darling, Mummy's here. I'll take you back to bed in a minute.'

Charlie darted a look of triumph at his father, and let go of Ruth's skirts. Please God let her take him up right now and forget about …

'Ha! Will's birthplace … Anne Hathaway's cottage …' She was off again. He kept terror at bay by trying to decide whether it would be worse to be forced to appear on *Big Brother* or *I'm A Celebrity*. At some point during his cogitations he noticed that Charlie was wandering around slurping strawberry yogurt from a large plastic pot decorated with bright pink cows that appeared to be in the terminal stages of CJD. What on earth …?

'You can't fool *me*, Jack! Soak up the ambience, my foot!' She thrust her face close to his, hissing. 'Do you think I don't *know* it's just an excuse for a glorified pub crawl?'

A glorified …? Relief flooded over him like a tidal wave. *She didn't know!*

'And you can take that silly grin off your face – if you think it's funny then you're even more stupid than I thought you were. Meanwhile, if you've got any other little plans you're proposing to corrupt the music master with I suggest you forget them.'

'No dear, of course I haven't.'

'And now if you don't mind I –'

There was a thin wail from the direction of the washing machine. Charlie sat slumped on the floor beside it, clutching the plastic pot as he jerked forwards and projectile vomited a stream of lumpy pink liquid onto the grubby lino.

'Now see what you've done! Poor little love – trying to comfort himself with Kiddie Kows after his nightmare!' Turning away, she scuttled towards Charlie, cooing. Jack gave him a reassuring, manly sort of nod: Charlie responded by eyeing him malevolently over Ruth's shoulder as, murmuring endearments, she gently removed the soiled pyjamas. For a hideous moment it seemed entirely within the realms of possibility that his small son's head would turn a hundred and eighty degrees and he'd start to intone obscenities in the devil's rasping tones.

'And another thing.' Ruth had straightened up now, and was clutching Charlie to her chest. 'You'd better look in on the girls when you come up, and make sure they've finished their World Affairs homework. I heard them giggling in their room over that Mr Bean video they're so fond of earlier. And you'd better have a look at the thermostat on the bloody boiler, it's playing up again. And don't forget to empty the dishwasher. There'll be trouble if I find it's still full when I come down in the morning.'

'Yes, of course, dear.'

As she reached the door, she turned and threw something at him. 'You can stick these in with your stuff. But make sure you give them a good rinse first, I don't want a lot of vomit clogging up the drum.'

She went out, banging the door behind her.

After Jack reckoned she'd been gone long enough not to be pulling one of her favourite tricks of leaving a room only to return silently a minute or two later – he'd been caught out more than once like that – he set the noisome bundle down gingerly on the counter. He was slowly unbuttoning his shirt when he became aware of a frenzied scratching and snuffling at the back door. Spike, wanting to come inside for the night. If Ruth found out there'd be merry hell to pay, but who was the boss round here, anyway? A man's home was his castle, wasn't it?

Quietly – no sense in courting trouble – he opened the back door. Spike entered, tail wagging furiously. Jack bent and rubbed the top of his rough, brindled head. Good old Spike! At least somebody loved him – *somebody* didn't want him around just to foot the bill for replica firearms or gold lamé crop tops or whatever they were called.

Spike pushed eagerly past his legs, nearly knocking him over.

From somewhere behind Jack came an obscene lapping sound, accompanied by deep grunts of pleasure. He turned slowly.

With a grin contorting his canine features, Spike was lapping up the cloudy curds of pink vomit.

CHAPTER TWELVE

'Hello?'

'Mum?'

'*Jack*? Wha ...what time is it? Are you all right? Oh God, have you told ...?'

'Mum, for goodness sake, what the hell are you rabbiting on about? What's going on? You weren't *asleep*, were you? It's only half twelve.'

'Sam? Yes, yes I was asleep. Fast asleep, very deeply asleep indeed, as a matter of fact – that sort of sleep where you have incredibly weird dreams and wake up babbling. Which is what I was doing then, you know, when I answered. Babbling. Because of this dream I was having about – about ... er ... Jack Straw, you know, the politician. I think.'

'Sorry, Mum.' He snorted with laughter. 'Though if you ask me that was no dream – that was a nightmare.'

'Pardon? ... Oh yes, I see, darling. Very good, I'll try and remember that. Anyway, what I mean is, don't take any notice of what I said just then, absolutely none at all, I was just –'

'Sure. Anyway, thing is, Mum, I've got some news.'

'News? What kind of ...? Oh darling! Oh, that's wonderful – I couldn't be more delighted! I *thought* there was something behind your setting the date for the wedding so soon! I couldn't be more thrilled! How's Lucy? Not feeling too sick, I hope –'

'Sick? Course not, Mum, she wanted this to get this sorted as much as I did. Thing is, I tried Google first –'

'Google?'

'But no joy. I don't mind admitting, I was gutted. Then Lucy came up with the idea of trying Internet Directory Enquiries. I found him almost straight away. '

'Found who, darling?'

132

'Whom, Mum, found *whom*. Dad, of course … Mum? … You haven't fallen asleep again, have you?'

'No, Sam. No, I haven't fallen asleep.'

'Got straight through, once we'd found the number. Bit weird at first, course, but once I'd explained who I was and told him about the wedding, and Lucy, and everything, it was a piece of cake.'

'Well, that's … that's … I'm sure he was absolutely … er … to hear you. Did he mention … me … at all?'

'Yup – he asked how the designing was going these days. Told him you were running a coffee bar in Brighton.'

'Oh.'

'Would have said culinary advisor if I'd been thinking straight, but I was feeling a bit – well, just a touch –'

'Of course you were, darling. Anybody would have in your position. So, what did he…?'

'Actually, I thought he sounded quite pleased. Anyway, got to go, Mum, Lucy's expecting a call from Tina, there's a bit of a problem about the choir boys' socks.'

'Ah.'

'Right. See you at Chez Gaston next week. Don't be late, Mum, and don't forget – no swearing and no jokes.'

'*Jawohl, mein Kapitän.*'

'Great. Lots of love. Bye.'

'Sam! *Wait*! What did he say?'

'Who?'

'Your … your …'

'Mum?'

'Sorry, darling, frog in my throat … Tony. Your father … Dad.'

'Oh, right. Yes. He's coming. Going to send him an official invitation as soon as they're printed. Gotta go, Mum, Tina'll get very upset if she can't get through.'

'Sam?'

'Gotta go.'

'Sorry, darling. Love you.'

'Right.'
'Sam –'
'*Mum*. Laters.'

CHAPTER THIRTEEN

'God, that feels *fantastic* ...'

Anna sighed with pleasure as Jack circled her nipples with feather-light kisses and began to move down her body, licking slowly as he went. They hadn't even bothered to eat the chicken salad sandwiches when he arrived, and he'd dispensed with the Donne altogether, ripping off her clothes almost the moment he walked in. It could only be a good sign. Apart from a quick phone call confirming that he could make it this lunchtime, they hadn't had a chance to talk since that last hideous meeting, when she'd thrown her wine at him. She winced at the memory. What on earth had got into her? How could she possibly have behaved so badly? How could she have been so heartless about the trouble he'd be in when he got home? Even worse – how could she have misjudged him so badly? Because he hadn't given so much as a monkey's cuss about sodding Ruth's reaction – he'd said so! And he really *did* want to come to Ireland with her – he'd said that too.

He was nuzzling her thighs, making appreciative noises. Fabulous. He must have got Ireland sorted out – he'd have told her as soon as he arrived otherwise.

'Mmm, you taste of vanilla, angel. Scrumptious ...'

Jack slid a finger inside her. Anna shifted slightly on the cold tiles, wishing she could make him see that it was a lot more comfortable for her if they made love on the rug in front of the dresser when the kitchen was the venue. For some reason (something to do with Lawrence, and spontaneity, though she couldn't remember exactly what) he always preferred to pull her down beside the dishwasher. Still, at least the music was romantic. A Schumann symphony had been playing on the radio when he arrived, and it was just coming to an end.

135

Meanwhile, he was kissing her again, and doing inventive things with his hands. She moaned. After a while, he moved on top of her. She was dimly aware of the music coming to an end, and a plummy male voice introducing the next programme as Jack entered her. She wrapped her legs tightly round him and closed her eyes, lost to everything but him now,

Suddenly he stopped moving.

'... *which opens at Stratford in August* ...'

'Jack?'

He lay motionless, letting her take the full weight of his body. It hurt. She opened her eyes – what on earth was wrong? Surely he couldn't have come already, especially now he'd got the hang of the counting trick she'd taught him?

'*... to tell us about the music. Also in the studio today we have Lara Tompkinson-Smythe, the well-known costume designer, whose interpretations will be generating considerable interest. Lara, since apparently these "costumes" will be practically non-existent, even for the main rôles, or parts, should I say, ha ha, forgive me – such as Oberon and Titania. Indeed, I think I'm right in saying they'll consist only of body paint – and precious little of that, if reports are true?*'

'*Yes, that's right, Armand. You see, my thinking is* ...'

Jack reared up, and stared wildly round the kitchen, face flushed, eyes bulging. Was he having a stroke? She clutched at him. 'Jack – please, darling – what is it? Where does it hurt? Shall I call an ambul –'

He rolled off her with a squelch and sat up. 'Jesus Christ – she'll hear it! She always has *Culture Carousel* on while she whips through the bloody Mensa crossword!' He buried his head in his hands. 'Ye gods, it was bad enough when she thought I was planning a pub crawl. If she thinks I was after an eyeful of tits and bums too I'll never hear the end of it! She'll have my dick on a fucking stick...'

Anna sat up slowly. 'By "she", you mean –'

He glared at her. 'Ruth, of course!' He put a hand protectively over his now shrivelled penis.

'But why on earth should she think –'

'Because I told her I was going to Stratford for the weekend to see their poxy production of puke-making fucking *Dream*, didn't I!'

Anna gave a whoop. 'But that's a great idea. I could come too! We could –'

He groaned. 'Anna, I'm not really going. I never had any intention of going. It was just an excuse to get me a weekend pass so I could go to Ireland with you.'

She threw her arms round him. 'Jack! Darling! I knew you'd do it! Thank you! Oh, thank you!'

He pulled away from her. 'It's no go, angel. Fell at the first hurdle, I'm afraid. Told her I was going with Rod, to pick up a few tips for the school prod. She went berserk – made it clear she thought we were just going for a beer-fest. The fact I had the best part of a bottle of red down my front didn't exactly help matters. Wouldn't be surprised if the cow's already phoned AA for some advice.'

'You mean … you aren't coming?'

'Not a snowball's chance in hell.'

She sprang to her feet. 'But I was counting on you, Jack! *Trust me*, that's what you said.' She began to pull on her clothes.

'Anna, darling …'

She shook her head mutely.

'Angel, don't let this come between us!' He jumped up. 'You don't know how much I wanted –'

'Oh, I think I know exactly what you wanted, Jack. You didn't even bother to eat your chicken sandwiches first. Shame really, I thought they looked quite good.'

'Darling, you're not being fair.' He plucked a sandwich from the plate and took a huge bite. 'Look, I'm eating one now. Mmm, delicious.'

'Not being *fair*?' She tried to fasten her bra. 'You think it was *fair* to let me assume everything was all right when you arrived with a smile on your face and a bloody great bunch of roses under your arm? Was it *fair* to make love to me as if everything was hunky-dory when all the time you knew there

137

wasn't a chance in hell of your coming with me?' With a sob she snatched up the flowers, snapped their stems in half and shoved them in the rubbish bin. 'For Christ's sake, Jack – *Tony's coming*. Sam phoned to tell me last night!' She burst into a storm of tears. 'How the hell am I going to …? I just don't think I can … I … you … he …'

Jack stood biting his lip for a moment, then suddenly, his face cleared. 'Angel, if you'd just given me a minute to finish that sentence. What I meant to say – what I was *trying* to say – was there isn't a chance in hell *yet*. That's it exactly. In a nutshell. My point precisely. Not *yet*.'

Anna wiped her wet cheeks with the back of her hand and gazed at him, eyes bright with hope. 'Not … yet? Jack? Do you mean …?'

'I mean it's never over till the fat lady sings, OK, angel?' He took a step towards her. 'Just give me a bit more time, that's all. I'll think of something.' He ruffled her hair. 'Count on me.'

Jack … *darling*.' She was in his arms. 'I'm so sorry! I should never have doubted you. You must think I'm an absolute –'

'Whoops! Now look what you made me do.' He glanced down at himself with a rueful smile. 'Looks like there's a bit of unfinished business here, too…'

Smiling tenderly, he pulled her down onto the tiles.

After Jack left, Anna was on her way back to the coffee bar when she stopped short in the hall. She went to the kitchen and retrieved the roses from the bin, trimmed the broken stems, found a vase, arranged the roses.

Placing them carefully in the middle of the table, she set off at a run for the bus stop.

Happy.

CHAPTER FOURTEEN

Declan turned off the main road into a side street lined with pebble-dashed council houses in varying stages of dilapidation. The straggly lime trees dotted along the uneven pavement served only to underline the air of general poverty. He'd been reluctant to accept the assignment when McGinty rang, but years of professional discipline had kicked in. He didn't need telling it would be the beginning of a very slippery slope indeed – once he started trying to avoid assignments he thought might be painful there was no telling where it would end. Anyway, sweet Mary and Joseph! Just because the kid at the swimming bath had upset him was no reason to start avoiding schools. Plus the talk was for kids – they weren't exactly going to be flashing up gut-wrenching images.

Time to get a grip, and just get on with the job.

He saw a sign ahead on his right: St Michael's Primary School *PLEASE KILL YOUR SPEED*. He slowed, and turned into a drive that led over tarmac in such a state of disrepair he feared the van's big end might go again to a cluster of low buildings. The buildings looked as if they'd been knocked up from flat-pack kits, all glass and right angles and pale blue panels, cheap materials that were holding up badly in the damp; scaffolding and a workmen's hut near the entrance showed that major repairs were under way. Declan parked the van beside a battered Morris Minor with a sticker that informed him in bright yellow letters that Jesus Loved Him.,

He got out and began to unload his gear. To his right, the asphalt gave way to the rough turf of a playing field; a great many small boys were running about screaming and kicking footballs while a harassed young man in a striped jersey chased after them shouting instructions and blowing a whistle. The teacher waved a hand to Declan who gave a thumbs-up in return, relieved that the staff were expecting him. As Declan watched, the sun came out, and he narrowed his eyes, revelling in the bright flashes of colour blurred by movement. After a moment, he glanced at his watch. Eleven fifteen. He was booked for eleven thirty; better check in at reception. Hefting his bag over his shoulder, he headed for the school's glass entrance doors.

The reception area – pale green, and smelling of plimsolls and disinfectant – was empty; but a glance at a brightly lettered sign on the noticeboard informed him that the talk on road safety was being given in the hall, the entrance to which was at the end of the corridor. There was bound to be someone there who could tell him where he should go. An exhibition of collages captioned 'Our Pets' had been taped to the walls. It looked as though boa constrictors and eagles were popular until he saw from the labels that the boa constrictors were enthusiastically rendered grass snakes, the eagles, outsized budgerigars. He was grinning when he pushed open the double doors and entered the hall.

Small children sat cross-legged in rows on the floor gazing with rapt attention at the young teacher, and a blackboard on which the Safe Cross Code was written out in bright red capitals. The teacher – with her coppery curls and short denim skirt he reckoned she looked hardly older than the kids – wore a glove puppet in the shape of a mop-haired small boy on her right hand, and a cross-eyed and extremely stupid-looking rabbit on her left. Boy puppet was quizzing rabbit puppet on the code; the rabbit was either squeaking the wrong answers or affecting to be unable to answer at all. In both cases, the kids were screeching the correct answers at the tops of their voices, to the teacher's approval. Two or three women were seated at the back of the hall, watching the proceedings. The plump one nearest Declan (whose iron-grey hair and fawn cardigan reminded him strongly of his mother) stood up as he approached, smiling as she saw the camera slung round his neck. 'Well now, young man. You'll be the photographer, I expect?'

He smiled back. 'Declan O'Halloran, *Galway Gazette*.'

'Shena McCarthy, headteacher. Now, we'll be done here soon.' She held up her hands in mock horror at a particularly vociferous roar from the kids. 'I mustn't complain. They're loving every minute, bless them, and to be sure there's nothing more important than teaching them road safety. Now, as I said, we're almost finished here. Shall we be going to the playground where the cyclists are going to be giving their little demonstration? And where the awards are going to be presented, of course.' Leaning down, she whispered something in her colleague's ear, then set off like a galleon in full sail towards the hall doors. Declan followed her obediently down the corridor, through reception and outside once more. A right turn took them past the bike shed to the deserted playground, where a fitful sun shone on a small table covered with a dark red baize cloth on which rows of badges and certificates had been neatly laid out.

Mrs McCarthy surveyed the scene with satisfaction, and turned to Declan. 'There. I always think scarlet adds a sense of occasion, don't you? Well, I'll leave you to get yourself sorted out. Will I be asking one of the dinner ladies to bring you out a cup of coffee?'

'Thank you – that would be very kind.'

'Our special guest is due any moment. I'll just introduce him to the children, and we'll be finished before you know it.'

She glanced up at the sky. 'We've certainly been blessed with a beautiful morning. Makes you feel good to be alive, doesn't it?' She trotted away.

Declan set his bag down beside the table, took a light meter from a side pocket and paced around, selecting the best spots for shooting the forthcoming cycling demonstration and awards presentation. The weather was, for the moment at least, perfect for the shoot.

'Mr O'Hare?'

He turned. A woman in a green overall with the smallest eyes he'd ever seen, set in a face the colour and consistency of suet, was standing beside him. She proffered a cup and saucer, the pale brown liquid in the cup overflowing liberally onto the garibaldi biscuit perched in the saucer. Something told him not to bother her with his correct name. 'Thank you, that's extremely –'

'Mrs McCarthy says you're the photo man from the paper. Sure, and that must be an interesting job. So...' She edged closer. 'Have ye ever photoed anyone famous, like?'

Declan was about to ask her politely to fuck off and let him get on with his work when he saw that beneath her wrinkled lisle stockings her legs were heavily bandaged from swollen knees to misshapen ankles. Parts of the yellowing crêpe were stained where some sort of ointment had seeped through. Jesus. He took the cup and thanked her, racking his brains to think of something that might make the long, painful trudge from kitchen to playground worth her while.

'Yup. Few days ago, matter of fact.'

Her eyes lit up.

'Brett Love. New doctor in *Heartbreak Hospital*?'

'Mary Mother of Jesus. *Brett Love*?' She crossed herself clumsily, eyes bulging with excitement. 'Ye never.'

He took a sip of coffee. 'Wow. Great. Thanks.' He slipped the dry half of the biscuit into his mouth and chewed hard, hoping it would take away the taste. 'Yeah, met Brett not long ago, actually.'

He was about to tell her about Brett's suspiciously orange tan, his refusal to sign autographs for the waiting crowd at the supermarket, and his inability to cut the yellow ribbon because his hand was shaking so much (which Declan was damn sure wasn't on account of his nerves), when he saw the eager expectancy on her face. So he told her instead about Brett's *fabulous* stretch limo, and his *really sharp* suit, and his *absolutely enormous* diamond pinky ring. His reward was in the sigh of pleasure with which this information was greeted.

'I'll be sure to tell me mother every word when I get home.' She peered over his shoulder. 'If it isn't Mrs M. herself, with the little ones. So. I'll be leaving you to your photoing. Be sure to say hello to Brett from Theresa next time you see him, now, won't you? ' She trudged away, carrying his empty cup carefully in both hands.

Smiling, Declan made a final check with his light meter and was about slip it back into his bag when the excited shouts of the approaching crowd of school children made him turn his head. The sun was in his eyes; if he squinted, he could make out the shifting mass of kids, and the taller shapes of their teachers, and Mrs McCarthy. He was about to wave a hand in greeting when he saw another shape beside the headmistress.

Walking towards him out of the sun – just a silhouette –but he'd know that walk anywhere …

'… Dec?'

He checked the rear-view mirror, slowing down to let a Kawasaki 750 overtake. The van was in the garage for its MOT; it should have been ready last night, but the mechanic was still farting about with the bloody brake shoes. The Fiat he'd rented for the weekend was nippy enough, but he wasn't about to take any risks. 'What, darlin'?'

'You're sure you like it? I mean, you're not just saying?' Maura tugged at the skirt of her dress; it barely covered her slim brown thighs.

Declan glanced sideways, then back at the road. 'Love it. Though seems to me it could be a tad shorter. I've never been one for the convent look, myself.'

She giggled, and leant across the arm rest that separated them. 'Shame we're in this flash motor, boy, or I'd teach you a thing or two about convent girls.' There was no arm rest in the van; Maura always rested her hand casually on top of his thigh when they were driving. Sometimes she made sure he had to pull over.

He grinned. 'Behave yourself, you scarlet hussy, or I won't take you to the cinema – or out to dinner afterwards, neither.'

Pretending to pout, she switched on the radio and fiddled with the dial, looking for music. It had started to rain again; Declan switched on the windscreen wipers. Ahead, the Kawasaki swept past a tractor then pulled in sharply as the Mercedes ahead of it put on a sudden burst of speed. Declan slowed his speed still further, happy to let the silly buggers get well ahead. Suddenly the car was filled with a burst of song as Maura found Radio Two; Adele's 'Make You Feel My Love' was playing. She clapped her hands. 'Hey, O'Halloran – they're playing our tune.'

It was the song that had been playing over and over again on the jukebox in the pub they'd gone to on their first date. In the end they'd been the only customers left, slow dancing cheek to cheek among the tables stacked with upended chairs. Finally the grinning landlord dried the last of the glasses, draped his cloth over the Guinness taps and steered them, still dancing, through the door. Maura tipped her face up to his as they stood in the porch and clung to him, eyes closed, waiting to be kissed. As he bent towards her, the wind blew a gust of rain into her face. It trickled down her face like tears; as he gently wiped them away with the back of his hand, she opened her eyes and smiled at him. Declan felt his heart pierced, and as he brushed his lips against hers he knew with absolute certainty she was the woman he wanted for his wife.

Maura was singing along with Adele in her high, sweet voice. The road ahead was clear, now; and the rain had stopped. Declan switched off the wipers, checked the wing mirrors and flicked a glance at his wife, overwhelmed with love at the sight of her sitting there in her rose-printed sleeveless dress and her silver sandals; his birthday girl, his princess. He smiled, sharply aware of the faint smell of her perfume, some sort of floral scent – rose? Lily of the valley? The smooth surface of the steering wheel beneath his hands, the newly rainwashed sky. Full of anticipation of the pleasures of the evening ahead, and the night to come after that.

The song came to an end. The DJ was making a joke about Adele's hairstyle and Declan was opening his mouth to ask

Maura if she wanted to eat Chinese or try the new Indian in Hart Street McGinty was always on about when a dark blue Subaru came into view round the bend a few yards ahead, going way too fast. Suddenly it swerved violently, veered over the central line and headed straight for them, the driver red-faced and singing at the top of his voice and waving at them cheerily.

Declan thought afterwards he was probably wrong about the singing; the fucking bastard must have been screaming, as you would when you suddenly realised you weren't going to be able to load a stack of CDs into the player and steer a heavy four-wheel drive simultaneously after all, because you'd spent all afternoon drinking Murphy's with your mates celebrating your win on the 1.45 at Aintree and were so fucking tanked you could barely walk straight, let alone drive. He'd probably been wrong about the waving, too – the bastard had thrown up his arms reflexively to shield his face.

Declan wrenched the wheel sideways, one hand on the horn; heard himself yelling, Maura screaming …

He wishes, oh sweet fucking Christ how he wishes, that the last sound he was ever to hear her make hadn't been that terrible screaming.

And then they hit.

The Fiat somersaults over and over again

or so it seems to Declan – it turns out at the inquest that it was, in fact, only the once

and finally comes to rest in a shower of glass.

Then silence.

Which is only broken when Declan realises that the passenger seat next to him is empty and sees the jagged hole in the scarred glass of the windscreen and starts to scream Maura's name over and over again – and he's out of the Fiat somehow and crawling on his hands and knees down the road, stones and sharp fragments of asphalt digging into his palms, ripping and tearing at the knees of his trousers, his good trousers, Maura will kill him when she sees, but there's no answer and the sun's gone in and the rain's pouring down again and somewhere he's dimly aware of the blue Subaru upturned on the other side of the road and there's still no answer and there's somebody inside the Subaru screaming for help but he doesn't care about him the bastard he only wants –

He only wants –

And then he sees her.

Lying neatly on her back beside the ditch, arms by her sides, hair fanning out over a tussock of grass as if it were a pillow, her rose-printed skirt drawn demurely, eyes closed, a single trickle of scarlet blood trailing down her pale forehead.

One of her sandals is lying beside her, the heel snapped clean off, one of the slender silver straps split in two and scraped clean of its glitter.

But that's all right, he can buy her some more when they get home, and he knows that if he holds her very tightly in his arms, rocking her gently, saying her name, it's only a matter of time until she wakes.

By the time the ambulance comes, and the police cars, and the crowd of onlookers left he hasn't noticed arrive have been sent firmly back to their own vehicles, a grey dusk is falling and the rain's washed the blood entirely from Maura's forehead and he's trying to strap the sandal back onto Maura's foot, which is ice cold now and stiff in his hand.

A policeman squats down beside him.

Tries to talk to him.

After a while, he takes the sandal from Declan's hand and places it carefully on the asphalt. He hugs Declan tightly, speaking to him firmly but kindly as the ambulance men pick Maura up and put her on a stretcher.

Cover her with a blanket.

Pull it up gently to cover her face.

Slide her into the ambulance.

And take her away.

Declan cannot stand. The policeman steers him to the side of the road, talking, always quietly and calmly talking, and sits down beside him, gripping his shoulder, until a very young policewoman approaches, tears streaming down her face, and offers Declan a Thermos cup of very strong, sweet tea.

He hasn't touched tea since that day.

And then another ambulance man arrives, rolls up Declan's sleeve and gives Declan a shot of something, and the rest of Declan's life begins.

The shape was closer now, talking to the headmistress, Mrs McCartney, no, McCarthy, and yes it was it was, he'd expected the special guest to be some local councillor but oh sweet Jesus it really was him and Declan bent double, overcome by memories and scrabbled frantically in his camera bag, pretending to search for something although the contents were simply a blur.

'Mr O'Halloran? May I introduce Sergeant O'Connor?'

Images flashed before Declan's eyes: glass shards on wet tarmac; a heart-shaped spill of petrol; a flattened clump of nettlewort; steam rising from a plastic Thermos cup. Slowly he straightened up and forced himself to meet Sergeant O'Connor's eyes.

O'Connor's relaxed smile faltered as he recognized Declan. He checked his pace for the briefest of moments before striding forward again. Declan forced himself to smile. O'Connor returned it.

Swallowing hard, Declan held out his hand. It was shaken firmly. 'I want to …'

'God rest her soul.'

'… thank you …'

'I heard the bastard got eight years.'

'… for all you did that day.'

'Good to see you working.'

'Life goes on …'

And then Mrs McCarthy was saying something, and a ragged phalanx of young cyclists were taking up their positions and Sergeant O'Connor was giving Declan an encouraging nod and taking his place beside the table. With a cheery smile he turned to the waiting cyclists and began to put them through their paces.

147

Declan stood for a moment, seeing nothing. Then gradually the world came into focus again.

One of the little kids sitting cross-legged on the ground in the front row had taken a toad from his pocket and was showing it furtively to his neighbour. The elderly lollipop lady had arrived early for her lunchtime shift and was leaning against the school gates having a fag.

Declan felt the sun warm on the back of his neck.

Life went on.

Picking up his camera, he began the shoot.

CHAPTER FIFTEEN

As the twenty-seventh of June approached, Anna's feelings about the impending meeting with her son's future parents-in-law swung from wild optimism (they would all hit it off so well they'd beg her to accompany them on their next world cruise) to abject despair (they'd insist the wedding was cancelled on account of her unsuitability as M-of-the-G). Fortunately the day before the meeting, a new Italian coffee machine was delivered to the coffee bar to replace the ancient Conas. Alastair had clearly ordered the most complicated design he could find – the bloody thing had more flashing lights and fancy levers than a dialysis machine and by the time Anna had made sense of the instructions she was exhausted. The others had just as much trouble as she did. Trish and Susie repeatedly produced cups of steaming hot water instead of coffee; Roxy kept forgetting how to switch off the froth dispenser, with unfortunate results. Anna was far too concerned about what she'd find at work on Thursday to focus on whether she'd make the grade with the O'Shaugnesseys.

Ripples of anxiety threatened to surface from time to time that evening as she prepared a herb omelette for her supper, but she managed to quell them with the aid of a couple of glasses of wine She went to bed early and, surprisingly, fell asleep as soon as she switched off the bedside lamp. Planning to make a day of it in London – the train fare was extortionate, so she might as well get her money's worth – she rose at dawn. The sky was clear, the birds were singing, the rose bushes beside Sam's old swing had become a riot of pale pink blossom overnight. Relieved to be feeling so calm, she showered, washed her hair, dressed in her favourite secondhand Armani trousers and best Victorian-style lace blouse, dabbed the last of Jack's Christmas

Mitsouko behind her ears, put her hair up, took it down again, did her make-up, changed the trousers in favour of a black linen pencil skirt, pulled on her Hobbs ankle boots, put her hair up again and set off for the bus to the station.

The train was crowded with commuters. Butterflies began to flutter in her stomach as soon as she sat down, as if they'd simply been waiting till she was actually en route to burst out. The paperback she'd bought at the station on modern wedding etiquette made matters worse and when, in desperation, she tried to practise the Inner Calm breathing techniques she made herself feel sick. She resolved to concentrate instead on the disasters featured on the front pages of the newspapers held up in front of her fellow passengers' faces. At least dinner with the O'Shaughnessys couldn't be as bad as war, or terrorism, or an evening with Robert Peston. That helped for a while. Next she decided to try a tip from a self-help book she'd seen recommended by Oprah: apparently the trick when in dire straits was to make a mental list of all the things that were going *right* in one's life.

So, one: Jack. The Ruth situation hadn't been mentioned directly since that dreadful lunch a few weeks ago when he'd said that thing about the fat lady singing, and how he just needed a bit more time. Things had been great between them since then, and she had no intention of spoiling them again.

Two: Sam. He'd been more than usually stuffy last night when he rang to check she'd really been joking about the ra-ra skirt and Roxy's cowboy boots, but it was entirely understandable – he was just nervous about this evening.

Three: Hmm – *was* there a three? Yes – of course there was. She grinned. Three was the fact that if – no, *when* – the coffee bar began to slowly fill up with bubbling foam she'd told Roxy to fetch Alastair to come and deal with it …

The train pulled into Victoria at last. Feeling positively cheerful, Anna ordered a skinny latte at Starbucks, resisted the offer of a free croissant, and sat idly contemplating the throng of tourists swarming over the concourse as she considered the day ahead. First, she'd take the Tube to South Kensington and walk to the V&A, where she planned to spend the morning in the costume display, followed by half an hour or so with the Indian miniatures. After that she'd head for the gift shop and stock up on postcards, then have a quick lunch in the excellent cafeteria. A visit to the matinée at the National Film Theatre to see a showing of *Jules et Jim* was next on the agenda, then she'd have a cup of tea and … and … head for Covent Garden. OK, no time to waste. With a smile at the harassed young mother struggling to stop her toddler pouring his orange juice over his head – how he reminded her of Sam – she set off for the Tube station.

Anna replaced the comb more firmly in the mass of dark curls piled on top of her head, applied a slick of lip gloss and regarded herself critically in the mirror of the ladies loo in Luigi's, a little Italian coffee house in Covent Garden market. Did the lip gloss make her look *unmotherly*? Nowhere had lip gloss been mentioned in the make-up advice for the M-of-the-G in *Bride*. Yes, the lip gloss would definitely have to go. She took a tissue from her bag and rubbed it off.

She was turning away from the mirror when she was stuck by a terrible thought. Naked lips might brand her as *ungroomed*, a sin in any self-respecting M-of-the-G's book tantamount to admitting to having a penchant for eating babies for breakfast, or indulging in a spot of devil worship with the neighbours on Saturday nights. She reapplied the lip gloss hastily, and glanced at her watch. Twenty-five past seven; definitely time to go. Fine – she was ready. In fact she was more than ready. As she left the coffee bar, much cheered by a wink and a '*ciao, bella*!' from the handsome young man behind the counter, and set off for Chez Gaston, she realised she was looking forward to the evening ahead. Her day had been perfect; the visit to the V&A had been a delight, she'd had a fantastic Ancient Egyptian salad for lunch she intended to try on her customers at Avant Art next week, and *Jules et Jim* had entirely restored her faith in love, life and people. She really must come up to town more often; she might become a bit less narrow-minded, less inclined always to expect the worst. Now she came to think of it, the O'Shaughnessys were probably just as nervous about meeting her as she was about meeting them ...

There was Chez Gaston, on the corner with the little bonsai trees in gold pots flanking the entrance. She crossed the road and smiled at the doorman as she passed. He didn't smile back, just looked down his nose at her and moved closer to one of the bonsai trees as if he thought she might be planning to steal it. Never mind. He probably had a sick wife at home, or he'd thrown away his lottery ticket and had just discovered it had the winning number. She moved on into the restaurant, a sea of starched white cloths, pink-shaded lamps and pink-and-white flower arrangements. A waiter glided up. 'Madame?' When she explained that she was joining the O'Shaughnessys, he lowered his eyelids deferentially and requested her to follow him.

He set off on a circuitous route to the other side of the room. Anna hurried after him, concentrating on not tripping over the chair legs of the diners. He came to a halt eventually, extended his arm in a theatrical gesture, bowed and slid away. Anna saw Sam, Lucy, sitting with a couple. She moved forward, smiling.

'Mum!' Sam was on his feet.

'Darling!' Should she go round the table and kiss him? No, that might embarrass him – better not. She settled for a little wave.

'Hello, Anna! Lovely to see you!' Lucy was smiling and waggling her fingers at her.

'Lucy!' She waggled her fingers back.

Suddenly Sam was beside her. She saw with a pang that his hair had been cut too short, and he'd cut himself shaving.

'Mum, let me introduce Lucy's mother, Mrs O'Shaughnessy.'

Anna followed the direction of his beaming gaze, and turned to meet her hostess, full of pleasure and expectation. Which was a pity, as she was entirely unprepared for the look of surprise followed by sheer dislike that flashed across the surgically lifted and sunbed-tanned features of the woman sitting on the opposite side of the table. Awash with jewellery that tinkled or rattled or chimed (or in the case of the charm bracelet that encased one scrawny bronze wrist, all three), she was encased in a confection of lavishly fringed white leather that bulged here and there in a disconcerting way. Her hair was bright orange, her lipstick magenta, her eyes bright and black, like a jackdaw's. As Anna held out her hand uncertainly the woman pasted a social smile into place and extended a beringed talon in response.

'Great.' Sam was still beaming. 'And this is Lucy's dad. My mum.'

The small pasty man sitting beside Lucy stumbled to his feet and leaned over the table, his hand eagerly outstretched. 'Mrs Hardy.'

'Anna, please.'

'Eamonn.' He took in the short skirt and ankle boots and looked away, blushing. 'Well, this is a surprise. I must say I expected Sam's mum to look more like a ... er ... mum.' He blinked at Sam. 'If I may say so, she's an absolute ...' He glanced at his wife, and was silenced with a look. He sat down quickly.

Sam was pulling out a chair for her. 'Sit next to Mrs O'Shaughnessy, Mum, you're bound to have loads to talk about.'

Anna eased herself into the high-backed pink plush velvet chair and risked a glance at Lucy's mother. She had picked up a menu and was perusing it suspiciously. Anna cast about for something to say. 'Well, Mrs O'Sh– '

'Tina.' She went back to the menu.

There was a silence, in which nobody looked at anybody else. Lucy passed Anna a menu. 'The whitebait here are terrific.'

Anna loathed whitebait; she couldn't bear all those tiny eyes staring accusingly up at her. 'Whitebait? Mmm, great! Fantastic!'

Sam smiled at her encouragingly.

The wine waiter had approached and was hovering at Eamonn's shoulder. Thank God; she'd kill for a glass of wine. 'Perhaps you'd like to order some drinks, sir?'

'Well, perhaps ...' He took the wine list. 'As it's such a special occasion ...'

Tina's head whipped up. 'What in the name of the Sacred Virgin are you thinking of, Eamonn? Have you forgotten you've taken the Pledge? Whatever would Father O'Malley say?' She shot out a veined, manicured claw, snatched the wine list from him and scowled at the waiter. She scanned the pages briefly and ordered a bottle of Sancerre.

The grower's name was familiar. Anna thought it was one she'd read about in a Sunday supplement recently whose wines cost more than a hundred pounds a bottle.

'And a large gin and tonic for me.' Tina sighed heavily. 'Not that I shall enjoy it, but the doctor insists I have it for my nerves.'

'Anna, what would you like?' Lucy smiled encouragingly.

'I'd love a very dry –'

Tina frowned. 'Now you don't want to be spoiling your palate for the wine.'

Anna sank back in her chair.

Tina inclined her head graciously at the waiter. He bowed, and tiptoed away.

Eamonn removed his glasses very carefully and began to polish them.

Anna smiled brightly at nobody in particular.

The evening had begun.

'The bridesmaids in pink taffeta, with mauve hair bows. There are eight, of course – did I mention that? I haven't made a final decision on their shoes yet, though I rather think they'll be gold lamé kitten heels.'

'Actually, Mummy, I –'

'Pass the cream, Eamonn.'

Anna lifted her wine glass to her lips, forgetting that it had been empty for the last hour (the bottle had been made to stretch between five) and set it down again. Her face was stiff with smiling. Tina had monopolised the conversation for the entire meal, alternating details of her plans for the wedding with a series of impertinent questions. 'What is it you do, exactly? Art World Culinary Advisor? Money in that, is there? Brighton? Renting, are you? No chips? Trying to lose a bit of that fat before the wedding, are you?' A pitying glance. 'Me, I'm lucky with my figure, I can eat anything I like.'

Determined not to let Sam down, Anna had done her best to be pleasant. Now and again he flashed her a smile, which made it all worthwhile. Eamonn remained mostly silent, though now and again he sent Anna a sympathetic look and she could have sworn that when Tina called for her fourth gin he made a most unseemly observation to his trout. Thank God there was just the coffee to get through now, before she made a quick exit for the ten thirty-five, pleading work in the morning. Suddenly, Tina flung down her spoon and hauled herself to her feet, her platinum ankle chains rattling.

'Just off to the little girls' room.' She bared her teeth at Anna threateningly. 'When I come back, I'll tell you about the hat I'm going to wear. People are going to be *very* impressed, I can assure you.'

She tottered away on her lizard-skin Manolos.

For a moment nobody spoke. Then with a collective sigh of relief, they all sat back in their chairs; Anna was pretty sure the others didn't even realise they'd done it. The moment Tina was out of sight, Eamonn beckoned the waiter over and muttered in his ear. With a grin, the waiter scurried away and was back almost at once with a tumbler full of pale amber liquid. Eamonn tossed it back as if it were medicine, thrust a couple of folded notes in the waiter's willing hand, and winked at Anna. Hell, she wished she'd thought of that. Sam and Lucy were whispering sweet nothings to each other and pretending they hadn't noticed; Anna guessed that it probably happened all the time. Looking much refreshed, Eamonn leaned forward. 'She's booked in for liposuction on Friday. Always makes the old witch even rattier that usual.'

Anna smiled, and he asked her with genuine interest about her job. She had begun to like him, as well as feel sorry for him, and she wanted to cheer him up. Since the anecdote in no way conflicted with Sam's fancy description what she did, she told Eamonn about the party of French pensioners who had spent the afternoon happily touring Avant Art in the firm belief that they were visiting Tate St Ives.

Eamonn laughed immoderately at this, his enjoyment possibly enhanced by the sudden rush of neat malt whiskey. He was shaking his head, gurgling quietly to himself when Lucy touched Anna's hand lightly. 'How's the poetry going? Sam told me you wrote – he said you'd had quite a lot published. I've often wondered, how do you actually go about writing a poem?'

Anna glanced at her son in astonishment. She'd always thought he'd have preferred it if she'd been into crochet, or bowls, or singing in the church choir. He was smiling at her proudly. With a lift of her heart, she began to answer Lucy. 'I don't think I ever actually plan to write anything. I just see something, and it sort of connects to something else, and –'

'Really, you'd think they'd have brought the coffee by now.' Tina plumped down in her chair, enveloped in a cloud of perfume so strong it made Anna want to gag.

'We haven't ordered it yet, dear.'

Tina scowled at her husband, clicked her fingers at a passing waiter, ordered coffee and another gin and began to rummage in her sequinned clutch bag.

Anna turned back to Lucy. 'With a poem I wrote recently, "Red Peppers", I suppose it was the link between the red juice spilling on the chopping board while I was preparing them and –'

With a cry of triumph, Tina whipped a fan of taffeta samples in various violent shades of pink from her bag and riffled through the samples. She held it out to Anna. 'That's what I'm planning for the bridesmaids. Set my lime brocade off a treat, so it will.'

Anna noticed that since the last dose of gin Tina's cut-glass vowels had broadened considerably. Also that despite her recent visit to the Ladies, one of her false eyelashes was coming slightly adrift.

'Actually Mummy –'

Tina frowned irritably at her daughter. 'Oh for the Lord's sake, Lucy, you're not going to start in again about wanting 'em in cream organdie and carrying posies of forget-me-nots or some such rubbish, I do hope?' She swung round to Anna. 'To be sure, have you ever heard of anything so dull?'

Anna thought cream organdie and forget-me-nots sounded absolutely perfect. She was about to say so when Sam, plainly sensing that trouble was imminent, leaned forward quickly. 'So, Mum, what are you planning to wear yourself?'

Anna could see that he regretted the words as soon as were out of his mouth. He was probably afraid she was going to say something embarrassing, like a red satin basque, or a flesh-pink PVC micro. He needn't have worried; she could see by the grim set of Tina's mouth and Lucy's anxious expression that this was no time for fooling about. Reluctantly passing up the opportunity to upstage Tina's lime-green brocade with electric-blue leopard skin, she uttered a carefree laugh. 'Honestly, darling, I haven't even thought about it yet.'

It was immediately clear that this was the wrong thing to have said.

Tina clutched at her throat. 'Not *thought* about it?' She thrust her head closer to Anna's, eyes wide in horrified disbelief, as if Anna had admitted to a predilection for S&M, or a lifelong heroin addiction. Even Lucy was looking mildly surprised.

'Well, no.' Christ. Suddenly her eye fell on the wine list, which still lay on the table – Anna thought the young wine waiter had probably been too scared to retrieve it. Embossed in gold letters on the pink leather cover beneath 'Chez Gaston' was the legend '*le choix juste*'. Anna covered it casually with her napkin. 'Though obviously when I say no, that's not precisely what I mean. Absolutely not. I mean that naturally

157

I've been giving the matter a great deal of very weighty consideration, and it's just that I feel I haven't arrived at *le choix juste* yet.'

Tina looked at her uncertainly and reached for her gin, the glittering charms on her bracelet jangling, the white leather fringes on her sleeve trailing in the purplish remains of her summer pudding.

'For me, it's a decision that will take time.' Should she risk it? She remembered the look Tina had given her when she arrived. Hell, yes. 'I'm afraid we haven't all been blessed with your unerring good taste, you know.'

As Tina nodded and took a slurp of gin, the eyelash detached itself altogether and fell on the tablecloth, where it lay like a dead spider. Anna hurried on to stop herself laughing. 'But you said you were going to tell me about the hat you'll be wearing?'

Tina set down her glass with a thump and wagged a finger in Anna's face. 'It'll be the talk of the wedding, to be sure. Picture a magnificent mauve and lime-green cartwheel, with giant velvet cabbage roses all round the brim and ...'

At last the evening came to an end. All in all it had gone rather well, Anna thought as she sank with relief into a corner seat of a carriage on the ten thirty-five. At least everyone had still been on speaking terms when she left, and Sam had breathed, 'Well done, Mum' into her ear as he kissed her goodbye. Job done, as Trish would say. Gazing out into the darkness through the grimy window she allowed her thoughts to drift to the more pleasurable memories of the day: six worn braid buttons on an eighteenth-century waistcoat, the soft green moss velvet thick with gold embroidery; a glowing slice of ripe, pink-fleshed fig in the Ancient Egyptian salad; the back of the head of a man in the queue at the National Film Theatre exactly like Jack's, the same shape and the same shade of grey hair; the expression on the face of a small girl in the piazza as she watched a busking clown.

There was a hoarse shout from the guard. Doors slammed, the train began to move. As they clanked and clattered through the outer London suburbs Anna returned to the memory of the day that she most wanted to preserve. In one of the V&A's Indian miniatures, a young girl waited at dusk in a tiny garden. The dark grass was richly studded with cornflowers and lilies, the trees were heavy with golden fruit, a crescent moon hung in the deepening sky. It was clear from the title of the piece that the girl was a princess awaiting her lover, but from the expression of agonised longing on her exquisite features the artist also made it painfully apparent that it was unlikely that her lover would ever arrive …

The train jolted its way over a set of points, jerking Anna back to the present. She'd missed Jack badly today. How she wished he'd been there to admire the waistcoat with her! If only it had really been him in the queue! How much easier dinner at Chez Gaston would have been to endure if he'd been at her side! Her thoughts returned to the Indian miniature; to the rich patterns and textures of the girl's spangled gauze skirts, her sleekly oiled hair, her pomegranate-red lips, the two doves billing and cooing at her jewelled, painted feet, the wicker gate set in the corner of the bay hedge, standing invitingly ajar …

The train began to pick up speed.

Anna sat lost in thought until they hurtled through Haywards Heath.

Then she began to hunt in her bag for her notebook.

CHAPTER SIXTEEN

'Hey, look, Roxy – over there, in Future Shock's window, next to the sign saying SALE.' Anna grabbed Roxy's arm.

Roxy's eyes lit up. 'The striped yellow dress? With the blue feather straps?'

'Are you mad? Course not, stupid – the beige suit.'

'Yeah, course.' Roxy sighed. 'The beige one.'

Anna glanced at her watch. 'Come on, we've just about got time if we hurry.' She hustled Roxy over the crossing and steered her through the crowd of lunch-time shoppers to Future Shock's window. They stood peering at the display of zany, colourful garments, expensive even at sale prices. The one exception to the weird stuff was a simply cut beige suit, with cream collar and cuffs and horn buttons.

'Hmm. 'S'not that bad, I s'pose, though it still beats me why you're so stuck on beige or bleedin' brown. It's a wedding, girl, not a funeral.'

'Look, Roxy, I've told you a hundred times. I'm the sodding Mother of the Groom, OK, and according to *Bride* that's the deal.'

'But …'

'No buts. We're going in. Anyway,' Anna glanced at the suit again, 'I rather like this.'

Roxy sniffed. 'Yeah, that's what you said about that chocolate-brown tent with the white sailor collar in Next yesterday, till it –'

'Turned out to be a maternity dress, yes, thanks, Roxy, I hadn't forgotten. Actually, I thought I looked quite nice in it.'

'You looked like a ruddy Sherpa.' She sighed. 'Come on, then. Let's do it.'

161

Roxy led the way into the shop. There were hardly any customers wandering about the vast, wooden-floored space, and as far as Anna could see, precious few clothes hanging on the rails. Presumably the watchword here was quality, not quantity, which made a change from the shops she and Roxy had spent their lunch breaks rummaging through during the past couple of weeks in a bid to find the perfect beige (or brown) garment. Roxy had insisted on accompanying Anna on these forays once she realised that Anna had been thoroughly demoralised by her visit to Chez Gaston. Anna had tried to laugh when she described the look Tina had given her when she arrived, but instead she'd burst into tears. Roxy spent hours trying to persuade Anna that the mad old bitch (Tina) had been jealous of Anna's natural attributes, rather than critical of her clothes. When this failed, she decided that Anna would need moral support on her search for an outfit and resolutely set out every lunchtime with her, refusing to take no for an answer.

They'd started in the chain stores. Anna had spent almost all her savings on Sam and Lucy's wedding present, which left very little for The Outfit. She'd been strolling in the Lanes the previous Sunday afternoon, and had stopped to look in the window of the antique shop where she'd seen the amethyst ring. If it was still there, maybe Jack …

It had gone, and set neatly in its place was a gold Victorian mourning ring. Anna was turning away, telling herself that only fools believed in omens, when she caught sight of a row of Venetian goblets on a narrow glass shelf to the right of the window. The tissue-thin globes were webbed with a delicate tracery of spun gold vine leaves, each faceted stem reflecting a rainbow of colours in the spring sunshine. She stood for a long time entranced, knowing that they were the perfect gift, and that she would buy them no matter what the price.

Unfortunately, the search for The Outfit had so far proved rather less rewarding. Spring was apparently the wrong time of year for beige and brown. Assistant after assistant bestowed pitying smiles at their lack of sophistication in such matters and suggested they return in October. In Oasis, Roxy lost her temper and informed the startled salesgirl that at this rate her friend would be in the loony bin by then. That had been last week. Since then, they'd been forced to move gradually upmarket in their quest, and had begun the rounds of Brighton's more exclusive boutiques.

Here, too, they'd drawn a blank. They'd just left Vanilla, a little store in the Lanes, where the assistant (who looked, Anna thought, more like a starving greyhound than a person) had barely been able to conceal her distaste at Anna's request, indicating with a pained gesture the pale green watered silk creations in the window. They'd been wending their way back to Avant Art, feet aching, tempers short, when Anna caught sight of the beige suit in Future Shock's window.

'Yah?' A stick-thin creature in a silver catsuit with inch-long purple-dyed hair was lounging against the counter, whispering seductively into a mobile phone. Anna blinked; she'd assumed the exotic creature was a customer. She glanced down at the faded jeans and pinstriped shirt she'd thought looked rather good when she put them on this morning; they now looked decidedly passé. And her hair could definitely do with a trim. She began to edge away. 'It's all right, thanks ...'

Roxy nudged her sharply in the ribs.

Anna swallowed. 'I mean I'd like to try on the suit in the window, please.'

The stick insect rolled her eyes and exhaled slowly, as if Anna had snatched her mobile phone from her hand, or demanded to try on the catsuit. Then, with the air of one exercising enormous patience, she cooed something into her phone, laid it on the stack of tissue paper beside the till and stalked over to the window. She wrenched the beige suit from the bald turquoise dummy, stalked back to Anna and thrust it into her arms. 'I'm not at all sure this will suit, size-wise.'

'Oh. Perhaps I could try another –'

'Last one left.' She sighed. 'Cubicles over there, 'kay?' She indicated a row of bleached calico curtains in the far corner.

'Attagirl.' Roxy winked at her. 'Give us a shout if you manage to get it on.' She sniffed. 'Though if you ask me, it'll make the Sherpa gear look positively daring.'

Anna made a face at her, and headed for a changing cubicle. As she slipped inside and drew the curtain behind her, she heard Roxy asking the stick insect innocently if they had any bedroom slippers, she was particularly keen on them tartan ones with pompoms on …

Grinning, Anna dropped her bag on the floor, shucked off her clothes and slipped into the skirt, not even bothering to look in the mirror. Beige really wasn't a colour she could get excited about and suits had never been her thing. Still, it was worth a try, and there were a couple of other places left to visit if this didn't work out, there was no point in panicking yet. She fastened the buttons and glanced up. She moved closer to the mirror. The narrow jacket fitted perfectly, the cream collar set off her light tan to perfection, the horn buttons added a touch of simple elegance. The skirt flared gently above the knee.

She drew in her breath.

Then stepped back quickly, frowning at her reflection. Wasn't the skirt a bit short? She twisted round, craning to get a glimpse of her back view. God, her bum looked enormous. Tina would look her up and down as if she was wearing a bin liner and say it was a pity she'd given up on that diet … She turned back again, scrutinizing the jacket. Didn't the sleeves pull ever so slightly under the arms? The assistant would say …

Suddenly the curtain was pulled back with a jerk. Roxy stood looking at Anna, eyes wide. 'Bloody 'ell, vicar – I think we just hit the jackpot.'

Anna tugged at the skirt. 'I don't know, Roxy – it's a bit short. And don't you think the jacket's rather tight?'

'Give us a break, girl, it fits you like a glove.' She brushed a piece of lint from a lapel, fluffed the hem. 'Could've been made for you.'

'But Tina'll say –'

'Sod flippin' Tina. Believe me, girl, that cow'll take one look and faint dead away from sheer bleedin' jealousy. You look gorgeous.'

Anna's heart lifted. 'Honestly?'

'Honest.'

'OK. I'll take it.'

'*Yesss*!!' Roxy clenched both fists and raised them in the air, then disappeared through the curtains once more.

Anna took off the suit and hung it carefully on the hanger. A pale blue price tag dangled from the skirt zip. The scrawled figures had been crossed out and rewritten so many times they were almost illegible. She half-closed her eyes and concentrated hard. No, it couldn't be! The suit was in a sale, for God's sake, she must be imagining that zero on the end ... She checked again, willing it to come out different this time. It came out different, all right: the '0' she'd thought was a smudge on the card was in fact a second zero, making the price even more astronomical.

Trying hard not to cry she got dressed and joined Roxy at the counter, where the assistant received the suit with a supercilious sneer. Anna smiled at her. 'Thanks so much – it's sweet, but I'm afraid the buttons simply aren't me.'

As Roxy opened her mouth to protest, Anna grabbed her arm and propelled her towards the door. Once they were outside she told her about the price. Roxy's expletives caused an elderly lady to scoop up her tartan-jacketed corgi protectively and make what Anna was pretty sure was an unscheduled sharp left turn into Rave Records. Grinning, Anna checked her watch. 'Five to one. Come on, we'd better hurry. Alastair'll have a fit if we're late back again.'

The lunchtime rush was just beginning when they returned. At two o'clock, Susie and Trish finished their shift and returned to college to face the ire of their tutor, who had not been pleased that the model of the Pompidou Centre they'd presented as the centrepiece of their term's coursework was constructed mainly from old cornflakes boxes and toilet-roll tubes. Anna and Roxy got down to tackling the washing up. By three, order was restored; the pots and pans were scoured, the plates and mugs were drying in the racks, the counters were wiped over; baskets of cakes and scones and fresh piles of yellow paper napkins had been set out ready for the tea-time crowd. A few customers – two plump matrons and a couple of leather-clad lesbians – lingered over the remains of their Dutch apple tart and fruit cake.

Anna and Roxy were taking advantage of the lull to relax with a couple of feta cheese baguettes and hot chocolates, which was all the new coffee machine would produce since Alastair lost his temper with the foam-production system. Roxy had been forced to call him down from his eerie to deal with the unstoppable torrent the day Anna went to London. Roxy passed Anna a brimming mug.

'That'll put hairs on your chest, love. Still, shame the cappucino wotsit's broken. Told his nibs not to keep hitting the lever with his shoe, but would he listen? Nah. I said to Ron …'

'Hi, Anna Bandanna. Lo, Rocksoff. Awright?' Alastair sauntered past the counter, looking pleased with himself. Anna returned the greeting, vaguely including the heavy-set blond man who was with him in her smile. The pair began to examine the exhibition of photographs at the other end of the gallery. Anna returned to her baguette, while Roxy read choice snippets from her *Daily Clarion* aloud to her.

'"She cut the arms and legs off sneaky husband Geoff's (42) suits. Then wronged wife Jeannie Havens (56) seized the strimmer from the garden shed and …"'

'Ace shit, innit?' Alastair stood near the counter, talking earnestly with his companion and gesticulating towards the photographs.

Anna sensed the blond man staring at her. His skin was tanned, his eyes pale blue, his suit crumpled black corduroy with smears of paint on the trousers. 'Indeed - pared to the bone.' He continued to look at Anna as he spoke.

'"… said neighbour Mrs Doris White (78). 'I was shocked, they always seemed such a nice …'"'

'Yeah. Gets you here, dunnit.' Alastair punched himself savagely in the solar plexus. 'No bullshit.'

Still staring at Anna, the blond man nodded. 'It's very fine.'

He and Alastair discussed the composition of several of the photographs, then Alastair slapped him on the shoulder. 'So, et's grab a coffee, take it upstairs while we kick a few ideas bout re-installing your shit in the Upper Gallery in December. Now, is this show going to be hot or is it going to be *hot*? Probably get you a slot on *Late Night Review*, and I'll be giving anuszczak a bell – *Sunday Times* art critic, *capisce*? Anyway, o far my thinking goes suspend "Sperm Zone" from the central irders, maybe light the scrotum with a couple of strobes –'

The conversation became alarmingly specific. Anna got up nd carried her plate and mug over to the sink and washed them p, trying not to think about the implications for anyone tanding beneath a monster stalactite entitled 'Blood Shit Tears nd Sweat' …

Alastair leaned over the counter, clicking his fingers mpatiently. 'Hey, couple of coffees here pronto, yeah?'

Roxy folded her newspaper, tossed it in the bin and got up, rinning.

'Fuck.' Alastair turned to his companion. 'Just remembered. Coffee no can do.'

The blond man raised a quizzical eyebrow at the gleaming offee machine.

Alastair ran his hand through his shock of green and pink triped hair. 'Kaput at the moment. Japanese make, see.'

'Ah.'

'Better make that two teas, then.'

As Roxy made the most of reeling off the list of herbal rews available, the blond man moved quietly along to the end f the counter where Anna was filling a basket with shortbread nd began to study the menu.

'… And then there's Rose Souchong. Lovely pink colour, hat is, tastes like scent. Dead good for PMT.'

'Give us a break. Two builders' brew, awright?' Alastair slouched over to his companion. 'Just going to take a wazz. Be right back.'

'*Jawohl.*' The blond man returned his attention to the menu. '… It is a most interesting list. Though I feel that something is missing.'

Anna glanced up. 'I'm sorry?'

He held her gaze. 'We are at the seaside, yet there are no oysters on the list.'

'Menu, love, not list.' Roxy threw three teabags apiece into two mugs and added hot water from the Ascot.

He ignored her, continuing to stare at Anna. 'Oysters … they are so …' he ran his tongue slowly round his lips '… sexy.'

Anna looked away, trying to remember if there was enough plain flour in the stock cupboard for tomorrow afternoon's griddle cakes.

'You want to go up Wheeler's, love.'

'Wheeler's?'

'Restaurant down the town. Dead pricey, but the fish is fab.'

'Ah.'

Anna could tell by his voice that he was amused. She risked a glance at him; he was waiting for it, and smiled as their eyes met. She blushed. Damn. Despite the paint stains, and the aggressively muscular build, and the arrogance, he wasn't entirely repulsive. In fact, in some ways – the tan, the blond hair, the strong, calloused hands – he was rather … The piece of shortbread she was holding slipped from her fingers and fell to the floor.

'*Bitte.*' He came round to her side of the counter. 'Allow me.' He knelt down beside her and gathered up the fragments of shortbread. Rising to his feet, he put the biggest piece in his mouth, closed his eyes and ate it with extravagant sounds of enjoyment, wiped his mouth with the back of his hand and opened his eyes. Looking at Anna, he put the rest of the shortbread into his mouth.

Anna looked away quickly and concentrated on fitting the lid back on the tin.

'So. This Wheeler's your colleague mentioned – where is it
o be found, please?'

While Roxy enthusiastically gave him directions Anna
busied herself hunting for the plain flour, and tried not to think
about Wheeler's. She'd been there several times with Luke, the
art history lecturer, and had fond memories of the trout with dill
mayonnaise, and shared desserts, and amorous chats over the
brandy and coffee … Damn, there wasn't enough plain flour for
griddle cakes; she'd just have to make flapjacks instead and
send Trish to cash and carry in the morning.

'… Cod 'n' chips from Bert's van by the pier. Ron's never
been a one for oysters, see.'

She couldn't remember when she'd last been out to dinner
with Jack. She stood clasping the plastic container of oats.
Stupid. They'd *never* been out to dinner.

'I wonder?' The blond man was beside her. 'Might I invite
you to accompany me there?'

'Pardon?'

'To eat oysters.'

He took the oats from her and set them down on the counter;
Anna tried not to notice the musky smell of his cologne as he
leaned towards her. She wiped her hands on her apron, trying
not to like the way he just did things without asking anyone's
permission. She didn't think he'd let her tie *him* up for a
minute. In fact he'd probably …

Roxy heaped sugar into the builders' brew, muttering out of
the side of her mouth as she stirred vigorously. 'Go on, girl.
You know you want to.'

'No really, I …'

Roxy flashed a dazzling smile at the blond man. 'Excuse my
friend a minute.' Grabbing Anna by the elbow, she hustled her
over to the fridge. 'What you waiting for, Anna, Prince bloody
Charmin'? Do you the world of good, a night on the town
would. Go on, girl – have a bit of fun while you got the chance.
Jump at it, if I was in your shoes. What the 'ell's stoppin' you?'

Anna thought of Jack. It wasn't *his* fault they never went
anywhere, or did anything – they simply couldn't risk being

seen. But soon all that would change. OK, so the right moment to tackle Ruth hadn't come yet, but he'd said only last week he was sure it would soon. And then they could go to Wheeler's every night, if they wanted to. She darted a look over Roxy's shoulder at the blond man. So what if he was the art world's latest big shot? She'd bet he'd never heard of John Donne, and he'd definitely never bring her roses – more likely a giant box of condoms and a light-up dildo. In fact, if she really thought about it she didn't care for blond men, and now she looked more closely she could see his hands were none too clean …

She blinked. What on earth was the matter with her? How could she have been so horribly flighty, even for a moment? So hideously fickle? Anyone would think she wasn't looking forward to seeing Jack this evening.

She disengaged herself from Roxy's grasp.

'Put some scones on the tray with the tea, could you? Thanks.'

She returned to the counter.

'I'm sorry, but I meant it. I can't.'

'*Can't*?' His eyes opened wide with astonishment; clearly the art world's latest hot shot wasn't used to being refused.

'No, honestly, I –'

'But *warum, Liebling*?' He grabbed her hand. 'After the champagne and the oysters, we could …'

She pulled her hand away.

He grabbed it back.

Oh God, this could take hours, and she still had the flapjacks to make. Suddenly there was a burst of laughter from the lesbians as one made a joke to her friend about the departing matrons.

She looked earnestly at her admirer. 'Honestly, I'm terribly flattered, any girl would be. It's just you see, the thing is … I'm gay.'

He looked back at her, eyes wide. 'You mean …?'

She nodded solemnly.

'*Mein Gott!* So you bat for the other team!' His face cleared. 'It is not that you are rejecting Liebermann?'

'Gosh, no.'

He nodded, satisfied. 'So – you are happy together? All three?'

'Tremendously.' She eyed the lesbians' greasy leather jackets and watched as one spat out a lump of pink bubblegum and pushed it into the other's mouth. Anna looked away quickly. 'Oh yes, we have some very jolly times.'

'Wa-hey! *Wunderbar*!' His eyes, Anna noticed, sparkled at the mere thought.

'Bruno!' Alastair hurried up. 'Awright, cock? 'kay, let's vamoose back upstairs and kick a few ideas about your "Mad Menses" piece. Thought we might install it in the men's john for a laugh, wotcha reck?' He seized the tea things and set off.

Giving Anna a lingering look, the blond man followed him. As he passed the lesbians, he winked at them and tapped his nose. They looked confused.

Her cheeks pink, Anna crouched down behind the counter and spent more time than was strictly necessary clearing up the shortbread crumbs; while she was emptying the dustpan into the bin, her eye fell on the discarded *Clarion*. She hadn't been listening when Roxy read out what 'wronged wife Jeannie' had done with the strimmer once she'd 'seized it from the garden shed', and she realised that she was quite keen to find out – it might give her an idea what to expect when Jack found the right moment to tell Ruth he was leaving. Roxy was busy explaining to a customer exactly why there was no cappuccino, and miming Alastair's attack on the machine in graphic detail. Anna took the opportunity to slip the newspaper into her bag.

Reading the article on the bus on her way home, she learned that Jeannie had 'savagely strimmed' all the blooms off her husband's prize rose bushes and 'dementedly decapitated' the scarecrow that stood guard over his soft fruit. She was 'hysterically heading' for the goldfish pond when the local vicar (Reverend Miles Sobers, 79) arrived on a routine pastoral visit and dissuaded her from further carnage. According to the final paragraph, illustrated by a blurred photograph of Jeannie (165, though hopefully that was a misprint) that made Myra Hindley

171

look like Princess Diana, Jeannie had quickly seen the error of her ways and now not only attended church regularly but was a mainstay of the Sunday School. 'WOW!!! Happy Ending or WHAT, Readers!!! – *ed'*, screamed the article's last line.

Well, it could have been worse – though maybe it would be a good idea to suggest to Jack that he hide the shears and any other dangerous tools before he broke the news of his departure. Anna was about to stuff the newspaper back in her bag when her eye was drawn to an article on the opposite page entitled 'Sexy Sindy's 50 – YES, 50!!! WAYS TO PEP-UP YOUR SEX LIFE!!!' Hell, she might as well read it – there were still two more stops to go, and who knew, maybe she'd learn something. She might even be able to persuade Jack to give the silk scarves a miss tonight …

She began to read.

'Fantastic cannelloni, angel. Great idea of yours, having separate nosh, though I can't say that rocket salad of yours looked exactly appetizing … Mind if I polish off the garlic bread?'

Anna pushed the basket towards him, smiling, and got up to replace *Songs for Swingin' Lovers* with Bryan Ferry's new album, which was if anything even smoochier. As she passed his chair he reached out an arm lazily and pulled her close. 'Let's skip dessert. How about going straight upstairs?'

As she bent down and kissed him, it occurred to her that it was ages since Donne had been so much as mentioned. She missed Donne. As she caressed the back of Jack's neck she wondered what on earth he'd make of Sexy Sindy. At least nobody could accuse them of getting stale, a major lapse as far as Sindy was concerned. She extricated herself and changed the CD. Good – that should set the mood nicely. Jack was already getting to his feet, leaning towards the candles to blow them out. She had to be quick. 'Actually, darling, I've got a surprise.'

'Honestly, Anna, I'm stuffed.' He glanced at his watch. 'Come on, let's go upstairs. I daren't risk being as late as I was last time, I could tell she didn't believe a word about the puncture.'

Last time she'd somehow managed to spill wine on the stocking binding his left wrist and it had taken hours to get the bloody knot undone. 'I meant I thought we could try something new.'

'Darling! Have you bought one of those leather masks? Great.' He headed for the door. 'Hope it's got a mouth zip, I've always thought –'

'No, I mean … different.' She leant seductively against the dresser. 'And I've got a feeling this is the best place for it.'

'But …'

'Think it might be a bit messy.'

She could see he liked that idea; she was quite keen on it herself. Plus the *Courier* advised taking it in turns, which she liked the sound of even more – though if they didn't get a move on, they'd run out of time and she wouldn't get a look in.

As usual.

'So, what do we do?'

'First, we take off our clothes.'

'Sounds good to me.'

When they were both naked he began to move towards her, arms outstretched. She held up a warning finger. 'Uh oh. Not allowed to touch.' The article emphasised how much more erotic the effect of this particular trick was if there was no embracing or kissing beforehand. Fine; what was good enough for Sexy Sindy was good enough for her. She took a cushion from the rocking chair and threw it on the lino near the fridge. 'Lie down, and make yourself comfortable.'

'He grinned. 'Yes, ma'am.' He lay down, his head resting on the cushion. 'What now?'

'Close your eyes.'

'Sure thing.'

Anna went to the fridge, removed the purchase she'd made at the corner shop on her way home – a family-size plastic pot of yoghurt, lavishly decorated with frolicking, bright pink cows – and knelt down beside Jack.

'Anna? What on earth …?'

She smiled. 'Wait and see.'

'But what do I have to …'

She put her hand gently over his mouth. 'Absolutely nothing, my darling. Just lie back and think of England, and leave the rest to me.'

She peeled the silver lid off the pot, and scooped out some of the contents. 'This might be a touch cold at first, but don't worry. I think you'll like it …'

She lowered her hand slowly. Waited a tantalising moment, then began to apply the fragrant pink cream to his suddenly erect penis.

'Anna! Oh god! Anna! *Don't stop…*!'

Stop? She had no intention of stopping. In fact, she was having nearly as fun as Jack obviously was. Well no, not quite as much, maybe; he was practically beside himself with ecstasy, and had been for the last half hour. And there was so much you could do! Licking, sucking, stroking, and when she cupped one hand round the shaft and sort of fluttered the fingers of her other hand round the head like *this* …

Kneeling on the floor was painful. As she shifted to a more comfortable position she knocked over the yoghurt pot; pink goo splattered over the lino. Damn. 'Hang on a sec – just going to get a cloth –'

'For god's sake, what …?' Jack opened his eyes.

Anna smiled seductively and held up the pot. 'Strawberry yogurt.'

Uttering a high scream, he shoved her aside and sat bolt upright, eyes bulging.

He grabbed a teacloth and scrubbed at himself. 'Yuk! Yuk! Strawberry –? There's *lumps*, urgh, it looks like … *Yuk*!' He checked his watch. 'Shit. No time to wash. Let's just hope I don't throw up on the way home.'

He pulled on his clothes, fast; bent down and kissed her briefly on the cheek. Shuddered as he caught sight of the yogurt-splashed lino, and almost ran towards the door. 'Call you tomorrow, OK?'

'Jack, I'm terribly sor –'

He was gone.

Anna sat gazing at the almost empty plastic pot – as she'd paid for it she'd imagined the fun she and Jack would have together – until the candles guttered out. Then she got up stiffly and flipped on the overhead light; the kitchen looked drab and lifeless in its harsh glare. Shivering, she pulled on her sweater. Scrubbed the floor. Washed up the supper things. If only she could phone him and apologise – she'd had no idea he was allergic to strawberries! She was tired, and there was a coach party booked for lunch at Avant Art tomorrow, but she knew she was too miserable to sleep. Tipping the last of the wine into her glass, she went into the living room and turned on the television. Anything would be better than lying in bed remembering …

First, she sat through what must have been the hundredth repeat of a sitcom about a charmingly disingenuous couple who were trying to make a go of living in the country. This was timely, as it kept her mind occupied deciding which of the two she'd kill first if offered the choice. As the maddening theme tune tinkled to its close, she was grateful that they'd prevented her from thinking about the expression on Jack's face as he left or the way he'd just sort of pecked at her instead of kissing her.

She turned up the volume as *Newsnight* began. Tonight she would listen to every word, instead of half reading a novel and redoing the polish on her toenails at the same time. By the end she'd be better informed about world affairs and hopefully sleepy, too. Things went well for about twenty minutes; the report on recent Japanese developments in organ transplantation proved to be fascinating. Unfortunately the report segued into film of an operation, complete with close-ups of details she'd very much prefer not to see. Hastily averting her eyes, Anna fumbled for the remote control and changed channels. This wasn't much better: an enormously fat woman was describing (with some relish, Anna thought) just how badly wrong her recent liposuction operation had gone, and just how much she was planning to sue the surgeon for. As she prepared to pull up her dress to exhibit the evidence, Anna changed channels again and got photographs of thunderous rain clouds as a pleased voice described just how bad the local weather was going to be during the coming week.

OK, she'd give it one last try, and if it turned out to be a documentary on vivisection, or an Open University programme on bridge for beginners, she'd watch an old DVD. She pressed the remote and found herself gazing at an intimate close-up of a couple, locked in passionate embrace. That was all she needed. She was about to switch off when the pair stopped kissing and began to argue heatedly in French. The camera pulled back to reveal powdered wigs and exquisite costumes, all jewelled silks and foaming lace. A few moments later it became clear that the setting was a sumptuous eighteenth-century chateau.

Anna was enchanted; she spoke very little French, but the cinematography was more than enough to hold her interest. Some while later, during a particularly long speech, her attention was caught by a courtier's gown. It was made of velvet, and an exquisite shade of delphinium blue – precisely the same shade, oddly enough, as her living-room curtains. What wouldn't she give to have a dress like that? Well, not exactly like that, obviously. But perhaps … a suit? With a narrow skirt reaching just above the knee, and a jacket with an elegant stand-up collar …

No, she couldn't possibly.

But blue was allowed for the M-of-the-G – one of those old bats had been wearing navy. And surely delphinium wasn't so very different.

She glanced back at the screen.

Oh yes, she could.

There was no time to watch the rest of the film – she had to make a start at once. She clicked off the television. Jumping to her feet, she ran to the bureau and began to search for her sketch pad and coloured pencils.

CHAPTER SEVENTEEN

Late spring became summer.

The weeks passed quickly. The coffee bar was busier than ever as tourists and foreign students flocked into town. Mercifully, Anna had no further contact with Tina apart from one late-night phone call in which she demanded to know whether Anna was quite clear about not wearing anything that would clash with lime green, and another which informed her that her room at the Grand Hotel had been booked but not paid for.

Things were going better than ever with Jack. For a while, Anna had made a point of reading Sexy Sindy's column, but since a debacle with the shower attachment and baby oil she'd managed to persuade Jack that they should put further experimentation on hold until they didn't have such time restrictions on their intimate moments.

Late summer quietly turned into early autumn.

The right moment to tell Ruth had almost come several times – last weekend Jack had actually begun to tell her, apparently, when there was a ring at the doorbell; it was the father of a girl in the twins' class, who'd come to complain about the pornographic films his daughter had let slip she watched with the twins when she came to tea. Obviously it was all a ghastly mistake, but by the time things were sorted out the moment had passed and Jack thought it wise to get on with making the Ovaltine, rather than persevere with his mission. 'Telling Ruth' hadn't been mentioned since.

Perhaps the happiest occasion had been last Sunday, when Sam and Lucy came to supper for the last time before the wedding. While they were having coffee, Anna passed Lucy the box that contained the Venetian glass. The look of joyful amazement on their faces as they unwrapped the first of the goblets and held it aloft in the soft glow of candlelight would remain in her memory for ever. If she'd had to walk to Ireland barefoot and wear a sack to the wedding the staggering price would have been worth it.

Then, of course, there was her suit. She'd taken down the curtains the night after she'd seen the French film, and washed and carefully ironed them. It had taken several evenings to complete the pattern. When the details were perfect she set to work, spending every spare moment measuring and cutting, turning and basting, hemming and edging. At night, she dreamed of darts and buttonholes, cuffs and seams. When the jacket was finished she celebrated by buying a tiny pill box hat, a pair of dark blue Italian shoes and a matching pair of gloves made of leather so fine they fitted like a second skin.

Three weeks later, she sewed the zip into the skirt and snipped the last tacking stitch from its dusky pink silk lining. It was four in the morning. She made herself a cup of tea, had a shower, put up her hair and fixed her make-up – it took a while, her hand was shaking with exhaustion – and then she tried on *le tout ensemble*.

Her first thought was that it was perfect.

Her second was that Jack wouldn't be standing by her side when she wore it.

As she turned away from the mirror, tears were running down her face.

Suddenly it was seven o'clock in the morning on Friday, the twenty-third of September, and she was running about the house like a mad thing, stuffing last-minute items into her suitcase, searching for her hairbrush, and trying to remember if she'd reminded Roxy to buy extra baguettes for the group of language-school students arriving at the coffee bar at lunchtime. She'd cancelled the milk, asked Mr Simwak-Kim to water the tomato plants and emptied the kitchen bin. Jack had come last night. After supper they'd made love and he'd promised to think about her every moment she was away. If only he was coming with her … But she mustn't think about Jack now, it would only make her sad. Quickly, she drank the rest of her coffee, rinsed out her mug and unplugged the toaster. There was her hairbrush, on the dresser beside the oil and vinegar containers. Great, all she had to do now was –

The phone rang.

Anna froze.

Father O'Malley, calling to ask whether the Mother of the Groom was prepared to take his special crash conversion course before the ceremony?

Tina, calling to say she'd decided puce was the perfect colour to offset lime green, she'd found the very dress for Anna and wouldn't take no for an answer?

Eamonn, calling to say a cordial goodbye; he could take no more and had decided to top himself?

She hurried into the living room and snatched up the receiver.

'Darling!'

'*Jack*?'

'Angel – I'm so glad I caught you before you left! I just had to call and …'

Anna sat down on the arm of the sofa, feeling suddenly faint. Jack calling so early could only mean one thing: he'd told Ruth. She jumped up again, overjoyed.

'Oh, I can't believe it! What hap –'

'… wish you luck, and Dan too, of course. I know everything's going to go absolutely brilliantly.'

She sat down again slowly, dimly aware of the letterbox rattling as the postman shoved a heap of letters through it.

'You know I'll be thinking of you absolutely every second, darling.' From somewhere in the background came a series of piercing screams, accompanied by dull, regular thumps and wild barking.

'What's going on, Jack – are you all right?'

'Get that jock strap off the dog *at once*, Charlie. You know football's forbidden in the garden since you broke Mrs Cooper's window again.' There were muffled shouts. The dull

181

thumps came nearer. 'Charlie! You'll hit some –' There was a cry, and the phone went dead.

'Jack? *Jack*…?'

The phone began to ring again. She snatched up the receiver; it buzzed dully in her hand. The ringing didn't stop. It took her a moment or two to realise it was the doorbell. The taxi! She slammed down the phone and ran back to the kitchen. Shoving her hairbrush in her pocket, she zipped her case shut, staggered with it into the hall, grabbed her jacket, gathered up the pile of post, shoved it into her bag together with the magazine and stash of chocolate she'd bought for the journey, and opened the front door.

Three minutes later she was on her way to the bus station, and the eight-thirty coach to Stansted.

'And if you'll be lookin' at this little red whistle here …' The stewardess whipped a plastic trinket which in Anna's opinion wouldn't have passed muster as a child's toy from a tiny pouch in the side of the yellow life jacket. '… sure and it'll summon assistance in the event of a marine emergency.'

She beamed down the aisle at the rows of helpless, seat-belted passengers like an infants' schoolteacher pleased with the good behaviour of her class. 'So I'll be wishin' you all a pleasant trip, and remindin' you to keep those seat belts fastened good and tight now till we're up and away and Captain O'Hara switches on the little red sign givin' us the go ahead to unbuckle – if he's managed to get it workin' again.' She gestured daintily at a sign on the cabin wall behind her.

Anna risked a sideways look at her neighbour, an ancient, sourfaced nun who had ignored Anna's polite good morning as she took her seat and continued to mutter what Anna assumed were prayers, but could have been voodoo curses to judge from her expression. She smelled strongly of cat's pee. Anna did her best not to breathe through her nose and tried to remember whether cats or chickens were ritually sacrificed in black-magic ceremonies. The Ancient had ignored the stewardess's safety lecture, concentrating instead on telling the beads of a clicking rosary she'd hauled from the depths of her capacious habit. The beads were huge – Anna hoped it was a rosary. The chance of it being a string of tiny shrunken heads was too high for comfort.

The idling engines began to hum. Anna felt sick; she'd always hated take-off. If only Jack was beside her, holding her hand and whispering sweet nothings in her ear, instead of this toothless old crone who looked like an extra from a Dennis Wheatley film. She glanced at the rows of passengers on the other side of the aisle. Everywhere she looked there were couples, talking and laughing, holding hands and kissing … Apart from her neighbour, she seemed to be the only passenger travelling alone.

The hum increased to a roar and the plane began to roll forward, gathering speed as the noise increased. Anna swallowed hard and clutched the arms of her seat, palms damp with sweat. Think of something nice, that was the thing to do. Right, Jack, yes, good. Let's see; what sprang to mind? Stockings. No, *please* not bondage, not while she was strapped in her seat like this, it only made her feel worse … The plane gathered speed, gave a final shudder, seemed to hesitate for a moment, then left the ground and slowly began to climb. Soon the pressure began to build in her ears. What if her eardrums burst? She squeezed her eyes shut, and tried to concentrate on Jack again. What the hell was that weird crackling noise? One of the engines must be on fire! She opened one eye a fraction and turned her head slightly to the window. The engines were fine, as far as she could see but the Ancient was irritably wrenching a sick bag from the seat pocket, swearing colourfully as several dog-eared travel brochures shot out at the same time and cascaded into her dusty lap. She began to vomit copiously.

Anna swallowed hard and forced herself to unclench her fists. She leaned back against the sticky plastic headrest.

She was on her way.

CHAPTER EIGHTEEN

Jack walked slowly down Beech Avenue. His head had been aching all day – he wouldn't be surprised if there wasn't some kind of brain haemorrhage going on after the whack he'd received from Charlie's football. He'd had a hell of an afternoon with the Arts Sixth; all they were interested in was exactly how often and in what positions Romeo would have shafted Juliet after he'd shinned up the balcony, whether Mercutio was gay, whether the Friar would have got done for murder and whether Capulet senior might have been having a thing with the Nurse.

It hadn't been a great week. It had kicked off to a lousy start on Sunday. Ruth had been glued to some documentary about divorce and he'd been sitting at the table pretending to mark essays but actually listening like a hawk. A lot of the people interviewed thought divorce was a jolly good thing if you'd had a gutful, and it occurred to him that he could casually instigate a discussion when the programme finished and then subtly direct the conversation round to his plans with Anna.

It hadn't worked out that way. The programme was coming to an end when there was a ring at the doorbell; it was the father of one of the twins' friends, Ruby. He'd assumed from the occasional sighting of Ruby as she disappeared, giggling, into the twins' bedroom that she was suffering from some fatal disease, but when he'd mentioned it to the twins they'd explained with studied patience that she was a Goth. Her father was relatively normal in appearance, apart from the fact that he was apoplectic with fury – he began to shout as soon as Jack opened the front door. Fortunately Ruth appeared then, and took charge; incredible as it seemed, the fellow had come to complain about his daughter watching porn films with the twins! Well, obviously Ruth was incandescent – in fact, he'd actually felt a bit sorry for Ruby's father, he was practically cowering in his chair – and she'd insisted on calling the twins down. Naturally, the whole thing was a complete misunderstanding, turned out the wrong film had been put into the Mr Bean box by mistake at the video rental shop. The girls hadn't realised what they were watching at first, of course – Jess said they'd thought it must be Mr Bean Goes to Hospital. Poppy nodded solemnly. 'Yeah, because of all the nurses.' Of course, as soon as they'd realised what it really was – 'Wow, like dis*gust*ing!' Jess shuddered. 'Yeah, *gross*.' Poppy rolled her eyes – they'd stopped watching and put on *ET* instead, and taken the offending video back to the shop the very next day.

Ruby's father apologized profusely. He left very soon after that.

Jack's pace slowed as he wondered (not for the first time) exactly what the content of this particular slice of porn might have been – adult films featuring nurses had always been something of a favourite of his. Maybe he could persuade Anna to dress up some time, and force him to have a very thorough check-up …

Nearly home. With a sigh, he hefted his briefcase to his other hand. It was heavier than usual tonight – he had scads of mock GCSE papers to mark. As he crossed the road he looked up. A plane was making its way across the cloudless blue sky; he wondered if it was going to Ireland. Shame he hadn't been able to have more of a chat with Anna this morning before she left. The blow on the head with the football had happened just as he was about to remind her how much he loved her. (He lifted a hand and prodded the lump gingerly. Maybe he should have a scan, just to be on the safe side?) Even more of a damn shame that he couldn't go with her – a couple of nights in a hotel really would have given them scope for some fun. Maybe he could have persuaded her to pretend to be a chambermaid, or something.

Blast, he'd almost passed the front gate.

As he opened the front door he was assailed by the usual racket; the television booming at top volume in the living room, Charlie barking madly somewhere, violent banging and crashing directly overhead as Ruth slammed about in their bedroom. He put down his briefcase and headed for the kitchen. With a bit of luck he could grab a can of beer from the fridge and sneak it into the garden before Ruth came down. He was passing the living-room door when he hesitated. The noise was so loud the walls were practically vibrating – if he didn't do something fast Mrs Cooper would be coming round to complain again. And this was setting aside the effect the racket was having on his headache – or brain tumour, which he wouldn't be at all surprised if it turned out to be.

He pushed open the door and went in.

The twins sprawled on the sofa, clad in carefully torn T-shirts reaching barely to their navels and white PVC shorts that revealed most of their buttocks. Jess, frowning with concentration, the tip of her tongue protruding from her lips, was pushing a needle through Poppy's right earlobe. Poppy was gazing at the television. Neither of his daughters looked at him as he entered. 'Jess! What the hell are you –?'

'Dad, isn't it obvious?' Jess glared up at him. 'I'm piercing her ear, OK? Everyone's doing it.'

'Ah. I see. Right, fine. Good.'

He glanced out of the window. He could see his son near the rockery, crouching over Spike. The dog was barking louder than ever and had his back legs tied together with what looked suspiciously like his best tie. Charlie appeared to be attempting to fix an elastic band round his testicles.

Jack sighed. He'd go and sort things out as soon as he'd dealt with the sound problem.

Head throbbing, he turned towards the television. A middle-aged actor in an unnaturally starched white medical coat, stethoscope slung ostentatiously round his neck, was pacing up and down his surgery. After a bit more pacing, he picked up a photograph of a beautiful woman from the corner of the desk and regarded it with an expression Jack assumed was meant to

187

convey anguish. Jack smirked; somebody should tell the guy it looked as if he was trying to remember his own name. He turned to the twins, intending to share this observation with them; they were staring at the screen, rapt. He blinked. Good god, wonders would never cease. He reached out discreetly to modify the sound.

'For chrissake, Dad, leave it. It's *Heartbreak Hospital*.'

'Yeah, geroff.'

'But girls, Mrs Cooper ...'

'Hey, Jess – what the –?' Poppy was frowning.

Jack followed her gaze.

The scene had changed to what was clearly intended to be a ballroom, since an enormous revolving glitterball dangled from the studio ceiling. Strobe lights beamed dramatically back and forth through the darkness, illuminating a glamorous young couple waltzing cheek to cheek.

'It's a flashback to Doctor Strong when he was young, right? Like he's remembering when he first met his wife – you know, Tara.' Jess breathed. 'See the guy? Brett Love. I mean *shit* – fuckin' A.'

Thank God Ruth wasn't around.

'Yeah, fuckin' A.'

The young hunk tossed back his gelled quiff and clasped his pneumatic teenage partner closer to his tux. 'This'll last like forever, right, Tara?' She winced as the stethoscope dangling rakishly from his breast pocket dug into her cleavage.

'Sure thing, Rock. Forever.'

They kissed and the twins sighed blissfully. Jack was pretty sure they didn't notice the glitterball jerk suddenly and drop a couple of feet, or the strobes reveal the fact that the hunk was wearing jeans and trainers below the tux. He hid a grin. With a bit of luck it would soon be over; he'd come back and turn down the sound then. He'd pretend one of the twins was wanted on the phone, or something, so he'd only have to deal with one of them fighting back.

The soaring violins ceased and the screen went blank for a moment. The ballroom was replaced by the surgery again where

188

Doctor Strong was still gazing at the photograph. Jack began to creep away – he was still in with a chance with that beer if he was quick.

He'd almost reached the door when the living room was filled with rich, manly tones.

'Tara! How could I ever have left you, precious girl? I know now what a fool I was – what a terrible, terrible mistake I made.' The actor gave a manly sob. 'How could I ever have thought Jolene could take your place? I'll find you again somehow, somewhere, if it's the last thing I do, and I'll make it up to you, my darling.' Another sob. 'I'll ask you to be mine once more.'

Jack turned slowly, horrified. Be mine once more?

What if Anna's ex-husband …?

The Doctor bent over his desk, shoulders shaking, as the credits began to roll. Once, Jack would have thought that he was certainly laughing.

Now … Now it was all he could do not to burst into tears himself.

CHAPTER NINETEEN

Anna gazed out of the taxi window in disbelief.

So where the hell had they filmed *Ryan's Daughter*? And what about *Barry Lyndon*?

Where were the rolling green hills and meadows, the picturesque stone-walled fields, the charming wayside grottos that featured big in every single film set in Ireland she'd ever seen? The view ahead consisted – as it had consisted for the last hour – of mile after relentless mile of grey road unspooling through a flat landscape of unremitting dullness. Now and again a grey house could be seen squatting at the side of the road, its ugliness highlighted by a garish red and white trim.

And what about the weather? Where were the gentian-blue skies illuminated by shafts of gentle autumn sunshine? The wispy lambswool clouds? The sodding rainbows? The sky was the colour of steel wool and it had been drizzling lightly but persistently ever since she got off the plane.

Unfortunately her expression had been interpreted by the taxi driver as admiration of his homeland, and he'd maintained a barely comprehensible running commentary since they set off. Every so often he'd catch her eye in the mirror and wink.

When she'd first seen him lounging beside his battered navy blue saloon, deep in the *Catholic Times*, she'd assumed he was awaiting the Ancient's arrival; since he looked exactly as she imagined her neighbour would look if divested of her habit there seemed a good chance that he was her brother. Anna was disappointed when the Ancient, looking positively invigorated by the rigours of the flight, strode straight past and climbed into a waiting car driven by a scared-looking nun who appeared to be about fourteen.

The taxi driver half turned in his seat, speeding up slightly as he gestured towards a grim fortress that was heaving into view through the rain-splattered windscreen. The cigarette that dangled from his bottom lip deposited a trail of ash down the front of his rust-coloured pullover.

Anna nodded enthusiastically; she'd learned early on in the journey that this was the only thing that would make him turn back and concentrate on the road ahead again. The fact that so far the only other vehicles they'd seen were a tractor and a very old man wobbling along on a bicycle miles from any sign of habitation did nothing to lesson her apprehension. On both occasions the taxi driver had swivelled round to draw her attention to their fellow travellers. They'd passed them both at top speed, the taxi veering wildly all over the road. As Anna cast a look back she saw the tractor plough into the nearside brambles; the old man nearly fell off his bike as he gave them the finger. The taxi driver waved heartily back through the rear window, and muttered something incomprehensible.

She'd stared at him dumbly, too terrified to speak.

He nodded encouragingly, and for want of anything else to do short of leaning over the bench seat, screaming, and grabbing the steering wheel, she'd nodded back.

The hideous building was looming closer. She nodded hard. 'Golly, yes! Absolutely!'

A prison? A remand home? A truly ghastly thought struck her; she gripped her bag even more tightly. Please please don't let him be saying and this, my dear lady, is your hotel. As he returned his attention to the road, she saw that a statue of the Virgin stood sentinel beside the high, closed gates. Thank God – it was a convent, not a hotel. Anna was almost sure the Virgin rolled her eyes disapprovingly as they shot past. She was about to return her gaze to the road ahead when she realised the driver was muttering and crossing himself piously. Would he glance in the mirror and expect to see her crossing herself too? Fortunately the controls required all his attention at that moment, as without indicating he accelerated and turned left into a narrow road that appeared between a telegraph pole and a battered green letterbox nailed to a creosoted post. After they had driven for a couple of miles the driver turned and beamed at her, jerking his head (dislodging a further spill of ash) at a green-painted sign ahead.

'Wow, yes! Great!' Anna nodded maniacally.

He turned back to the road again.

They drove on. Any hopes Anna had of her destination being imminent were dashed as time passed and dusk began to fall. But the countryside had gradually changed from a featureless plain to gentle, wooded hills – now and again a stone wall could be glimpsed, and once she caught sight of a little stream bubbling along at the side of the road, though there were no signs of any human habitation. She glanced at her watch: seven o'clock. God, she was hungry. At least she should be able to get a good dinner. As Tina had expounded at some length in her last telephone call, the Grand Hotel was famous throughout Ireland for the excellence of its cuisine. The great and the good frequently sojourned there, and she had it on good authority from her friend Thelma, who was very high up in party planning, that Queen Mary had once almost stayed there. She was about to search in her bag for the brochure Tina had sent (along with details of the terrifyingly high tariff and a sharp reminder about not clashing with lime green) when the taxi veered sharp right. They sped beneath a stone arch and along a winding track bordered by iron fencing buckling beneath the weight of massive laurels. Over a pair of cattle grids, and the track became a gravelled drive. Anna clutched her bag again, and began to feel excited as she made out what looked like a miniature castle in the near darkness, its turrets and towers silhouetted against the sky, lights glimmering here and there from its shadowy bulk. A moment later the taxi swept past a display of topiary animals or birds – it was impossible to tell – grouped artistically round a circular flowerbed and came to a halt at the bottom of a curving flight of steps lit by a pair of antique lanterns, only one of which was functioning. The driver turned round, looking pleased with himself, and named an astronomical sum in euros. Anna was too grateful to have arrived in one piece to question it and paid up, adding a ridiculously large tip. She waited for him to get out, open her door and remove her luggage from the boot. It soon became apparent that in his view, none of this was part of the arrangement. Lighting another cigarette from the butt of the last he drummed his fingers impatiently on the steering wheel, clearly anxious to be on his way back to the heady fleshpots of Knock.

Anna took the hint. It took a moment to fix the handle back into its socket once she'd managed to get her door open, and quite a lot longer to wrestle the boot open and haul out her suitcase, but at last she managed it. With a cheery blast of the horn, the taxi accelerated away into the night, scattering clouds of dust and causing a flurry of rooks to rise from the trees, shrieking indignantly.

Picking up her suitcase, Anna took a deep breath and watched by a pair of stone lions, began to climb the steps. The wet stone was cracked and covered with yellowing lichen; she tripped and almost fell more than once. At the top she pushed open one of the heavy walnut double doors. A very thin old man in a maroon jacket was watching her expressionlessly through the engraved glass panel; at the last moment he reached out a trembling hand and held it open. She entered, smiling her thanks, and set down her case with a sigh of relief.

The foyer was large, featuring a great many mirrors in elaborately leafed and curlicued gilt frames and vases of salmon pink gladioli perched on insubstantial-looking wrought iron stands. At first glance it appeared extremely grand; closer inspection revealed that the mirrors were silvered, the gilt was tarnished, the gladioli were beginning to wilt and the wrought iron could do with a dust. An oil painting of a racehorse hung over the marble fireplace; a cigarette butt had been tossed in the empty hearth and what looked like (but surely couldn't be?) a used condom lay in the grate. Smiling gamely, she looked back at the elderly man who flickered his tortoise-lidded eyes in the direction of the deserted reception desk. As she rang the little brass bell and waited for someone to appear she wondered why he didn't sit down and rest on the faded plum velvet love seat beneath the largest mirror – he certainly looked exhausted. Perhaps he was a famous Irish author politely waiting for his wife to emerge from the Ladies, or an American tourist waiting for the rest of the group to come down and join him for cocktails in the bar before they went into dinner?

'Yes?'

A young woman in a black dress, her eyebrows plucked into faint arcs, her hair bleached the colour and consistency of straw, stood behind the desk gazing at her blankly; a gold brooch pinned to her breast vouchsafed the information that her name was Bernadette. It took Anna the best part of a quarter of an hour to persuade Bernadette that no, she wasn't with the Golden Wedding anniversary party (that explained the old man then); yes, she had booked, she was part of the O'Shaughnessy wedding party, the Mother of the Groom, actually; no, she didn't need to park her car in the hotel carpark; and yes, she would like someone to take her suitcase up. She accepted the key to Room 103, signed the register, picked up a handful of brochures from the display beside the dish of imperial mints and smiled her thanks at Bernadette, who responded with a distant twitch of her sugar pink lips in Anna's direction and a queenly gesture to the old man, who to Anna's horror lurched forward and tried to lift her suitcase.

'God, no, please – I can wait for a member of staff.'

Bernadette sighed. 'Patrick is the bellboy, Madam.'

The *bellboy*? The poor old bugger must be eighty at least. Anna reached out and tried to prise the handle from his liver-spotted grasp. He shot her a look of pure venom and tightened his grip. Anna gave up, and made great play of perusing one of the brochures while he concentrated on hoisting the suitcase a couple of inches above ground level and tottering to the lift. She soon wished she hadn't. Tina had already informed her that Fergustown was only five miles away, but the map on the front of the brochure, all laughing tankards of Guinness and winsome leprechauns, made it look horribly near. The thought of Tina lurking so close by was chilling.

Quelling the urge to throw the leaflet into the grate along with the condom she hurried over to the lift, where the aged bellboy was crouched over her suitcase in what appeared to be the final stages of a heart attack. As she entered he made a lunge for the control panel and with a wheeze the door closed and the lift began to judder slowly upwards, stopping now and again as if to remember what it was supposed to be doing before sighing and continuing its shaky ascent. The silence during the third halt was broken by the bellboy farting. Anna felt her cheeks go pink. Quick, think of something to say. 'Gosh, I'm starving.' Now she came to think of it she really was – she'd had nothing since breakfast except a can of lukewarm Coke and a cellophane-wrapped slice of something unidentifiable on the plane. A glass or two of wine and some decent food would restore her flagging spirits considerably. 'Still, I've come to the right place, haven't I? I hear the food here is fantastic. Must say I'm really looking forward to dinner.' She mimed exuberant expectation, almost losing her balance as the lift began to jerk and heave upwards again.

He stared at her as if she'd said she was looking forward to having a couple of male strippers and an effigy of the Pope sent to her room. There was a ping as the lift stopped and the doors rattled open, drowning his reply as he staggered with her suitcase into the corridor and headed for Room 103 at the far end. Something about being close to heaven, was it? Oh, how awful. Still, given his age and his undoubted religious devotion, he'd probably meant it in a *good* way.

It wasn't until she'd over-tipped him, and accepted from his shaking hand the yellowing sheet of paper headed Information for Guests that Anna realised what he'd said.

The dining room closed at seven.

CHAPTER TWENTY

'Stop playing with your food, Jack, and eat properly. And while you're about it you can finish Charlie's.' Ruth leant across the kitchen table and scraped a cold hamburger, half a fried tomato with most of the flesh sucked out and several peas his son had spat out in disgust, onto her husband's plate.

Jack eyed the revolting mess miserably, speared a pea and put it in his mouth. At least it was quiet, apart from the sound of Ruth masticating. The twins were currently refusing to eat anything except cucumber, which meant they'd graced the table for about two minutes, and Charlie had doused his pile of oven chips with ketchup, hoovered down the lot in three seconds flat and repaired to the garden to 'be nice to Spike'. Ruth had smiled fondly as he departed; Jack felt too depressed to do more than hope 'being nice to Spike' would stop short of actual dismemberment. He speared another pea, thought better of it, put it back and began to rearrange the pile with the blade of his knife.

'*And make you mine again.*'

Sweet fucking, sodding Jesus. What if Michael – no, Martin – Christ, what was the bastard's name? Tony, right, yes, that was it. What if he took one look at Anna and decided he wanted her back? What if she took one look at Tony – and for all he knew the creep was an oily sweet-talking two-timing jerk like that stupid prat of a doctor – and decided she felt the same?

'Jack.'

The smooth sod was probably blond and tanned like that ruddy wanker too, after all he'd been living in Australia for years.

'There's something I …'

He pushed the peas around faster.

They'd probably sit together in the church. If that didn't rekindle old memories and revive the old spark nothing would! Anna would be looking fabulous – he couldn't remember exactly what she'd be wearing, hadn't she mentioned some sort of frock or something she'd fixed up herself? – and smelling of that perfume she always wore, and she'd have her hair up, and he'd bet she'd be wearing those stockings with the lacy bits at the thighs that made him sweat just thinking of them, and that randy little bastard of an ex of hers would …

Glancing down he saw he'd formed the peas into a T; he grabbed the ketchup and doused the T in ketchup. It looked like blood.

Good.

He'd run a hand down the smooth curve of her bum while they were leaving the church and he'd grab her and squeeze her to his manly chest moaning, 'How could I have left you, precious girl …?'

'I'm speaking to you, Jack.'

Anna would look at him with tears in her eyes and, quick as a flash, the bastard would steer her into a pew …

'*Jack.*'

… throw her down, pull up her skirt and …

He drew in his breath sharply and threw down his fork.

'Ruthie, it's no good. There's something I've simply got to –
'

'Oh for heaven's sake stop interrupting me, Jack. There's something I've got to bloody tell *you.*'

He closed his eyes. She was going to complain about the mess he'd made with the sodding tomato sauce, follow that up with a brief discourse on the shocking waste – had nobody told him about famine in the third world and didn't he realise the *price* of ketchup …

'I'm leaving you.'

… and finish with detailed instructions on how she wanted her post-prandial coffee made. He knew how she wanted her post-prandial … hang on a minute. *'Leaving you.'*

198

He must be hallucinating. It was incredible what stress could do to you. Or maybe (he clutched a hand to his head) the brain tumour was kicking in already?

'Jack? Did you hear what I said?'

He opened his eyes slowly. Ruth was sitting opposite him, knife and fork placed neatly together on her plate. She was wearing a red and white candy-striped blouse he'd never seen before and she'd done something different to her hair. Christ. It must be a tumour – she looked almost human. Still, he might as well enjoy the fantasy while he could – the spell could break any moment and he'd be thrust back into harsh reality. OK. He'd roll with it.

'You're ... *leaving* me?'

'That's correct.'

Wow. He'd had dreams like this – so real you could swear it was really happening till you woke up and smelled the toast burning and heard the kids fighting and Ruth shouting at the milkman.

'I'm going to live with Peregrine.'

Eh?

'Peregrine Anstruther-Jones.'

Hey – this was *fun*. 'Who?'

She sighed. 'Do *list*en, Jack. Peregrine Anstruther-Jones. He's the father of Friday's five-to-seven GCSE maths retake. It's Gideon's fifth attempt – the poor boy simply can't get the hang of multiple fractions, no matter how loudly I shout – so I've been going to the house for some time. I got into the habit of having a small gin and orange with Perry post-lesson last term while we discussed Gideon's learning difficulties.'

A small gin? He almost laughed aloud. Ruth never drank alcohol.

'One thing led to another, and somehow we found ourselves ...'

In his fantasy she'd had a fringe cut. That figured – it almost hid the way her eyebrows grew together in the middle.

'And of course we're both passionate about cacti ...'

And her blouse was fastened at the neck with a brooch he'd never seen before.

'… and Rodgers and Hammerstein.'

It seemed to be some kind of dog. A Scottie, was it? It was hard to see because of the way its eyes glittered under the harsh overhead light. *Wow*. This must be what being on drugs must be like.

'Agatha Christie's novels, and the *Telegraph* crossword.'

She'd always refused to let him buy the *Guardian*, so he had to make do with the copy in the staffroom at school – it was crumpled and coffee-stained most days by the time he got to it, and the best bits had been torn out. And now it was featuring in this waking fantasy – obviously his feelings had gone deeper than he realised. Let's see how far he could push this. Ruth always complained he used too much ketchup, didn't she? Right. Get a load of *this*, poppet. Reaching for the plastic bottle, he squeezed it hard over the congealed hamburger remains. It proclaimed its emptiness with an aggressive hiss. This wasn't the way fantasies were supposed to go. He tapped his head to give things a bit of a jog and squeezed the bottle again. It responded with a volley of loud, wet farts.

'Stop playing with that bloody bottle and bloody *listen*, will you?' Ruth leaned forward and jabbed him in the back of his hand with the plastic blade of the Kiddie's SAS Kombat Knife that was the only implement Charlie would use at table these days. It hurt. He looked down to see a pinkish gouge on the back of his hand, oddly realistic for a dream. *Christ on a pogo stick*! *This was really happening*.

No, surely, it couldn't be.

He swallowed hard and cleared his throat. 'We seem to be out of ketchup, dear.'

The little smile that had been playing about her lips – surely that wasn't lipstick she was wearing? – disappeared as she snatched the bottle out of his hand and banged it down on the table. 'Isn't that absolutely *bloody* typical!' She leaned forward, screaming into his face. 'I tell you I'm leaving you, and all you've got to say is *we seem to be out of bloody ketchup, dear*?'

Outside in the garden, Spike began to howl; the hideous racket blending seamlessly with the moans and yells from the twins' room which Jack assumed was a current hit single.

'Let me tell you, Jack, that's exactly why I'm leaving. Not just because I'm sick of …'

He noticed absently that Ruth's whiteheads had cleared up.

'… your pathetic apology for a bloody career. And not just because I've had enough of having absolutely no support whatsoever with the children or the fact that you never lift a hand to help in the house …'

Her eyes filled suddenly with tears; she dashed them away angrily.

'… or the way you pick your nose while you're watching television and insist on keeping your bloody socks on in bed. I'm leaving you because I'm sick of being treated like a bloody servant, Jack.'

That was a bit rich – he distinctly remembered making her a cup of tea the day she came home from hospital after having the twins. 'I must say that's a bit –'

'Don't interrupt. Perry treats me like a person, Jack. A *person*. If Perry ran out of ketchup would he come whining to me? No, he would not; it would go straight on to his weekly Ocado order. Frankly, I can't wait to move into The Grange. It's enormous, so there'll be plenty of room for the children – in fact, Perry's already surround sound and Apple TV in the girls' rooms.'

Suddenly he realised the brooch was a gift from poxy, pervy, pustulating Perry. So that was why the Scottie dog's eyes shone so brightly; they were diamonds.

'And he's ordered a pedigree puppy for Charlie. He knows how much he adores animals.'

'But we've already got a dog.'

'No, Jack, *you've* already got a dog. You're keeping Spike. He'd be entirely out of place at The Grange.'

Rising to her feet, she picked up the empty ketchup bottle and dropped it in the bin. The clatter it made as it hit the side made him jump, finally underlining the fact that he was awake

201

and fully conscious and that – thank you, thank you, thank you God – this really was no dream. He wanted to laugh; he wanted to cry. He wanted to run up and down the kitchen whirling like a dervish, howling ecstatically. Glancing up he saw that Ruth was leaning against the draining board with folded arms and regarding him through narrowed eyes, waiting for a reaction. Christ. If she knew he was practically wetting himself with joy she'd crucify him and have a quick snack of the remains on toast later, while she watched *Question Time*.

Quickly he sank his head in his hands tried to think of something sad: the look on Spike's face when he dropped him off at Blue Cross in a couple of days should do the trick. It could take years for him to find a new owner ... Jack's eyes began to sting and his nose filled with mucus. Not bad, Teale – he could give that soap actor lessons any day. He peered through his fingers. Ruth was turning away, looking pleased with herself, and reaching for the jar of dandelion coffee. The thing was not to overdo the shaking shoulders and remember to ...

'The children will get on terribly well with Perry. He hasn't met them yet, of course, but I know it will be fine. And of course once I'm actually living there I'll get Gideon through that exam in no time.'

Good Christ, Poovy or Piggy or whatever his name was wouldn't know what had hit him.

'It doesn't mean you can abdicate your responsibilities, Jack. I'll expect half the value of this house ...'

If the poor bugger had any sense he'd be having a moat dug and filled with sharks and an electrified portcullis installed.

'... and maintenance for the children.'

Jack gave a whoop of laughter at the thought but managed to disguise it as an agonised sob. Time to get out while the going was good; he couldn't keep this up for ever. Shaking his head numbly as if in shock, he pushed back his chair and stumbled to the door, keeping a hand over his eyes and groping for the handle the way he'd seen Olivier play Oedipus after he'd had his eyes put out.

202

Ruth was calling after him sharply, 'And another thing, Jack …'

But he was gone, the door swinging shut behind him as he bounded up the stairs, lightheaded with joy. *Ruth* was leaving *him*! Not only was he off the hook – he had the moral high ground as well! Hell, he'd probably be able to get off library duty for weeks on the strength of his grief! And as for the timing –it was well-nigh perfect, for what could be more natural after being hit by such a bombshell than to feel the need to get away for a spot of solitary contemplation?

Trying hard not to break into song, he extricated a holdall from the welter of junk beneath the bed, blew the worst of the dust over Ruth's pillow, tipped the corpse of a large spider lurking in its pocket into the toe of one of her peach mules and began to pack.

This time tomorrow he'd be in Ireland.

CHAPTER TWENTY-ONE

Anna scanned the rest of Information for Guests. There seemed to be no offer of room-service after the kitchen had closed. Not even a sandwich. She concentrated on looking on the bright side of being found dead from starvation on the morning of her son's wedding. At least it would be obvious that she had taken her diet seriously.

She resolved to ignore the grinding hunger pangs and enjoy the other pleasures of staying at The Grand. The luxurious en-suite bathroom ... the delights of the hospitality mini-bar ... With relief she remembered that the brochure said something about a welcome basket. Now that really *would* raise the spirits. It was bound to be all cream satin bows and crackling cellophane and exotic fruit and chocolates and champagne and ... No, they'd put the champagne in the fridge, wouldn't they? She'd fortify herself with a sip of chilled bubbly and a chocolate or two, then set about unpacking. Picking up her case, she pushed open the door of her room.

And almost dropped her case.

Room 103 was vast, but that was its sole claim to grandeur. A narrow bed lurked in the far corner, a lurid print depicting the crucifixion hanging lopsidedly above the oak headboard. Opposite the bed stood a kidney-shaped dressing table, a portable television perched at one end, a corpse-green Bakelite teasmade at the other. The only other furniture was a gigantic wardrobe, a small rattan coffee table with a matching armchair and the smallest refrigerator Anna had ever seen. The cushion on the armchair was embroidered with the martyrdom of St Sebastian but the wool had frayed around St Sebastian's loin cloth, creating an exuberant ejaculatory effect disconcertingly at odds with the saint's peevish expression.

Anna grinned, then wrapped her arms round herself as she realised she was shivering. The grimy sash window was open at the bottom, letting in a damp, chilly air – one of the curtains had come adrift from its hooks and hung at half-mast. Beneath the windowsill a sign bearing the legend 'Out of Ordure' hung from the radiator's dripping tap. Just for a moment, she allowed fatigue and disappointment to wash over her, before pulling herself together. Was she a mouse or a Mother of the Groom?

Straightening her back, she strode purposefully over the wasteland of dusty blue carpet printed with faded gold fleur-de-lis, slammed the window shut then headed for the fridge. After a brief but violent tussle the door swung open to reveal, not the champagne she'd been hoping for, but a single bottle of mineral water lying on its side beside an empty ice tray. If it wasn't for the fact that Tina would get to hear of it, with repercussions that didn't bear thinking about, she'd make her feelings felt in no uncertain terms on TripAdvisor. She kicked the fridge door shut, hard.

Definitely time for a spot of deep breathing to promote Inner Calm. Oh, bugger Inner Calm. Anna trekked back to the dressing table and plugged in the teasmade. If only Jack was here! No, she mustn't go down that road. She'd have to make the best of what was on offer. If she stuffed St Sebastian into the gap at the bottom of the door where yet another icy draught came whistling through, switched on the lamp on the unit beside the bed – that flesh-pink plastic box beside it must be the phone and radio thingy – and pinned the curtain up, the place would feel positively cosy. Well, a bit less like Alcatraz, anyway. And she could see now that the door beside the bed was labelled Bathroom. As soon as she'd hung up her suit and drunk her tea, she'd have a soak in a nice hot bath, and pamper herself with all the hotel freebies.

Cheered again, she unzipped her case and began to unpack.

Twenty minutes later Anna returned to the bedroom in rather lower spirits. The bathroom had been even more spartanly appointed than the bedroom. An antediluvian water heater had spewed warmish water into the veined clawfoot bathtub, clanked alarmingly several times then given up. The luxury freebies consisted of a single wafer of unperfumed soap and a plastic bathcap patterned with bright green starfish. So certain had Anna been of the five-star lifestyle awaiting her at The Grand she'd packed neither towels nor dressing gown, an omission she regretted as she dried herself on the thin hand towel provided by the management.

Quickly she took a set of clean underwear from her case and pulled her clothes back on again, avoiding looking at the teasmade, which had exceeded the water heater's performance by refusing even to pretend to be operational. God, she was hungry. She was about to have another go at the teasmade when she noticed a leatherbound book beside the bedside lamp. The room service menu – of course! Why didn't she think of that before? What about a Grand de-luxe club sandwich – or maybe a Grand de-luxe Special Grill, with a Grand de-luxe side salad of her choice? She was about to dial when a line of swirling gold script at the bottom of the page caught her eye.

'*No Room Service between 8.00pm-8.00am*'

Anna glanced at her watch. It was five past nine.

She'd read somewhere that the thing to do when faced with suicidal thoughts was Keep Busy. Right. She'd hook up the sodding curtain, which would not only improve its appearance but would also ensure that she wasn't woken at the crack of dawn by sunlight streaming into the room.

Good.

Excellent.

Dragging the rattan chair over to the window, she climbed onto the seat, and from there onto the window sill, and grasped the corner of drooping chocolate-brown polyester in her left hand. She was fumbling for the plastic rings on the curtain rail when she heard a car engine. Or rather, engines; glancing down from her precarious perch she saw that car after car was sweeping into the forecourt below. Christ. Must be more wedding guests – Tina had told her proudly that several of the more far-flung relatives and most of Sam and Lucy's London

207

friends would be staying at the Grand. Car doors slammed, voices floated upwards as greetings were exchanged. Anna jumped down, not caring that she'd pulled the entire curtain with her, crouched below the windowsill and peered out.

Several Tina clones were stalking across the gravel, screeching greetings at each other, fluffing out their fake furs and rattling their jewellery. The rain had stopped; moonlight gilded their ankle chains and highlighted their hair; silent husbands and sullen children trailed behind them. Apart from them, joking and jostling, were tall glossy girls exuberantly air-kissing each other in greeting and sharp suited young men exchanging high fives – the IT contingent.

Anna watched until the doors swung closed behind the last guest and the forecourt was silent again, aware that not a single person had arrived alone.

Oh, Jack …

Anna had never phoned him at home for obvious reasons, and he had insisted that Anna should only ring his mobile in the direst of emergencies. Well, tonight was an emergency – her heart was about to break from loneliness. Folding up the curtain, she placed it neatly on the windowsill and went over to the phone.

Half an hour later, she admitted defeat. An outside line was more than the flesh-pink plastic could cope with. Each time she tried she found herself connected either to a local radio phone-in programme: '*Well and hello there, caller! And what views will you be wanting to share in our unbiased discussion on the terrible crime of abortion?*'; or the local garda '*Is that you again, Mrs Murphy? And it's good news I have for ye. Tigger's been spotted under a car in Keats Road, so he has, and Officer O'Leary's on his way to the scene right now.*' Anna decided that enough was enough. She glanced at her watch again. Nearly ten. If only she could ring Sam, just to let him know she was thinking of him, say goodnight and God bless. Chances of being able to get through to the Bald Eagle, the local pub where he and his best man plus the ushers were staying, were clearly zero, and anyway they'd probably have got Sam legless by now ...

Best to have an early night. And if she looked on the bright side that meant she'd a) get warm and b) have some much needed beauty sleep. She could watch television. With a bit of luck there'd be a really scary horror film – *Nosferatu* would fit the bill nicely – that would make her feel positively grateful that Tina and the relatives from hell were the worst she'd have to cope with tomorrow.

She undressed, cleaned her teeth, piled all her clothes plus the curtain on top of the bed, jumped in, remote control in hand, made herself as comfortable as she could against the thin, slithery pillows, and pressed the on-button.

She gave up more quickly, this time. It only took about three minutes to realise that the only programmes on offer were a local news channel, an Irish soap and a hardcore porn film featuring donkeys. Throwing back the covers, she leapt out of bed, dug the by now slightly crumpled magazine and battered stash of chocolate out of her bag, slid back under the covers, beat the pillows into submission once more and settled down, feeling almost happy. At least she was on safe ground here; a magazine would require no new batteries, no dead fuses would need replacing, no defunct plugs demand rewiring. With a sigh, she opened the magazine and was confronted by a full-colour double-page spread with the headline, THE HIDDEN COST TO YOUR HEALTH OF AN AFFAIR.

Anna hurled the magazine across the room, enjoying the splintering as it hit the teasmade and sent it crashing to the floor.

Switching off the lamp, she lay grimly counting the stars dusting the rectangle of velvet sky visible through the uncurtained panes of glass until at last, worn out, she fell asleep.

CHAPTER TWENTY-TWO

Midnight.

Declan sat in his garden, enjoying the scents and shadows of the country darkness. The drizzle had stopped while he'd been indoors developing the film he'd taken that afternoon – mostly studies of the shifting grey clouds reflected in the rain butt. There'd been leaves and dead insects floating in there, too; the shapes and textures had been extraordinary. After he'd finished he'd cleaned up the workroom, and come outside to clear his head before he organised his gear for tomorrow.

Tomorrow! Jesus Christ, the thought of photographing another bloody wedding was enough to make him want to throw up. He tilted the bottle of Guinness to his mouth. A wedding should be a private affair, like his and Maura's had been, not a West End stage production with a cast of thousands and more attention paid to the Heal's gift list than the meaning of the ceremony.

The things you saw in this game. At a bash he'd done in County Mayo last year – he'd needed the cash so he could splash out on a decent present for his parents' Golden Wedding – he'd seen the bride's father rogering the chief bridesmaid in the back of his Bentley Continental in the hotel car park. He'd nipped back to the van to get some more film when he'd noticed the car rocking and through the back window a flurry of bright pink silk and mottled flesh mingled with black pinstripe and grey hair. His automatic response had been to raise the Pentax slung round his neck and start shooting – the colour contrast had been superb, and the car window had created a perfect frame for the composition – when two contorted faces had reared up against the glass and he understood exactly what he was looking at. He'd given an apologetic wave of his arm –

apologetic? Why the hell was *he* apologising? – and got the hell back to the reception. The bride's mother had been in the kitchen bawling out the caterers when he walked past. She'd caught one of the waitresses sneaking a prawn vol au vent or something. He drained the Guinness and sighed. By the sound of it, tomorrow's do wouldn't be a whole lot better – from her phone calls it sounded as if all Nita, or Zita, or whatever the woman's name was, cared about was outdoing the Royal family in the pomp and circumstance stakes. Last time she'd phoned she'd been bleating about the florist complaining about her late night phone calls. He grinned. If he'd been the florist he'd have told her exactly where she could shove her buttonholes …

Ah well. It was all part of life's rich pattern.

He got to his feet and stood gazing at the stars glittering silently in the sky above the distant mountains.

After a while, he went inside and started to pack his camera bag.

CHAPTER TWENTY-THREE

Very early next day, a smart white, unmarked van sped into the service area of The Grand Hotel and swerved to a halt. The driver, a young man sporting a quiff that would have put Elvis to shame, crepe soles so thick Little Richard would have killed for them and a shoelace tie that would have had Lee Van Cleef weeping with envy, leapt out and regarded himself critically in the cracked wing mirror. Licking his fingers he applied spittle to eyebrows and sideboards, and checked his front teeth for any errant remnants of breakfast. Satisfied, he adjusted his balls with a practised gesture and wiped his nose (the morning was chilly) on the back of his sleeve.

Whistling, he hurried round to the back of the van, threw open the doors and began to unload stack after stack of smart white, unmarked boxes onto the gravel.

Meanwhile, several miles along the road from Knock airport, an old grey Morris Minor full of giggling nuns was coming to a halt outside a grey stone convent. The nuns waved delightedly as Jack, unshaven, dishevelled, and clasping his holdall tightly against his nether regions (he'd never know whether the fat one with the horsy teeth had meant to grope him as he climbed in), extricated himself from the back seat.

He waved goodbye as the Morris was swallowed up by the thorn-crowned black gates. Checking his watch for the hundredth time since he got off the plane, he took up position by the side of the deserted highway and stuck out his thumb.

Anna woke with a start and tried to remember where she was. She raised herself up on an elbow and the sight of the semi-curtained window, the coffin-like wardrobe and the heap of

213

green plastic shards and rusting metal coils that had once been the teasmade did the trick pretty quickly.

It all added up to only one thing.

Today was the day.

She closed her eyes again and tried to keep calm. The thought of the perils and trials, the pure terrors that lay ahead were enough to make a yogi hyperventilate. Yogi. Indian. Breathing exercises! Yes, that was the thing! It was clear to her now that these had failed before because there had been too many distractions. If you were lying flat out in bed with your eyes closed they were *bound* to work.

In ...

Must remember to make the bloody switchboard get hold of Sam at the Bald Eagle, so she could send him huge love, and wish him all the luck in the world.

Out ...

Would the creases have hung out of her suit? Had she packed her spare tights?

In ...

Should she sing along with the hymns in church and risk being at least half a verse behind the rest of the congregation or maintain a serene and dignified silence?

Out ...

Down the corridor the lift door clanged shut; seagulls flew past her window screaming raucously; and her stomach rumbled so loudly she thought for a moment it was thunder.

Anna opened her eyes. Bloody Indian healers! As soon as she got home she was going to ring breakfast TV and complain.

Flinging back the covers, she leapt out of bed and began to get dressed. Maybe breakfast would help ...

In the hotel kitchen, the van driver put a pile of smart, white, unmarked boxes onto a counter and turned with a show of elaborate cool as the door to reception opened and Bernadette sauntered in yawning. Affecting a start of surprise as she saw the driver, she sashayed over and plugged in the kettle with a

214

toss of her straw curls (she'd been up since five with the curling tongs in preparation for this encounter) and a moué of her thickly glossed lips. (Guaranteed to 'Drive Men Wild', the ad said, and Bernadette's faith in ads was second only to her faith in the Holy Trinity.)

'Oh hiya. Didn't realise you did your round this early – I wasn't expecting to see anyone yet.'

The delivery man shrugged. It had looked dead good when he practised in the mirror last night but he'd been on his tod then, hadn't he, so it had been easy.

'So d'you want a coffee, then?'

He ran a finger round the back of his collar, and tried to speak.

Bernadette shrugged. It had looked pretty good when she practised in the mirror last night, especially when she flicked a sort of sideways look under her lashes. 'It's no bother. I'm having one.'

He checked his quiff and ran a hand over his shirt front. 'Yeah. Why not?'

Bernadette checked her lip gloss with the tip of her tongue. It was passion-fruit flavoured – guaranteed to have 'em 'Dropping Like Flies'. As she turned away to fetch the mugs, she took the opportunity to unfasten another button on her white blouse.

Eight o'clock: Anna had spent the last hour and ten minutes having a stand-up blanket bath in the freezing bathroom and washing her hair. By the time she was dressed (in her good trousers and her best Oasis sale sweater – the wedding wasn't until twelve and she wasn't going to take any risks with the delphinium blue velvet) she was faint with hunger. There was no way she was going to have breakfast in the dining room, it would be full of the Tina contingent and IT guys. She checked the room service brochure. Yup – there it was; up and running at 8.00 a.m. Great. She'd have a pot of coffee and a Grand de-luxe half-grapefruit followed by a Grand de-luxe mixed grill and several Grand de-luxe slices of toast. She felt better already.

And wasn't that a faint glimmer of sunshine behind the trees over there?

Smiling, she pressed the button marked Reception.

After half an hour, having found herself connected to various guests' bedrooms, directory enquiries and the speaking clock, she replaced the receiver carefully, picked up the leatherbound tome and threw it very hard at St Sebastian. Feeling slightly better, she picked up her bag and marched to the door. It was clear there was nothing for it; if she didn't want to pass out on the steps of the sodding church she was going to have to put in a personal appearance at reception and bloody well *demand* service.

After a lack of response to her summons for the lift, she hurried down the stairs and crossed the deserted foyer. The gladioli had wilted further since last night, and the condom-like object still lay in the grate. The reception desk was unmanned, but the door behind it stood ajar, affording a glimpse of marble-topped counters and an industrial-sized fridge. Must be the kitchens. There was a hell of a racket going on. Some sort of TV drama, by the sound of it, all shouting and *feckin'* this and *feckin'* that – probably an Irish version of *Eastenders*. She reached out and was about to ring the bell when something hit the other side of the door with a thud and the noise escalated sharply. A roar was followed by a high scream of fear.

Anna gasped: violence was clearly imminent. She looked around for help, but the foyer was still deserted. Suddenly a slight figure with a madly bobbing quiff and crepe-soled shoes sprinted across the doorway, hotly pursued by a much larger figure in tweeds loudly promising his quarry a lingering and feckin' painful death. Anna clapped a hand to her mouth. She couldn't have Lucy and Sam's wedding day ruined by a murder! Banishing the thought that leapt unbidden to her mind – unless of course the victim was bloody Tina – she darted round the end of the reception desk and ran into the kitchen.

CHAPTER TWENTY-FOUR

'I'll have yez guts for garters, ye randy little rat! Leavin' the feckin' boxes on the feckin' ground for the feckin' cats to pillage while you try 'n weasel yer way into Bernadette's feckin' knickers! I'll kill yez – so help me, I'll feckin' kill yez!'

The figure in tweeds lunged at his terrified prey. Bernadette, watching wide-eyed from the shelter of the huge cream-coloured fridge, so ancient Anna thought it must surely be the original prototype, squealed with terror. Seizing the gibbering delivery man by his sky-blue polyester lapels, his persecutor shook him like a terrier worrying a rabbit, screaming incoherently and shaking with fury. Anna could stand it no longer. Rushing forward she grabbed the big man's right sleeve and yelled at Bernadette to fetch the hotel owner.

As Bernadette shrieked, '*Eejit*! Mr O'Flynn *is* the hotel owner!' the big man scowled and attempted to shake Anna off. The delivery man took advantage of the momentary lull in hostilities to slip from his attacker's grasp. Gibbering, he raced for the open back door. Red-faced and panting, his tormentor succeeded in dislodging Anna and, cursing, lumbered after him. As he disappeared Anna heard a door slam and an engine burst into life. With a violent crashing of gears and a defiant blast of the hooter that made Bernadette smile a small and secret smile, the delivery man made his escape.

Anna gave a sigh of relief. Now she might finally get some breakfast. The best thing would be to carry on as if nothing had happened, tell Bernadette politely but firmly that she'd like breakfast brought to her room at once and ask how she could get an outside line so she could ring Sam.

She smiled brightly. 'Well, that *was* an interesting start to the day, wasn't it? Now, I wonder if I might order ...'

There was a roar behind her. 'An' you can tell yer weasley feckin' little friend to get out, too, Bernadette! I'd've had the bugger if it hadn't been fer ...'

The receptionist's plump hands flew to her mouth. 'But she's not my friend, Mr O'Flynn. She's –'

'An' what will we be givin' the buggers for their feckin' puddin' now, eh? Answer me that if yez can!'

Anna turned. The large man stood by the back door, trembling with rage and pointing to the courtyard beyond dramatically. She took a step back. Really, this was a bit rich. Didn't he realise she was a guest? And not just any old guest, either, for heaven's sake – hell, she was the ... Before she knew it he'd surged forward and grabbed her arm. As Bernadette fluttered and wrung her hands ineffectually, savouring every moment to regale her best friend Siobhan with later, he frogmarched Anna outside, coming to a halt beside a trail of horribly battered and chewed once smart, white unmarked boxes that lay strewn over the gravel.

Beside them lay scattered a great many tiny gold pots.

A movement near the sparse yew hedge at the other end of the courtyard caught her eye. A couple of large tomcats with distended stomachs lay beside it, the biggest one licking its lips and, Anna was pretty sure, grinning. The hedge failed to screen the jumble of lidless dustbins behind; it was clear that they'd just breakfasted off the remains of last night's dinner. With an oath, the large man bent down, picked up a sharp stone and hurled it at the cats; it missed by a mile. Anna was about to scream for help – fading quietly away from starvation was one thing, being battered to death by a madman quite another – when her captor suddenly crumpled. Letting go of her arm, he sank down beside an ornamental Victorian urn and burst into noisy tears.

'Feckin' randy van drivers ... feckin' crème feckin' brûlées ... feckin' weddins ...'

Weddings?

Crèmes fucking brûlées?

Just a minute, hadn't Tina said something about crèmes brûlées being Lucy's favourite pudding? Evidently they were to feature big in the wedding breakfast, and the gold pots were being delivered for use as individual containers. Great idea – they'd look brilliant. As she contemplated the wreckage, the madness of the last few minutes began to make sense. Clearly the man sobbing his heart out beside her was terrified of telling his chef what had happened. Everyone knew chefs were a temperamental lot, look at Gordon Ramsay, he'd probably have hung drawn and quartered his entire staff with his bare hands if *his* gold pots had been mucked up. It was up to her to make him see that it really wasn't such a disaster after all. In fact if they moved fast, the chef need never know what had happened.

Crouching down, she began to gather up the pots.

'Please don't be upset – they're fine, really, look!'

She held one out to him. He shook his head violently, then burst into fresh paroxyms of sobbing. *Wow*. Chef must be really something. 'Honestly, all they need is a quick rinse and –'

He looked up at her fiercely. 'And what, eh? No good servin' empty feckin' pots, is it?'

Anna sat back on her heels and stared at him, nonplussed.

'Feckin' cats.' He hiccuped. 'Ate the feckin' lot.'

So the pots had been full! How odd that they'd been delivered. Obviously some arcane Irish country recipe had been handed down through the chef's family for centuries – he'd had the mixture bubbling away in an iron pot deep in the woods all night and the driver had just been popping them over to the fridge to be chilled. No wonder The Grand's owner was so upset.

She tried again. 'I do see how awful it is for Chef after all his hard work, but let's look on the bright side? It's still early – there's plenty of time for him to knock up a replacement …'

He covered his face with his hands, and broke into fresh sobs. 'If this gets out, we'll be feckin' ruined.'

'Ruined? Look, it'll be fine. All your chef has to do is …'

Raising his head, he stared at her hopelessly. 'There is no feckin' chef.'

Anna gazed back, astonished. 'No feckin' chef? But?'

His voice sank to a whisper. 'All the victuals are supplied by commercial caterers.' He cast a swift look over his shoulder. 'Frozen.' A tear ran down his bulbous strawberry nose. 'So there's no feckin' chef. Just Connor.'

'Connor?'

'Used to be the under-gardener till I put him in charge of the microwaves. Never cooks anything except guests' breakfast toast, and he's planning to put a stop to that soon. Going for le continental petit-whatd'yemacallit, so he'll only have to microwave the rolls.'

'Ah.' She thought for a moment. 'But surely you must have stock?'

He snorted. 'Not two hundred and fifty portions of anything, for feck's sake. There's mebbe thirty or so portions of that sorbet muck kickin' about in the deep freeze. Always shift a lot of those on Saturday nights. Few apple tarts ...'

Anna bit her lip; it wasn't exactly wedding fare. She thought of the elaborately printed gold menus Lucy had told her about excitedly when they last met, the dessert wine Eamonn had been despatched to France to select personally, the scene Tina would create if a slice of apple tart was placed in front of her after the lobster bisque and the pheasant royale, instead of the pudding she'd expressly ordered.

She would have to do something. Mouth set determinedly, she straightened her shoulders.

Alarmed by the glint in her eyes, O'Flynn lumbered to his feet and backed away.

Anna darted forward and grabbed his lapels. 'OK. Here's what we're going to do ...'

'All right, so it's money yez want. How much d'ye want to keep shtum?'

Anna laughed. 'Money? It's not about *money*, for Christ's sake.' She let go of his lapels. 'Look, there's not much time if we're going to ...'

If *we're* goin' to what? He backed away; he wasn't going to have anything to do with this madwoman. He halted, struck by a thought. If it wasn't about money, what the feck *was* it about? 'So why's yez so concerned about the feckin' puddins, then?'

Anna smiled. 'Because I'm the Mother of the feckin' Groom, Mr O'Flynn, that's why.' She brushed a speck of gravel from her sleeve. 'Now, let's get to work, shall we?'

Turning on her heel, she headed back to the kitchen.

CHAPTER TWENTY-FIVE

An hour or so later, on a road some distance from The Grand Hotel, a gleaming red convertible sped past Jack as he stood dejectedly in the drizzling rain that had begun again shortly after the slurry cart dropped him on the verge.

He was still standing there half an hour later, thumb outstretched, when it shot past in the opposite direction.

It didn't stop.

Meanwhile, Anna was sitting on her unmade bed, scribbling notes for a poem about the taxi journey from the airport and finishing her breakfast. The Grand de-luxe mixed grill had been surprisingly good, considering the meadow-fresh mushrooms, hand-reared country-bred bacon rashers, dew-fresh tomato halves and dawn-gathered free-range egg had spent the last six months stashed in Nosh Anon's freeze storage unit on a Belfast industrial estate before being delivered to The Grand and into Connor's microwave. Before it was brought to her room, borne tremblingly aloft on a silver salver by a waiter who made the bellboy look positively youthful, Bernadette had managed to secure Anna an outside line. She spent several happy minutes chatting to a hungover Sam, managing not to remind him to comb his hair and clean his teeth before setting off for the church, and making a point of telling him how much she was looking forward to the wedding breakfast.

She'd just finished the last mouthful of de-luxe crunchy crusty wholemeal toast when the phone rang. Reaching for the flesh-pink box, she snatched up the receiver, full of hope. 'Jack? Oh darling, I'm so glad to hear you! You wouldn't believe how much I miss you – the hotel's unbelievable, an absolute hell hole, and –'

'This is your receptionist Bernadette calling from the reception desk at reception.' Somewhere in the background Anna could hear the lift doors opening with a clang and the sound of the Tina contingent complaining about the weather. Bernadette's piercing tones dropped to a hoarse whisper. 'Mr O'Flynn says to inform you he's *back with the goods*.'

Anna found herself gripping the receiver tightly, infected by the mood. 'Message received. I'm on my way, reception.'

'Copy that, contact. Over and out.' There was a ping, and the phone went dead.

Jack was sitting on the verge, head in hands, wet through, when a gold Mercedes hurtled past in the direction of The Grand. He staggered to his feet, thumb extended.

Too late.

Anna bustled about the kitchen, hair pinned on top of her head and sleeves rolled up, heaving copper saucepans that had hitherto served a merely decorative function down from their hooks on the stained plaster walls, and lining them up on the black marble counter beside the rickety New World gas cooker. She grinned as she set about hunting in the beetle-infested cupboards for wooden spoons and mixing bowls; it seemed only too likely that Christopher Columbus had discovered the cooker on his travels. In fact, she thought, a cauldron suspended over a wood-burning fire would have been more in keeping with the kitchen's positively Dickensian air. Apart from a battalion of modern microwave ovens ranged above the gold-rimmed crockery and crates of dented silverware, the grumbling, juddering fridge was the only contemporary feature, though the flypaper suspended above the enormous freezer had been fashioned in a crude silhouette of Winston Churchill.

She was washing out an enormous flowered jug that would come in useful when it came to portioning out the mixture when O'Flynn came puffing through the back door bearing a stack of cardboard egg trays so high only his bulging eyes and damp grey hair were visible above them. With an oath, he set them down beside the vats of double cream, the cartons crammed with giant bars of best quality dark chocolate and the bottles of Grand Marnier already arrayed on the blackened oak refectory table that ran almost the length of the kitchen, and wiped his forehead on a handy dishcloth. 'That'll be the last of the stuff, thank God. So, will we be ready to begin, then?'

They certainly were, though there was now a slight change to the menu. The chances of producing perfect crèmes brûlées were practically zero; the egg yolks, sugar and cream mixture was sure to curdle as she brought it to the boiling point, and anyway, there simply wouldn't be time to shove it in a bain marie for an age before chilling it. And then there was all the palava with the blow torch – ha, like the kitchen even *had* a blow torch ... Chocolate mousse was the obvious answer.

Anna handed him a plastic apron, barely noticing that it was emblazoned with the torso of a naked woman, complete with three dimensional nipples and scarlet navel gem stone (no doubt the property of Connor, who'd left straight after his breakfast shift, pleading a sick great aunt) and tied a tea towel stencilled with rather less inflammatory robins round her own waist. 'Right, let's make a start. If we can get them in the fridge by eleven, we're in with a chance.'

They set to work.

As he observed Anna zipping to and fro between work top and stove, breaking chocolate into chunks, cracking and separating eggs, peeling lids from cartons with cheerful efficiency, allocating him the simplest tasks but never failing to thank him when they were accomplished, O'Flynn's manner began gradually to change from grudging acceptance to something very close to respect. And when Anna, failing (not surprisingly) to locate an egg whisk, and instead of throwing a tantrum as Connor would have done (having seen rather too many celebrity chefs on TV) merely shrugged and said it was no problem, they could make do with forks, he poured them both a coffee cup of Grand Marnier and invited her with a full heart and a catch in his throat to call him Desmond.

Happy to be doing her absolute best for the person whose wellbeing had always been paramount in her life – Sam – Anna clicked her cup to Desmond's with a smile, said she'd be delighted if he'd call her Anna and promised, to his childlike delight, to teach him the trick of separating the yolks from the whites using only one hand.

The florist's van had arrived at the service entrance, the waiters had begun to rearrange the tables in the dining room and the maids were scuttling backwards and forwards with armfuls of starched linen when the gold Mercedes swept into the courtyard and came to a halt in a spray of gravel at the bottom of the entrance steps.

Adjusting the epaulettes on the shoulders of his dusty jacket, the ancient bellboy winched a smile into place and tottered down the steps to greet the new arrivals.

'God, no, Desmond – things go wrong all the time, honestly.' Anna lifted the last bowl of melted chocolate from the microwave and set it down beside the others on the table, admiring Desmond's wrist action as, using both hands, he beat savagely at two copper bowls of foaming egg whites using a clutch of battered forks as improvised whisks. The kitchen, pleasantly warm now, and smelling delightfully of vanilla and cocoa beans, was a hive of activity as they went about their preparations. A minion was washing the little gold pots at the low stone sink, another was drying them and setting them out in neat rows at the end of the refectory table; both were listening wide-eyed to Anna's stories of life at Avant Art as they worked. Music was playing cheerily in the background on Connor's portable radio – Desmond, unaware of the stifled giggles of the staff, had burst into song when 'My Boy Lollipop' had ripped through the airwaves a few minutes earlier.

Anna carefully measured brandy into the bubbling chocolate, and began to stir.

'Another time a coachload of Russian cultural officials showed up on the wrong afternoon. Roxy and I were alone in the gallery – Alastair was in London, checking out a new installation at the ICA, Fart Art, I think it was.'

Desmond grunted, and topped up his coffee cup from the open bottle beside him. 'Beggar sounds a right feckin' ponce, if you ask me.'

'Think you're probably right there. Anyway, we had to think fast. There'd have been hell to pay if we'd let on we weren't expecting them, they'd come to decide whether to allow Avant Art to show some of their own up and coming young artists – things were really on the line.' She added more brandy to the chocolate, and glanced at the mountains of egg white beginning to burgeon in the great copper bowls. 'Ease off a bit, Desmond, or they'll be too stiff to use – soft clouds are what we need, not bloody great Alpine peaks.'

'Sorry. So, what happened with the Ruskies, then?'

Anna grinned. 'Roxy took them on a tour of the exhibitions – parroted some of the junk Alastair comes out with and managed to steer them past the "Interactive Orgasm" installation – while I knocked up a quick batch of borscht and shot out to Tesco's for a couple of jars of rollmops.'

Desmond roared with laughter.

'Those egg whites are coming on a treat. OK, I'll mix the yolks into the chocolate while you stir, then I'll add the cream.'

Bernadette rolled her eyes at the florist, who was replacing the gladioli with sprays of white roses and carnations (dead cold for a wedding, in Bernadette's opinion. When she got married she was going to have red and orange, like Madonna) and reached for the phone. It was the first moment she'd had to herself all morning, what with all the wedding guests complaining about their breakfast coffee being instant, and the hot water running out, and the lift not working and that – if she didn't talk to Siobhan soon she'd go mental, she really would. Popping an imperial mint into her mouth, she dialled the number. Thing was, Siobhan was an expert on men; she'd know exactly what Bernadette should do next to ensure the delivery man didn't swerve from his quest. Though that quiff was going to have to go, no way was she going to have hair gel smeared all over fanny when they …

A ping from the bell jolted her back to consciousness. Sugar, *another* bleddy guest wanting to complain. Swear to God, sometimes she wished she'd gone into chiropody like her mother had wanted. With a sigh, she set down the receiver with exaggerated patience and looked up.

A tanned, middle-aged man, groomed to within an inch of his life, drummed his fingers on the fan of brochures beside the sweet dish. Clinging adoringly to his arm was a stunning, world-class bimbo in her early twenties; nipped, tucked and suctioned to improbable proportions, implanted, injected and extensioned to Barbie-like perfection.

Bernadette goggled at them. She confided to Siobhan in the Fox and Ferret that evening, Blake and Crystal in those endless reruns from *Dynasty* her gran was always watching weren't even *in* it. Pulling herself together, she shoved her mint imperial down the side of her cheek with a forefinger and gave them her best receptionist's smile. 'Good morning, sir, madam. How can I help?'

'G'day. I think you'll find we have a reservation.' The man squeezed his companion's raspberry-pink chiffon-clad bottom, puckered his lips at her in an extravagant kiss, then turned back to Bernadette. 'The name's Hardy.' He puffed out his chest, which filled out the jacket of his cream linen safari suit just a little too fully, looking pleased with himself. 'Tony Hardy.'

CHAPTER TWENTY-SIX

'Oh yes, Mr Hardy, we received your email. We've been expecting you.' Bernadette unhooked the key to Room 34 from the patchily gilded pegboard behind her and handed it across the desk with a gracious smile. She clicked her fingers at the bellboy, who having made three trips to the Mercedes' boot to retrieve the new arrivals' luggage was lurking by the lift trying unsuccessfully to unwrap a Fisherman's Friend.

'Thanks, sweets.' Tony leaned across the desk. 'Wonder if you could tell me what room Anna Hardy's in?' He smirked. 'Only polite to introduce my lady ex-wife to my lovely fiancée before the kid's wedding, wouldn't you say?'

Bernadette gazed at him, glassy-eyed. He was the Anna woman's *ex*? Didn't look at all her type. She shrugged. Oh well, better give him Anna's room number, let them sort it out between them. With a bit of luck she could find an excuse to nip up to the second floor later, and listen to the row. She was riffling through the register to check Anna's room number when the door to the kitchen swung open behind her and one of the staff hurried through and on towards the dining room, where she was scheduled to fold a hundred and fifty napkins into swans. Before it closed again Tony caught a glimpse of Anna, cheeks flushed, hair escaping in delicate wisps from its pins, stirring something in a bloody great bowl and laughing up at a fat bastard in a kinky apron who was doing something weird to something in *two* bloody great bowls.

As the door swung open once again under its own momentum, Anna raised her arm to push a lock of hair out of her eyes, caught sight of the ex-husband she hadn't seen for nearly twenty years, and dropped her wooden spoon.

Tony's jaw dropped. As the door clicked shut he did an exaggerated double-take, eyebrow raised as incredulously as if he'd caught a glimpse of his ex-wife pole dancing.

There was a short pause. Then the door opened and Anna emerged, *sans* robin-printed tea towel, sleeves rolled down, hair smoothed into place. Bernadette crammed several mints in her mouth, eyes swivelling greedily from Anna to Tony, whose companion waited, smiling politely at the open register. Tony favoured Anna with a pitying smile.

'Say, hello there. If it isn't good old Annie. Grand to see you again. But,' he did the incredulous leer thing again, 'what on *earth* are you doing in the hotel kitchen?'

Anna felt her hands clench involuntarily. No no *no* – that wasn't the way at all; she mustn't let him bait her. And she wouldn't comment on his ridiculous Australian accent. Wishing the ancient Indian healer was there to admire her astonishing mastery of emotions she concentrated on producing a sophisticated smile. 'Hi, there.' She gave what she hoped was a casual shrug. 'Cooking's what I do professionally these days.' She chose to ignore Tony's disbelieving shake of the head. 'The Grand's chef's world famous, of course, and the kitchen here's just to die for – I simply couldn't resist popping in for a professional pow-wow.' Trying not to think of the beetle-infested cupboards, she gave a little gurgle of helpless pleasure.

A frown marred Tony's brow for a second, then the smile resumed service as he reached out an arm and yanked the Barbie lookalike to his side. Anna blinked; she hadn't realised they were together. 'I want you to meet someone very special, Anna. My fiancée, Tara-Louise – this is Anna, my ex.'

Anna's eyes widened. 'Fiancée? But you didn't mention any fiancée in your reply to Lucy and Sam!'

He nuzzled Tara-Louise's ear. 'Decided to keep it as a fabulous surprise.'

Tara-Louise giggled prettily.

The trick was to never show the buggers they'd surprised you. When she got back to Brighton she was going to tell that breakfast television show to axe the Indian and take her on

230

instead. She took a deep breath. 'But that's wonderful! Congratulations!'

Tony squeezed Tara-Louise's bottom again. 'Y'know things couldn't be better. Life's been just one long success story ever since I got my shit together and struck out for the outback.'

Anna restrained a shriek of fury and with an effort willed herself to smile.

'Got my own chain of graphic design agencies in Sydney, as a matter of fact, and boy, are they successful.' He winked at Tara-Louise. 'Oh yes. Very successful indeed.'

Tara-Louise giggled obligingly.

'A huge house with a swimming pool, three cars … Life simply couldn't be better.' He looked at Anna with concern. 'And you're … *cooking*, you say?'

Much more of this and she'd knee him in the balls.

'Well, hardly cooking.'

She laughed lightly, as if the mere idea were preposterous. 'No, I'm with Avant Art – Brighton's answer to the Tate, you know – in a culinary advisory capacity.' Thank you, Sam. She managed the little gurgle of pleasure again.

'Oh.' A world of condescending dismissal was invested in the single syllable. 'So you're not designing, then?'

What did I just say, cloth ears? 'Not a tremendous amount these days, no. But I write a lot of poetry. It's taken the place of all that, so I don't really miss it.'

'Oh, well.' He smirked. 'It's not as if you ever actually got anywhere with it, is it?'

Anna felt the blood rush to her cheeks. Furious, she was about to respond when she noticed Tara-Louise looking anxiously from one to the other. Poor girl – none of this was her fault, and she must be exhausted from the journey. She gave her a friendly smile. 'But enough about me – what do you do, Tara-Louise?'

'I –'

Tony gripped his fiancée's slender upper arm possessively. 'She's a neurosurgeon.'

Anna's jaw dropped.

Another smirk. 'Blonde, beautiful *and* brainy, right? Not only Miss Melbourne 1991 but MD, too, not to mention FSABS, Fellow of the Society of Australian Brain Surgeons, natch, as well.' He looked solemn. 'I don't mind telling you, she's a whizz with a laser. In fact she was in theatre operating right up until a couple of hours before we left; an emergency craniostomy – or was it a lobotomy, precious?'

Before Anna could tell Tara-Louise that she had definitely been lobotomising the wrong bloke, the kitchen door swung open. Desmond stuck his head round it, looking anxious.

'Anna! *Psst,* Anna! Think the egg whites are almost there, but it's tricky ...' He made frantic beckoning signs and disappeared.

Anna had never been so glad to see anyone in her life. She gave a rueful smile. 'I dunno – these five-star, Paris-trained chefs! Oh well, I suppose I'd better go and sort him out ...' She began to back round the corner of the desk. 'Lovely to see you again, Tone.' He'd always hated her calling him that. 'Tara-Louise – look forward to meeting up again later.'

Waving cheerily, she disappeared though the door.

Tony stared after her, looking extremely annoyed. Suddenly he pulled his fiancée to his chest and kissed her vigorously. 'Whaddya say to a few tinnies and a quickie, precious, before we get our glad rags on?'

Tara-Louise nipped playfully at his earlobe. 'Whatever you say, big boy.'

Entwined in a passionate embrace, they headed for the lift.

Her eyes as big as saucers, Bernadette watched them go. As the lift door clanged shut, she reached for the phone. Siobhan was going to bleddy *die.*

CHAPTER TWENTY-SEVEN

Eleven fifteen.

Anna stood at the top of the steps at the hotel's main entrance, ready to leave for the church. Back home in Brighton, Anna had planned her timetable for the morning of her son's wedding with the utmost care, as advised by the writer of the M-of-the-G article. Now Brighton seemed light years away, on another planet. The *Bride* article routine had been scheduled to take three hours, from the first pluck of the tweezers to the final spritz with the perfume. Her morning hadn't exactly gone to plan. By the time she escaped from the kitchen she had had less than half an hour to get ready. She'd been in such a rush she'd hardly had time to check the results in the ill-lit bathroom mirror, and would have been amazed if she'd known how beautiful she looked. Her hair, upswept in a smooth chignon, shone beneath the little pillbox hat; her skin glowed beneath its faint dusting of translucent powder. The exquisitely tailored delphinium-blue velvet suit, over which she'd laboured so long, fitted perfectly. It was set off by the corsage of tiny cream orchids that had been delivered earlier, with a handwritten note from Sam that she dared not read because tears would have made her mascara run and there would be no time to repair the damage.

The taxi she'd asked Bernadette to book to take her to the church was due at eleven fifteen. As she waited, she watched the guests milling in the forecourt below gradually sort themselves out and climb into their cars. As the last of the preening Tina coterie and bragging IT faction disappeared down the drive, hooting at each other and jostling aggressively for right of way, she tried to relax – the events of the last couple of hours had been taxing, to say the least.

At least the *mousses chocolats au Grand Marnier* had gone well. She had to agree with Desmond that they were a total feckin' triumph. He'd called her back to the kitchen at exactly the right moment; the egg whites were of the right consistency, neither too soft nor too stiff. She'd folded them quickly into the chocolate mixture, then decanted the frothing concoction into the flowered jug; she and Desmond had taken it in turns (Desmond delighted as a child to be allowed to help) to fill the rows of waiting tiny gold pots. They were chilling now – rich, dark and delicious, perfumed faintly with Grand Marnier – in the depths of the ancient fridge. She smiled. A feckin' triumph indeed, though she said it herself.

But the same could not be said of the meeting with Tony. She shuddered every time she thought about it – which, unfortunately, was roughly every thirty seconds or so. She'd known it would be difficult. She'd been prepared to shed a tear for old times' sake, even. And of course she'd expected him to look different – twenty years would naturally have taken its toll. But bloody hell – that ludicrously affected Aussie accent! The cringe-making slang! And as for that ridiculous safari suit! She'd bet the pockets were full of compasses and Swiss army knives and collapsible billabongs or whatever they were called. She wouldn't be surprised if he was planning to wear one of those leather bush hats festooned with dangling corks to the wedding …

And as for Trixie-Labelle, or whatever her name was, she made the Stepford Wives look positively lackadaisical in their attempts at man-pleasing. And this Katie Price lookalike was a *brain surgeon*? It was a bit like discovering that Marilyn Monroe held a PhD in quantum physics, or that Victoria Beckham had been awarded the Nobel Prize for Literature. Typical bloody Tony not to have warned anyone about her. How on earth was Sam going to take it? And what the hell would the O'Shaughnessys make of her?

Oh, if only Jack … No. She mustn't think about Jack now, or she'd cry.

Anna straightened her back, took a tiny lace-edged handkerchief from her bag and dabbed at her eyes. Where the hell was that taxi? She looked at her watch. *Half past eleven?* She ran back into the foyer.

Bernadette looked up warily from her emery board as Anna approached, scenting trouble. However, being the youngest of eleven children had had its effect. She had been an expert in the art of denial from an early age. Whenever any accusation was hurled – especially when she was guilty, whether of stealing the week's milk money from the tobacco tin or filching her eldest sister's new lipstick – she specialised in an expression of injured innocence of which any RADA graduate would have been proud. This was her expression as the realisation sank in that in her hurry to speak to Siobhan that morning she'd entirely forgotten to make Anna's taxi booking. (She'd also omitted to arrange for the lift repair man to call, but that wouldn't come to light until the following week when an elderly American banker would find himself trapped between floors for several hours and have a heart attack as a result). Declaring her certainty that he must surely be about to arrive at any moment, she advised Anna to resume her post on the steps while she investigated.

Ten minutes later, there was still no sign of it. Desperate, Anna was prepared to force Bernadette to put a call through to the Garda and make them send a police car, if necessary, when two young men, the IT contingents, emerged. Dressed to kill in suits so modish they looked positively old-fashioned, they cantered down the steps animatedly discussing the latest development in Japanese electronics. Ignoring Anna, they sauntered towards a sleek black BMW Z4, the only car remaining in the forecourt. Without even thinking about it, Anna found herself in hot pursuit, begging hysterically for a lift.

Agreeing with barely a glance in her direction, they continued their discussion as the owner held open the nearside door for her and with a jerk of his head indicated the luggage shelf behind the low-slung bucket seats.

She took a deep breath. Preserving her modesty as much as possible under the circumstances – which wasn't easy given the tight space, the shortness of her skirt and the lacy-topped black stockings that made Jack seem somehow less far away – she clambered in and crushed herself into the tiny space.

There was a short but appreciative silence. Then, grinning, her benefactors climbed in after her and, with a roar, they set off.

The journey was uncomfortable, but thanks to the driver's predilection for speed and total disregard for either his own or his passengers' safety, mercifully brief. Fergustown proved to be a pleasant little Georgian spot; as they shot over the peaceful river and through a main street lined with intriguing little shops, Anna reflected that had it not been her son's wedding day, she'd have liked to stop and look around. Despite her worst fears, St Aloysius was well signposted, and in a wide, tree-lined street with ample parking space. The BMW snaked easily into a space between a silver Rolls (one of Tina's brothers-in-law) and a vintage forest-green MG (Sam's boss). Thanking the driver, who showed a reluctance to let her continue unaccompanied, Anna hurried through the garlanded church lychgate and up the path. There were a few guests ahead of her, still trickling through the open church doors. A photographer sat in the shadows of the porch, head bent, loading film into a camera in an unhurried kind if way.

God, what on *earth*? That had to be the biggest, maddest, *pinkest* straw hat she'd ever seen – forget cartwheels, think fairground big wheel. Not only was it huge, it had giant scarlet and mauve cabbage roses bedecking the brim. It probably had little fairy lights that flashed on and off when darkness fell … Must be some madwoman on day release from the local loony bin. The poor thing might have been jilted on her own wedding day and been attending the nuptials of strangers ever since like a modern-day Miss Haversham. Please God let her get past and into the church without being stopped to listen to some harrowing story …

Head down, Anna had almost made it inside when she felt a hand claw at her arm. She turned quickly. 'Look, I'm afraid I really can't stop.'

'So, you've got here at last. I must say we've all been getting quite worried about you.'

It was Tina. If the hat was alarming, the rest of the outfit was positively bowel-chilling: a skin-tight lime green brocade dress with a plunging neckline revealing a good deal of mottled cleavage, topped by a skimpy gold lamé bolero. Anna didn't dare to check out the shoes. She was digging her nails into her palms in an effort not to break into hysterical laughter as it was, and backless gold mules with six-inch cobra-skin heels set off with rhinestone ankle chains were definitely more than she could cope with right now. Tina was looking her up and down critically. 'That's a very strange shade of blue. Puts me in mind of the mould you get on cheese. So what would you call that, then? Diesel?'

'Delphinium. Well, if you'll excuse me, I'd better go in. I wanted to say hello to Sam, before ... before ...' Her throat closed. Smiling blindly, she shook her arm free and entered the church.

Anna had expected St Aloysius to be all gold, incense and elaborately carved masonry, with stained glass windows of unbearably worthy saints and plastic lilies and ferns in every lace-doilied niche. She was utterly unprepared for the scene that met her eyes. The church was a cool haven, with pale flagstones and elegant columns soaring to a high, vaulted stone roof. The windows were simple arches of clear amber glass. Bowls of white roses and lily of the valley had been placed here and there, and tiers of white candles graced the steps to the altar, where a plain gold crucifix shone. The pews were packed; the organ was playing her favourite Bach prelude.

Her eyes filled with tears.

'Welcome to our little church.'

The voice was low and unctuous. An elderly priest, silver haired and stooping, was regarding her thoughtfully. What was the form here? Was she supposed to bow? Kiss his ring?

'Father O'Malley. Delighted to meet you.'

He held out his hand, and Anna found herself quite liking him until she noticed his eyes fix unwaveringly on her bosom as he took her hand in his and held it a little too long. Mercifully Jezza, one of the ushers, and one of Sam's oldest friends (they'd gone snowboarding together last winter; the photos had nearly given Anna a heart attack), stepped forward at that moment, grinning. 'Hi, Anna. How's it going?'

Disengaging herself from Father O'Malley, she turned. 'Jez, lovely to see you'

'Big day, no?'

'It certainly is.' Tears started to well. Oh, for God's sake. She must pull herself together. He handed her an Order of Service, gave a little bow. 'This way, Mrs Hardy. Looking stunning, if I may say so! Let me show you to your pew.'

He led her down the central aisle. Anna was an only child, and her parents had died within six months of each other five years ago, but a surprising number of her more distant relatives had made the journey, booking accommodation at various hotels in Fergustown. There was Grandma Taylor, and Aunt Gwen, perusing a prayer book disapprovingly. And that looked like Barbara in the angora beret and looking fidgety – Anna hoped she wouldn't light up in church.

She smiled as she passed, looking forward to seeing them all later, as the usher came to a stop. He was about to show her to her place when she caught sight of a handsome young man in immaculate morning dress, his grey and silver tie perfectly knotted, his matching cummerbund testament to a faultless sense of style, his face grave. Beside him sat another young man. Wasn't that JT, Sam's friend from Oxford? But JT was Sam's best man. Which could only mean … she looked at the handsome young man again, and realised it was Sam.

She turned to the usher. 'Excuse me, I think I'll just … if you don't mind … have a quick …'

'Of course.' Smiling, he stepped aside. Anna approached her son hesitantly. 'Darling …?'

'Mum.' Sam rose to his feet; she would never forget the look of relief on his face.

Anna embraced him, willing herself not to cry. As they hugged, over his immaculately tailored shoulder, she caught sight of Advancing Years Action Man, in a white satin suit, black silk shirt and salmon-pink bow tie, swaggering down the aisle towards them. A vision in skin-tight rainbow silk trotted a few paces behind, trying to keep up. She stiffened.

Sam followed her gaze. 'Mum? Is that …?'

Managing a smile, she nodded, kissed him lightly on the cheek, and gave him a little push in Tony's direction. Sam squared his shoulders and approached his father, holding out his hand.

Anna busied herself with the Order of Service for a few moments. When she looked up again, Sam and Tony were beaming at each other, hands pumping frantically. Resentment washed over her for a fraction of a second, to be followed an instant later by relief so great her hands shook. It was going to be all right.

Relief was followed by gratitude – to who or what, she neither knew nor cared. Fortunately it was entirely appropriate that her face should be wreathed in smiles; the thing was to suppress the snort of laughter that threatened to burst forth every time she caught sight of the white satin get-up. She risked a glance at Sam but his attention was now focused on the vision in rainbow silk who had finally caught up with her escort and was clinging onto his arm, puffing prettily and batting eyelashes so thick with mascara Anna wondered how she could see out of them.

'I'd like you to meet Tara-Louise, sport.' He goosed Tara-Louise's bottom, beaming proudly. 'My fiancée.'

Sam's eyes widened. 'Your …?'

Anna reflected that the last time she'd seen her son look that surprised was when he was seven and she'd given herself blonde highlights on the spur of the moment one winter afternoon when he was at school. Surprise on that occasion had been followed by howls of outrage; this morning it was supplanted by a deep blush as Sam, keenly aware of the risk to his physical equanimity an embrace would almost certainly engender since the rainbow silk left nothing to the imagination, gave Tara-Louise a manly handshake, too.

'So,' Tony surveyed the little group with a pleased smile. 'Here we all are, then. Beaut.'

Anna was racking her brains to think of a suitable reply when she was saved by a dramatic increase in the buzz of conversation among the congregation. There was a swish of expensive fabrics as women swivelled round, a muffled clatter as prayer books were knocked off pews. The organ fell silent, followed a moment later by a flurry of activity at the church door.

'Bloody hell, it's the bride!' An usher seized Tony and Tara-Louise by the arm and propelled them into the pew behind Sam and JT. As the organ struck up the first chords of the Wedding March, the usher, panicking, thrust Anna into position on Tony's other side, then moved discreetly to a side aisle, congratulating himself on his managerial abilities and hoping nobody would notice him texting Tokyo during the service about some shares he was thinking of offloading.

Anna sat down, her back ramrod straight, looking directly ahead and gripping her bag so tightly the clasp bit into her flesh. The golden cross gleamed back at her from the altar, reflecting the deep golds and burnt oranges of the candles' steadily burning flames in the depths of its burnished metal. She found the sight oddly comforting, and she'd composed herself to the point where she thought she could just about cope with things when she felt a sharp jab in her ribs. She risked a glance at Tony; he was staring towards the back of the church. He smirked at her. 'Hey, nice sheila.'

Anna was about to tell him that Sam's intended's name was Lucy, when she realised 'sheila' was yet another of Tony's Aussie-slang affectations. Gritting her teeth, she smiled cheerfully. The best way of dealing with it (though not the preferred method, which would have been to hit him sharply over the head with a blunt object) was to do what she used to do with Sam when he was a small boy and tried to annoy her by tipping his dinner over his head when it wasn't to his liking: viz, totally ignore it. As Mendelssohn rang gloriously through the church, the congregation rose as one to their feet. Anna rose with them.

Followed by a horde of tiny, giggling bridesmaids, pageboys and a stressed-looking matron of honour doing her best to keep order, the bride was processing slowly up the aisle, more beautiful by far than anything conceived of in *Bride*. Beside her, leaning heavily on her arm, tottered Eamonn, white with terror.

Anna blinked: that couldn't *possibly* be Tina's old wedding dress Lucy was wearing. The gossamer-fine guipure lace clung to Lucy's curves, the tight sleeves ended in long points over the back of her hands, the train swept out dramatically behind her to form a fishtail. A foaming veil spangled with tiny brilliants was held in place by a tiara that flashed as Lucy turned her head to acknowledge her guests with a smile so radiant it all but eclipsed the diamonds. As she drew abreast of Anna, she bowed her head slightly and smiled into her eyes. Anna returned the smile, full of love for her prospective daughter-in-law. And she saw the look of wonder on her son's face as his bride took her place beside him.

Beside her, Tony whipped out a large handkerchief patterned with luminous red and yellow kangaroos and trumpeted noisily into it. A bright pink straw cartwheel swivelled angrily in their direction.

Grinning, she leaned towards her ex-husband. 'Yeah, *beaut*, cobber.'

Smiling beatifically, Father O'Malley stepped forward, hand raised in benediction as creaking and groaning, the great doors swung closed at the back of the church and the service began.

CHAPTER TWENTY-EIGHT

Declan sat on a tombstone, gazing at a clump of dandelions.

The only way to get through these occasions was to try to feel nothing at all, and he was doing fine so far. It was the usual sort of wedding, with the usual sort of crowd, and the couple themselves seemed pleasant enough, though the old bat – Christ, why didn't someone tell her she looked like something out of a pantomime? Widow Twanky sprang to mind – was an even worse pain than he'd expected. The smallest pageboy had been wriggling around crying piteously just before the bride arrived, obviously desperate for a wee. Instead of nipping the poor little bugger pronto into the bog, or whipping him behind the nearest tombstone, she'd grabbed his hand, bent down and whispered something very quietly in his ear. Declan didn't know what she'd said, but the kid had been dead white when the old bat let go and pranced off to bollock the organist for not playing fast enough, or whatever, and he sure wasn't wriggling any more. No wonder her poor bastard of a husband looked as if he was going to top himself any minute …

The gravestones were getting him down. There was a tiny spider trying to get to the top of the cherub's head on the one nearest him. He'd almost make it, then get confused by the patch of lichen on the cherub's nose and slip back to its chipped and pitted sandstone chin.

Declan picked a blade of grass and held it patiently until the spider climbed aboard, then decanted the little creature carefully onto the top of the cherub's head. It sat motionless for a second or two before scuttling away out of sight as if it couldn't believe its luck.

He glanced at his watch.

Twenty past twelve.

It shouldn't be long now.

CHAPTER TWENTY-NINE

Half an hour later, the church doors were thrown open and the bells began to peal wildly. As the sun showed its face for the first time that morning the happy couple emerged, followed by the congregation ecstatically throwing confetti. Declan had positioned himself perfectly in the centre of the path a few yards from the porch and, pausing only to check his light meter, he set to work.

Anna let herself drift to the edge of the crowd, her face stiff with smiling, forcing herself to nod and shake hands with complete strangers.

'Isn't the bride just simply …'

'… the Vidor, so frightfully emotional.'

'… with Sam up for the Zircon contract – you know, he really is one top …'

'… where the loo is? One of the pageboys has just shat himself.'

'I love your suit, do tell me, where did you …?'

The more adventurous guests spilled into the graveyard, pastels and furs and top hats nodding and bobbing among the cypresses, reading aloud the inscriptions on the weathered memorials with appropriately witty substitutions (the IT faction) and tweaking any recent floral tributes into pleasingly symmetrical alignment (the Tina contingent).

Suddenly a space cleared in front of Sam and Lucy where they stood arm in arm, smiling as though they'd never stop, greeting well-wishers. Embracing, Lucy holding out her left hand to admire the narrow platinum wedding band sparkling in the sunlight, accepting congratulations, laughing and embracing again. Anna gazed at her son with pride and sadness as he kissed his new wife and whispered something in her diamond-studded ear. The gap closed again, and she retreated to the church porch, where she concentrated on reading the Mothers' Union poster about the forthcoming autumn jumble sale pinned on the porch wall and a request for funds for urgent repairs to the church roof.

Eventually it was time for group photographs. The key members of the party arranged and rearranged themselves, the bridesmaids and pageboys milling about, screaming and fighting, safe from adult censure as soon as their photograph was done. Declan was switching to his favourite Canon digital when he looked up and saw Anna standing silent and absolutely alone in the midst of the joyful cheers, the hearty congratulations. He would remember for the rest of his life that first sight of her.

As he watched, touched by her beauty and air of separateness, he saw the old Bat with the Hat (Nita? Zita?) swoop over, sink her orange talons into the woman's upper arm and drag her over to the enormous group of bickering relatives jockeying for position. Wincing on her behalf, he saw the woman in blue (what was that colour? Cornflower? No, delphinium. They had always been his favourite flowers, delphiniums) snap into defensively cheerful mode and allow herself to be shoved into the middle of the mêlée. He stepped forward involuntarily to ... to do what precisely? He stopped. He was being ridiculous. Anyway, duty called. He must make the best of the sun while it lasted. He set to work.

As soon as the group photographs were over, Lucy and Sam left for the reception. Their guests began to drift away to their cars, calling loud *au revoirs* (the IT faction) and 'see yez back at the ranch' (the Tina faction). Declan took several impromptu shots then gathered up his equipment, sprinted back to the van and set off for the hotel.

As the crowd thinned, Anna found herself alone again.

'Nice little service, wasn't it?' Tony stood beside her, Tara-Louise at his side. Tiny bows of the same material as her dress nestled among her lavish hair extensions; her wet-look lip gloss perfectly matched the sugar-pink stripes, her turquoise eye shadow the blue. 'You've got to admit he's done well for himself, our kid. Well, see you back at The Grand. Must say I could use a few tinnies.'

Tara-Louise smiled at Anna. 'I love weddings, don't you? And isn't her frock something? Would that be polyester, do you reckon?' She frowned. 'Though my friend Tracy-Sue had a cocktail frock like that once, and she said it itched so bad she …'

'Hey, Tara-Louise – she doesn't want to hear all that crap.' Smiling fiercely, Tony drew his fiancée's arm through his and clamped it sharply to his side. 'But hey, Anna, where's your wheels?'

'I …'

'You don't mean – you ain't gonna tell me …' He studied her with pitying incredulity. 'You got no wheels?'

Anna shrugged in what she hoped was an unconcerned manner. 'Nope.'

He narrowed his eyes. She knew that look; it meant he was closing in for the kill. 'I couldn't help noticing earlier. No date, either?'

'Oh, that's a shame! All on your own-eeh-oh at your son's wedding! Wasn't there a neighbour you could ask, or something?' Tara-Louise gazed at her, her eyes dark with sympathy. Anna wondered briefly what Mr Simwak-Kim would make of the raucous Tina faction; he had quite enough trouble coping with Western women as it was.

'No …' Oh, Jack. 'Well, the thing is there *is* someone …' For Christ's sake! Don't even *think* about going there. 'No.' She cleared her throat. 'No, there wasn't.'

Smirking, Tony stuck out his chest. 'Shame. Looks like you'd better bum a lift in the Merc.'

'No, really, thanks but …'

Seizing her arm with his left hand, Tony set off in the direction of the gold Mercedes parked opposite the lychgate, Tara-Louise clattering along gamely on her scarlet strappy sandals gripped firmly on his other side. After much ostentatious play with the remote key, and ignoring with set jaw

247

the blaring alarm that started up as he opened the passenger side and which took more than three minutes to silence, he gestured towards the suede-covered luggage rack behind the butterscotch leather seats. Anna didn't even hesitate. With the casual air of one to whom projecting gear levers, loose coils of seat belt strap, slews of maps, travel rugs and bottles of mineral water were mere trifles, she manoeuvred herself into the tiny space, smiling sweetly when Tony stuck his head over the back of the driver's seat and observed that if she'd worn stockings like that in his day he might have stuck around a bit longer. Anna survived the journey back to The Grand by trying to decide which of the Tina faction she'd least like to be marooned on a desert island with – a tough one – and which of the males encountered that morning she'd least like to have sex with – no contest: Father O'Malley.

A waiter (hardly more than eighty, by Anna's reckoning, and thus a mere junior) was waiting to greet them in the forecourt, overflowing now with parked cars. Lime-green helium balloons bearing the entwined initials S&L had been tied to potted shrubs in a festive manner, giving them the air of having been afflicted by some rare and virulent blight. Muttering darkly to himself, the ancient waiter conducted them down a side path to the grounds at the back of the hotel, where the reception was already in full swing. He accepted Tony's tip of what looked to Anna suspiciously like five pence with a look of contempt so great she had to restrain herself from hugging him.

'Hey, some shindig.' Tony stood gazing about him with a satisfied air. He seized Tara-Louise's hand. 'Time to put away a few tubes of the amber fluid before we get down to the tucker, I reckon.' Without a backward look he disappeared into the crowd, pulling his fiancée after him.

If the scenes in the churchyard after the wedding had been jolly, the reception was a positive riot. Guests milled about the vast central lawn, downing glasses of Pimms stuffed with veritable salads of brightly coloured fruit and sipping from brimming flutes of champagne – indeed, in some cases, both – and getting in the way of the harassed-looking waitresses bearing salvers loaded with small squares of toast topped with lime green and orange swirls. Large numbers of Eamonn's business colleagues and important clients had recently arrived (who knew what profitable contacts might be established?) and were recognisable by their too-blue, too-tight suits and hearty laughter. Several insalubrious and therefore inconsequential members of what was clearly a Tina-relatives' sub-faction (not important enough to be invited to the church, but useful inasmuch as they stoked the main players' self-importance) were also present, and were recognisable by their tendency to take two every time a dish of cocktail sausages or tray of drinks was proffered.

As Anna tried in vain to catch a glimpse of the bride and groom among the crowd, the elderly swing band dressed in boldly striped blazers and boaters, and stationed strategically by the drinks table, broke into a passionate albeit slightly off-key rendition of 'Love is Here to Stay', one of Jack's favourite tracks on their *Songs for Swingin' Lovers* CD. Anna bit her lip. Damn and blast them to hell, she'd been doing fine until then. She grabbed a flute of champagne, downed it, slammed the glass back on the tray and took another. The waiter responded with a supercilious smile, and hurried away.

Walking purposefully, as if she had somewhere very important to be, and gripping her glass tightly, Anna headed for the Scot's pine at the edge of the lawn, nodding politely to people as she passed. Beneath the shelter of the great tree's branches the air was still and deliciously scented; the effect was as calming as a cool draught of lemonade. Setting her glass down carefully in the rough grass she drew a tiny notebook and pencil from her bag and after a moment, began to write.

The last of the early morning rain clouds finally vanished; the pale sun rose higher in the sky, giving old ladies and long-estranged relatives a useful topic of polite conversation.

Declan moved through the crowd, observing, recording. He'd been keenly aware of Anna's presence from the moment she arrived, and her sadness whenever she thought she was unobserved. He'd taken several shots of her already, and intended to take several more.

Eamonn, thinking himself unobserved, crept into the hotel forecourt and on towards the circular flowerbed beside the drive. Drawing a crumpled sheaf of scribbled notes from an inner pocket he began to declaim his speech to a topiary peacock, unaware that Bernadette was watching, convulsed, from the staff loo window.

Kate, the matron of honour, thinking herself unobserved, slipped behind a clump of hydrangeas badly in need of pruning and downed the medicinal gin she kept in a Venetian perfume bottle in her handbag for such occasions. If that bastard Ben didn't propose to her soon, she'd ... she'd ...

Father O'Malley, thinking himself unobserved, slithered into the shrubbery beside the tennis court, gripping the oldest, fattest waitress firmly by the waist.

Desmond, in full morning dress now, sauntered through the crowd greeting the guests in a lordly manner and doing his best to look as if he hadn't a care in the feckin' world. Where the feck was Anna? Thank Christ! There she was, holding an empty glass and talking to some old bird about the weather. He hurried over, made some mad remark about the sunshine to the old bird, who nodded thoughtfully, then sidled up to Anna and whispered urgently in her ear. Anna stood frowning at the ground for a moment, then whispered a reply. Bidding a polite goodbye to the old bird who was still, apparently, chewing over his comment on the sunshine, they hurried off to the kitchen.

In the kitchen, wearing an impressively formal chef's hat somewhat at odds with the plastic apron, Connor screeched orders at the waitresses loading the microwaves with the Foil 'n' Freeze banquet the hapless delivery man had delivered early that morning. Desmond watched approvingly for a moment, then went over to the fridge; Anna followed, her stomach churning. Opening the door with a flourish, he drew out a tray of little gold pots. Anna took it gingerly – examined it – and let out a little whoop of joy. The Grand de-luxe *mousses au chocolat Grand Marnier* looked delicious – chilled to perfection, each pot brimming with a delicate froth of airy bubbles.

She handed the tray back to Desmond, who placed it reverently in middle of the refectory table.

'Feckin' great. But …?' He looked at her questioningly.

She nodded solemnly. 'Something's missing.'

'Right. Like I said, it's my opinion they need tartin' up.' He chewed at a thumbnail. 'Could get Bernadette to nip round the empty Pimms jars and collect up the maraschino cherries?'

Anna opened her bag and took out a brightly coloured carton. 'Or maybe …' She shook the contents onto the table, laughing as Desmond shouted with delight. Scattered across the dark wood was a glittering heap of tiny gold bells – the wedding confetti she'd been too upset to throw at the appropriate time, and for which omission she was now wholeheartedly grateful.

They stood beaming at each other for a second, then, with the utmost care, they set to work.

CHAPTER THIRTY

Half an hour later, Anna headed back to the reception, well satisfied with her handiwork. Two hundred and fifty gold pots of *mousse au chocolat Grand Marnier* that had been merely charming were now quite exquisite – or 'feckin' fantastic', as Desmond had put it as he'd slid the trays carefully back into the fridge. Each little pot of froth was now topped with a pair of tiny golden bells, the perfect decoration for a wedding breakfast dessert.

'Would yez look at that!' said an elderly waitress as she shuffled past bearing a stack of soup plates, tears of delight in her eyes. 'If it's not like some puddin' from the fairies' feast!'

Job done, thought Anna, as she negotiated her way through the crowd of guests outside which, fuelled by a steady intake of Pimms, seemed to have become markedly more animated during her absence. As she accepted a glass of champagne from a passing waiter she caught sight of Sam and Lucy in the distance, talking with Grandma Taylor. Anna smiled; they were probably enquiring discreetly where she'd bought the expensive but hideous set of Popular Cat Breeds place mats she'd sent as a wedding present so that they could exchange them. She was about to go over and join them when a very elderly man (one of Eamonn's important clients, if she remembered rightly) quavered up to the little group, bowed and began to make flirtatious advances to the old lady. It was clear from Grandma Taylor's response that she was not entirely averse to this. Grinning, Sam kissed her on the cheek and putting his arm round Lucy, discreetly withdrew. Anna was about to wave and catch their attention, when Sam pointed out someone in the crowd to Lucy. Anna saw that it was Tony and Tara-Louise; as she watched, Sam began to shepherd Lucy towards them.

Anna sighed. She was about to go in search of Barbara and hear the latest instalment in the saga of the crazed dope fiends who'd moved into the Islington flat below hers (a perfectly pleasant couple of medical students, according to Brian, Barbara's long-suffering husband) when she saw a bright pink straw hat, so enormous it knocked other guests headgear askew, making a beeline for Sam and Lucy from the opposite direction. Sam had begun to talk to Tony and Tara-Louise while the hat was still several feet away; as he introduced his new wife Anna saw it come to an abrupt halt. Suddenly her view was blocked by a couple from the IT faction arguing loudly about the merits of Mark Zuckerberg's management style. Stepping swiftly round them, Anna was just in time to see Tina bristling as she looked Tara-Louise up and down.

Lips thinned to invisibility, ankle chains rattling with rage (or quite possibly envy of the stripey bows and matching make-up) Tina watched sourly as Sam nodded at something his father said and Lucy made some pleasantry to Tara-Louise. They were chatting together when Tina stalked over and attached herself to the group. Conversation stopped at once, and more introductions were made, a touch less enthusiastically this time. Anna could tell that the conversation was stilted and, from Tina's body language, that she was being less than friendly to Tara-Louise, until suddenly Tony said something proudly to her and Tina reared back in surprise. She shook her head slightly as if to clear it – causing the Hat to wobble alarmingly – then engaged Tara-Louise in exaggeratedly animated conversation.

Anna drained her glass again, and was about to accept another from a hovering waiter's proffered tray in an attempt to raise her spirits, when a dessicated creature swaddled in bright orange fox furs caught her eye. It occurred to Anna with a pang of homesickness how much Roxy would love the fox furs, which were topped by a hat consisting almost entirely of plastic fruit. The wearer was so ancient she made Grandma Taylor seem a mere strip of a girl, so Anna was even more surprised to see her throw herself passionately at Tina in an apparent attempt to throttle her.

Anna had long been surprised that Tina had survived so long without a contract being taken out against her. This development was a thrill. Anna grabbed another glass from the waiter, hoping very much that nobody would take it into their heads to intervene. She was disappointed when, after a short tussle, it became apparent that Tina's assailant (from her mad banshee screeches, clearly a close relative) was simply drunk as a skunk and wanted Tina to lead her to another Pimms. fast.

Evidently deeming that the wisest course of action was to mime tolerant understanding until she could have the old girl thrown into The Grand's cellars for the rest of the reception, then taken out and shot, Tina waved a fluttering farewell to the surprised group. Then, pinning her still ranting relative in an armlock of steel, she scuttled away.

Bugger. Still, Tina's relative didn't look one to be easily deflected, and would cut up rough when no more Pimms was forthcoming. Hopefully she had a sten gun concealed beneath the furs, or better yet, a grenade. Anna looked at the new bride, expecting to see her dealing with the situation with a shrug and a light laugh but Lucy's attention was elsewhere. Clutching at Sam's arm she was gazing with concern at someone on the edge of the crowd: her father. As Anna watched, Lucy said something politely to Tony and Tara-Louise, grabbed Sam's hand and hurried off through the crowd towards him.

Anna sighed. Was she *ever* going to get a quiet word with her son and her new daughter-in-law? She was about to go in search of Barbara again (hearing about the dope fiends always cheered her up) when she became aware that Tony was waving enthusiastically at someone in the crowd – so enthusiastically, in fact, that it was obviously some long-lost friend. Anna looked around, surprised; she hadn't realised he knew anyone there. People were looking at her oddly. Why? Was there something wrong with …? Just a minute. She looked back at Tony; he waved with renewed vigour. Oh dear, it was her attention he was trying to attract. Nothing for it; better go and see what he wanted before he broke into an Australian version of a Maori haka.

Trying to look amused in a sophisticated sort of way, and concentrating on not tripping over the mole hills that littered the lawn or stepping in the plentiful cat turds, she strolled over.

'Hey, Annie. Just saying to Tara-Louise here, can't be much fun having to stand around solo with an empty glass all day at your own son's wedding. Let's do the decent thing and call her over.'

'Actually, I ...'

'So, you're still living in Brighton then?'

'Yes, I ...'

He flashed his teeth at Tara-Louise. 'Strewth, you wouldn't believe what a dump that place is, Princess. Practically still in the Dark Ages – most exciting thing you can do there is buy a stick of rock and visit the goldfish in the aquarium.'

Anna was stung. 'There's the theatre, and the cinemas – and the sea ...'

Tony roared with laughter. 'Jeez, pommie sea'd freeze the balls off a brass monkey. When we say sea we mean the good ole bright blue Indian Ocean, right, Tara-Louise?'

Tara-Louise looked doubtful. 'I guess, honey. I've never really been sure what it's ...'

'Beach so hot you get a tan just by thinking about it, right, Tara-Louise?'

'Well I guess you'd have to actually take your clothes off if you –'

He slapped her bottom hard. 'Not that we bother to hit the beach much. Hell, why would you when you've got your own bloody great pool at the bottom of your yard. And when I say yard, I mean acres of it, lush green grass and massive palm trees and ...'

Droves of starving man-eating tigers and wild boar hunting in packs, hopefully.

'Sounds great.' Anna gripped her glass tightly. 'Well, I really must be –'

He shot her a look. It was another expression she recognised: the message was *I'm going to hurt you now, but I'm going to pretend I don't know I'm doing it*.

'Must say I was surprised to hear you were in – what was it? – yeah, catering, these days.'

'I –'

'Shame. You used to have such big ideas.' He shook his head sadly. 'Guess there's only room for serious talent out there these days.'

'Look –'

'Gotta say I'm glad *I'm* not chopping up cabbages for coleslaw all day in some tin-pot art gallery passing itself off as Brighton's answer to the Albert Hall.'

'Tate.'

'Yeah. Feel real chuckered I've made it so big in graphics. Still, you know what they say.' He shrugged. 'Talent will out.'

Anna thought of her starred first in fabric design and the stream of work offers he'd refused to let her accept. She gripped the glass harder.

'Yup, got my very own chain of graphics agencies. Stretch right across Australia.'

He puffed out his chest. Anna wondered if anybody had ever actually burst from self-regard. Still, no worries – Tara-Louise was on hand to stitch him up again.

'Great.' She began to edge away. 'Well, I must be …'

'And as for a relationship, hell, I guess Tara-Louise – world-class babe in anyone's book, plus a shit-hot brain surgeon to boot – says it all about my prowess in *that* department.' He ran a forefinger down the front of Tara-Louise's ample chest. 'Ain't that right, Princess?'

Tara-Louise had been gazing absently into the middle distance; she jumped as Tony pulled her close.

'Betcha thinking about one your patients, aren't you, Princess?' He rolled his eyes at Anna. 'Happens all the time.'

Tara-Louise giggled self-consciously, and kissed him on the cheek; he made no attempt to wipe away the glistening pink smear of lip gloss.

'See? Tony glared at Anna. '*She* certainly isn't complaining about anything.'

Anna thought about having sex with Tony. It didn't take long; there wasn't very much to remember.

'And you're here all on your lonesome.' He smirked. 'Now don't get me wrong, but I figure you want to give a bit of thought as to why that might be.'

Because sodding Jack couldn't get a sodding late pass from sodding Ruth so he could come with me, OK?

'Cos I reckon it's the clobber. Your chassis's not in bad shape, considering, but you wanna take a tip from Tara-Louise here. Go for a bit of glitz, a bit of colour ...'

I know everything's going to go absolutely brilliantly, angel.
Oh yes, brilliantly.

Be thinking of you absolutely every second, darling.
But that's not enough.

'... oomph that hair up a bit ...'
Jack ... why aren't you here?
Her eyes filled with tears.

'Well, I think her hair's dinkum. And personally,' Tara-Louise pulled away from her fiancé, 'I think working in a caff's neat, too.' She directed a blinding smile at Anna.

Willing herself not to cry, she tried to smile back. 'Thanks. Really must be going now – things to do, people to ...'

'It's Englebert, bejasus!' With a glad but tremulous cry, one of the most senior of Eamonn's business colleagues launched himself at Tony, seized his hand and began to pump it violently up and down. Pimms splashed over Tony's white satin tux from the enormous tankard clutched in his assailant's other hand. 'Know yez anywhere! Bin me top favourite ever since *Please Release Me*! And to think O'Shaughnessy never gave us so much as a hint he was acquainted, much less said yez was attendin' the nuptials, sly divil!'

Pale with loathing beneath his tan, Tony began to back away, pulling the would-be fan with him since he steadfastly refused to relinquish his grip. Still pumping, he began to bawl questions about Englebert's recent musical activities. Anna

258

noticed with pleasure the sprig of mint dripping down her ex-husband's bow tie, and the segment of satsuma lodged in his soaking lapel.

'Cripes!' Tara-Louise looked fearfully at Anna. 'You reckon he's escaped from some loony bin?'

'Hell, no. No need to worry. The old boy's just Irish – pretending to think they know you is a tremendous compliment. Tony'll be thrilled.'

'Oh, right.' She still looked alarmed.

Panicky yelps now punctuated the eager inquisition taking place a few feet away. Anna smothered a grin – keep talking. 'I must say your work sounds absolutely fascinating, Tara-Louise. As a matter of fact I was watching a documentary on television a few weeks ago about brain surgery. Amazing, the advances they're making. Everything's so hi-tech – I couldn't believe the microsurgery stuff. There was a studio discussion afterwards. You know, experts arguing about the pros and cons of new treatments, patients who'd actually had the operations …'

The debate had been riveting, and Anna had been genuinely interested. As she outlined the gist of the programme, and the questions and issues raised, Anna found herself sincerely wanting to hear Tara-Louise's views. 'Seems to me it's impossible for a lay person to decide, so I'd be really interested to hear your opinion.'

Tara-Louise gazed at her. If she hadn't known she was an expert, Anna would have said she looked bemused. It must be because she was concentrating.

'Uh …'

Anna looked away, so as not to distract her. Tony had somehow managed to manoeuvre his would-be fan close enough to them to overhear the conversation; he looked none too pleased at what he'd heard. Well, bugger that; she'd show him there was more to her than coffee machines and coleslaw. She turned back to Tara-Louise. 'The latest treatment mimics a cardiac angioplasty, apparently –'

'Mmm.'

'Only here they thread a catheter through the body's arteries and introduce it into the brain aneurysm …'

'Uh huh?'

'Yes, and then they fill it with pliable …'

'Uh …'

'… coils, made of some sort of material developed in the space race, I think they said.'

'… huh?'

'And sort of seal it.'

'*Wow*.'

Tony gave a strangled squawk. Wresting himself from his admirer's grasp, he leapt to Tara-Louise's side and smiled fiercely at Anna. 'Doncha just *love* the way she's so cool?' He grabbed his fiancée's elbow. 'Nobody'd guess in a million years you were a brain surgeon yourself, Princess.' Twisting round smartly, he zapped Eamonn's colleague with the smile. 'Just got to have a word with my backing group here, grandad. Be over to autograph your pension book in two shakes of a dingo's twat, OK?'

Satisfied, the old man trotted away.

Ignoring Tony, Anna continued to talk about the programme. Galvanized into action by her fiancé's presence, Tara-Louise began to nod or shake her head interestedly at frequent intervals, occasionally repeating something Anna had said with an earnest expression.

'… patients' blood pressure, but they said that hasn't been quantified yet.'

'Cripes no, mate.'

'So what kind of post-operative complications would you expect, then?'

'Excuse me?'

'I was wondering what problems might arise after the op.'

'Problems? … After the op?' Tara-Louise was staring at her like a rat in a trap.

Tony jabbed her hard in the ribs.

'Oh, you mean like *after* the op? Well, let's see …' Frowning, Tara-Louise nibbled at a perfectly French-manicured

260

fingernail. Suddenly her face lit up. 'Hey. Bet you'd have the bastard of a headache.'

'*Oh, for chrissakes*!' Tony clapped his hand to his forehead with a strangled scream.

Tara-Louise bit her lip. 'Screw, did I get that wrong, Tiny?'

'Wrong? *Wrong*? Bastard of a headache? What the fuck happened to all the frigging medical terms we practised on the frigging plane?'

Hmm … call her picky, but it had occurred to Anna that 'bastard of a headache' wasn't exactly the response you'd expect from a brain surgeon.

'And it's Tony! *Tony*! How many times have I got to tell you, you stupid frigging cow?' He saw Anna's expression, and attempted a laugh through gritted teeth.

In fact, now she came to think of it …

She began to put two and two together, and she was opening her mouth to ask some searching questions when she saw Sam and Lucy approaching, holding hands and positively glowing with happiness.

'Mum!' Letting go of Lucy's hand, Sam put his arms round her and hugged her. 'Didn't get a chance to say it earlier, but you look fantastic. Can't tell you how… how …' His voice thickened. Holding her away from him, he looked directly into her eyes. 'Just want to say thank you.' He hugged her again. 'For … you know …' His grip tightened. 'Everything.'

Anna ruffled his hair, painfully aware that it was probably the last time she'd ever make that small, maternal gesture, and hugged him back so hard the starch in his snowy shirt front crackled.

Then she put him gently away from her.

Lucy held out her hand to show Anna her ring as Sam approached Tony, who'd been watching the little scene, scowling. 'Dad?'

His father eyed him warily.

Sam took a deep breath. 'Just want to say how glad – no, how *proud* I am that you're here.'

Anna willed herself not to look away. She was to be glad for the rest of her life that she didn't, as Sam slung his arm round his father's shoulders and made the leap from child to man in front of her eyes.

'Better late than never, eh, Dad?' he grinned.

Relief flashed across Tony's face and was gone. 'Good to be here, sport – son. Say, heard the one about the lady photographer in the jungle …?' Clapping Sam heartily on the back, he launched into a long and involved joke about the sexual predilections of gorillas.

Declan clicked the shutter, thanked the smallest bridesmaids for being so patient, handed out the pink sugar mice he kept in his pockets for rewards on such occasions and looked after them, grinning, as they scampered away. He caught sight of the Woman in Blue, as he'd come to think of her. Saw the pain on her face as she gazed at a young man – hey, wasn't that the groom? – and a tall blond bloke who had the groom in fits.

He raised the camera and took yet another shot of her.

'Honestly, Anna, Sam's father coming to the wedding really has made his day, you know.' Lucy gripped Anna's hand, eyes shining, then turned to Tara-Louise. 'And Mummy thinks it's *super*, having a real surgeon in the family!'

Still laughing (Anna dreaded to think what the joke's punchline had been) Sam gave his father a friendly shove, reached for Tara-Louise and planted a kiss on her cheek. 'Well, I'll know where to come now, won't I?' he grinned. 'Lucy – my wife – is always telling me I need a brain transplant. *My wife* … Mmm. I rather like the sound of that …' Reaching out, he drew Lucy to him and kissed her.

As Tony looked away, he caught Anna's eye; she looked back at him levelly. Tara-Louise looked from one to the other, biting her lip and plucking at her hair extensions with an air of desperation. Suddenly she took a shaky step forward and tapped Sam on the shoulder. 'Look, mate, I gotta tell ya …'

The trials and terrors, the frequent despair and constant deprivations of the last twenty-five years rocketed though Anna's head like a tape on fast-forward.

How glad I am. How proud I am. For you know, Mum ... Everything.

She swallowed hard. If she loved her son, she'd give him this last gift.

Keep what she'd just learnt to herself.

Laughing lightly, she slipped her arm round Lucy's delicate, lacy waist. 'Hey, don't worry – he's only kidding.' Looking directly at Tony, then at Tara-Louise, she emphasised her next words. 'You don't have to tell him.' She managed another laugh. 'I'm pretty sure Sam knows brain transplants aren't possible.'

'Huh?' Tara-Louise's brow furrowed; clearly this was news to her. 'They ...'

Grabbing a canapé from the tray of a passing waiter with a cry of 'Great tucker, sport!' (and ensuring forever Australians' reputation for ill-breeding with the staff of The Grand) Tony shoved the delicacy between his fiancée's perfect, glossy lips.

Sam glanced at his mother uncertainly, clearly hoping she wouldn't be upset by witnessing what was clearly some private love game peculiar to his father and his fiancée. Seeing his anxiety, Anna responded with a radiant smile. Then, restraining herself from seizing the tray and braining her ex-husband with it and throttling him with his bloody luminous kangaroo hanky, she made her final effort for her son. Gritting her teeth, she slipped between Tony and Tara-Louise and linked arms tightly with them both. 'I just want you to know,' she smiled sunnily up at each of them in turn, 'that *I* think it's great you're both here, too.'

Amid cries of 'Beaut, Anna' (Tara-Louise), 'Nice one, Mum' (Sam), 'Oh Anna, what a lovely thing to say' (Lucy) and 'No sweat, mate' (a profusely perspiring Tony), everyone embraced everyone else.

At last Anna disentangled herself. 'And now, if you'll all excuse me, I need the loo. See you later, Tony, Tara-Louise.'

She backed away, fluttering her fingers à la Tina at Lucy. 'Back in a jiff.'

Sam was grinning at her. 'I'll grab you some more champagne, Mum.'

She smiled at him gratefully. 'Lovely, darling.'

She didn't start to run until she was sure she was lost to view among the crowd, but stopped suddenly as she cannoned into some guy with his back to her.

'Sorry, I'm so sorry …' Please God she hadn't made him spill red wine all over himself.

He turned, and lowered the camera he'd been holding. Phew, not red wine, thank goodness. Of course – it was the wedding photographer. She'd noticed him taking photos of her several times, maybe Sam had asked for some specially. He grinned at her. She couldn't help but notice his black hair in need of cutting, angular jaw, dark brown eyes …

'No worries – reckon I've got quite enough shots of Widow Twanky over there already.' He nodded his head in Tina's direction; she was bending down, frowning, delivering a lecture to the youngest bridesmaid.

Widow Twanky? Anna burst out laughing.

'Oops, sorry, she'll be your son's relative now – apologies. Sure, I bet she's an absolute charmer when you get to know her.'

'Oh, absolutely …'

They looked at each other for a moment. Anna stirred reluctantly. 'Well, I must be …'

'Declan O'Halloran.' He held out his hand.

Anna took it. It was big, square, and warm – comforting. 'Anna Hardy. Mother of the groom.'

He grinned. 'I know.'

She turned away. 'I must be getting on, if you'll excuse me, Mr …'

'O'Halloran'.

O'Halloran? Where had she heard …?

'Just want to say what a beautiful colour your outfit is. Delphinium, I think that would be?'

264

She turned back. 'Why yes, it is! Thank you!'

They looked at each other a moment longer.

Then she hurried away.

Mercifully, the foyer was empty. The roses and carnations had brightened it up considerably and the carpet had been vacuumed, though it occurred to Anna as she hurried past that the effect might have been improved if the vacuum cleaner had been put away afterwards rather than left in the corner by the lift.

The walls of the Ladies were bilious green marble, the bevelled mirrors above the grimy washbasins were dusty, the brass fittings tarnished, the grubby roller towel dangled limply to the tiled floor. The musty air was freezing, and the slightest sound echoed. No matter; she was the sole occupant, which meant she could compose herself without having to chat about fur stoles and six-inch heels to some crazed member of the Tina faction or incomprehensible hi-tech matters to some glossy twenty-something IT exec.

The first thing she had to do was calm bloody down, and the best way to do that was just breathe slowly and deeply until she felt better. Simple, really. Stepping out of her shoes, she laid her bag on the marble counter, trying to avoid the pools of liquid soap and tangles of unidentifiable hairs. Now… in and out … Good. Excellent. And again … in and out …

She was drawing in another deep breath when she caught sight of herself in the mirror. Smeared and spotted it might be, but not smeared and spotted enough to prevent her from seeing that her pillbox hat was tilted at a rakish angle, several curls had come loose from their moorings and her nose was shiny. Bugger, bugger, *bugger*. Still, no good getting worked up about that now. Probably no-one had noticed. So concentrate, now, and it's slowly … In and …

So you're not designing, then?

… ooooout –

Not as if you actually got anywhere with it, is it?

With a shriek of rage, Anna snatched up her shoes and hurled them with all her force at the mirror. They hit with a satisfying *thwack*, but far from cracking the glass into the scarred and splintered shards she'd hoped for they slid limply down the pinkish smears of hair lacquer and mists of eau de cologne and fell with a dispirited plop into the washbasin. Jesus Christ – breathing wasn't going to even *begin* to make her feel better. *Bastard* – she should have throttled him with his fluorescent bloody kangaroos. She began to bang her head against the mirror; this she found, helped quite a lot.

She was still banging away when she heard the door open behind her, and footsteps clacking across the floor. Christ. Quickly, she jerked her head back a couple of inches and pretended to be checking her eye make-up in the mirror as the footsteps came to a halt beside her and the new arrival started to do something energetic to her hair. By sheer good fortune, Anna's bag was within reaching distance on her other side. Taking out her mascara, she applied another coat, humming in what she hoped was a casual, light-hearted fashion. Found her eyeshadow, and smoothed on a touch more. Licked the tip of her little finger and smoothed her already smooth eyebrows. Damn, there wasn't much more she could fix with her head tilted back and her eyes half-shut – but the figure beside her showed no signs of going. But that must mean her head-banging hadn't been spotted. In which case she could powder her nose, fix her curls, straighten her hat and get the hell out of there. Taking care to keep up the humming, she rummaged busily in her bag for her powder, straightened up, looked in the mirror – and met Tara-Louise's eyes.

'Hi there, Anna.'

'Tara-Louise! Gosh, I didn't realise it was you.' From the look on her face she had seen the head banging.

'Just came to spritz some more Glamagloo on my extensions and do a bit of backcombing. Jeez, I tell you, they're more trouble than flaming implants.'

'Ah.' Sod her shiny nose, and she didn't care if the rest of her hair collapsed and her hat fell down the lav. 'Well, I'm just going to pop into the loo.'

'Strewth, some dunny this is, isn't it? Like something out of a horror film, you know, that *Shining* one, where Warren Beattie – no, Jack Nicholson …'

'Golly, yes. Anyway, if you'll excuse me.'

'Anna?'

Tony's going to laugh himself sick when I tell him what I saw.

Turning away, Anna headed briskly for a stall.

Tara-Louise followed her. 'I just wanted to say –' She stopped and swallowed. 'Look, Tiny …'

'Tony.'

'Yeah, sorry. Tony'll kill me if he finds out I've blown the gaffe, but the way he's always knocking you makes me want to chunder, I'm not kidding.'

Chunder? Didn't that mean throw up? Anna turned round slowly. Tara-Louise stood gazing at her, twisting her hairbrush, its pink shell-encrusted back twinkling in the dim light like some unlikely Fabergé jewel. 'Pardon?'

'It gets right up my jacksie, mate.'

'It does?'

'Yeah. If I was you I'd get dirty with him. Give him a good smack in the mouth. The way that whacker treats sheilas, honestly …' Turning back to the mirror, she began to backcomb her fringe vigorously. 'I don't mind telling you, I'm sick of it. Plus I've had it up to here with the way he always makes me let him wear the maid's uniform every time we have a naughty.'

'He does?'

'Yeah, the flaming mongrel. So here goes …' Laying down her brush, she swivelled round to face Anna again. 'Not only is yours truly not a brain doctor – I'm not his flaming fiancée, either.'

Anna returned slowly to the washbasins. 'You're not?'

'No way, mate. Hired me from a flaming agency, didn't he?'

'Agency? You mean as in ...' Anna swallowed. '*Escort agency*?'

'Yeah. Elite Escorts of Sydney. Must have cost him a fortune for a whole week, plus he booked Special Services. Though we flew tourist, mean bastard.'

That was Tony, all right. Now Anna knew she wasn't kidding.

'But why? I mean surely he could have brought a girlfriend?'

Tara-Louise burst out laughing. 'Are you joking? He's got his girlfriend minding the store while he's away. Mate of mine lives pretty close to it, Candy-Chantelle – she works for another agency – so I got her to take a look. Always useful to know what the bloke's got going on at home, in my line, though gotta say Candy-Chantelle didn't say much – couldn't speak for laughing.' She adjusted an extension. 'Must be a real dog.'

Chassis's not in bad shape, considering

Removing her hat, Anna began to unpin her hair. She needed something to do with her hands to stop them shaking, and anyway she'd have to take it all down before she could pin it up again.

Beside her, Tara-Louise turned to the mirror and scrutinised her reflection. 'Strewth, my right eyelash's starting to go walkabout.' Taking a tiny tube of glue from a compartment in her bag, she unpeeled what appeared to be a row of tarantula legs from her eyelid and began to repair the damage. She giggled. 'Oh, and he hasn't got a chain of design agencies, either.'

Hairpins showered into Anna's washbasin. 'He hasn't?'

'Cripes, no.' Tara-Louise affixed the tarantula legs to her eyelid once more and pressed them firmly into place. 'Just a corner shop in Newcastle.'

'*Newcastle*?'

'Little suburb just outside Sydney. Jeez, what a dump.'

And you're cooking, *you say.*

Anna picked up the pink hairbrush and began to tug it savagely through her hair.

Tara-Louise examined her other set of lashes critically, then turned her attention to her lip gloss. 'Rubbish, these cheap brands. If that's wet look, I'm the Pope's salsa instructor.' Sighing heavily, she produced a turquoise plastic pot, applied more, then tilted her head on one side thoughtfully. 'Though to be fair, he did say it had a photocopier.'

A corner shop.

A photocopier.

But hang on – this trip must have cost him a fortune. Air tickets (albeit tourist class), car hire, hotel room ... And there was a good chance the size-too-small safari suit and flashy tux had been bought specially for the occasion – there couldn't be a lot of call for either in the suburbs of Sydney.

Anna laid the hairbrush down very carefully on the counter.

Getting Tony to part with money had always been like trying to part a heroin addict from his fix.

She remembered their first meeting. She'd been standing in the canteen queue at college when the tall, blond Jude Law-lookalike ahead of her had flashed a blinding smile and started chatting. After five minutes he'd asked her to lend him a fiver until his grant came through. Hard up herself, but already fatally smitten, she'd lent him a tenner and bought him lunch. He never repaid the tenner, or reciprocated the lunch, but she'd attributed that to his preoccupation with his Work. Before she knew it, he'd moved his few belongings into her bedsit and she was cooking him supper every night. Not long after that, she'd found she was pregnant.

Marriage hadn't changed things. The first Christmas they were married, she'd asked if she could have as a present a secondhand hoover she'd spotted for sale in the *Brighton Argus* small ads. He'd smiled vaguely, criticised at length the brilliant riot of sunflowers on the fabric design she'd just completed and asked where supper was. On Christmas morning he'd placed an enormous gift-wrapped box under their tiny tree; inside, wrapped in layer after layer of festive wrapping paper (she could remember even now her excitement as she ripped them off, sure that he'd decided to surprise her with something much more exciting) was a red plastic dustpan and brush.

Fatherhood hadn't changed things. She'd been the only new mother on the ward whose husband never brought flowers – or anything else, for that matter – at visiting time …

Unless he'd recently undergone conversion to some religious faith (unlikely in view of the unpleasant remarks he'd made about her job/appearance/solo status) or discovered he had some ghastly terminal disease (unlikely in view of the burgeoning paunch and aggressively healthy tan) there was some ulterior motive behind his visit. She turned abruptly to her companion. 'Tara-Louise? Why's he doing all this?'

Tara-Louise applied a final slick of gloss, her forehead furrowed in thought. Then she replaced the lid on the little pot and regarded Anna earnestly in the mirror. 'Reckon the bastard thinks he's got something to prove.'

Anna looked away and started to wind her hair into a chignon; Tara-Louise pencilled a beauty spot above her upper lip. Anna was trying to deal with a particularly troublesome curl when she caught Tara-Louise's eye in the mirror.

'Well, the bugger's dead right about one thing, anyway.' Tara-Louise shovelled her makeup back into her bag with a flourish. 'He has.'

They stared at each other for a moment, then started to laugh.

It was some time before they managed to stop; whenever Anna hiccupped to a halt, Tara-Louise would relate some anecdote about the journey from Sydney ('… mile high club – he just wouldn't take no for an answer. Trouble was …') and whenever Tara-Louise managed to regain control, Anna would regale her with memories of her marriage ('Pink rash. He was absolutely convinced he'd got …'). After some time Anna looked at her watch. 'Christ – the wedding breakfast'll be starting any minute. We'd better be getting back. I'll just finish fixing my hair.'

Tara-Louise inspected her critically. 'No offence, but it looks a heck of a lot better down. It looked great when you were brushing it. Why don't I …?' Quickly, she unpinned Anna's hair and arranged it in a glossy curtain around her shoulders. 'There you go.' Tara-Louise surveyed the result with satisfaction. 'Eat your heart out, Julia Roberts. Take a look, mate.'

Taking a tissue from her bag, Anna wiped the mirror clean.

Her eyes were clear, her cheeks pink from laughing. The blue velvet glowed, the corsage of tiny cream orchids lent *le tout ensemble* a festive air. She looked, it occurred to her with surprise, happy. She was about to pick up her bag when she was struck by an appalling thought. 'Christ, Tara-Louise – Tony'll have fed Sam the whole pack of lies by now. God knows what it'll do to him if he finds out the truth – he's over the moon everything's turned out so well. And Lucy, too.' Not to mention sodding Tina, who'd probably order sodding Father O'Malley to annul the union on the spot if she discovered that the extent of Tony's design franchise was a single corner shop in a Sydney suburb and that his fiancée was actually a high-class escort rented for the wedding.

'No worries there, mate – we're flying back tomorrow.' Tara-Louise handed Anna her bag, picked up her own and winked at her. 'And you can bet no-one's gonna hear a chook's cheep about any of this from *me*.'

Anna kissed her on the cheek.

Arm in arm, they hurried out of the Ladies.

271

CHAPTER THIRTY-ONE

The Grand Hotel's enormous dining room, with its flaking mushroom-distempered walls, high cracked ceiling and beige polyester drapes, normally had the allure of a station waiting room. Today, however, it was transformed. A great many round tables draped with white damask cloths, set with polished crystal glasses and shining silverware, had been placed in clusters round the room; in the centre was a smaller table bearing a cake composed of so many elaborately iced and curlicued tiers that Anna finally gave up trying to count them. Fronds of delicate greenery spilled over the silver plinth, rose petals had been scattered liberally over the table's pale pink cloth. Tall beeswax candles glowed everywhere, softly illuminating the bowls of cream roses set at the centre of the guests' tables, winking off the crystal and silver.

The effect was magical.

Everyone had gathered for the wedding breakfast, and the room was filled with the hubbub created by the (mostly) cheerful guests as they argued, laughed and (occasionally) broke into song. Three longstanding family feuds were repaired, and a new one was begun: two flirtations among the IT faction developed promisingly, one of them being consummated in the gents between the first and second courses and resulting in a pregnancy that led to marriage the following Christmas. One of the plumper waitresses had her bottom pinched frequently by an elderly business colleague of Eamonn's so drunk that when she finally slapped his hand he slid quietly off his chair with a loud fart and thence under the table, where he fell asleep and wasn't found until next morning when the cleaner was hoovering.

If Tina had scored a personal triumph with the decor of the top table, where the gold-embossed tablecloth was liberally swagged with lime-green ferns and the roses were a violent tangerine hue, she had, thought Anna grimly as she lifted her glass to her lips, excelled herself with the seating plan; there might be no way she could keep the Mother of the Groom off the top table but at least she could make sure she was seated between the wedding breakfast companions from hell. Anna spent the first course listening to Lucy's Great Uncle Liam recount in great detail his problems with his new dental plate, which he removed and brandished in her face whenever he wished to demonstrate a particularly startling point – the way one of the croutons accompanying the lobster bisque had wedged itself between the bright pink plastic palate and a glistening false molar, for example, or the Pimms stains that had dulled the silver wires and which he wagered no amount of scrubbing with lav cleaner would remove.

Since Great Uncle Liam was Lucy's godfather, and had let Anna know as she sat down that he hadn't yet made up his mind whether he would be leaving the considerable fortune he'd amassed from manufacturing plastic light-up models of Jesus (the top of the range version had a flashing crown of thorns and stigmata that glowed in the dark, apparently) to his god-daughter or the local cats' home, she was only too aware of the need for forbearance. Mercifully his attention had been claimed by his other neighbour as the waiters placed their pheasant royale before them. Her stomach rumbling with hunger, Anna was cutting into the tender meat with a sigh of relief when she felt a hand on her knee. Jesus Christ. Tina had placed Father O'Malley on her right, with instructions no doubt to grill Anna on her religious beliefs and bring her Into the Fold by the time liqueurs were served.

Unfortunately Father O'Malley appeared to be more interested in matters corporeal, and she spent the next half hour swatting his clammy hand away from her thigh with one hand while forking up anything on her rapidly cooling plate that didn't require cutting (which eliminated everything except the peas and a couple of baby carrots) with the other. He was leaning towards her bosom with a gleam in his eye, yellowing forefinger poised to finger her corsage, when a sweating waitress leaned between them in order to remove their empty plates. Anna took the opportunity to turn swiftly to Great Uncle Liam, incontestably the lesser of the two evils, and enquire with urgent concern how his plate had stood up to the pheasant. Delighted at her interest, he began a lengthy illustrated answer involving the shreds of semi-masticated poultry currently trapped between the upper mandibles. Restraining herself from wiping away the gravy that was dribbling down his hoary jowls and onto his wing collar, and keeping an interested smile firmly in place, Anna allowed her thoughts to wander.

The present company might leave something to be desired, but they were the personification of charm compared to bloody Tony. It would be a long time before she forgot the lengths he'd gone to get what he obviously considered to be his revenge, or she forgave the insulting remarks he'd made. Right now she could see he had his arm slung round Tara-Louise's shoulders, and was recounting an anecdote about the time he'd fought a white shark – 'teeth big as harpoons and sharp as razors, mate' –to a small, white-faced pageboy. According to Tony he'd stunned it with a fearless karate chop before finishing it off with the hunting knife strapped to his calf; tossing the corpse casually aside to be devoured by its hungrily lurking shark relatives – 'cunning as dunny rats, sharks are, mate'.

As the pageboy ran off in tears in search of his mother, Tony roared with laughter and clicked his fingers at a passing waiter for another Fosters.

Anna leant forward anxiously – to see Tina smiling approvingly at Tony, glass raised, little finger crooked.

'Just what the little shite –' she swigged at her wine, '– pardon me, *lad*, needs. Told him I'd cut his willy off if he didn't wait for a pee till after the service. Burst into tears then, too. Eamonn's nephew – well, you can see the family resemblance, can't you?' She dabbed at the corner of her mouth with her napkin. 'I simply shudder to think what he'll be like when he grows up. Talk about lack of spunk. Well, I mean, look at his uncle.' She darted a venomous look at Eamonn, hunched beside her, leafing through his notes with shaking hands, then turned sharply towards Tara-Louise, causing her hat to slip forward over her eyes at a rakish angle. 'I wonder – is there any treatment you could suggest, Doctor? Drugs, perhaps? Or electric shocks …?'

Anna missed Tara-Louise's response as at that moment a hand tapped her shoulder lightly.

'Anna, just to let yez know.' Desmond stood beside her chair. He bent down, grinning. 'Had a word with her ladyship before the bisque. Told her senior management had decided to change crèmes brûlées to Grand de-luxe Chocolate Mousse Grand Marnier …' He dug her in the ribs, snorting with laughter. 'Wait for it – oh Mary and Joseph and Jesus, bless us.' Plucking a shocking pink silk bandanna from the breast pocket of his morning coat he wiped at the tears of mirth that ran down his face '… *feckin' Royale.*'

'Desmond! You didn't!'

'Feckin' did.' He leaned closer. 'Told the old cow 'tis what Prince Charles and Lady Di had for their nuptial pud. Said t'was a deadly secret vouchsafed to me by Connor, who used to be the Royal Dessert Maker till he got the call from The Grand.' He mopped at his eyes. 'I tell yer, thought she was goin' to wet herself, so I did.'

Anna started to laugh.

'Gotta go – t'is time to fetch 'em in. Jest thought you'd like to know.'

And he was gone, striding towards the doorway where the two youngest waitresses waited, each holding a silver tray bearing a glittering pyramid of tiny gold pots. As Desmond reached them he struck a match and lit the little bouquet of sparklers he'd positioned at the apex of each pyramid. Then to gasps of delight from the guests and a round of applause that as far as Anna was concerned made all the tribulations of the morning worthwhile, the waitresses solemnly entered the dining room. Followed by Desmond, bowing in dignified acknowledgement of the compliments of the guests, they began to distribute the mousses.

276

'... some feckin' newfangled cream they just brought out that's s'posed to shrink 'em, but they're still the size of grapefruit and the spray did more for me itching. Demand to be put back on it, so I did, but when Doctor O'Flynn took a squint up me back passage she discovered ...'

Having disposed of his dessert by the simple expedient of lifting the pot to his lips and downing the contents in a single slurp, Great Uncle Liam had abandoned discussion of his plate in favour of a discourse on his Problems with Piles. Anna lifted a spoonful of mousse to her lips, looked at the foaming chocolate bubbles and laid the spoon quickly down again. She was casting about for a polite way of changing the subject (to what? the horror of hernias? the perils of prostate?) when she heard the welcome sound of a spoon being tinkled gently but insistently against crystal. Thank God – the speeches. She looked up. Desmond was standing behind Eamonn's chair, and imperiously tapping a spoon against an empty wine glass. Gradually silence fell, punctuated now and again by occasional rumbling belches and bursts of flatulence.

'Good afternoon, ladies and gentlemen, and welcome to the Grand Hotel, priceless gem in the glittering diadem that is Irish hospitality, rare orchid among the exotic blooms otherwise known as Irish five-star hotels, and introducing *Mousse de Luxe Royale* ...' He bowed deeply in Tina's direction. She responded, causing her hat to tip even further forward. She swore, then recalling herself, adjusted it regally. '... queen of majestic desserts. Welcome, on this most splendid of occasions, to the wedding breakfast of Mr and Mrs Samuel M Hardy.'

There was a moment's silence. Then, led by the IT contingent, there was a burst of applause. It swelled as the relatives joined in; reached a crescendo as Eamonn's business colleagues and clients followed. Suddenly all the guests (apart from those incapacitated by mental infirmity or alcohol, or in several cases, both) were on their feet, turning towards the bride and groom, clapping and cheering. Sam and Lucy rose, hands tightly clasped, and smiled and waved at their well-wishers, illuminated in the sudden shaft of sunlight that shone through the window behind them and looking for all the world, thought Anna, like the prince and princess in some exquisite fairy tale.

Declan, leaning against the mantelpiece, raised his camera casually. Took a single shot.

Silver tinkled against crystal again. 'And now,' Desmond indicated Eamonn with a lordly gesture, 'pray silence for the Father of the Bride, Mr Eamonn O'Shaughnessy.'

The applause subsided and the guests sat down as the sun went in again. Eamonn, cowering in his chair beside Tina in a haze of cigarette smoke, looked round wildly as an expectant hush descended. 'Me? ... It's *me*? Now? ... *Already*? But ...'

Wordlessly, Tina reached out a claw and yanked him to his feet. He stood shaking, his notes rattling like autumn leaves in his nerveless hand. After a moment he stubbed out his cigarette, picked up his glass and drained it. Looked at his waiting audience, reached for Lucy's glass and drained that too, opened his mouth and tried to speak. Failed. Coughed. Tried again.

'Afternoon. Ladies. Gentlemen. Great pleasure to. Yes.' He squinted at his notes.

Tina leant towards him, eyes narrowed to glittering slits, hissing. 'Up! Speak *up*!'

He jumped, and dropped his notes on the table. 'Willco.' He looked up, eyes bulging with terror. 'Notes gone, so share with you all l'le story about m'daughter Lucy when l'le tiny baby. Mother – m'beautiful lady wife here – went to hairdresser – this in days before Tina wore wig, see ... forgot to take baby with her when she left! Thing is, Lucy perf'ly happy all mornin. No crying t'all – not *t'all* —till mother came to c'lect her!'

There was an embarrassed stir among the guests. Puce with rage, Tina scrabbled among the detritus of the wedding breakfast, snatched up his notes and shoved them violently into his hand.

''Kay. Try 'gain.' Eamonn peered at them. 'Still can't make it out ...'

He held the tattered scraps towards the nearest candle just as Tina thrust it towards him. The edges caught, slowly at first, then flaring suddenly into a brilliant yellow blaze. There was a collective gasp of horror. Shaking his head sorrowfully, Desmond moved forward, picked up Eamonn's wedding speech by an as yet undamaged corner and dropped the flaming mass into a handy water jug beside the orange roses. Eamonn stood goggling. He was about to subside, shaking, into his chair, ready for whatever the Good Lord saw fit to visit him with next – he should've known he'd never get away with his visits to the betting shop on Fridays, or the strip club every Monday when Tina thought he was at Rotary – when he heard hoarse shouts, accompanied by a dull, repetitive thumping. Slowly he raised his aching head and gazed round the dining room. Feck! Great Uncle Liam was banging his empty pudding pot on the table like a baby banging his rattle in his high chair and shouting, 'Speech! Speech!' at the top of his voice.

Mary Mother of Joseph. No sorry, Lord, no offence, *Jesus*, deliver him! If he disappointed Great Uncle Liam, Lucy wouldn't get the money from the light-up Jesuses! All right, so Lucy wouldn't care a fig but Tina would make his life even more of a hell! She might even start insisting on her conjugal rights again like she did that time she found that copy of *Knave* in his briefcase!

The noise was getting louder. Sam and Lucy's friends had started to join in, and his colleagues were banging on their tables, too.

'Mr O'Shaughnessy? Eamonn?' Young husband of Lucy's – nice boy, could see he made Lucy very happy – was leaning over, grinning, handing him a glass of wine. 'Go for it, sir!'

Eamonn hesitated. Then he grinned back. Downed the wine, and did as he was bid.

''Kay. Lessee. Tell you l'le joke.' There was a roar of approval from what he now thought of as *the crowd*. ''bout l'le street in Belfast. One side of street, Catholic shops. Other side's Protestants. On one side's Catholic cobbler, other side's Protestant cobbler. Lotta competition between 'em, right? Constantly vyin to outdo each other, get the picture? 'kay. Anyway, one day Catholic cobbler puts up a sign over his shop – great big gold crown, plus "BY APPOINTMENT TO HER

MAJESTY" in bleddy great red letters. So the Protestant cobbler comes out.'

The crowd was silent. Rapt.

'"How come you're puttin up a sign like that?" he says. Catholic cobbler replies "I had to make her Royal Majesty a pair of shoes." Not to be outdone, the Protestant cobbler says "Well, I had to make her Royal Majesty *two* pairs of shoes." And he goes and gets a ladder and he puts up a sign with an even *bigger* bleddy crown on.'

Eamonn picked up his glass, took a deep pull and wiped his mouth on the back of his sleeve. Looked at his audience. 'And underneath in bleddy great red letters "BY APPOINTMENT TO THE QUEEN *AND COBBLERS TO THE POPE*."'

There was a second's silence. Then the dining room erupted in a roar of joyful laughter, punctuated by whistles and catcalls and yells demanding more.

Anna looked about her, helpless with mirth. Beside her, Father O'Malley sat motionless, rigid with embarrassment. Tina was scrabbling furiously at her husband's sleeve, trying to make him sit down. He shook her off. 'Thank you, thank you. Lessee … this one's about St Peter. Greets new intake of the recently deceased. Baptists, this time. So St Peter welcomes them, makes 'em feel right at home then takes 'em on a tour of Heaven …'

He was off. At a signal from Desmond, waiters began to circulate once more, filling glasses, offering cigars and chocolates to the enthralled guests. Sam put his arm round his helplessly giggling wife. People were relaxing; IT whizzes were exchanging grins with Eamonn's business colleagues, elderly relatives were sending 'isn't he a caution' smirks to each other as they listened with guilty pleasure to this new joke. Silver paper chocolate wrappings littered the stained and wrinkled tablecloths; the roses were beginning to droop, the candles burning low. Anna took a sip of wine, enjoying the respite from the attentions of her neighbours. Great Uncle Liam was hanging on to Eamonn's every word, eager as a child to hear the punchline, Father O'Malley continued to stare straight ahead.

'"Sure and it's a grand place, Heaven," said St Peter to the Baptists as they reached the end of their tour.' Eamonn solemnly regarded *the crowd* once more.

'"Now if you'd like to follow me I'll be showin' you to the Baptist quarters down the end of this corridor here." He beckoned 'em to follow him. They came to an oak door, tall and pointy and studded with cherubs and crucifixes and suchlike in flashy gold leaf. St Peter stopped and put a finger to his lips. "If yez wouldn't mind bein' silent as we pass the door." One of the group, braver than the rest, raised his hand. "If yez don't mind me askin', sorr – why would we have to do that, now?" St Peter lowered his voice. "T'is where we keep the Catholics." He smiled. "And they t'ink they're the only ones up here."'

Eventually the uproar died down; Eamonn was only allowed to sit down when he promised to do another turn later, after the cake had been cut. Desmond, scarlet in the face and wheezing with the effort of restraining his mirth, tinkled a teaspoon against the glass again. 'And now pray silence for –' he hiccupped, '– the groom, Mr Samuel Hardy!'

Applause and cheers greeted Sam as he rose to his feet. Anna looked away as he began to speak. She knew if she looked at him she would cry, not, this time from sadness but from pride, and today of all days she would not embarrass her son. She concentrated hard on the napkin in her lap and her fruitless efforts to turn it back into the immaculate swan it had been at the start of the meal.

'… my mother.'

Bugger, this was impossible – it looked more like a pregnant budgerigar than a bloody swan. If she could just get this fold here to fit under that bit there …

'Mum?'

She looked up. Sam was looking straight at her. He was smiling, but his eyes were full of tears. 'I just want to say …' He swallowed hard. 'I just want to thank you for everything, Mum. For always being there. For never letting on how hard it must often have been. For making it possible for me to grow up to be the man my beautiful Lucy chose to marry.' He raised his glass of champagne to her, then turned to the guests. 'My Mum, Anna.'

The guests rose to their feet, smiling, and joined him in the toast.

It was a while before she composed herself enough to take in the rest of Sam's speech. He must have made some jokes, because people were laughing, and at some point he raised his glass briefly to Tina, who was unfortunately too busy castigating a clearly unrepentant Eamonn out of the side of her mouth to respond.

'I'd like to finish by saying how proud and happy I am to have my father and his fiancée,' beaming, he turned to Tony and Tara-Louise, 'here with us today.'

Tony thrust out his chest with a smirk; Tara-Louise winked at Anna. Grinning, Anna raised her glass in a silent toast. As Sam sat down to more cheers and applause she glanced down at her lap. If she just tucked this little flap in *here* … so, and folded and refolded that fold *there* under the wing … so … Hey presto! A perfect swan.

Gently she placed it on her side plate, and let it sail away.

At last the speeches were over, and hand in hand, Sam and Lucy approached the centre table and cut the cake, accompanied by Tina issuing orders and getting in the way. As instructed, Declan had taken several photographs from all possible angles, and was about to take the only shot he was personally interested in (of the happy couple by chance exactly mirroring the stance of the tiny bride and groom atop the highest tier) when he saw a dishevelled figure appear at the window in the background of his shot. He clicked the shutter and lowered his camera. Unobserved by the guests, now crowding round the happy couple, the figure was frantically signalling.

At him? No. Must be someone at the table behind him – Declan turned, just in time to see Anna catch sight of the man at the window. Her hand flew to her mouth. Grabbing her bag, she almost ran out of the room.

'You there, Mr Photographer,' Tina was waving her tangerine leather pocket book at him, screeching imperiously. Her hat was tilted precariously, her magenta lipstick had been recently been renewed but without the benefit of a mirror and the lime-green brocade was adorned with a large blob of chocolate mousse. 'I'm about to sample the cake – we simply must have a record for posterity! I think a close-up from the left, yes?'

Without a shred of doubt, lady. A shot like that would probably win him worldwide fame, since it said more than words ever could on the subject of weddings. But first …

He hurried after Anna.

Anna raced out of the hotel, down the steps and round the corner to the row of grimy dining-room windows. She searched about her frantically – there was no sign of the mackintoshed figure she'd glimpsed. Was she going mad? Did she only imagine …? Oh God, maybe it hadn't been him after all. She'd read somewhere that if you desperately longed to see someone the mind could play strange tricks. Perhaps she'd been hallucinating, what with her overwrought emotions, and the champagne, and – but no! Look! Over there …

A figure emerged from a clump of rhododendron bushes, beckoning madly. It *was* Jack. He'd *come*! With a cry she ran to him and threw her arms around his neck. 'Jack! Jack! Oh, I can't believe it's you.' She covered his face with kisses, running her hands through his sodden hair, murmuring endearments.

'Darling, angel,' Jack kissed her back passionately. Wow – that was more like it. Almost made the rigours of hitching worthwhile. God, he hated the Irish, the only lift he'd been offered in the last couple of hours had been from a lousy tractor, if you didn't count the ancient yokel who'd offered him a lift on the crossbar of his rusty bike, silly old fart. What a welcome – the old trouser snake was certainly making itself felt in no uncertain manner. Anna looked fantastic in that little blue velvet skirt, with that fuck-me hat with its sexy little wisp of

283

black veil. With a bit of luck he might be able to get her to sneak into the rhododendrons with him in a minute. Mmm – he felt rather like Richard Gere in that film about the bloke who came back from the war. Pity Jodie Foster was so small and thin – no meat on her, reminded him of – hey, steady, Teale, the old trouser snake was deflating fast. He squeezed Anna's bottom.

'Oh Jack, I've got so much to tell you! You just won't believe everything that's happened –'

He smiled ruefully. 'Me too, angel.'

She held him away from her and gazed at him. God, he must have been through hell with bloody Ruth. He looked terrible, even worse than after that time he'd try to teach the War Poets to the lower fourth and they all said they were pacifists and spent the whole lesson playing with their Game Boys as a mark of protest. His eyes were bloodshot; he hadn't shaved; for some reason there was straw in his hair and his mac was covered in oil. She hugged him. 'But everything's all right now you're here.'

They began to kiss again.

Declan rounded the corner of the hotel and stopped dead. Somehow the moment he saw Anna that morning he had a feeling ... And when she'd bumped into him earlier, he'd kind of thought that maybe ... Nothing he could put his finger on for sure, but just for a while there he'd thought, no, *felt*, that was it – as if he ... she ... no, *they* ...

He turned away. Go back and get that shot of the old bat eating cake, man. It's what you're good at.

All you're good for.

Anna held Jack away from her again, overcome with relief. She took in the way his hair seemed more thickly striped with grey than ever (what had that cow Ruth done to him?) and flopped into his eyes, the way his shirt was stained and wrinkled (she'd look after him now, poor lamb), the way sleep caked the corners of his red-rimmed eyes. (He was probably already missing his beloved kids. She only hoped she'd be worthy of such a sacrifice.) She kissed him gently. 'So this means …?'

He nodded gravely. 'Yes, Anna. I've left Ruth.' He bowed his head. 'For you.'

For her! She could hardly believe what she was hearing – it was a moment she had truly thought would never come. She closed her eyes, hating herself for ever having doubted him.

Jack heaved a sigh. Better get this over with, she'd be bound to want to know the whys and wherefores, they always did, then with a bit of luck they could have a quick one two in the bushes and head inside for some nosh. 'I just couldn't take it any more, angel. Love, pain – the whole damn thing.' Wasn't that the title of some play? Thank God he wasn't talking to Ruth – she'd have spotted it right away. 'Anyway, thinking of you going off on all your ownio to your son's wedding, well, that was simply too much to bear. Teale, I said to myself, it's got to stop here and now. Enough's enough. Are you a man or a …' Christ. How did the rest of it go? Louse, yes, that was it. '… or a louse. So I strode into the kitchen and told her I was leaving.'

'You mean … just like that?'

'Yup. Just like that. Told her I couldn't live without you any more and she'd just have to make the best of it.'

'But what – surely she must have …'

'Oh, terrible scene. Terrible.' He frowned, recalling way Ruth had screamed at him about the ketchup; the way she'd kept thumping the table while she listed his faults; the way she'd jabbed him in the back of the hand with Charlie's knife. 'Bloody woman was a complete virago. She tried to stab me, actually.'

Anna gasped, and held him close.

'But I stood firm.' He stroked her bottom again. He was feeling pretty firm right now, frankly.

'It must have been awful, darling.'

'It was, angel.' He remembered the Scottie dog's flashing eyes – the red and white candy-striped blouse. He shuddered. 'It was.'

She held him closer, murmuring endearments.

285

'But now, my angel …' He slipped a finger between the buttons of her jacket. 'Now love is here to stay.'

'Oh, Jack! I never thought it would happen. I never thought Ruth would let you go!'

His stomach rumbled. Christ, he was hungry. 'Me neither.' His feet were freezing; his shoes were soaking. Ruined. And he'd never get these oil stains out of his mac. He shook his head angrily. 'What she sees in sodding Peregrine I'll never know.'

There was a moment's pause.

'Peregrine?'

He snorted. 'Bastard'll change his tune after a month or two of the twins drying their G-strings in the microwave and monopolising the bathroom for months on end … Still, at least it means you and I can have the house, angel … Oh, yes, I almost forgot. They're leaving Spike, too.'

Anna was very still.

'Who's Peregrine?'

'Father of one of her precious private maths pupils. Loaded, by all accounts.' He gave a bark of laughter. 'Must be deaf, dumb and blind into the bargain, if he's asked Ruth to go and –'

'What, Jack? Go and *what* …?'

'You know, shack up with him.'

'You mean he's asked her to *marry* him?'

'Christ, I don't think he'll go that far. If you ask me the bastard just wants a bit of free coaching for his idiot son.'

'So Ruth's …'

'Oh yes, I nearly forgot. They've both got a thing for cacti, apparently.'

'Ruth's leaving *you*?'

'Well, put it that way if you like.'

'Dear God! When I think of all the times you swore you were going to tell her.'

'Matter of fact, I was just opening my mouth to give her the glad news when she jumped in with the Perry stuff.'

'So you mean *Ruth* wants …'

He gave her a rueful smile. 'Typical.'

'*Ruth* said …'

286

'Oh, come on, angel – why does it matter who said what and who to? To whom, rather.' He tried to take her in his arms. 'The main thing is I'm here now. Can't tell you what hell the journey was to get to you – it's taken days! Made that god-awful film *The Road* look like *Mary Poppins*! Even had to take a lift in some vile slurry cart.'

'Oh Jack! I'm sorry!' She moved into his embrace. 'I'd no idea – honestly, it's fantastic that you went through all that just for me.'

'True love or what?' He scowled. 'Bloody nightmare it was, forced to hitch-hike like some vagrant …'

'Never mind, sweetheart, you're here now.' Tenderly, she picked a clump of straw out of his hair.

'Never *mind*?' He scowled at her. 'Going to cost a fortune to get this mac cleaned and my bloody shoes are a write-off. At least I won't have bloody Ruth on my back asking questions. Till Perry gives her the push of course and she comes running back, and I'm forced to …'

There was a silence.

'To what, Jack?'

When you've been together for ages you just sort of get into the habit.

'Hey, come on, angel, what is this, the Inquisition?' He tweaked the straw from her fingers and stuck it in her lapel. 'Tell you what, let's make mad, passionate love among the rhododendrons. You know we always said how romantic it would be to make love in the open air.'

She pushed him away. 'You never intended to tell Ruth you were leaving her, did you Jack? You're only here now because she told you she was leaving *you*!'

'Oh for God's sake, Anna. What difference does it make?'

'What *difference* …?' She stared at him in disbelief. 'You lied to me, Jack.' She thought of all the other times he'd lied to her – not done what he'd said he would, let her down. 'And the minute she decides she wants to come back, you'll …'

She gave a cry of pain. He was worse than bloody Tony.

Declan, walking slowly back to the hotel entrance, heard the cry. He stopped.

'How could you, Jack?'

'Angel, believe me …'

'Believe you? I'll never believe anything you say ever again.'

'Angel, you're overtired. The stress of the wedding's got to you. But I know what you need …' He drew her to him.

'No, Jack, I don't …'

'Come on, trust your Uncle Jack.'

'No.'

'Darling, you know you want to. Nobody'll see us from the hotel, if that's what you're worrying about. What a dump, by the way, no wonder you're feeling down. A spot of the old two-backed beast's just what the doctor …'

'*No*, I said!' Anna pushed him away from her as hard as she could. Arms flailing, he fell backwards with a crash among the rhododendron bushes. He lay motionless for a moment on the wet, dark earth as raindrops showered down on him from the thick, glossy green leaves, then struggled to his feet, covered with bits of broken twig, and staggered out again.

'Anna!' A limp sac of bright pink rubber was clinging to his sleeve. Good God! It was a condom. What a stroke of luck – if he made a joke about it, Anna would see the funny side and relax a bit. He held it out to her. 'Hey! Looks like they knew we were coming!'

'Just go, Jack, all right?'

'But darling …'

She turned away.

With a defeated sigh, he retrieved his case from behind the bush where he'd stashed it when he arrived. There was a sodding great oil stain down the side – damn tractor, he was glad now he hadn't given the driver a tip. Bloody Irish … And what was vile smell? He looked down. There was shit all over his shoes. They were in more of a mess than ever. Christ, they were his best brown suede ones – he'd never get it all off! Bloody cats … He looked at Anna. Her back was still turned, so there was no point in giving her his little boy smile, but it was worth one more try. 'Anna?'

She shook her head.

'I'm going now.'

She didn't move.

Bloody women. He began to slink away.

As he disappeared out of sight past the rhododendrons, Anna turned – made to go after him –...

must be deaf dumb and blind.

She stopped herself.

Declan stood watching helplessly, concerned at seeing Anna so distressed.

The scrap of pink rubber lay on the grass where Jack had thrown it. Lord, they were everywhere – was there something in The Grand's water? She could see now it was the same as the one she'd seen in the foyer fireplace the night she arrived. Was it only yesterday? It seemed like years. God, she'd been deliriously happy then compared to the way she felt now. There seemed to be writing on it; odd, she'd never seen writing on a condom before. Maybe it was a warning from the Pope, or something. She bent down. A lot of stars, and something about ears ... Picking it up between thumb and forefinger, she stretched it out. In gold ink rendered almost illegible by the recent rain, she could just make out the words MARY AND JOSEPH, 50 HAPPY YEARS. Fifty happy ...? Of course! It wasn't a condom – it was a balloon from the Golden Wedding party that had been held at the hotel on Friday night.

She stared at it, tears running down her cheeks.

Once she'd been certain a day would come when there'd be a party with champagne, and cake, and balloons bearing the legend ANNA AND JACK, JUST MARRIED.

She'd been a fool.

After a while she went and sat down on a nearby bench; she'd have to compose herself before she could even think of going back to the reception. Better clean herself up a bit, too. She couldn't recall tears and snot being mentioned among *Bride*'s 'Natural Look Suggestions for the Mother of the Groom'. After a futile dab at her eyes with the cuff of her sleeve, she rummaged in her bag in search of a tissue. Notebook ... diary ... wallet ... keys ... make-up bag ... pens ... fruit gums ... Oh, for God's sake, there must be one here somewhere. She groped irritably down to the next layer. Old notebook ... spare tights ... tampons ... old Avant Art brochures ... envelopes ... Oh, this was ridiculous. She'd have to turn the whole thing out, she'd be here till dark at this rate. Quickly, she upended the bag onto the bench, fielding the contents deftly as they threatened to spill over the edge onto the wet grass. At last, a tissue. A bit grubby, with what looked like a very old toffee stuck to one corner, but absorbent, nevertheless. She'd blotted the worst of the mess from her face and was reaching for her make-up bag when she caught sight of the envelopes that had spilled out with the rest of the junk. Odd that they were unopened ... Of course, it was the mail she'd stuffed in her bag yesterday morning when the taxi came. Listlessly she picked them up and riffled through them. Pretty much par for the course; a couple of bills, a postcard from Greece depicting a temple against an impossibly blue sky from her friend Polly, and a stiff white envelope bearing the logo WILD HORSES in bright scarlet.

WILD HORSES, as in well-known poetry press.

WILD HORSES, as in well-known poetry press to which Barry had submitted twenty-five of her poems.

Anna almost laughed aloud. It had to be a rejection; everyone knew it took months for submissions to the major poetry presses to be considered. They'd replied too quickly for it to be anything else. Still, after the day she'd had she simply didn't care. Ripping open the envelope, she took out the letter.

Dear Ms Hardy,

Further to receiving your submission of twenty-five poems, we are pleased to inform you that we would like to discuss with you the publication of a collection of your work, to be entitled subject to your agreement The Rules of Love *(with reference to the key sonnet included in your submission). We should be interested to see any new poems that you might have completed, with a view to their inclusion.*

We shall be in touch in the next two weeks to arrange a meeting.

With all best wishes,

Roger Johnson (editor)

Jack had been right about one thing; the stress of the wedding had definitely got to her. For a minute she'd actually thought the letter said they were going to publish her work. Oh well, be grateful for small mercies – at least nobody had been there to see her make a fool of herself by misinterpreting it. Better read it through once more and check.

She scanned the letter again.

Put it down.

Picked it up.

Read it a third time, very slowly.

Let it fall from her nerveless fingers.

Then with a whoop that caused the rooks to scatter from a nearby copse in alarm, and the hotel cats to burrow deeper beneath the rhododendron bushes as they slept off their lunch of filched pheasant bones, she jumped to her feet, and radiant with joy, threw her bag high into the air.

Declan gazed at Anna, transfixed, mentally registering the action as an exquisite montage of black and white stills, but – for almost the first time in his professional life – ignoring the camera slung round his neck.

This was a moment he wanted to share, not record.

He couldn't remember when he'd last felt like that, God help him. He was desperate to know what she liked to eat. Did she drink Guinness? What was her favourite book? Colour? Animal? Did she like *Father Ted*? Did *Burn After Reading* dissolve her in tears of mirth, too? Did she like to travel?

Not to put it too fine, as his friend Finn would say, he wanted to get to know her. Too see her smile like that, one day, for him.

Slowly, he started to walk towards her.

He'd begin by asking her name.

Anna finished shoving her belongings back in her bag and looked up, startled. It was the wedding photographer, Declan – Declan O'Halloran. Tina must have sent him to look for her, probably time for yet more group photographs. Damn. She hoped he hadn't seen her making a fool of herself …

The publisher's letter was still lying on the grass where it had fallen. Picking it up quickly, Anna thrust it into her bag.

Then, trying to look composed, she went – slowly at first, but for some reason she could not for the life of her explain, with gradually increasing speed – to meet him.

THE END

I Do?
Karen King

Local journalist Cassie is getting married to hot-shot, reliable Timothy and his mother Sylvia nicknamed 'Monster-in-Law' wants to plan the entire wedding. When Sylvia books the exclusive ID Images to take photographs of the extravagant do, Cassie has no idea what she's walking into.

The elusive JM, ID Images' newest photographer, just so happens to be Jared, Cassie's first love and ex-fiancé, who broke off their engagement to travel and take photos of far-reaching wonders. He's back to pay for his next wild adventure.

Cassie decides it's best to pretend not to know him, but when she's asked to write an article for her newspaper, she's tasked with a column surrounding all things wedding related. When Cassie jokingly writes a column meant for herself depicting her situation, a co-worker submits it in place of the real article and it's soon making headlines, with readers asking the age old question - Who Will She Choose?

For more information about **Anna Legat**
and other **Accent Press** titles
please visit

www.accentpress.co.uk